THE PORTABLE
Romantic Reader

The Viking Portable Library

Each Portable Library volume is made up of representative works of a favorite modern or classic author, or is a comprehensive anthology on a special subject. The format is designed for compactness and for pleasurable reading. The books average about 700 pages in length. Each is intended to fill a need not hitherto met by any single book. Each is edited by an authority distinguished in his field, who adds a thoroughgoing introductory essay and other helpful material. Most "Portables" are available both in durable cloth and in stiff paper covers.

THE PORTABLE

Romantic Reader

EDITED, AND

WITH AN INTRODUCTION, BY

HOWARD E. HUGO

New York

THE VIKING PRESS

PN
6014
H84

THE ROMANTIC READER
Copyright © 1957 by The Viking Press, Inc.
First published in 1957 by The Viking Press, Inc.

Viking Portable Library Edition
Issued in 1960 by The Viking Press, Inc.
625 Madison Avenue, New York, N. Y. 10022

TENTH PRINTING FEBRUARY 1974

DISTRIBUTED IN CANADA
BY THE MACMILLAN COMPANY OF CANADA LIMITED

ACKNOWLEDGMENTS

The editor wishes to thank the following for their kind permission to reprint excerpts from the works listed below:

The Citadel Press: *The Poetry and Prose of Heinrich Heine,* edited by Frederic Ewen; copyright 1948 by The Citadel Press.

The Liberal Arts Press, Inc.: *Reason in History* by Hegel, translated by Robert S. Hartman; copyright 1953 by The Liberal Arts Press, Inc.

Liveright Publishing Corp. and Chatto & Windus Ltd.: *The Red and the Black* by Stendhal, translated by C. K. Scott-Moncrieff, copyright renewed 1953 by George Scott-Moncrieff; *On Love* by Stendhal, translated by H. B. V., copyright renewed 1954 by Liveright Publishing Corporation.

Oxford University Press, Inc., and Faber and Faber, Ltd.: *Goethe's Faust, Parts I and II,* translated by Louis MacNeice; copyright 1951 by Louis MacNeice.

Pantheon Books Inc.: *Hölderin's Poems,* translated by Michael Hamburger, copyright 1952 by Pantheon Books Inc.; *Poems of Baudelaire,* translated by Roy Campbell, copyright 1952 by Pantheon Books, Inc.

William Reeves Bookseller Ltd.: *The Life of Chopin* by Franz Liszt, translated by John Broadhouse.

Rinehart & Company, Inc.: *The Sorrows of Young Werther* by Goethe, translated by Victor Lange; copyright 1949 by Victor Lange.

SBN 670-60539-5 (hardbound)
SBN 670-01064-2 (paperbound)

LIBRARY OF CONGRESS CATALOG CARD NUMBER: 57-9499

PRINTED IN THE U.S.A. BY THE COLONIAL PRESS INC.

CONTENTS

Prologue:
What the Romantics Said about Romanticism

Part One: The Man of Feeling

THE PLEASURES AND PAINS OF SENTIMENT

THE ROMANTIC IN LOVE

Part Two:

The Romantic Hero and the Fatal Woman

THE HISTORICAL HERO: NAPOLEON

THE OUTSIDER

THE HERO'S CONSORT: THE FATAL WOMAN

THE METAPHYSICAL QUESTER

Part Three: The Romance of the Past

ROMANTIC HELLENISM

ROMANTIC PRIMITIVISM, OR THE NOBLE SAVAGE

THE ROMANTIC VOYAGE

Part Five: The Romantic Revolutions

THE REVOLUTION IN MANNERS AND MORALS

Revolutionary Years: 1789, 1830, 1848

Part Six: The Romantic Artist

Imagination: The Poetic Principle

The Artist in Person

Introduction

"Romantic" and "Romanticism" are troublesome words. It is small consolation for the common reader—all of us—that they were perplexing when they first appeared. True, the modern colloquial usage of "romantic" evokes fairly specific sentiments. "Isn't it romantic!" began a song from a musical comedy that was popular many years ago. The exclamation makes us think of moon-June-spoon, of the happy endings of Hollywood productions, of the soap operas that spin out sentiment for months and years, and of the pleasant romances that comprise the bulk of novels and magazine stories. From this rich world one might conceivably build a Romantic reader, but it would be an anthology quite different from this volume, where the editor, with academic circumspection, has stayed between the restricting dates of approximately 1770 and 1848. Within this span lies what subsequent historians have called the Romantic Movement. The dates may properly be disputed; but no one would deny that there was a cluster of ideas and attitudes in Western Europe and America that deserves a descriptive name, even if some writers have preferred to speak of "Romanticisms" rather than to employ the term in the singular.

To associate "romantic" with amorous activities and preoccupations is not wrong; so far as Romanticism is concerned, it is only too limited. The Romantics were often singularly concerned with the passion strangely labeled as tender, and one section of this *Reader* offers a selection of passages illustrating how they felt about

1

it. But, as a quick glance at the table of contents will show, politics, philosophy, nature, the past, the hero, art and the artist—to single out a few categories—all exhibited a peculiar Romantic cast, one that has always been easier to illustrate than to define in comprehensive terms.

To equip the word Romantic with a capital letter, as we have gradually been doing, is to shout it a little louder, not to give any explanation. We know that something happened from the late eighteenth century through the first half of the nineteenth to shatter a fairly homogeneous pattern of ideas, attitudes, behavior, and expression. In his introduction to the Viking Portable *Reader* that deals with the earlier period, Mr. Crane Brinton has eloquently pointed out the dangers of over-simplifying the Age of Reason. It too was an age containing diversities as varied as those we tend to attribute to the Romantics, with their principle of extreme individuation. Still, the range of feelings engendered by reason (and by its poor cousin, reasonableness) possessed a vague consistency. In praising reason the men of that age found a convenient way of uniting the highest aspirations of the human intellect with basic common sense and prudential activity.

The Romantic movement never possessed even this fuzzy unity. We speak more frequently of a movement, in the case of the Romantics, than of an "age" or "period," perhaps because our terminology is unconsciously influenced by Romantic rhetoric. All periods are really movements in time; but the exponents of Romanticism seemed unusually aware that theirs was a moment of flux, of organic change and growth, while they undertook to revolt against what they regarded as the fixed, outworn canons of preceding generations. Add to this deliberate choice of the organic, or changing, or illogical, an equally calculated desire of the Romantics to abandon uniformity—"I am not made like

anyone I have ever met; I even venture to believe that
I am not made like anyone now alive," announces Rousseau at the beginning of his *Confessions*—and the task
of exact or complete definition becomes almost impossible. The quotations in the Prologue to this volume
indicate how currents, cross-currents, and minor eddies
obscured the direction of the tide. Partisans and de-
tractors crossed party lines with baffling rapidity.

In all truth there were few individuals, within the
near-century from which we have chosen texts, who
thought of themselves as Romantics (whereas many
audacious men of letters in the eighteenth century had
been convinced that they represented an age of reason
or an enlightenment). A small group of German intellectuals and artists living around Jena in 1800 were the
first to exhibit glimmerings of Romantic self-consciousness. Although the English Lake poets—Wordsworth,
Southey, and Coleridge—embraced a common literary
cause at about the same date, they were not allied to
the Lake District and hence to one another until some
years after most of their most representative poetry had
been written. In the 1820s and 1830s Paris abounded
with *cénacles* and salons where the leading young artists
congregated. At that time the members were aware of
mutual bonds created by artistic rebellion and occasional
political allegiances, but it was not until decades later
that Hugo and Gautier would talk in retrospect of their
youthful Romanticism. Between 1830 and 1850 the
New England Transcendentalists, with Emerson as their
leader, incorporated much English and Continental
thought into their ambitious programs for philosophic,
social, and artistic reforms—ideas we now would call
Romantic—but Emerson would have been shocked at
being so described. Thoreau was too independent ever
to wish partnership in any cultural firm. Poe, Whitman,
Melville, and Hawthorne—save for the friendship of
the last two—worked in isolation, mainly unaware of

affinities with European contemporaries and forerunners. We sympathize with their posthumous dismay—and with that of Blake, Goethe, Hölderlin, Vigny, and Byron, to mention a few names at random—if they have discovered that posterity has placed them all together in an age, a school, an epoch, a movement.

Somehow a lowest common denominator, perhaps tiny in magnitude, was shared by all. The selections in this volume, and the groups into which they have been assembled, try to prove this modest assertion. Whatever Romanticism was we may best observe by seeing how its practitioners felt about six major areas of experience: the passions that move men, the heroic types in which the movement invested its sympathy, the past, the world and nature apart from man's achievements, revolt and reform, and the artist and his vocation.

THE MAN OF FEELING

The Enlightenment, that climax to the Age of Reason, had underscored the idea that all the major phases of experience fell into rational schemes comprehensible to the human mind. Man was no doubt irrational. One need only read Swift or Voltaire to catch the despair these keen intellects felt about human shortcomings. Yet rationality was the aim; and for them and less brilliant contemporaries those parts of the psyche related to the feelings and the passions were not relevant when ultimate values were at stake. If laws about the cosmos, society, the arts, and the nature of man were ever to be established, these had to be rules intelligible to the mind and to common sense.

How can we account for the reaction against such a beautiful rationalism that developed during the Romantic movement? Perhaps the eighteenth century flew too high, and those who claimed the highest place for reason inadvertently disclosed its final limits and possible inadequacy. To watch the progress of the eighteenth century is to observe the gradual intrusion of such terms as intuition, inspiration, taste, the moral sense, sensibility, and to note their slow victory over a drier vocabulary. It would be foolish to assert that men suddenly started feeling and stopped thinking. At the same time one cannot deny that *feeling* came to take on dimensions hitherto ignored or minimized.

To this strange triumph the contributions were various. Intuitive processes are always private and yet universal, the property of all men despite superficial differences in rank, station, education, and mental abilities. The Age of Reason had discovered its ideal in the philosopher-gentleman who represented a kind of modern equivalent of Plato's philosopher-king. But with the rise of the middle class, both the social status and the learning and cultivation enjoyed by the gentleman meant less and less to the young man in search of a better world. Thus the real Rousseau, the fictional Werther and Harley (*The Man of Feeling*), all share at least two traits: acute emotional sensibility, which raises them above their less sensitive brothers, and an awareness of not belonging to the existing social order. The former trait took on many later configurations and names as the *philosophe* turned into the solitary dreamer: spleen, melancholy, the blue devils, *Weltschmerz, le mal du siècle*. What the Middle Ages had labeled acedia, the grave sin of spiritual sloth and despair, came to be the mark of spiritual distinction—a prerequisite for the genius, a necessity for the man of fashion. And when the social revolutions of 1789, 1830, and 1848 destroyed old orders only to create new systems for the organization of men, the same individuals were left to contemplate the ashes of their hopes—they for whom these same cataclysms had once seemed promises of liberation and fulfillment.

The Romantic man of feeling dwelt in a world of emotions where sadness predominated over happiness.

Here he ramified the eighteenth-century cult of sensibility and diverted it into a single mournful channel. Laurence Sterne, writing his praise of "dear sensibility" in *A Sentimental Journey* (1768), showed that all experiences, pleasurable and painful, could be enriched when the heart was free to pour out tears or laughter. The Romantics strove to prove that sensibility was not equated with happiness. The Romantic *isolato* rarely laughed; if he did, it was after the manner of Byron: "And if I laugh at any mortal thing, / 'Tis that I may not weep." The wry smile covers up the catch in the throat and the incipient sob. In *Julie, ou la Nouvelle Héloïse,* Rousseau's young hero Saint-Preux comments poignantly, "For me there is only a single way to be happy, but there are millions of ways to be miserable."

The "tender passion"—love—came to crown all other feelings. Romanticism *is* so very romantic. Despite the elegance, finesse, and social decorum we associate with the Augustans, the court of Louis XIV, and the entire eighteenth century, these were times when love emerges surprisingly earthy and lusty. We may think we are emancipated in our sexual attitudes and conduct, having been exposed to the theories of Freud and the tabulations of Kinsey. But Fielding's novels still dismay the fastidious schoolmarm forced to teach these classics; Shakespeare's ribaldry draws nervous laughter from sophisticated audiences; and to produce plays by Wycherley and Congreve in many American cities would be to incur the wrath of Watch and Ward societies just slightly younger than Boston's own. The Age of Reason had pursued the topic of seduction with intellectual audacity until little more remained to be said. Few twentieth-century authors can match Boswell's casual *libertinage* in his *Journals,* the dissection of the psychological elements in the art of love and amorous conquest by Choderlos de Laclos in *Les Liaisons Dangereuses*

(1782), or the anatomization of the methods of sexual satisfaction by the Marquis de Sade in the 1790s.

Against such franchise Romanticism rebelled. As it did so often, here it joined novelty with a return to the past. When Mme. de Staël introduced German literature to her French readers shortly after the turn of the century, one of her attacks on the proponents of the Enlightenment was their insufficient recognition of the charms and the reality of love. She extolled the Age of Chivalry less for its heroic aspects than for a manifestation of love as material for serious literature. It was time to turn once more to the gentler qualities of man's sexual instincts.

Centuries earlier Socrates had described the ladder of love in Plato's *Symposium,* where it began on the physical and erotic level finally to achieve complete spirituality in the realm of the Idea, the One, the Good, and pure Beauty. The Middle Ages and the Renaissance gave birth to the fascinating doctrine of courtly love, *cortezia* in Italian, *Hohe Minne* in German. Is it excessive to suggest that Romantic love meant a resurgence *mutatis mutandis* of an attitude, mystical and intuited, which intervening ages of rationalism had intellectualized out of existence? The supreme expression of courtly love is doubtless to be found in Dante's *Divine Comedy:* the author's love for Beatrice is transmuted into the highest recognition of God's "love that moves the sun and other stars." Romantic writers were seldom able to define the deity or their own aspirations with the clearness that Dante achieved. The sea of Christian faith was at the full in 1300; its long, withdrawing roar was heard five hundred years later. Yet the spiritual quests were similar and the reality of the exploration was equally affirmed. The Romantics suggested, as had Dante, that love was a route by which the time-bound individual might learn a vision of ultimate truth, a glimpse of that world which stands behind or above our meager existences. Hence love was a state of being that was eagerly to be coveted, not for purposes of physical satisfaction, but rather because the attraction of one soul for another was a guarantee that the entire universe was permeated with similar energy and spirit.

Naturally such hyperbolic sentiments were not owned by an entire generation or several generations. And even outstanding late-Romantic representatives, such as Heine, Byron, and Stendhal (particularly the last), seemed to display a skeptical ambivalence. "Love we must," said these three in a figurative chorus . . . but is it possible or merely a chimerical ideal concocted by poetic souls?" Nevertheless the amorous legacy left by Romanticism is rich. The literature of the tough-minded 1920s and 1930s abounds in heroes and heroines whose superficial sexual freedom masks a yearning for love as a genuine spiritual entity and a belief in this same truth which gainsays any physical materialism. Even today's young men and women still speak of "falling in love." The socio-economic jargon they employ—marriage of in-groups and out-groups, inner-directed and outer-directed personalities—may be less harmonious than Shelley's dulcet tones in the *Epipsychidion*, but the intention is not very different.

THE ROMANTIC HERO

I want a hero: an uncommon want,
When every year and month sends forth a new one,
Till, after cloying the gazettes with cant,
The age discovers he is not the true one.

Byron's lines from *Don Juan* are cogent and ironic when we remember that he created several impressive Romantic heroes (Childe Harold, Manfred, Don Juan) and that the legend he left behind him gave posterity still another. Taine once observed that every epoch tries to locate its particular "ruling personage" or "notable character," the figure that "contemporaries invest with their admiration and sympathy," in short, the hero. The Greek poet Pindar long ago asked, "What god, what hero, what man are we to celebrate?" He was assured of an answer in the person of the ancient warrior or athlete. The Greek epic and tragedy also created heroic types—Achilles, Odysseus, Oedipus—whose careers we still follow with humility and astonishment. More recently Ezra Pound has queried, "What god, man, or hero / Shall I place a tin wreath upon?" He is not alone among modern intellectuals in seeking a new heroic type when the gold standard seems to have been totally abandoned. From ancient times to our own the social leveling of the hero is relatively easy to discern. The captains and the kings depart. Shakespeare's King Lear (1606) is transformed into Balzac's retired noodle manufacturer, Père Goriot (1834), and subsequently into Willy Loman, hero of Arthur Miller's *Death of a Salesman* (1949). Democratization, the emphasis on egalitarian similarities between men rather than on their distinguishing differences, has made the hero increasingly difficult to define.

Voltaire once dryly commented, "I don't like heroes; they make too much noise." The Age of Reason was rationally unsympathetic to individuals who threatened to burst the confines of an orderly society, whether they were real or fictive. The rapier carried by the Renaissance courtier became the small-sword decoratively worn by the eighteenth-century nobleman on ceremonial occasions. What better emblem could stand for the decline of the hero as a fighting man? Both the Chesterfieldian gentleman and the honest, upright tradesman came to serve as models—one for the aristocracy, the other for the *bourgeoisie*. They fulfilled Voltaire's demand for essentially quiet types.

The developments conspiring to disrupt such relative passivity were various. We single out two. The sheer

stress on individualism led to an increasing preoccupa-
tion with uniqueness, and hence to a weakening of the
conviction that men resembled each other or that such
solidarity was ultimately to be desired. A second development of the years following 1789 was the near-
total destruction of aristocratic molds, which were never
again to be repaired. Social disruption created a new
class of young men released from ancient and restricting
social hierarchies, each one of them—insofar as he
realized his condition—anxious to find the career open
to his talents.

The phrase reminds us of the meteoric rise of the man
who seemed to prove that the hero was not dead: Napoleon. His success, even his final defeat, became a paradigm and pattern for those whose aspirations were non-
military. The few texts in this volume concerned with
Napoleon try to sketch his *charisma*. Balzac, constructing *The Human Comedy,* blandly stated that he was
completing with the pen what Napoleon began with the
sword. Dante had written a *Divine Comedy* when the
Imitatio Christi enjoyed sole supremacy. In an age of
secularity the imitation of Napoleon rivaled any divine
antecedent. Through Napoleon, Romanticism discovered a quality—greatness and genius or contrariwise he
proved an hypothesis already current. That the decisions
of men in a position of power could alter events was
nothing new, but the phenomenon of Napoleon tran-
scended the acts of his predecessors. No wonder that
philosophers of history, Hegel the foremost, used him
as an example of the great man who momentarily embodies the world spirit at certain crucial turning points.

The assertion of greatness and genius carries with it
credentials of isolation and suffering. The albatross portrayed in Baudelaire's poem is sublimely beautiful only
when it soars alone in the sky. On deck among ordinary
humanity it becomes a figure of fun. The destiny of the
genius, as Romantic generations found, is to be anni-

hilated by the very society whose goals he has helped to reach, whose hopes he has articulated. The messiah becomes the outlaw, the scapegoat, the outsider. The necessary egotism of the Romantic hero may be capable of sustaining him temporarily. At the end he must go down before the collective onslaughts of his fellowmen. Perhaps here is a distinguishing feature of all Romantic heroes. The hero of the Greek epic, the mediaeval knight and *preux chevalier,* and the Renaissance aristocrat with his scholar's learning and courtier's ease—all were ideals created by societies in which the major metaphysical, social, and psychological premises were shared by everyone. The Romantic heroes lived their lives when traditional beliefs about the nature of the cosmos on one level, the organization and community of men on another, were brought to question. Even the contours of the mind seemed no longer to follow the intellectual pattern which the Age of Reason thought it discerned. Locke's *tabula rasa,* that blank slate upon which sense impressions are subsequently inscribed, is a far cry from the deep abysses of the soul or the irrational world of dreams into which we plunge with Poe, Novalis, Melville, and Coleridge.

Outlaws and outsiders, *isolati* and rebels, fatal women and temptresses, sensitive souls and devoted artists bearing the contumely of society: the catalogue is long and various. Perhaps most interesting for the modern reader is what we have called the metaphysical quester. It can be said that the great tragic hero of any period—Oedipus and Hamlet are two—pursues his own investigations into the ultimate nature of things only at the last to suffer a glorious defeat. *We* inject such a philosophical interpretation; the author's aim may have been humbler. Certain Romantic heroes seemed designed by their authors solely to follow an absolute quest after final truth, and Goethe's *Faust* stands out as foremost among many. What is possibly new after the eighteenth century is Romanticism's placing the burden of metaphysical speculation on *belles-lettres* as well as on formal philosophy. Certainly Romanticism did not exclude the latter. The names of Fichte, Schelling, and Hegel (with Kant as a bridge) continue a line of abstract thought from Spinoza, Leibnitz, Berkeley, and Hume. But there is a vast difference between Pope's versifying philosophy in the *Essay on Man*, and Melville's composing the story of the biggest fish that ever got away and meanwhile creating, in the course of the hunt after Moby Dick, his own divine comedy and human tragedy. We shall have more to say about the Romantic imagination.

THE ROMANCE OF THE PAST

In the Romantic period, the past was revisited with a new zeal and necessity. One such return was to the world that neo-classicism had marked out for its own, the ancient world of Greece and Rome. The other was unique in that on the whole the Age of Reason had ignored the Middle Ages (the adjective "Dark" is indicative of Enlightenment attitudes toward Europe between the fall of Rome and the rise of New Learning) and the misty regions of the pagan and early Christian North. These were felt not to be separate cultures; they were not cultures in a strict sense at all. (Today we have gone further when we speak of African cultures or those of New Guinea, an extension of cultural franchise that would have shocked the Romantics.)

First consider pagan antiquity. The Greek gods never died. Ancient Greece has reinvigorated the thought of every epoch, although there were times when the light from Hellas seemed to burn low, as during the first ten centuries after Christ. The neo-classicism we associate with a portion of the Age of Reason was aware of its debt to the past. What then was Romantic Hellenism? How did it differ from its predecessor?

Perhaps it was less a difference than an intensification, when more information about classical civilization was revealed. The "new" science of archaeology opened up two Graeco-Roman cities (Herculaneum in 1738, Pompeii a decade later), and men were able to see these artifacts of antiquity without the accretions of succeeding ages, which would obscure original monuments, as in the case of Rome. "No other disaster ever yielded such pleasure to the rest of humanity as that which buried Pompeii and Herculaneum," commented Goethe. The Germans seemed especially beguiled by such physical remains, all the way from Winckelmann in the 1750s to Schliemann excavating what he hoped were the topless towers of Ilium on the plains of Troy. One critic has suggested a Teutonic homesickness for a motherland to accompany the Fatherland. Yet we must remember the Elgin marbles and Keats.

Literary scholarship meant that lost or forgotten classics were rediscovered and corrupted texts were emended—scholarly labors that led to a richer comprehension of the Greek tragic playwrights, of Homer and Pindar. Gradually it became evident that the Romantic Hellenists sought to find a canonical civilization in Greece; an age of total social, political, moral, and aesthetic perfection such as the most ardent neo-classicist never dreamed; an imaginary kingdom and an Arcadia where hearts troubled by the present might seek nourishment from the glorious past. They made at least two contributions of great value. Around 1800 the Schlegel brothers perceived the subtle shadings between Greek culture and the Roman and Hellenistic periods that arose from it. For the latter they reserved the negative qualifications of formal and decadent. In this discrimination the Schlegels were not alone, nor were they in another trenchant observation. Neoclassic critics had always stressed the plastic serenity of Greek art, the repose and harmony. Winckelmann thus spoke more for them than for later interpreters when he made his famous remark about Greek art: "A quiet grandeur and a noble simplicity." Romantic Hellenists found this only partially true as slowly they concentrated on the irrational elements. The Dionysiac had greater appeal than the Appolonian. The Romantics may have exaggerated their novel perception, and modern classical scholarship has occasionally blossomed with strange fruits produced when the Freudian ego blends with Apollo, the god of light, and the id is made synonomous with Dionysus, the deity whose activity is associated with the wine barrel and libidinous freedom; but bizarre variations do not destroy a great theme. These Romantic *aperçus* were brilliant and original. Never before had critics noticed the balance in Greek tragedy between man's desire to assert rational claims over inchoate experience and his simultaneous perception that the gods, the fates, the given elements in life, were permeated with mystery and terror.

We can only be amazed when we remember the penury of contact the most ardent Romantic Hellenists had with the culture they admired and with its geographical center. Compared with the book knowledge of a modern student of the classics, theirs was scarcely above average. André Chenier, transition figure between neo-classicism and the movement we have been sketching, was foremost among French poets in his efforts to pour new wine into old Grecian bottles; but he never left France. Hölderlin, greatest Hellinist among the Germans, remained in northern Europe—unlike the hero of his novel *Hyperion,* who bitterly discovered eighteenth-century Hellas to be a miserable copy of the glorious realm he had imagined. Shelley spent his last days in northern Italy. Goethe's famous voyage to the South took him as far as Sicily. Byron alone saw Greece, only to die there at Missolonghi. In no way does this diminish the magnitude of their endeavors. The Renaissance brought ancient classical masterpieces back into the main line of Western thought. The Enlightenment made them part of a working tradition. The function of Romanticism was a further appraisal of Greece, in an effort to recapture a unity the modern world had lost.

More radical was the slow revelation of another tradition—that of the Celtic, Scandinavian, Teutonic North, which existed in polar relation to the Mediterranean. We may be puzzled by the popularity of MacPherson's Ossianic poems, but we cannot ignore the hold these gloomy verses of doubtful authenticity had on Goethe, Byron, and Napoleon, not to mention thousands of less famous readers. Their melancholy and elegiac tone struck responsive chords in hearts already attuned to sweet sensibility. They spoke of an age that seemed morally superior and nationally closer to modern Europe than was Greece. Historians discovered information about societies long forgotten; Scandinavian mythology produced a pantheon of gods as various as Zeus's family. Poets wrote translations and imitations of the Norse *Eddas* and the tales and songs of the Nibelungs—those works in which ancient Celts, Saxons, Teutons, Vikings, and Northmen warred as strenuously and poetically as ever the Greeks and Trojans. And the disparate races were placed under the convenient heading of "Gothic."

This was mainly a pagan world existing during the first five or six centuries after Christ. The greater gap to be filled belonged to the high Middle Ages, with which the Gothic also came to be identified. When Gibbon said, "The schools of Oxford and Cambridge were founded in a dark age of false and barbarous science," his words expressed the attitude of the Age of Reason toward those times that stood between modern man and classical antiquity. By the close of the eighteenth century, however, such patronizing language was no longer the fashion. Nationalism was replacing cosmopolitanism; the *citoyen du monde* of the Enlightenment was giving way to the German, French, or English patriot; and the roots of a national past were located not in Greece and Rome—except for the Greeks and Italians—but in the days of Richard Coeur de Lion, Friedrick Barbarossa, Louis XI, and Robert the Bruce.

Moreover, philosophic and religious developments played important roles in what might otherwise seem an artistic, literary change of interest. Those for whom the light of reason shone brightest were chiefly deists— believers in some sort of God, but a God who resembled an impersonal cosmic clockmaker, the prime mover of Newton's universe. Some rationalists went further in the direction of philosophical skepticism. But one feels both deism and skepticism to be played out for many intellectuals by 1800. (Naturally there always had been practicing Protestants and Catholics; we speak of the extremes.) A definite Christian revival took place in all quarters, spurred on when the excesses of the French Revolution and its aftermath were interpreted by many as the logical, horrifying outcome of secular and "enlightened" thought. Novalis, Burke, Chateaubriand, and Coleridge compose a curious group. Whether they talked of cathedrals or conservatism in church and state, of tradition, loyalty, or duty, they pleaded for a return to Christian principles and thus represented a movement of which the Gothic revival was both a product and a contributing cause.

ROMANTIC NATURE

From classical antiquity through most of the eighteenth century the word nature had meant the sum total of existence, the entire cosmos and its laws and activity. When the so-called cult of nature arose in the Romantic Movement, the term had already come to mean something more limited in its connotations: the world apart

from man's achievements, the landscape and countryside, the sea and the mountains.

The philosopher-gentleman could enjoy the country
as a brief respite from strenuous city life with its *beau
monde*, salons, coffeehouses, wit and conversation. But if
you read Voltaire or Dr. Johnson, how seldom you find
them speaking of the attraction of woods and flowers,
the pleasure of walking! Johnson's tavern chair was the
throne of human felicity; a great city was the school for
studying life; he could never, as he said, "exchange
London for the obscurity, insipidity, and uniformity
of remote situations." Those who enjoyed the country
were fit for the country. Voltaire loved his garden at
Ferney; but it, like a more intimate Versailles, was laid
out on exact formal principles, and the hand of man restrained any unruly "natural" tendencies.

The Romantics moved out from the boudoir and
salon to the field and hillside, just as for them the delights of social interchange were supplanted by private
reverie, melancholy introspection, and the contemplation
of the overflowing heart. Doubts about progress, civilization, and the primacy of intellect were augmented when
it seemed likely that men were better in a state of nature.
Perhaps the noble savage, the child, the simple unedu-
cated rustic still partook of the Golden Age when mankind had hearts rather than purses of gold; when there
were no *mine* and *thine*, no artificial laws, no hierarchy
among persons. In vain did rigorous minds fight a rear-
guard action, and Voltaire—speaking of Rousseau—
refuse to go down on all fours to become an infant
once again. Humanitarian and democratic tendencies
were too powerful. When the franchise was finally
extended to the poor and humble, it was partly because
they were felt to inculcate values that were not possessed by those of intellect or social rank.

Those "presences of nature" about which Wordsworth rhapsodized had still more cogency for certain select and dedicated souls. The eighteenth-century philosophers had made much of natural theology as opposed to revealed theology; that is, they held that the presence of God in the universe could be proved by an examination of the structure of the world. Since the world appeared to act in accordance with general scientific laws, and laws are created by intellects, reasoning by analogy would lead to establishing an Intelligence who made the cosmos and has continued to stand behind its operations. This was quite in keeping with deistic tenets. Pantheism, the philosophic attitude of so many Romantics, approached the problem very differently. (The origins of pantheism are, of course, much older than the eighteenth century: in early Greek thought, in classical Stoicism, and, during the Age of Reason, in the writings of Spinoza.) As one might expect, generations convinced of the primacy of intuitive thinking, of the eyes of the soul seeing farther and deeper than the eyes of the mind, found the analytical method of rationalism uncongenial or at best severely limited. Hence Wordsworth feels a "sense sublime" behind external phenomena. Not only were nature and mind exquisitely fitted, but they were parts of a Mighty Mind, the Oversoul of Emerson, an immanent God manifested through all forms of nature. Those initiates who, like Pope's "poor Indian," could see God in the clouds, required no superior intellectual powers for their sacred task; indeed, the meddling intellect impeded the possibility of true vision. Such notions of the pantheists indicated a reversion to a special and very private mysticism; and it is no wonder that institutionalized religions condemned their doctrine, or that the older Wordsworth deprecated his own youthful pantheistic exuberance when he became a pillar of the Church of England. It is interesting too that this way of looking at life found more enthusiastic adherents in northern Protestant countries such as Germany and England than in Catholic France or Italy.

One brief comment about the Romantic voyage, which we have somewhat doubtfully placed under the larger heading of "Nature." What was its particular cachet? After all the voyage is as old as Western literature, if one recalls Homer's *Odyssey*. The Grand Tour was undertaken by many young men in the eighteenth century to fill out their education and teach them the ways of polite society. But there is a huge difference between Boswell, traveling about the Continent in the 1760s to improve his taste, meet the great minds and the socially prominent, and, incidentally, to indulge in highly instructive love affairs; and Byron, who described the pageant of his bleeding heart in *Childe Harold*, the record of a trip made to find out if any region on sea or land was capable of providing the proper environment for the passionate, melancholy, isolated Romantic ego. The Romantic voyage was always away from the known, conventional and dull civilization toward the exotic and mysterious, where there was the promise—alas, not the fulfillment—that there the jaded and misunderstood soul might discover peace after struggle and a port after stormy seas. Then we come to those curious Romantic voyages of the mind and the imagination, quests that we normally associate with the world of dreams—Poe's tales, Coleridge's *Ancient Mariner*, Melville's *Moby Dick*—works that look forward to Rimbaud's *Drunken Boat* or even to the bizarre universe of Franz Kafka and the castle that is forever out of reach. "Anywhere out of this world . . ." The final goal has to be death.

THE ROMANTIC REVOLUTIONS

Already so much has been said about Romantic revolt that any additional commentary may be superfluous, and the selections in this volume are self-explana-

tory. There is, however, one observation that might
be offered. Previous ages had made no special demands
on the intellectual or the artist to take a definite political
stand. Men of letters often fought for causes—Dante
for the White Guelfs in fourteenth-century Italy, Cervantes against the Turks at Lepanto—or they became
political pamphleteers, like many of the English Augustans. But there seemed to be no necessary connection
between two spheres of activity, the active and the
contemplative. From 1789 through 1848, the social
upheavals posed a problem that is still with us. At a
time when certain critics pointed to a *necessary* relation
between art and society, and Heine condemned the art
of certain German Romantics for being Catholic and
politically reactionary, the role of the artist-intellectual
became more complicated. He was faced with a conflict
between art for art's sake and art for the sake of society.
If he chose the first, the artist stayed *au dessus de la
mêlée*, as the embodiment of Thomas Mann's Unpoliti-
cal Man. What cared he for the base struggles of the
rest of less-gifted mankind? Like Baudelaire's albatross,
he soared on the wings of creation in a region of pure
ideas and pure feelings. Yet this fine detachment seemed
increasingly difficult to maintain in a world where the
man of letters depended on a new literate, middle-class
audience. With the disappearance of the patronage
system in the Renaissance and the eighteenth century,
there also passed away the small aristocratic, cultivated
audiences that were a guarantee to the writer's own
taste. On this issue the Romantics split, and the fissure
has never been repaired. In our own day the controversy
about Ezra Pound points to its permanence.

Our Romantics fall into one camp or the other, or
some remain indecisively in the middle. Keats, for
example, was the dedicated soul whose poems and
letters reveal little concern with contemporary social
events. Shelley burned to be, in his own words, an

unacknowledged legislator of the world. Goethe's temperateness kept him aloof both from the nationalism of his younger contemporaries, during the Wars of the Liberation, and from the repercussions of the French Revolution that reached Germany in the 1790s. Of all the selections, perhaps Vigny's *Journal of a Poet,* most poignantly describes the state of mind of the intellectual torn between the events of 1830 and his desire to live a life of artistic creativity and contemplation. Or we could cite an anecdote about Heinrich Heine. This self-styled soldier in the war for humanity, who had looked forward so eagerly to the overthrow of tyranny and corruption, said that when the 1848 insurrection broke out in Paris, he went to the Louvre and wept at the foot of the Winged Victory.

THE ROMANTIC ARTIST

In the *Phaedrus,* Socrates tells of the divine madness, *mania,* that impels the poet; and before him other Greeks were convinced that the artist, at his highest moments, was driven by numinous inspiration to achieve the beauties that were unobtainable by any other mortal. It is good to remember that the older Plato expels many poets from his ideal Republic. The reasons were various, but one was that their inspirative claims made them a menace to civil order. Throughout history the artist has justified his activity by maintaining the dignity of his lofty calling, and the defense always contains overtones of the *Phaedrus,* naturally with cultural variations. Art is not mere pleasure: the artist is no simple entertainer, for he reveals a world of beauty by which our own existences are made meaningful. And the attackers come back with ammunition supplied unwittingly by the *Republic:* artists at best decorate life, and at worst they threaten morality. To quote an old critic, "Poets are liars, wantons, and wasters of men's time."

The Romantic movement was the last time that artists threw down the gauntlet to society and challenged their opponents to open warfare. The fight is not over, but then perhaps Romanticism is not entirely dead either. The superiority of intuitive over ratiocinative processes in the psyche meant that the imagination, like the mysterious phenomenon of love, was exalted to a position it had rarely enjoyed in the past. The passages in this reader from Coleridge's criticism and Wordsworth's *Prelude* underscore the primacy of the imagination not merely as the essential ingredient in a work of art, but as the means by which the artist—and possibly the reader or spectator as well—catches some glimpse of absolute reality. Whether Romantic art actually succeeded in achieving this bold metaphysical certainty is not the issue. We can only marvel at the temerity of the quest.

Pope, Dryden, Racine, and Voltaire did not feel that any special uniqueness accrued to them because they were writers: what they did seem to feel was only pride in their craft, annoyance at any ill reception their works might have received, and a certain pardonable intellectual satisfaction at their fame. By the end of the eighteenth century a new type of artist began slowly to emerge, and ordinary men found him puzzling. Goethe's play *Torquato Tasso* (1789) is one of the first delineations of the creative individual who feels himself a marked man. Genius is his, as well as the respect of his benefactors; and gladly they bestow the laurel crown upon his brow. But he feels an apartness from them that they cannot be expected to understand. The play ends with his nervous outburst. He leaves the Renaissance court where he has tried to find happiness, and we are left with the hope that eventual maturity will provide an adjustment. Here is the basic theme, and the real and fictional lives of subsequent Romantic artists were counterpoints over this *cantus firmus*. Goethe was

later to write, "And when man is mute amid his torments, / A God gave me the gift to utter what I am
suffering." But it was a gift with a string attached, as so
many Romantic artists regarded this boon of self-
catharsis. Add to this burden the conviction that the
artist was a guide to society, but that society often
scorned its saviors; add the increasing difficulties of
physical existence in a workaday, middle-class world
where only "practical" activity is rewarded—and you
have the artist's problem. Like so much of Romanticism,
it is still with us.

* * *

"Never apologize, never explain." Some rare souls
may abide by this stern and cynical injunction. The
anthologist cannot. He wars with his conscience while
he chooses and edits. He fights future imaginary battles
with unknown readers whose taste and judgment he
predicts will conflict with his. Instead of providing brief
selections from many authors, this volume might have
confined itself to a few masterpieces of Romanticism.
In that case, it might have been an equally interesting
reader, and a more eloquent tribute to a period of unusual intellectual and artistic attainment, but it would
have been aimed at another target than the one chosen
here.

Again I mention Crane Brinton. "An editor of one of
these Readers," he says, "must keep the choice of the
best subordinate to the choice of the characteristic, the
representative, must make no mere anthology but rather
a sampling of the variety and range of human culture
at a given time." Where does one find the characteristic
and the representative? Modes and fashions, social history, is one answer. It may be that all too little such
material has been included. Writers of second-rate importance are valuable—those to whom the teacher
awards the B-minus and the non-honors grade of C. They

often reveal the climate of opinion one suspects to be
closer to that of ordinary men and women; they register more accurately the aspirations of most of us, harsh
as the truth may be. Great men of letters, intellectuals,
and artists in this sense are dangerous. They annoyingly
threaten to dissolve clear patterns and cultural clichés.
Yet surely these titans articulate the inchoate feelings of
their contemporaries. Goethe, for example, spoke for his
age when he created Faust; Taine described Goethe's
hero as the ruling personage of the day. At the same
time it would be hazardous to claim that an entire
generation or several generations explicitly proclaimed
themselves to be Faustian.

Texts dealing with metaphysics, logic, epistemology,
and ethics may seem conspicuous in their absence. The
omission was deliberate. Romanticism broadly defined
showed a bias against abstract thinking, even while it
produced its own anti-abstract abstractions; and much
of the burden of such theoretical speculation was placed
upon imaginative creation. If authors writing in English
own an impressive majority, still they speak directly to
the reader without the medium of translation. Moreover, the English Romantics (not so much the Americans) preserve their nation's dislike of extremes and a
conservative tendency to be eclectic. They built fewer
figurative and actual barricades. Their manifestoes,
rarely as they appeared, were still more rarely anything but temperate. The "characteristic and representative" may emerge from them with a degree of calmness
seldom attained by their Continental colleagues.

For slighting Russian, Italian, Spanish, Polish, and
Scandinavian authors, the editor pleads two extenuating
circumstances. The first was originally voiced by Dr.
Johnson in reply to a question once directed at him.
"Ignorance, pure ignorance." More seriously, it can be
argued that Romantic contributions from these regions
were less valuable and original than the products of the

four countries we have chosen. Pushkin and Lermontov; Manzoni, Foscolo, and Leopardi; Zorrilla, Larra, and Espronceda; Slowacki, Krazinski, and Mickiewicz; Oehlenschlaeger and Wergeland—all have a legitimate claim to a place in any Romantic reader. Nevertheless, in many cases they derived more than they originated, or their roles in the Romantic movement were ambiguous. These are fighting words, but the editor stands by his decision.

Many suggestions by others have been gratefully incorporated. Most thanks must go to Malcolm Cowley, whose firm, mature judgment was a sure guide when my own wavered. He suggested just enough pruning to keep the paths clear. I hope friends and former teachers will recognize ideas, books, and authors for whom they acted as mentors: Jean Seznec and Sir Maurice Bowra (Oxford), John W. Miller (Williams), Joaquín Nin-Culmell (Berkeley), Renato Poggioli and Harry T. Levin (Harvard). Henry Aiken, James W. Fowle, I. Bernard Cohen, Henry C. Hatfield, and Edward Morris (all of Harvard) provided valuable bibliographical aid. Mrs. Leslie S. Keay struggled with assorted texts and manuscripts.

☙ ☙ ☙ ☙ ☙

SUGGESTIONS
FOR FURTHER READING

As Crane Brinton suggested in the *Portable Age of Reason Reader*, the volumes that deal with this period included in the series entitled *The Rise of Modern Europe* (edited by William L. Langer, published by Harper and Brothers, New York) are richly informative. The lengthy bibliographical essays and miscellaneous comments offer the interested reader most of the information he may require about the age—factual, cultural, and intellectual.

> Brinton, Crane. *A Decade of Revolution, 1789-1799* (1934).
> Bruun, Geoffrey. *Europe and the French Imperium, 1799-1814* (1938).
> Artz, Frederick B. *Reaction and Revolution, 1814-1832* (1934).

Another volume in the series—dealing with the years between 1832 and 1848—is in preparation.

The list of books that follows in no way pretends to be definitive or exhaustive, but it tries to be suggestive. The necessary limitation of texts in English is severe; much of the best writing about Romanticism has been in French and German. The thankless task of translating such works awaits future zealous scholars.

The categories of suggestions for further reading are tentative; their contents spill over any neatly erected partitions. The demands of constricted space forbid the inclusion of material relevant to specific authors, and certainly this is a loss. Critical studies of such figures as Goethe, Wordsworth, Hugo, Melville, and Chateaubriand—I single out authors at random—have often been most provocative in delineating the contours of a movement so protean, tenuous, and confusing.

In many instances, the choices were dictated by a personal preference for authors whose approach stimulated interest in Romanticism, even if one might disagree with their final conclusions and attendant hypotheses. Romanticism elicited all too seldom the calm responses we associate with cultural historians; the battle about it is still on, and it has taken on the configurations of an old family quarrel, where original sources are forgotten amid the heat of partisan interests.

Two other riders are appended. When a large volume or set of books (such as Höffding's *History of Modern Philosophy*) is suggested, naturally only those portions apposite to the period are intended. And any duplication of the list of suggested reading in the *Age of Reason Reader* is deliberate. It is relatively easy to excise discussions posterior to Romanticism, as we come implicitly to define it. But the roots go deep, and demand nourishment that no simple chronology can forbid.

I. General Works: Philosophy, Politics, Economics, and the History of Ideas

Aiken, Henry. *The Age of Ideology*. New York: Houghton Mifflin Co., 1956.

Babbitt, Irving. *Rousseau and Romanticism*. New York: Houghton Mifflin Co., 1919.

Barzun, Jacques. *Romanticism and the Modern Ego*. Boston: Little, Brown & Co., 1943.

Bate, Walter Jackson. *From Classic to Romantic*. Cambridge: Harvard University Press, 1946.

Bentley, Eric R. *A Century of Hero-Worship*. New York: J. B. Lippincott Co., 1944.

Borgese, G. A. "Romanticism," *Encyclopedia of the Social Sciences*, Vol. XIII. New York: Macmillan Co., 1934.

Bowra, Sir C. Maurice. *The Romantic Imagination*. Cambridge: Harvard University Press, 1949.

Brinton, Crane. *Ideas and Men*. New York: Prentice-Hall, Inc., 1950.

Bury, J. B. *The Idea of Progress*. Rev. ed. New York: Dover Publications, 1955.

Cassirer, Ernst. *The Problem of Knowledge: Philosophy, Science, and History since Hegel*. New Haven: Yale University Press, 1950.

Collingwood, R. G. *The Idea of History*. Oxford: Clarendon Press, 1946.

———. *The Idea of Nature*. Oxford: Clarendon Press, 1945.

Fairchild, H. N. *The Noble Savage: A Study in Romantic Naturalism*. New York: Columbia University Press, 1928.

Gooch, G. P. *Studies in Modern History*. London: Longmans Green, 1931.

———. *History and Historians in the Nineteenth Century*. London: Longmans, Green, 1935.

Hayes, Carleton. *Historical Evolution of Modern Nationalism*. New York: R. R. Smith, 1931.

Halévy, E. *Growth of Historical Radicalism*. London: Faber & Gwyer, 1928.

Höffding, Harald. *History of Modern Philosophy*. 2 vols. New York: Dover Publications, 1955.

Kohn, Hans. *The Idea of Nationalism*. New York: Macmillan Co., 1946.

Lovejoy, A. "On the Discriminations of Romanticism," *Essays in the History of Ideas*. Baltimore: Johns Hopkins, 1948.

——— *et al. A Documentary History of Primitivism*. Baltimore: Johns Hopkins, 1935.

Lucas, F. L. *The Decline and Fall of the Romantic Ideal*. Rev. ed. Cambridge, England: Cambridge University Press, 1948.

Praz, Mario. *The Romantic Agony*. New York: Oxford University Press, 1933.

Rougemont, Denis de. *Love in the Western World*. New York: Harcourt, Brace & Co., 1940.

Ruggiero, Guido de. *History of European Liberalism*. New York: Oxford University Press, 1927.

Sabine, G. H. *A History of Political Theory*. New York: Henry Holt & Co., 1950.

Saunders, J. J. *Age of Revolution*. New York: Roy Publishers, 1949.

Schumpeter, Joseph. *History of Economic Analysis*. New York: Oxford University Press, 1954.

Wellek, René. "The Concept of Romanticism in Literary History," *Comparative Literature*, I, 1949.

Whitney, Lois. *Primitivism and the Idea of Progress*. Baltimore: Johns Hopkins Press, 1934.

SCIENCE

Bush, Douglas. *Science and English Poetry*. New York: Oxford University Press, 1950.

Butterfield, Herbert. *The Origins of Modern Science*. New York: Macmillan Co., 1951.

Dampier, Sir William Cecil. *A History of Science*. 3rd ed. Cambridge, England: Cambridge University Press, 1942.

Whitehead, Alfred North. *Science and the Modern World*. New York: Macmillan Co., 1948.

Wolf, A. *A History of Science, Technology, and Philosophy in the Nineteenth Century*. London: Allen & Unwin, 1938.

AESTHETICS AND CRITICISM

Abrams, M. H. *The Mirror and the Lamp: Romantic Theory and the Critical Tradition*. New York: Oxford University Press, 1953.

Bosanquet, Bernard. *History of Aesthetics*. London: S. Sonnenschein, 1892.

Gilbert, Katherine, and Kuhn, Helmut. *A History of Esthetics*. New York: Macmillan Co., 1939.

Nahm, Milton C. *Aesthetic Experience and Its Presuppositions*. New York: Harper & Brothers, 1946.

―――. *The Artist as Creator*. Baltimore: Johns Hopkins Press, 1956.

Wellek, René. *A History of Modern Criticism*. 2 vols. New Haven: Yale University Press, 1955.

THE ARTS, OTHER THAN LITERATURE

Barzun, Jacques. *Berlioz and the Romantic Century*. 2 vols. Boston: Little, Brown & Co., 1950.

Brown, Calvin S. *Music and Literature*. Athens, Georgia: University of Georgia Press, 1948.

SUGGESTIONS FOR FURTHER READING   31

Friedlander, Walter. *David to Delacroix*. Cambridge: Harvard University Press, 1952.

Hauser, Arnold. *The Social History of Art*. New York: Alfred A. Knopf, Inc., 1951.

Lang, Paul Henry. *Music in Western Civilization*. New York: W. W. Norton & Co., 1941.

Leichentritt, Hugo. *Music, History, and Ideas*. Cambridge: Harvard University Press, 1938.

Richardson, Edgar P. *The Way of Western Art*. Cambridge: Harvard University Press, 1939.

Sachs, Curt. *The Commonwealth of Art: Style in the Arts, Music, and the Dance*. New York: W. W. Norton & Co., 1946.

Whitley, William T. *Art in England: 1800-1820*. Cambridge, England: Cambridge University Press, 1928.

―――. *Art in England: 1821-1837*. Cambridge, England: Cambridge University Press, 1930.

III. Separate Countries

ENGLAND

Beach, Joseph Warren. *The Concept of Nature in Nineteenth-Century English Poetry*. New York: Macmillan Co., 1936.

Beers, H. A. *History of English Romanticism in the Eighteenth Century*. New York: Henry Holt & Co., 1948.

Bernbaum, Ernest. *A Guide through the Romantic Movement*. 2nd ed. New York: Ronald Press, 1949.

Brailsford, H. L. *Shelley, Godwin, and Their Circle*. New York: Henry Holt & Co., 1913.

Brinton, Crane. *The Political Ideas of the English Romanticists*. Oxford: Humphrey Milford, 1926.

Somervell, D. C. *English Thought in the Nineteenth Century*. London: Methuen, 1929.

Stokoe, F. W. *The German Influence on the English Romantic Movement*. Cambridge, England: Cambridge University Press, 1926.

Summers, Montague. *The Gothic Quest*. London: Fortune Press, 1938.

Willey, Basil. *The Nineteenth-Century Background*. London: Chatto & Windus, 1949.

GERMANY

Aris, Reinhold. *Political Thought in Germany: 1789-1815*. London: Allen & Unwin, 1936.

Brandes, Georg. *Main Currents of Nineteenth-Century Literature*, Vol. II. New York: Macmillan Co., 1906.

Dewey, John. *German Philosophy and Politics*. New York: G. P. Putnam's Sons, 1942.

Hentschel, Cedric. *The Byronic Teuton*. London: Methuen & Co., 1940.

Reiss, H. S. *The Political Thought of the German Romantics*. Oxford: Blackwell's, 1955.

Robertson, J. G. *History of German Literature*. Rev. ed. New York: G. P. Putnam's Sons, 1931.

Santayana, George. *Egotism in German Philosophy*. New York: Charles Scribner's Sons, 1916.

Silz, Walter. *Early German Romanticism*. Cambridge: Harvard University Press, 1929.

Viereck, Peter. *Metapolitics: From the Romantics to Hitler*. New York: Alfred A. Knopf, Inc., 1941.

FRANCE

Clement, N. H. *Romanticism in France*. New York: Modern Language Association, 1939.

Draper, F. W. M. *The Rise and Fall of French Romantic Drama*. London: Constable & Co., 1923.

Engel-Janosi, Friedrich. *Four Studies in French Historical Writing*. Baltimore: Johns Hopkins Press, 1955.

George, Albert G. *The Development of French Romanticism: The Impact of the Industrial Revolution on Literature*. New York: Syracuse University Press, 1956.

Manuel, Frank E. *The New World of Henri Saint-Simon*. Cambridge: Harvard University Press, 1956.

Soltau, Roger. *French Political Thought of the Nineteenth Century*. New Haven: Yale University Press, 1931.

UNITED STATES

Matthiessen, F. O. *The American Renaissance.* New York: Oxford University Press, 1941.

Mayer, Frederick. *A History of American Thought.* Dubuque, Iowa: William C. Brown Co., 1956.

Parrington, V. C. *Main Currents of American Thought.* New York: Harcourt, Brace & Co., 1930.

Pritchard, John Paul. *Criticism in America.* Norman, Oklahoma: Oklahoma University Press, 1956.

To suggest other anthologies may suggest an embarrassment of riches for the reader. Yet the following collections contain sources which this editor found valuable; indeed, he incorporated their material in some instances. No one has a monopoly within the Romantic movement, and certainly any compounding of selection is desirable. In all instances the prefatory essays are rewarding; twice this list breaks the rule, that non-English works may not be mentioned.

Bate, Walter Jackson. *Criticism: The Major Texts.* New York: Harcourt, Brace & Co., 1952.

Baumer, Franklin Le Van. *Main Currents of Western Thought.* New York: Alfred A. Knopf, Inc., 1952.

Grigson, Geoffrey. *The Romantics.* London: Routledge & Kegan Paul, 1942.

Guthrie, Ramon, and Diller, George. *French Literature and Thought since the Revolution.* New York: Harcourt, Brace & Co., 1942.

Mack, Maynard, general editor, *et al. World Masterpieces.* 2 vols. New York: W. W. Norton & Co., 1956.

Stenzel, Gerhard. *Die Deutschen Romantiker.* 2 vols. Salzburg: Das Bergland Buch, 1954.

Wright, Raymond. *Prose of the Romantic Period: 1780-1830.* London: Penguin Books, 1956.

The excerpts to which anthologies are of necessity committed are bound to fill both editor and reader with partial dissatisfaction. After a diet of snippets, where the choice of even these morsels is queried, one hungers for entire works and more substance. (This tantalization is, of course, one aim of any anthology.)

For many years certain publishers have reprinted standard texts of imaginative, critical, and expository writing in relatively cheap editions—the Bohn Classics, Oxford World's Classics, E. P. Dutton's Sons' Everyman's Library, the Viking Portable Library, Modern Library (Random House), the Classics Club (W. J. Black), and the University Classics (Packard & Co.). There much material relevant to the Romantic movement is readily available. Recently we have seen an incredible increase in the production of paperback reprints: Croft Classics (Appleton-Century-Crofts), Rinehart Editions, Library of Liberal Arts (Liberal Arts Press), Pocket Books, Mentor Books (New American Library), Hafner Library of Classics, Gateway Editions (Henry Regnery), the English Penguin and Pelican books, Contemporary Affairs Series (Beacon), Anchor Books (Doubleday), Anvil Books (Van Nostrand), Vintage (Knopf), Compass (Viking), Meridian, Grove Press, and others. About half the volumes of the Viking Portable Library are now available in paper, and more are being issued.

Thus the following list of titles is appended for that reader anxious to read more extensively, whose purse is thin, and for whom the resources of a large public library are not easily obtainable. In the interests of brevity, only primary texts are mentioned. Critical works about Romanticism—some already suggested—may also be found among the various paperback series.

Balzac, Honoré de, *Père Goriot* (Rinehart, Penguin, Everyman).
Blake, William, (Viking Portable, Rinehart, Everyman, Modern Library, Oxford World's Classics).
Brontë, Emily, *Wuthering Heights* (Pocket Books, Rinehart, Modern Library).
Byron, George Gordon, Lord (Modern Library, Penguin, Rinehart).
Chateaubriand, *Atala and René* (University of California paperback).
Coleridge, Samuel Taylor (Viking Portable).

Dumas, Alexandre, the elder, *Three Musketeers* (Everyman).

Emerson, Ralph Waldo (Viking Portable, Rinehart).

English Romantic Poets (Penguin; *Viking Portable Poets of the English Language*, Vol. IV).

Flaubert, Gustave, *Sentimental Education* (Everyman); *Madame Bovary* (Pocket Books, Modern Library, Rinehart, Penguin).

Goethe, Johann Wolfgang von, *Faust Part I* (Penguin, Crofts, Oxford paperback, Rinehart); *Werther* (Rinehart); *Conversations with Eckermann* (Everyman).

Hawthorne, Nathaniel (Rinehart, Viking Portable).

Hegel, Georg Wilhelm Friedrich (Library of Liberal Arts).

Hölderlin, Friedrich (New Directions).

Hugo, Victor, *Notre-Dame* (Everyman, Modern Library).

Irving, Washington (Rinehart).

Keats, John, *Poems* (Modern Library, Crofts, Penguin, Rinehart); *Letters* (Anchor).

Melville, Herman (Viking Portable); *Moby Dick* (Pocket Books, Rinehart, Modern Library); *Tales and Poems* (Rinehart).

Poe, Edgar Allan (Rinehart, Everyman, Viking Portable).

Rousseau, Jean Jacques, *Confessions* (Penguin, Everyman); *Social Contract and Discourses* (Everyman); *Émile* (Everyman).

Scott, Sir Walter, various novels (Rinehart, Everyman, Oxford World's Classics).

Shelley, Percy Bysshe (Rinehart, Everyman, Oxford World's Classics, Modern Library).

Stendhal: *The Red and the Black* (Penguin, Modern Library); *Charterhouse of Parma* (Anchor); *Henri Brulard* (Vintage); *Letters to the Happy Few* (Grove).

Thoreau, Henry David (Modern Library, Rinehart, Viking Portable).

Vigny, Alfred, Comte de, *The Military Necessity* (Grove).

Walpole, Horace, *The Castle of Otranto* (Everyman: *Shorter English Eighteenth-Century Novels*).

Whitman, Walt (Viking Portable, Rinehart).

Wordsworth, William (Rinehart, Oxford World's Classics, Everyman, Penguin, Crofts, Modern Library).

BIOGRAPHICAL LIST
OF AUTHORS

Austen, Jane (1775-1817). English novelist and satirist, whose novels of manners and morals ally her more with the Age of Reason than with Romanticism.

Bage, Robert (1728-1801). English paper manufacturer, author of six novels, he sought in *Hermsprong* to popularize notions about "natural man."

Balzac, Honoré de (1799-1850). French novelist, whose numerous novels in *The Human Comedy* attempted to portray the whole of society in France, from the Empire through the July Monarchy.

Baudelaire, Charles (1821-1867). French poet and critic, officially labeled a "Symbolist" by literary historians, who nevertheless represented the extremes of Romanticism.

Beethoven, Ludwig van (1770-1827). German musician, whose nine great symphonies and various other compositions epitomize Romantic endeavors in that art. His life serves as a paradigm for the unhappy Romantic artist.

Berlioz, Hector (1803-1869). French composer, who with Franz Liszt was the greatest exponent of program music in the century. When Wagner is added, the three musicians represent the canonization of music as a leading Romantic art form.

Blake, William (1757-1827). English poet, painter, engraver; visionary and mystic; creator of private mythologies in his prophetic books; self-educated rebel against what he considered to be eighteenth-century materialistic and mechanistic philosophy.

Brentano, Clemens (1778-1842). German poet, novelist, and editor (with Achim von Arnim) of *The Child's Horn of Plenty* (1808), a collection of folk songs.

Brontë, Charlotte (1816-1855). English novelist, chiefly remembered for *Jane Eyre* (1847).

36

Brontë, Emily (1818-1848). English novelist and poet, whose poems first appeared in 1846 with those of her sisters Anne and Charlotte. Her unorthodox novel *Wuthering Heights* (1847) received only mild critical attention on publication.

Byron, George Gordon, Lord (1788-1824). English poet, dramatist, and satirist; aristocrat and rebel. His life and works established him as the model for a particular Romantic hero; his iconoclasm appealed to an entire generation.

Carlyle, Thomas (1795-1881). Scottish historian, essayist, and polemicist, whose fame rests principally on his *French Revolution* (1837), *Sartor Resartus* (1833-1834), and *On Heroes, etc.* (1840).

Chamisso, Adelbert von (1781-1838). German poet, novelist, botanist, soldier in the War of the Liberation. From 1815 to 1821, he circumnavigated the world pursuing his scientific studies.

Chateaubriand, François René, Vicomte de (1768-1848). Pioneer of French Romanticism; man of letters, statesman, ambassador. His *Memories from Beyond the Grave* (pub. 1850) offer a rich storehouse of information about the movement.

Chatterton, Thomas (1752-1770). Lay clerk at Bristol Cathedral, this English poet and antiquarian committed suicide at seventeen. The poems he "discovered," by the fifteenth-century monk Thomas Rowley, were later demonstrated to be a forgery.

Coleridge, Samuel Taylor (1772-1834). English poet, critic, and philosopher. Collaborated with Wordsworth in *The Lyrical Ballads* (1798); studied in Germany and provided an intellectual connection between the thought of the two countries. The most provocative of English Romantic critics on the subject of art and the imagination.

Cooper, James Fenimore (1789-1851). American novelist who presented Europe and America with the picture of the frontiersman and the noble savage in his *Leatherstocking Tales* (1823-1841).

De Quincey, Thomas (1785-1859). English novelist and critic, one of the first writers for *Blackwood's Magazine,* friend of most of the poets of the Lake School.

Desprès, Jean-Baptiste Denis (1752-1832). French playwright; translator of Lewis's *The Monk* and Mrs. Radcliffe's *Mysteries of Udolpho*.

Deschamps, Émile (1791-1851). French critic who founded *The French Muse*, an early Romantic periodical to which such writers as Hugo, Vigny, and Nodier contributed.

Disraeli, Benjamin, First Earl of Beaconsfield (1804-1881). English statesman, prime minister, leader of the Young England movement in the 1840s, and novelist.

Dumas, Alexandre, the Elder (1803-1870). French playwright and novelist, among whose historical novels *The Three Musketeers* (1844) is best known.

Eichendorff, Joseph, Freiherr von (1788-1857). German poet, novelist, and critic; author of *From the Life of a Good-for-Nothing* (1842).

Emerson, Ralph Waldo (1803-1882). American philosopher and man of letters; leader of the Transcendental Movement in New England; close friend of Thoreau; the main intellectual bridge between Europe and America during the second third of the century.

Flaubert, Gustave (1821-1880). French novelist, whose writings alternate between Romantic historicity and exoticism, and the realistic technique of his most famous book, *Madame Bovary* (1856).

Fouqué, Friedrich, Freiherr de la Motte (1777-1843). German author, member of a French émigré family, Prussian officer in the war against Napoleon.

Gautier, Théophile (1811-1872). French poet, novelist, critic, and literary historian. Early associated with the Romantic school, he later became one of the leading writers in the Parnassian movement, for which his preface to *Mademoiselle de Maupin* became a kind of manifesto.

Goethe, Johann Wolfgang von (1749-1832). German man of letters whose activities ranged through all the literary genres, philosophy, the natural sciences, and practical statecraft. Most of his life was spent at Weimar, which became a center for pilgrimages by all of Europe's intellectuals. Officially no "Romantic"—he decried the excesses of the younger generation writing ca. 1800-1830—he contributed largely to the attitudes and theories of the movement, from his early "Storm and Stress" days until his death.

Gray, Thomas (1716-1771). English poet, scholar, Cambridge professor; in his later years devoted to Icelandic and Celtic studies; best remembered for his *Elegy Written in a Country Churchyard* (1750).

Hawthorne, Nathaniel (1804-1864). American novelist whose tales blend Puritanism, Transcendentalism, and a feeling for the Gothic "terror" in a strange amalgam. Friend of Melville; later consul at Liverpool and traveler in Italy.

Haydon, Benjamin Robert (1786-1846). English historical painter; friend of Keats and Wordsworth; one of the first to give the Elgin marbles their just acclaim.

Hazlitt, William (1778-1830). A leading English critic of the time; member of the Wordsworth-Keats-Lamb circle.

Hegel, Georg Wilhelm Friedrich (1770-1831). German philosopher whose ideas about the workings of the historical process dominated nineteenth-century thought, and to whom Marx served as a curious—albeit rebellious—disciple. His lectures included studies of metaphysics, history, law, logic, and aesthetics.

Heine, Heinrich (1797-1856). German poet, critic, satirist; an exile in Paris for most of his life. *The Romantic School* (1836) is still one of the best studies of that movement, written by one at once sharing and chary of its tendencies.

Hölderlin, Friedrich (1770-1843). German poet who was insane through his last forty years. Perhaps the outstanding German Hellenist, whose works aspired to recreate the spirit of ancient Greece in the modern world.

Hugo, Victor (1802-1885). French man of letters whose name is synonymous with Romanticism, and whose many plays, novels, poems, and essays explored all the contours of the movement; a youthful monarchist and sentimental medievalist. His later liberalism caused his exile during the reign of Louis Napoleon (in his phrase, "Napoleon the Little"). *Hernani* and the Preface to *Cromwell* were manifestos for French Romanticism.

Immermann, Karl (1796-1840). German playwright, novelist, and theater director.

Irving, Washington (1783-1859). First author to be hailed by Europeans as indigenously American; historian, essayist, novelist, and Continental traveler.

Keats, John (1795-1821). English poet, whose three small volumes of verse published in his short life established him as one of the leading Romantic lyricists. His life (he was born the son of a stable-keeper, was the unhappy lover of Fanny Brawne, and died of tuberculosis), like Beethoven's, served as a pattern for the Romantic artist.

Lamb, Charles (1775-1834). English poet, essayist, and critic who was acquainted with most of the major English Romantics. The nineteenth and early twentieth centuries seemed to exaggerate his status, both as critic and personality.

Lewis, Matthew Gregory (1775-1818). English practitioner of the Gothic novel of terror, friend of Scott, Byron, and the prince regent. His chief fame rests on *The Monk,* which earned him his sobriquet, "Monk" Lewis.

Liszt, Franz (1811-1886). Hungarian-born pianist virtuoso, composer, and theorist, who came to Paris at the apogee of French Romanticism to become one of the movement's leading partisans. His daughter Cosima—born out of a liaison with the Comtesse d'Agoult—later married Wagner.

Mackenzie, Henry (1745-1831). Scottish man of letters. The popularity of *The Man of Feeling* (1771) tends to obscure his role as mediator between early German Romantic drama and the English public. He also was chairman of the committee to investigate the authenticity of MacPherson's *Poems of Ossian.*

MacPherson, James (1736-1796). Scottish scholar who purported to discover the Gaelic poems by the third-century poet Ossian, from 1760 to 1763, including the epics *Fingal* and *Temora.* Doctor Johnson challenged their authenticity, which later was proved questionable; Goethe, Blake, Byron, Thoreau, and Napoleon were among the many admirers of Ossian.

Marggraff, Herman (1809-1864). German playwright, poet, novelist, and historian.

Maturin, Charles (1782-1824). Irish novelist and playwright, author of several Gothic novels.

Melville, Herman (1819-1891). American poet and novelist, who started as a writer of sea stories and tales of South Sea adventure. *Moby Dick* (1851), considered by many critics to be the greatest American novel, marked the commencement of his popular decline for the contemporary public.

Musset, Alfred de (1810-1857). French poet and dramatist, author of some of the few comedies produced by French Romantics, celebrated biographically for his love affair with George Sand.

Nerval, Gérard de (Gérard Labrunie, 1808-1855). French poet and novelist, Romantic eccentric, author of curious dream literature prefiguring Surrealism, a bridge between Romanticism and the Symbolist movement.

Nodier, Charles (1780-1844). French novelist, founder of the first Romantic *cénacle* or salon where the principal writers, including Hugo, gathered in 1823; author of several fantastic and Gothic tales.

Novalis (Friedrich von Hardenberg, 1772-1801). German author whose tales and poems (*Heinrich von Ofterdingen, The Disciples at Saïs, Hymns to the Night*) reflected his interest in strange myths, Christianity, mysticism, geology, and mineralogy, and his love for his dead teen-age fiancée, Sophie von Kühn.

Peacock, Thomas Love (1785-1866). English novelist and minor poet, satirist of some of the excesses of Romanticism, friend of Shelley. Peacock's positivist essay provoked that author's *Defence of Poetry* (1821). Scythrop, in *Nightmare Abbey,* is probably modeled on Shelley.

Poe, Edgar Allan (1809-1849). American poet and author of supernatural tales; leading representative of the "Gothic" in America; early practitioner of detective fiction.

Radcliffe, Ann (1764-1823). English novelist, whose *Romance of the Forest* (1791) and *The Mysteries of Udolpho* (1794) inspired scores of Gothic imitators.

Rellstab, Ludwig (1799-1860). Minor German critic and novelist.

Rousseau, Jean Jacques (1712-1778). French philosopher, musician, novelist and man of letters, whose writings have traditionally been regarded as seminal for later Romanticism.

Saint-Simon, Claude Henri de Rouvroy, Comte de (1760-1825). French social theorist who expounded plans for international, social, and political reform. His disciples included many of the prominent French Romantics in the 1820s and 1830s.

Schiller, Johann Christian Friedrich von (1759-1805). German dramatist, historian, poet, and aesthetician. His youthful "Storm and Stress" writings were later superseded by a more restrained idealistic humanitarianism, where Kant was a strong influence. Goethe was a close friend.

Schlegel, Friedrich von (1772-1829). A leading German Romantic theorist whose ideas were popularized by his brother, August Wilhelm. His writings on Greek, Indic, and modern literature established a mode of thinking for his contemporaries and successors.

Scott, Sir Walter (1771-1832). Scottish poet, dramatist, novelist, and publisher. His collection of folk songs and ballads, *Border Minstrelsy* (1802-1803), contributed to the revival of folk verse as a serious form of art; his many novels, including *Waverley* (1814), *Ivanhoe* (1819), and *Kenilworth* (1821), determined the pattern for most historical novels in the nineteenth and twentieth centuries.

Sénancour, Pivert de (1770-1846). French novelist. *Obermann* (1804) was largely ignored until the 1830s, when a later generation of Romantics found it a source of melancholy inspiration.

Shelley, Mary Wollstonecraft (1797-1851). English authoress, daughter of the philosopher William Godwin; Shelley's second wife.

Shelley, Percy Bysshe (1792-1822). English poet, second-generation Romantic along with Byron and Keats—both his friends; political revolutionary and Utopian, despite the nineteenth-century characterization of him as "an ineffectual angel."

Spiess, Christian Heinrich (1750-1799). Minor German dramatist and novelist.

Staël, Anne Louise Germaine de (1766-1817). French woman of letters whose chief role was to introduce German thought to France; friend of the Schlegel brothers,

Goethe, the critic Sismondi, Benjamin de Constant, etc. At one time Napoleon exiled her from Paris.

Steffens, Heinrich (1773-1845). Norwegian-born, German-educated writer; member of the Young Romantic group at Jena in 1799.

Stendhal (Henri Beyle, 1783-1842). French novelist, journalist, music and art historian. His affection for eighteenth-century thinkers, the realism of his novels, his disdain for the commonplace aspects of French Romanticism, make him difficult to categorize as a Romantic. In this he resembles Byron and especially Heine.

Thoreau, Henry David (1817-1862). American essayist and poet; the rebel par excellence against any sort of conformity; close friend of Emerson, and strongly influenced by Transcendentalism; later admired by the English Fabians, Tolstoy, and Gandhi.

Trelawney, Edward John (1792-1881). English adventurer, friend and biographer of both Byron and Shelley.

Vigny, Alfred, Comte de (1797-1863). French dramatist, poet, writer of historical novels; officer in the Army during the Restoration, until 1827; close in spirit to another nineteenth-century stoic, Matthew Arnold.

Vitet, Ludovic (1802-1873). French critic and politician, early partisan of the Romantics; contributor to the Romantic journal, The Globe, in 1824.

Walpole, Horace, Fourth Earl of Orford (1717-1797). English traveler and literary amateur; lived from 1747 at Strawberry Hill, Twickenham, which he made into "a little Gothic castle."

Wellington, Duke of (Sir Arthur Wellesley, 1769-1852). English statesman and soldier; victor over Napoleon at Waterloo; prime minister from 1828 to 1830.

Whitman, Walt (1819-1892). American poet, early champion of free verse, spokesman for American aesthetic and intellectual freedom from Europe.

Wordsworth, William (1770-1850). English poet, youthful admirer of the French Revolution and the radical philosophy of William Godwin; collaborator with Coleridge in The Lyrical Ballads (1798); poet laureate in 1843.

CHRONOLOGICAL TABLE, 1740-1851

DATES	POLITICS AND WAR	SCIENCE AND PHILOSOPHY	ARTS AND LETTERS	DATES
1740-80	Maria Theresa, Empress of Austria and the Holy Roman Empire			1740-80
1740-86	Frederick II, the Great, King of Prussia			1740-86
1750			J. S. Bach: Art of the Fugue	1750
1751-54		Franklin's experiments with electricity		1751-54
1751-80		The Great Encyclopedia published in France, 35 vols.		1751-80
1752			Handel: Jephta	1752
1755			Dr. Johnson: Dictionary of the English Language	1755
1756			Burke: On the Sublime	1756
1756-63	Seven Years' War			1756-63
1757		Helvétius: On the Mind	Gray: Odes	1757
1758				1758
1759			Voltaire: Candide	1759
1760-1820	George III King of England			1760-1820
1761			Rousseau: Julie, or the New Héloïse	1761
1762		Rousseau: Social Contract	MacPherson: Fingal	1762
1762-96	Catherine II, the Great, Empress of Russia			1762-96
1764		Voltaire: Philosophical Dictionary	Walpole: Castle of Otranto	1764

Date	Politics & History	Science & Philosophy	Arts & Letters
1766			Lessing: Laocöon; Goldsmith: Vicar of Wakefield
1768			English Royal Academy of Arts; Sir Joshua Reynolds, president
1770	Warren Hastings governor of India	Hargreave's spinning jenny; Holbach: System of Nature; Watt's steam engine	
c. 1770			Rousseau: Confessions
1770-88			
1771			Mackenzie: Man of Feeling
1773-85			
1774	Louis XVI King of France	Priestley's experiments with oxygen (dephlogisticated air)	Goethe: Werther; Gluck: Iphigenia in Aulis
1774-93			Beaumarchais: Barber of Seville
1775	American Revolution		
1775-83			
1776		Adam Smith: Wealth of Nations	
1776-88			Gibbon: Decline and Fall of the Roman Empire
1777			Chatterton: Rowley Poems
1778	Alliance between France and the American colonies	Buffon: Epochs of Nature	
1779		Hume: Dialogues Concerning Natural Religion; Mesmer: Animal Magnetism (hypnotism)	
1780-90		Lamarck's studies in chemistry	
1781		Kant: Critique of Pure Reason	Schiller: The Robbers

DATES	POLITICS AND WAR	SCIENCE AND PHILOSOPHY	ARTS AND LETTERS	DATES
1783		Herschel: Motion of the Solar System in Space		1783
1786			Burns: Poems	1786
1787	American Constitutional Convention in Philadelphia		Mozart: Don Giovanni	1787
1787-88		The Federalist		1787-88
1788		Blake: There Is No Natural Religion	Haydn: Oxford Symphony	1788
1789	Fall of the Bastille; beginning of French Revolution	Bentham: Morals and Legislation	Blake: Songs of Innocence	1789
1790		Burke: Reflections on the French Revolution		1790
1791			Boswell: Life of Johnson	1791
1792-1815	France at war: the Coalitions and Napoleon			1792-1815
1793	Execution of Louis XVI	Godwin: Political Justice; Dalton: Meteorological Observations		1793
1793-94		Paley: Evidences of Christianity; Whitney patents cotton gin	Radcliffe: Mysteries of Udolpho	1793-94
1794	Reign of Terror in France		David: "Rape of the Sabines"	1794
1795		Schiller: Simple and Sentimental Poetry	Goethe: Wilhelm Meister's Apprenticeship	1795
1795-96			Lewis: The Monk	1795-96
1796		Condorcet: Progress of the Human Mind		1796
1798		Malthus: Principle of Population	Wordsworth and Coleridge: Lyrical Ballads	1798

Year	Political	Science / Philosophy	Arts / Literature
1799	Napoleon First Consul of France	Novalis: Christendom or Europe	Haydn: Creation; Hölderlin: Hyperion
1802		Chateaubriand: Genius of Christianity	
1803	Louisiana Purchase		Austen: Northanger Abbey
1804	Napoleon crowned Emperor of France		Beethoven: Third Symphony ('Eroica')
1805	Battles of Trafalgar and Austerlitz		Beethoven: Fidelio
1805-1806			
1807		Hegel: Phenomenology of the Mind	Wordsworth: Prelude
1807-1808		Fichte: Speeches to the German Nation	
1808			Arnim and Brentano: Child's Horn of Plenty; Goethe: Faust, Part I
1808-14	Peninsular War in Spain and Portugal		
1809		Lamarck: Zoölogical Philosophy; Soemmering invents the telegraph	
1810-13			Goya: "The Disasters of War"
1812-14	War between England and the United States		
1812-15			Grimm brothers: Fairy Tales
1812-18			Byron: Childe Harold
1814		Stephenson's locomotive	Scott: Waverley; Chamisso: Peter Schlemihl
1814-15	Congress of Vienna		
1815	Waterloo		

DATES	ARTS AND LETTERS	SCIENCE AND PHILOSOPHY	POLITICS AND WAR	DATES
1816	Rossini: Barber of Seville	Owen: New View of Society		1816
1817		Coleridge: Biographia Literaria; Ricardo: Principles of Political Economy		1817
1818	Keats: Endymion			1818
1819	Keats: major odes; Géricault: "Raft of the Medusa"	Schopenhauer: World as Will and Idea		1819
1819-24	Byron: Don Juan			1819-24
1820	Lamartine: Poetic Meditations; Shelley: Prometheus Unbound			1820
1821	Shelley: Defence of Poetry	Saint-Simon: Industrial System; James Mill: Elements of Political Economy		1821
1821-29			Greek War of Independence	1821-29
1822-23	Heine: Lyrical Intermezzo			1822-23
1822-31		Hegel: Philosophy of History		1822-31
1823			Monroe Doctrine	1823
1824	Beethoven: Ninth Symphony ("Choral")			1824
1825				1825
1826	Cooper: Last of the Mohicans Weber: Oberon	Niepce's camera experiments		1826
1827	Hugo: Preface to Cromwell			1827
1828	Schubert: Seventh Symphony			1828
1830	Hugo: Hernani; Berlioz: Fantastic Symphony		Revolutions in France, Belgium, Poland, etc.	1830
1830-33		Lyell: Principles of Geology		1830-33
1830-44		Comte: Course of Positive Philosophy		1830-44
1831	Hugo: Notre-Dame; Dumas: Antony; Stendhal: The Red and the Black	Faraday's dynamo		1831

1832	English Reform Bill		Goethe: Faust, Part II
1833		Keble's sermon initiates the Oxford Movement	
1834		Strauss: Life of Jesus	Balzac: Père Goriot
1835-36		Tocqueville: Democracy in America	
1835-40			
1836			Musset: Confessions; Heine: Romantic School
1837	Queen Victoria's accession		Carlyle: French Revolution; Dickens: Pickwick Papers
1838			Poe: Arthur Gordon Pym
1839			Stendhal: Charterhouse of Parma
1840		Carlyle: On Heroes and Hero-Worship	
1841		Newman: Tracts for the Times	
1843		Kierkegaard: Either/Or; J. S. Mill: A System of Logic	
1845			Schumann: Piano Concerto; Wagner: Tannhäuser
1846			Berlioz: Damnation of Faust (opera-oratorio)
1846-48	War between Mexico and the United States		
1847			E. Brontë: Wuthering Heights
1848	Revolutions in France, Austria, Germany, Italy, etc.; gold discovered in California	Marx-Engels: Communist Manifesto; J. S. Mill, Principles of Political Economy	Thackeray: Vanity Fair
1849	Completion of constitution of the German Empire	Thoreau: Civil Disobedience	
1851	Coup d'état of Louis Napoleon; Great Exhibition in London		Melville: Moby Dick

PROLOGUE

What the Romantics Said about Romanticism

NOVALIS
(Friedrich von Hardenberg)

[from *Fragments*]

1798

The world must be made romantic. Then once more we shall discover its original meaning. To make something romantic is nothing else but a qualitative potentialization. In such an operation, the lower self becomes identified with the higher self. We ourselves are this series of qualitative potentials . . . Insofar as I render a higher meaning to what is ordinary, a mysterious appearance to what is customary, an infinite look to the finite, I am romanticizing. . . .

Nothing is more romantic than what we customarily call the world and fate.

Trans. H. E. H.

51

JOSEPH VON EICHENDORFF

[FROM *Halle and Heidelberg*]

1857

Romanticism was not merely a literary phenomenon. It undertook much more: to effect an inner regeneration of the whole of existence, as Novalis had proclaimed. What was later called *The Romantic School* was indeed only a detached branch of the already sick tree.

Trans. H. E. H.

JOHANN WOLFGANG VON GOETHE

[FROM J. P. Eckermann, *Conversations with Goethe*]

[April 2, 1829]

"A new expression occurs to me," said Goethe, "which does not ill define the state of the case. I call the classic *healthy*, the romantic *sickly*. In this sense, the *Nibelungenlied* is as classic as the *Iliad*, for both are vigorous and healthy. Most modern productions are romantic— not because they are new; but because they are weak, morbid, and sickly. And the antique is classic—not because it is old; but because it is strong, fresh, joyous, and healthy. If we distinguish 'classic' and 'romantic' by these qualities, it will be easy to see our way."

[April 5, 1829]

Goethe also told me about a tragedy by a young poet. "It is a pathological work," said he, "a superfluity of sap is bestowed on some parts that do not require it, and drawn out of those standing in need of it. The subject was good, but the scenes I expected were not there; while others that I did not expect were elaborated with assiduity and love. This is what I call pathological, or even 'romantic'—if you would rather speak after our new theory."

[March 21, 1830]

"The idea of the distinction between classical and romantic poetry, which is now spread over the whole world and occasions so many quarrels and divisions, came originally from Schiller and myself. I laid down the maxim of objective treatment in poetry, and would allow no other; but Schiller, who worked quite in the subjective way, deemed his own fashion the right one, and to defend himself against me, wrote the treatise upon *Naïve and Sentimental Poetry*. He proved to me that I myself, against my will, was romantic, and that my *Iphigenia*, through the predominance of sentiment, was by no means so classical and so much in the antique spirit as some people supposed.

"The Schlegels took up this idea, and carried it further, so that it has now been diffused over the whole world; and everyone talks about classicism and romanticism—of which nobody thought fifty years ago."

Trans. J. Oxenford.

ÉMILE DESCHAMPS

[FROM *The French Muse*]

1824

This entangled lawsuit between the classicists and the romantics is nothing else but the eternal battle between prosaic spirits and romantic souls.

Trans. H. E. H.

FRIEDRICH VON SCHLEGEL

[FROM THE *Athenäum*]

1800

Romantic poetry is a progressive universal poetry. Its destiny is not merely again to unite all the separated classes of poetry, and to place poetry in contact with philosophy and rhetoric. Soon it shall and should blend and mix poetry with prose, genius with criticism, art-poetry with natural-poetry; make poetry lively and sociable and make society poetic; poetize wit; replenish and satisfy the outer forms of art with solid creative material from each separate art; animate everything by the vibrations of humor.

Trans. H. E. H.

JEAN-BAPTISTE DENIS DESPRÈS

[FROM *The Globe*]

1825

Let us say that romanticism is the conveying of spirituality into literature.

Trans. H. E. H.

NOVALIS
(Friedrich von Hardenberg)

[from *Letters*]

1798

The Romantic studies life the way a painter, a musician, and an engineer study color, sound, and stresses. This diligent study of life defines the Romantic, just as the diligent study of color, sound, and stresses defines the painter, musician, and engineer.

Trans. H. E. H.

GEORGE WILHELM FRIEDRICH HEGEL

[from the *Introduction to the Philosophy of Art*]

1820-29, pub. 1835

The Romantic form of art annihilates the unity of the spiritual idea with its sensuous form; it returns, although on a higher plane, to the difference and opposition between idea and form—a difference which symbolic art left unresolved. Classical art reached the loftiest degree of perfection which any sensuous process of art could ever realize. If classical art displayed any defects, these were innate to art itself, and were the limitations of art. . . .

Romantic art dissolves the ideal of classical art, which is the latter's visible unity. Romantic art has acquired a content far richer than that of classical art and its mode of expression. . . .

In brief, the essence of Romantic art lies in the artistic object's being free, concrete, and the spiritual idea in its very essence—all this revealed to the inner

rather than to the outer eye. . . . This inner world is
the content of Romantic art; Romantic art must seek its
embodiment in precisely such an inner life or some reflection of it. Thus the inner life shall triumph over the
outer world; triumph over it in such a way that the
outer world will itself proclaim the former's victory, by
which sensuous appearance must sink into worthless-
ness. . . .

Trans. H. E. H.

FRIEDRICH VON SCHLEGEL

[FROM THE *Athenäum*]

1800

I must place the real center, the essence of Romantic
fantasy, in Shakespeare. From there I seek and find
the Romantic in the older modern writers; in Shakespeare, Cervantes, Italian poetry, in every age of chivalry, in love, in fairy tales—in all those items from
which both the thing itself and the word are derived.
Up to the present time, this is the sole means possible to
provide an antithesis to the classical poetry of antiquity.

Trans. H. E. H.

KARL IMMERMANN

[FROM *Memoirs*]

1840

The Romantic school had its greatest influence on
poetic souls and on small coteries. No real literary
careerist could withdraw himself from its spell, for it
proclaimed itself to be a necessary stage in the development of German literature.

But popular this school could never be. It was not

based on the actual present, but rather generated out of a longing for something nonexistent—in all truth, a longing that had for origin a very delicate and aesthetic need. This "enlightened" century verbalized pure chivalry, Catholicism, the world of the fairy tale, mysticism: verbalized so successfully that it never was able to gaze on the true mirror-image of these ways of life.

Trans. H. E. H.

LOUIS VITET

[FROM *The Globe*]

1825

In a word, Romanticism is Protestantism in the arts and letters.

Trans. H. E. H.

VICTOR HUGO

[FROM THE PREFACE TO *Hernani*]

1830

Romanticism, badly defined so many times, when all is said and done is only—and here is its real definition, if you view Romanticism from its militant side—liberalism in literature.

Trans. H. E. H.

HEINRICH STEFFENS

[FROM *My Experiences*]

1840-44

The Middle Age was emphasized [by Romanticism] in all its strength: elevated, indeed, far higher than that real epoch which, when it was called upon to perform great and mighty deeds, had actually lost itself weakly in empty abstractions and in a few superficial ideas. . . .

Especially was the Madonna honored as the divine woman, by means of all the illusions produced by poetry. After Tieck, August Wilhelm Schlegel, and Novalis had made her the source of poetic consecration, we watched all the young poets kneel before the altar of the Madonna.

Trans. H. E. H.

PIVERT DE SÉNANCOUR

[FROM *Obermann*]

1804

The romanesque seduces lively and flourishing imaginations; the romantic alone suffices those deep spirits, those endowed with true sensibility. Nature abounds in romantic effects in the simple countryside. These are destroyed when ancient lands are extensively cultivated.

Trans. H. E. H.

CHARLES NODIER

[FROM *A Report on Byron's "Vampire"*]

1820

Our imaginations are . . . so in love with the lie that they prefer a startling illusion to the description of some pleasing emotion, natural as the latter may be. This last resort of the human heart, tired of ordinary feelings, is what is called the *romantic* genre: strange poetry, but a poetry quite appropriate to the moral condition of society, to the needs of surfeited genera-

tions who cry for sensations at any cost and believe
that they are not paying too dearly in terms of the
generations yet to come. For primitive poets and their
elegant imitators, the classicists, the ideal was found
in the perfection of our human nature. The ideal for
romantic poets is found in our sorrows.

Trans. H. E. H.

STENDHAL
(Henri Beyle)

[from *Racine and Shakespeare*]

1823

Romanticism is the art of offering people literary
works which are capable of giving them the greatest
amount of pleasure, in the present condition of their
habits and beliefs.

Classicism, on the contrary, presents them with literature which gave the greatest amount of pleasure to their
great-grandfathers.

Sophocles and Euripides were pre-eminently romantics. To the Greeks assembled at the theater in Athens,
they gave tragedies intended to procure the greatest
possible pleasure—in terms of the ethical customs of
that race, its religion, its preconceptions about everything relevant to the dignity of man.

To imitate Sophocles and Euripides today, and claim
that the imitations will not make a Frenchman of the
nineteenth century yawn: that is classicism.

I have no hesitation in claiming that Racine was a
Romantic. To the nobles at the court of Louis XIV, he
gave a true picture of the passions, tempered by the
extreme dignity then in fashion. . . . You do not find
this dignity anywhere in the Greeks. It is due to this

same dignity, which today must leave us cold, that
Racine was a romantic.

Shakespeare was romantic because, first, he showed
the English in the year 1590 those bloody catastrophes
brought about by civil war; and then—to quiet down
these dismal spectacles—a mass of delicate pictures of
the activity of the heart, nuances of the most delicate
passions. . . .

ALL GREAT WRITERS WERE ROMANTICS IN THEIR OWN
DAY.

Trans. H. E. H.

FRANZ LISZT

[FROM *The Life of Chopin*]

1852

Soon after [Chopin] arrived in Paris in 1832, a new
school of both literature and music began. Youthful
talent came forward to shake off old-fashioned theories
with startling power. Scarcely had the political ferment
of the first year of the July Revolution subsided when
questions were raised about arts and letters which
aroused universal interest and attention. *Romanticism*
was the order of the day; and a stubborn fight ensued
both pro and con. How could any truce have been
possible between one side, who would not admit that
it was possible to write in forms other than those
established; and those in the other camp who contended
that an artist should be allowed to choose such forms
as he felt best suited to express his ideas, any rule about
form being located in the appropriateness of a form to
the sentiments to be expressed—every varying shade of
emotion naturally requiring a different mode of expression? The former declared their faith to be in some
permanent form whose perfection represented absolute

beauty. . . . The latter, on the other hand, denied that immaterial beauty could ever own any fixed, absolute form: those different forms revealed by history seemed to them to be tents erected along the endless road of the Ideal—mere temporary stopping places reached by genius in various epochs, beyond which their heirs had ever to advance. . . .

Those who watched the fires of genius consume the ancient, worm-eaten, and crumbling skeletons all attached themselves to that school of which Berlioz was the most gifted, audacious, and brilliant representative. This school Chopin joined.

Trans. H. E. H.

WILLIAM HAZLITT

[FROM *Lectures on the English Poets*]

1818

Mr. Wordsworth is at the head of that which has been denominated the Lake school of poetry; a school which, with all my respect for it, I do not think sacred from criticism or exempt from faults, of some of which faults I shall speak with becoming frankness; for I do not see that the liberty of the press ought to be shackled, or freedom of speech curtailed, to screen either its revolutionary or renegado extravagances. This school of poetry had its origin in the French revolution, or rather in those sentiments and opinions which produced that revolution; and which sentiments and opinions were indirectly imported into this country in translations from the German about that period. Our poetical literature had, towards the close of the last century, degenerated into the most trite, insipid, and mechanical of all things, in the hands of the followers of Pope and the old French school of poetry. It wanted something to stir it up, and

it found that something in the principles and events of
the French revolution. From the impulse it thus received, it rose at once from the most servile imitation
and tamest common-place, to the utmost pitch of singularity and paradox. The change in the belles-lettres was
as complete, and to many persons as startling, as the
change in politics, with which it went hand in hand.
There was a mighty ferment in the heads of statesmen
and poets, kings and people. According to the prevailing notions, all was to be natural and new. Nothing
that was established was to be tolerated. All the common-place figures of poetry, tropes, allegories, personifications, with the whole heathen mythology, were instantly discarded; a classical allusion was considered as
a piece of antiquated foppery; capital letters were no
more allowed in print, than letters-patent of nobility
were permitted in real life; kings and queens were de-
throned from their rank and station in legitimate tragedy or epic poetry, as they were decapitated elsewhere;
rhyme was looked upon as a relic of the feudal system,
and regular metre was abolished along with regular
government. Authority and fashion, elegance or arrangement, were hooted out of countenance, as pedantry
and prejudice. Every one did that which was good in
his own eyes. The object was to reduce all things to an
absolute level; and a singularly affected and outrageous
simplicity prevailed in dress and manners, in style and
sentiment. A striking effect produced where it was
least expected, something new and original, no matter
whether good, bad, or indifferent, whether mean or lofty,
extravagant or childish, was all that was aimed at, or
considered as compatible with sound philosophy and an
age of reason. The licentiousness grew extreme: Cory-
ate's Crudities were nothing to it. The world was to be
turned topsy-turvy; and poetry, by the good will of our
Adam-wits, was to share its fate and begin *de novo*.
It was a time of promise, a renewal of the world and of

letters; and the Deucalions, who were to perform this feat of regeneration, were the present poet-laureate and the authors of the Lyrical Ballads. The Germans, who made heroes of robbers, and honest women of cast-off mistresses, had already exhausted the extravagant and marvellous in sentiment and situation: our native writers adopted a wonderful simplicity of style and matter. The paradox they set out with was, that all things are by nature equally fit subjects for poetry; or that if there is any preference to be given, those that are the meanest and most unpromising are the best, as they leave the greatest scope for the unbounded stores of thought and fancy in the writer's own mind.

VICTOR HUGO

[FROM *The Preface to Cromwell*]

1827

The same sort of civilization, or to use a more precise although more extended expression, the same sort of society, has not always occupied the world. In its entirety the human race has grown, developed, matured, just like any one of us. It was a child, it became a man; we are now spectators to its imposing old age. Prior to that era called antiquity by modern society, there existed another era called *fabulous* by the ancients, which might be more exact to name *primitive*. Therefore let us look at three great successive orders within civilization, from its origins to our own day. Hence, since poetry is always superimposed on society, we shall try to fathom out in terms of the structure of the former what must have been the character of the latter in these three great ages of the world—the primitive period, the antique period, the modern period. . . .

It was then [in the Christian era] that poetry took a big step, casting its eye on events at once impressive and laughable, and under the influence of the spirit of Christian melancholy and the critical philosophy we have just been sketching; a decisive step, a step which, like an earthquake's tremor, changed the entire face of the intellectual world. Poetry set about to do what nature does, to blend in with nature's creations, while at the same time not mixing them all together: shadow and light, the grotesque and the sublime—in other words, the body with the soul, the animal with the spiritual. . . .

Here you must allow us our conviction; for we have just shown the characteristic traits, the fundamental differences, which to our way of thinking separate the modern world from that of antiquity, living form from dead form; or, to make use of vaguer but more accredited language, separate *romantic* literature from *classical* literature.

Trans. H. E. H.

MADAME DE STAEL

[FROM *Concerning Germany*]

1813

The word *romantic* has been lately introduced in Germany, to designate that kind of poetry which is derived from the songs of the Troubadours; that which owes its birth to the union of chivalry and Christianity. If we do not admit that the empire of literature has been divided between paganism and Christianity, the north and the south, antiquity and the middle ages, chivalry and the institutions of Greece and Rome, we shall never succeed in forming a philosophical judgment of ancient and of modern taste.

Some French critics have asserted that German literature is still in its infancy; this opinion is entirely false: men who are best skilled in the knowledge of languages, and the works of the ancients, are certainly not ignorant of the defects and advantages attached to the species of literature which they either adopt or reject; but their character, their habits, and their modes of reasoning, have led them to prefer that which is founded on the recollection of chivalry, on the wonders of the middle ages, to that which has for its basis the mythology of the Greeks. The literature of romance is alone capable of further improvement, because, being rooted in our own soil, that alone can continue to grow and acquire fresh life: it expresses our religion; it recalls our history; its origin is ancient, although not of classical antiquity. Classic poetry, before it comes home to us, must pass through our recollections of paganism: that of the Germans is the Christian aera of the fine arts; it employs our personal impressions to excite strong and vivid emotions; the genius by which it is inspired addresses itself immediately to our hearts, and seems to call forth the spirit of our own lives, of all phantoms at once the most powerful and the most terrible.

It is said there are persons who discover springs, hidden under the earth, by the nervous agitation which they cause in them: in German poetry, we often think we discover that miraculous sympathy between man and the elements. The German poet comprehends nature not only as a poet, but as a brother; and we might almost say that the bonds of family union connect him with the air, the water, flowers, trees—in short, all the primary beauties of the creation.

When I began the study of German literature, it seemed as if I was entering on a new sphere, where the most striking light was thrown on all that I had before perceived only in a confused manner. For some time past, little has been read in France except memoirs and novels, and it is not wholly from frivolity that we are become less capable of more serious reading, but because the events of the revolution have accustomed us to value nothing but the knowledge of men and things: we find in German books, even on the most abstract subjects, that kind of interest which confers their value upon good novels, and which is excited by the knowledge which they teach us of our own hearts. The peculiar character of German literature, is to refer everything to an interior existence; and as that is the mystery of mysteries, it awakens an unbounded curiosity.

The new school maintains the same system in the fine arts as in literature, and affirms that Christianity is the source of all modern genius; the writers of this school also characterize, in a new manner, all that in Gothic architecture agrees with the religious sentiments of Christians. It does not follow however from this, that the moderns can and ought to construct Gothic churches; neither art nor nature admit of repetition: it is only of consequence to us, in the present silence of genius, to lay aside the contempt which has been thrown on all the conceptions of the middle ages; it certainly does not suit us to adopt them, but nothing is more injurious to the development of genius, than to consider as barbarous everything that is original.

Trans. anon (London: John Murray, 1814).

HEINRICH HEINE

[from *The Romantic School*]

1833

While I announce this book as a sequel to Madame de Staël's "De l'Allemagne," and extol her work very highly as being replete with information, I must yet recommend a certain caution in the acceptance of the views enunciated in that book, which I am compelled to characterize as a coterie-book. Madame de Staël, of glorious memory, has here, in the form of a book, opened a salon, in which she received German authors and gave them an opportunity to make themselves known to the civilized world of France. But above the din of the most diverse voices, confusedly discoursing therein, the most audible is the delicate treble of Herr A. W. Schlegel. Where the large-hearted woman is wholly herself—where she is uninfluenced by others, and expresses the thoughts of her own radiant soul, displaying all her intellectual fireworks and brilliant follies—there the book is good, even excellent. But as soon as she yields to foreign influences, as soon as she begins to glorify a school whose spirit is wholly unfamiliar and incomprehensible to her, as soon as through the commendation of this school she furthers certain Ultramontane tendencies which are in direct opposition to her own Protestant clearness, just so soon her book becomes wretched and unenjoyable. . . .

But what was the Romantic School in Germany?

It was naught else than the reawakening of the poetry of the middle ages as it manifested itself in the poems, paintings, and sculptures, in the art and life of those times. This poetry, however, had been developed out of Christianity, it was a passion-flower which had blossomed from the blood of Christ. I know not if the melancholy flower which in Germany we call the passion-flower is known by the same name in France, and if the popular tradition has ascribed to it the same mystical origin. It is that motley-hued, melancholic flower in whose calyx one may behold a counterfeit presentment of the tools used at the crucifixion of Christ— namely, hammer, pincers, and nails. This flower is by no means unsightly, but only spectral: its aspect fills our souls with a dread pleasure, like those convulsive, sweet emotions that arise from grief. In this respect the passion-flower would be the fittest symbol of Christianity itself, whose most awe-inspiring charm consists in the voluptuousness of pain. Although in France Christianity and Roman Catholicism are synonymous terms, yet I desire to emphasize the fact that I here refer to the latter only.

I refer to that religion whose earliest dogmas contained a condemnation of all flesh, and not only admitted the supremacy of the spirit over the flesh, but sought to mortify the latter in order thereby to glorify the former. I refer to that religion through whose unnatural mission vice and hypocrisy came into the world, for through the odium which it cast on the flesh, the most innocent gratification of the senses were accounted sins; and, as it was impossible to be entirely spiritual, the growth of hypocrisy was inevitable. I refer to that religion which, by teaching the renunciation of all earthly pleasures, and by inculcating abject humility and angelic patience, became the most efficacious support of despotism. Mankind now recognizes the nature of that religion, and will no longer allow itself to be put off with promises of a Heaven hereafter; it knows that the material world has also its good, and is not wholly given over to Satan, and now they vindicate the pleasures of the world, this beautiful garden of the gods, our inalienable heritage; and just because we now comprehend so fully all the consequences of that absolute spirituality, we are warranted in believing that the Christian-Catholic theories of the universe are at an end, for every epoch is a sphinx which plunges into the abyss, as soon as its problem is solved. . . .

The political condition of Germany was particularly favorable to the tendencies of the ROMANTIC SCHOOL, which sought to introduce a national-religious literature, similar to that which had prevailed in Germany during the middle ages. "Need teaches prayer," says the proverb; and truly never was the need greater in Germany. Hence the masses were more than ever inclined to prayer, to religion, to Christianity. No people is more loyally attached to its rulers than are the Germans. And more even than the sorrowful condition to which the country was reduced through war and foreign rule, did the mournful spectacle of their vanquished princes, creeping at the feet of Napoleon, afflict and grieve the Germans. . . .

We would have submitted to Napoleon quietly enough, but our princes, while they hoped for deliverance through Heaven, were at the same time not unfriendly to the thought that the united strength of their subjects might be very useful in effecting the purpose. Hence they sought to awaken in the German people a sense of homogeneity, and even the most exalted personages now spoke of a German nationality, of a common German fatherland, of a union of the Christian-Germanic races, of the unity of Germany. We were commanded to be patriotic, and straightway we became patriots—for we always obey when our princes command.

Trans. S. L. Fleischman (New York: Henry Holt, 1882).

THEOPHILE GAUTIER

[FROM *History of Romanticism*, "First Encounter"]

1874

Of those [in Paris in 1830] who answered Hernani's horn-call and enrolled as his attendants on Romanticism's rough mountain-top, where they valiantly defended the passes against the attacks of the Classicists, there survive only a small number of veterans, who are disappearing each day, just as are medals from St. Helena. We had the honor to be enrolled in those youthful companies who fought for ideality, for poetry and freedom in the arts, with an enthusiasm, a courage, and a devotion unknown today. A radiant leader remains standing amid his glory like a statue on a brazen column, but the memory of obscure soldiers is soon lost; and it is the duty of those who were a part of that great literary army to tell the tales of exploits now forgotten.

Present generations must imagine only with great difficulty the intellectual effervescence of that age; a movement much like that of the Renaissance was in progress. The sap of a new life flowed impetuously. Everything germinated, everything budded, everything burst all at once. Flowers released giddy perfumes; the air itself was intoxicated, and we were mad with lyricism and with art. It seemed as if we had just discovered a long-lost secret; and that was true, for we had rediscovered poetry.

One cannot imagine to what degree of insignificance and paleness literature had attained. Painting was scarcely any better. David's last pupils spread out their insipid colors on old, commonplace Graeco-Roman canvasses. Classicists found this perfectly beautiful; yet before such masterpieces, their admiration did not prevent them from putting their hands in front of their mouths to conceal a yawn—something, however, that did not make them any more indulgent toward the artists of the younger school, whom they called tatooed savages and whom they accused of painting with "a drunken brush." But we did not let their insults drop to the ground unnoticed; we answered back with *mummies* in place of their *savages,* and both sides scorned each other completely. . . .

Chateaubriand may be considered as the ancestor, or, if you prefer, the Sachem of Romanticism in France. He restored the Gothic cathedral with his *Genius of Christianity;* in *The Natchez* he opened up great nature, till then hidden; in *René* he invented melancholy and modern passion. Unfortunately, precisely to this poetic soul were lacking the two wings of poetry—verse—and these wings Victor Hugo possessed with a huge span, as he flew from one end of the lyrical sky to the other. He rose, he glided, he described circles, he romped with a liberty and strength reminiscent of the flight of an eagle.

What a marvelous age! Walter Scott was then in the full bloom of his success; we initiated ourselves into the mysteries of Goethe's *Faust*, which according to Madame de Staël's expression contained everything and even a little more. We discovered Shakespeare through Letourneur's slightly patchy translation; and Lord Byron's poems, *The Corsair, Lara, The Giaour, Manfred, Beppo, Don Juan* came to us from the East, which at that time was not yet banal. How young everything was; new, strangely colored, how intoxicating and strong the flavor! Our heads spun; we seemed to be entering into worlds unknown. . . .

Without yet being affiliated with the Romantic troop, we already gave our hearts to it! The preface to *Cromwell* gleamed in our eyes like the Stone Tablets on Mount Sinai, and its arguments seemed to us to be irrefutable. The insults rendered by little classical periodicals against the young master, whom we have considered ever since then, and rightly so, to be France's greatest poet, put us into a furious rage. . . .

In the Romantic Army, as in the Army of Italy, everyone was young.

The majority of the soldiers had not yet attained their majority, and the oldest of the troops was the commander in chief, twenty-eight years old. At that time, this was the age of both Bonaparte and of Victor Hugo. . . .

Trans. H. E. H.

ALFRED DE MUSSET

[FROM *Letters of Dupuis and Cotonet*]

1836

The first two years we thought that *romanticism*, as a manner of writing, only applied to the theater, and that it distinguished itself from classicism because it did away with the unities.

But suddenly we were taught (I think it was in 1828) that there was a romantic and a classical poetry, a romantic novel and a classical novel, a romantic ode and a classical ode. What can I say? A single verse, a single, unique verse, can be romantic or classical, depending upon the idea you have about it.

When we heard this news, we could not sleep a wink all night. . . .

Tired of examining and weighing opinions, finding always nothing but empty phrases and incomprehensible professions of faith, we came to believe that this word *romanticism* was merely a word. We found it to be beautiful, and it seemed too bad that it meant nothing. The word looks like *Rome* and *Roman,* like *roman* [i.e., the novel] and *romanesque;* perhaps it is really the same thing as *romanesque.* So, at least, we were tempted to think. . . .

From 1830 to 1831 we believed romanticism to be the historical genre; or, if you will, that mania lately possessing our authors to call characters in novels and in melodrama Charlemagne, Francis I, Henry IV, instead of Amadis, Orontes, or Saint Albin. . . .

From 1831 to the following year, we then thought it was the *intimate* genre everyone was speaking so strongly about. We watched the historical genre being discredited, yet romanticism was still very much alive.

But despite all the pains we took, we were never able to discover just what this intimate genre was. . . .

From 1832 to 1833, it came to mind that romanticism might be a system of philosophy and of political economy. It was certainly true that writers then had a predilection to speak in their prefaces about the future, about social progress, humanity, and civilization. We thought the cause of such a style was the July Revolution. Furthermore, it is hard to believe that there is anything really new in being a republican. . . .

Romanticism, my dear sir? Certainly it is neither a scorn for the unities, nor an alliance between the comic and the tragic, nor anything at all you might suggest. In vain you snatch at the wings of a butterfly, and the dust that collects on them is all that stays on your fingers. Romanticism is the star that weeps, the wind that wails, the night that shivers, the flower that flies, and the bird that exudes perfume. Romanticism is the unhoped-for ray of light, the languorous rapture, the oasis beneath the palm-trees, ruby hope with its thousand loves, the angel and the pearl, the willow in its white garb. Oh, sir, what a beautiful thing! It is the infinite and the star, heat, the fragmentary, the sober (yet at the same time complete and full); the diametrical, the pyramidal, the Oriental, the living nude, the embraceable, the kissable, the whirlwind.

Trans. H. E. H.

PART ONE

The Man of Feeling

THE PLEASURES AND PAINS OF SENTIMENT

Feeling is everything.
 —Johann Wolfgang von Goethe

Pride in the Heart

[FROM *The Sorrows of Young Werther*]

JOHANN WOLFGANG VON GOETHE

1774

May 10, 1771

A wonderful serenity has taken possession of my entire soul, like these sweet spring mornings which I enjoy with all my heart. I am alone, and feel the enchantment of life in this spot, which was created for souls like mine. I am so happy, my dear friend, so absorbed in the exquisite sense of tranquil existence, that I neglect my art. I could not draw a single line at the present moment; and yet I feel that I was never a greater painter than I am now. When the lovely valley teems with mist around me, and the high sun strikes the impenetrable foliage of my trees, and but a few rays steel into the inner sanctuary, I lie in the tall grass by the trickling stream and notice a thousand familiar things: when I hear the

humming of the little world among the stalks, and am
near the countless indescribable forms of the worms and
insects, then I feel the presence of the Almighty Who
created us in His own image, and the breath of that
universal love which sustains us, as we float in an
eternity of bliss; and then, my friend, when the world
grows dim before my eyes and earth and sky seem to
dwell in my soul and absorb its power, like the form of a
beloved—then I often think with longing, Oh, would I
could express it, could impress upon paper all that is
living so full and warm within me, that it might become
the mirror of my soul, as my soul is the mirror of the
infinite God! O my friend—but it will kill me—I shall
perish under the splendor of these visions!

May 12

I know not whether some deceiving spirits haunt
this spot, or whether it is the ardent, celestial fancy in
my own heart which makes everything around me seem
like paradise. In front of the house is a spring—a spring
to which I am bound by a charm like Melusine and her
sisters. Descending a gentle slope, you come to an arch,
where, some twenty steps lower down, the clearest
water gushes from the marble rock. The little wall
which encloses it above, the tall trees which surround
the spot, and the coolness of the place itself—everything
imparts a pleasant but sublime impression. Not a day
passes that I do not spend an hour there. The young
girls come from the town to fetch water—the most
innocent and necessary employment, but formerly the
occupation of the daughters of kings. As I sit there, the
old patriarchal idea comes to life again. I see them,
our old ancestors, forming their friendships and plight-
ing their troth at the well; and I feel how fountains and
streams were guarded by kindly spirits. He who does
not know these sensations has never enjoyed a cool rest

at the side of a spring after the hard walk of a summer's day.

May 13

You ask if you should send my books. My dear friend, for the love of God, keep them away from me! I no longer want to be guided, animated. My heart is sufficiently excited. I want strains to lull me, and I find them abundantly in my Homer. How often do I still the burning fever of my blood; you have never seen anything so unsteady, so restless, as my heart. But need I confess this to you, my dear friend, who have so often witnessed my sudden transitions from sorrow to joy, and from sweet melancholy to violent passions? I treat my heart like a sick child, and gratify its every fancy. Do not repeat this; there are people who would misunderstand it.

May 9, 1772

I have paid my visit to my native place with the devotion of a pilgrim, and have experienced many unexpected emotions. Near the great linden tree, a quarter of an hour from the town, I got out of the carriage and sent it on ahead so that I might enjoy the pleasure of recollection more vividly and to my heart's content. There I stood, under that same linden tree which used to be the goal and end of my walks. How things have changed! Then, in happy ignorance, I sighed for a world I did not know, where I hoped to find the stimulus and enjoyment which my heart could desire; and now, on my return from that wide world, O my friend, how many disappointed hopes and unfulfilled plans have I brought back!

As I saw the mountains which lay stretched out before me, I thought how often they had been the object of my dearest desires. Here I used to sit for hours,

wishing to be there, wishing that I might lose myself
in the woods and valleys that now lay so enchanting and
mysterious before me—and when I had to return to
town at a definite time, how unwillingly did I leave this
familiar place! I approached the town; and recognized
all the well-known old summerhouses; I disliked the
new ones, and all the changes which had taken place.
I entered the gate, and all the old feelings returned. I
cannot, dear friend, go into details, charming as they
were; they would be dull reading. I had intended to
lodge in the market place, near our old house. As I approached, I noticed that the school in which, as children, we had been taught by that good old lady, was
converted into a shop. I called to mind the restlessness,
the heaviness, the tears, and heartaches which I experienced in that confinement. Every step produced
some particular impression. No pilgrim in the Holy Land
could meet so many spots charged with pious memories,
and his soul can hardly be moved with greater devotion.
One incident will serve for illustration. I followed the
stream down to a farm—it used to be a favorite walk
of mine—and I paused where we boys used to amuse
ourselves making ducks and drakes upon the water. I
remember so well how I sometimes watched the course
of that same stream, following it with strange feelings,
and romantic ideas of the countries it was to pass
through; but my imagination was soon exhausted. Yet I
knew that the water continued flowing on and on . . .
and I lost myself completely in the contemplation of the
infinite distance. Exactly like this, my friend, so happy
and so rich were the thoughts of the ancients. Their
feelings and their poetry were fresh as childhood. And
when Ulysses talks of the immeasurable sea and boundless earth, his words are true, natural, deeply felt, and
mysterious. Of what use is it that I have learned, with
every schoolboy, that the world is round? Man needs

but little earth for his happiness, and still less for his final rest.

I am at present at the Prince's hunting lodge. He is a man with whom one can live quite well. He is honest and simple. There are, however, some curious characters about him whom I cannot quite understand. They are not dishonest, and yet they do not seem thoroughly honorable men. Sometimes I am disposed to trust them, and yet I cannot persuade myself to confide in them. It annoys me to hear the Prince talk of things which he has only read or heard of, and always from the point of view from which they have been represented by others.

He values my understanding and talents more highly than my heart, but I am proud of my heart alone. It is the sole source of everything—all our strength, happiness, and misery. All the knowledge I possess everyone else can acquire, but my heart is all my own.

Trans. Victor Lange (New York: Rinehart & Co., 1949).

Tears on All Occasions

[FROM *The Man of Feeling*]

HENRY MACKENZIE

1771

He had taken leave of his aunt on the eve of his intended departure; but the good lady's affection for her nephew interrupted her sleep, and early as it was next morning when Harley came down stairs to set out, he found her in the parlour with a tear on her cheek, and her caudle-cup in her hand. She knew enough of physic to prescribe against going abroad of a morning with an empty stomach. She gave her blessing with the draught; her instructions she had delivered the night before. They consisted mostly of negatives; for London, in her idea, was so replete with temptations, that it needed the whole armour of her friendly cautions to repel their attacks.

Peter stood at the door. We have mentioned this faithful fellow formerly: Harley's father had taken him up an orphan, and saved him from being cast on the parish; and he had ever since remained in the service of him and of his son. Harley shook him by the hand as he passed, smiling, as if he had said, "I will not weep." He sprung hastily into the chaise that waited for him: Peter folded up the step. "My dear master (said he, shaking the solitary lock that hung on either side of his head), I have been told as how London is a sad place." He was choked with the thought, and his benediction could not be heard—but it shall be heard, honest Peter! —where these tears will add to its energy.

In a few hours Harley reached the inn where he proposed breakfasting; but the fulness of his heart would not suffer him to eat a morsel. He walked out on the road, and gaining a little height, stood gazing on that quarter he had left. He looked for his wonted prospect, his fields, his woods, and his hills: they were lost in the distant clouds! He penciled them on the clouds, and bade them farewell with a sigh!

[Harley visits a madhouse and sees a young girl who has lost her lover.]

Though this story was told in very plain language, it had particularly attracted Harley's notice; he had given it the tribute of some tears. The unfortunate young lady had till now seemed entranced in thought, with her eyes fixed on a little garnet ring she wore on her finger: she turned them now upon Harley. "My Billy is no more!" said she, "do you weep for my Billy? Blessings on your tears! I would weep too, but my brain is dry; and it burns, it burns, it burns!" She drew nearer to Harley. "Be comforted, young lady," said he, "your Billy is in Heaven." "Is he, indeed? and shall we meet again? and shall that frightful man (pointing to the keeper) not be there?—Alas! I am grown naughty of late; I have almost forgotten to think of Heaven; yet I pray sometimes; when I can, I pray; and sometimes I sing; when I am saddest, I sing:—You shall hear me, hush!

"Light be the earth on Billy's breast,
    And green the sod that wraps his grave!"

There was a plaintive wildness in the air not to be withstood; and except the keeper's, there was not an unmoistened eye around her.

"Do you weep again?" said she. "I would not have you weep; you are like my Billy; you are, believe me; just so he looked when he gave me this ring; poor Billy! 'twas the last time ever we met!—

" 'Twas when the seas were roaring—I love you for resembling my Billy; but I shall never love any man like him." She stretched out her hand to Harley; he pressed it between both of his, and bathed it with his tears. "Nay, that is Billy's ring," said she. "You cannot have it, indeed; but here is another, look here, which I plated today of some gold-thread from this bit of stuff; will you keep it for my sake? I am a strange girl;—but my heart is harmless; my poor heart; it will burst some day; feel how it beats!" She press'd his hand to her bosom, then holding her head in an attitude of listening—"Hark! One, two, three! Be quiet, thou little trembler; my Billy's is cold!—But I had forgotten the ring." She put it on his finger. "Farewell! I must leave you now." She would have withdrawn her hand; Harley held it to his lips. "I dare not stay longer; my head throbs sadly: farewell!" She walked with a hurried step to a little apartment at some distance. Harley stood

fixed in astonishment and pity! His friend gave money
to the keeper. Harley looked on his ring. He put a
couple of guineas into the man's hand: "Be kind to that
unfortunate." He burst into tears, and left them.

[*Harley's death-bed*]

Harley was one of those few friends whom the malev-
olence of fortune had yet left me: I could not therefore
but be sensibly concerned for his present indisposition;
there seldom passed a day on which I did not make
inquiry about him.

The physician who attended him had informed me
the evening before, that he thought him considerably
better than he had been for some time past. I called
next morning to be confirmed in a piece of intelligence
so welcome to me.

When I entered his apartment, I found him sitting on
a couch, leaning on his hand, with his eye turned upwards in the attitude of thoughtful inspiration. His look
had always an open benignity, which commanded esteem; there was now something more—a gentle triumph
in it.

He rose, and met me with his usual kindness. When
I gave him the good accounts I had had from his physician, "I am foolish enough," said he, "to rely but little,
in this instance, upon physic: my presentiment may be
false; but I think I feel myself approaching to my end,
by steps so easy, that they woo me to approach it.

"There is a certain dignity in retiring from life at a
time, when the infirmities of age have not sapped our
faculties. This world, my dear Charles, was a scene in
which I never much delighted. I was not formed for
the bustle of the busy, nor the dissipation of the gay:
a thousand things occurred, where I blushed for the
impropriety of my conduct when I thought on the
world, though my reason told me I should have blushed
to have done otherwise.—It was a scene of dissimula-

tion, of restraint, of disappointment. I leave it to enter
on that state, which I have learned to believe, is replete
with the genuine happiness attendant upon virtue. I
look back on the tenor of my life, with the consciousness
of few great offences to account for. There are blem-
ishes, I confess, which deform in some degree the picture. But I know the benignity of the Supreme Being,
and rejoice at the thoughts of its exertion in my favour.
My mind expands at the thought I shall enter into the
society of the blessed, wise as angels, with the simplicity
of children." He had by this time clasped my hand,
and found it wet by a tear which had just fallen upon it.

A Man of Very Strong Passions

[FROM THE *Confessions*]

JEAN-JACQUES ROUSSEAU

1770-78

[*1712-1719*]

I am commencing an undertaking, hitherto without
precedent, and which will never find an imitator. I
desire to set before my fellows the likeness of a man in
all the truth of nature, and that man myself.

Myself alone! I know the feelings of my heart, and I
know men. I am not made like any of those I have seen;
I venture to believe that I am not made like any of those
who are in existence. If I am not better, at least I am
different. Whether Nature has acted rightly or wrongly
in destroying the mould in which she cast me, can only
be decided after I have been read.

Let the trumpet of the Day of Judgment sound when
it will, I will present myself before the Sovereign Judge

with this book in my hand. I will say boldly: "This is what I have done, what I have thought, what I was. I have the good and the bad with equal frankness.

I have neither omitted anything bad, nor interpolated anything good. If I have occasionally made use of some immaterial embellishments, this has only been in order to fill a gap caused by lack of memory. I may have assumed the truth of that which I knew might have been true, never of that which I knew to be false. I have shown myself as I was: mean and contemptible, good, high-minded and sublime, according as I was one or the other. I have unveiled my inmost self even as Thou hast seen it, O Eternal Being. Gather round me the countless host of my fellow-men; let them hear my confessions, lament for my unworthiness, and blush for my imperfections. Then let each of them in turn reveal, with the same frankness, the secrets of his heart at the foot of the Throne, and say, if he dare, 'I was better than that man!'" . . .

I felt before I thought: this is the common lot of humanity. I experienced it more than others. I do not know what I did until I was five or six years old. I do not know how I learned to read; I only remember my earliest reading, and the effect it had upon me; from that time I date my uninterrupted self-consciousness. My mother had left some romances behind her, which my father and I began to read after supper. At first it was only a question of practising me in reading by the aid of amusing books; but soon the interest became so lively, that we used to read in turns without stopping, and spent whole nights in this occupation. We were unable to leave off until the volume was finished. Sometimes, my father, hearing the swallows begin to twitter in the early morning, would say, quite ashamed, "Let us go to bed; I am more of a child than yourself."

In a short time I acquired, by this dangerous method, not only extreme facility in reading and understanding what I read, but a knowledge of the passions that was unique in a child of my age. I had no idea of things in themselves, although all the feelings of actual life were already known to me. I had conceived nothing, but felt everything. These confused emotions which I felt one after the other, certainly did not warp the reasoning powers which I did not as yet possess; but they shaped them in me of a peculiar stamp, and gave me odd and romantic notions of human life, of which experience and reflection have never been able wholly to cure me. . . .

How could I become wicked, when I had nothing but examples of gentleness before my eyes, and none around me but the best people in the world? My father, my aunt, my nurse, my relations, our friends, our neighbours, all who surrounded me, did not, it is true, obey me, but they loved me; and I loved them in return. My wishes were so little excited and so little opposed, that it did not occur to me to have any. I can swear that, until I served under a master, I never knew what a fancy was. Except during the time I spent in reading or writing in my father's company, or when my nurse took me for a walk, I was always with my aunt, sitting or standing by her side, watching her at her embroidery or listening to her singing; and I was content. Her cheerfulness, her gentleness and her pleasant face have stamped so deep and lively an impression on my mind that I can still see her manner, look, and attitude; I remember her affectionate language: I could describe what clothes she wore and how her head was dressed, not forgetting the two little curls of black hair on her temples, which she wore in accordance with the fashion of the time.

I am convinced that it is to her I owe the taste, or rather passion, for music, which only became fully developed in me a long time afterwards. She knew a prodigious number of tunes and songs which she used to sing in a very thin, gentle voice. This excellent woman's cheerfulness of soul banished dreaminess and melancholy from herself and all around her. The attraction which her singing possessed for me was so great, that not only have several of her songs always remained in my memory, but even now, when I have lost her, and as I grew older, many of them, totally forgotten since the days of my childhood, return to my mind with inexpressible charm. Would anyone believe that I, an old dotard, eaten up by cares and troubles, sometime find myself weeping like a child, when I mumble one of those little airs in a voice already broken and trembling?

. . . I have spent my life in idle longing, without saying a word, in the presence of those whom I loved most. Too bashful to declare my taste, I at least satisfied it in situations which had reference to it and kept up the idea of it. To lie at the feet of an imperious mistress, to obey her commands, to ask her forgiveness— this was for me a sweet enjoyment; and, the more my lively imagination heated my blood, the more I presented the appearance of a bashful lover. It may be easily imagined that this manner of making love does not lead to very speedy results, and is not very dangerous to the virtue of those who are its object. For this reason I have rarely possessed, but have none the less enjoyed myself in my own way—that is to say, in imagination. Thus it has happened that my senses, in harmony with my timid disposition and my romantic spirit, have kept my sentiments pure and my morals blameless, owing to the very tastes which, combined with a little more impudence, might have plunged me into the most brutal sensuality. . . .

I am a man of very strong passions, and, while I am stirred by them, nothing can equal my impetuosity; I forget all discretion, all feelings of respect, fear and decency; I am cynical, impudent, violent and fearless; no feeling of shame keeps me back, no danger frightens me; with the exception of the single object which occupies my thoughts, the universe is nothing to me. But all this lasts only for a moment, and the following moment plunges me into complete annihilation. In my calmer moments I am indolence and timidity itself; everything frightens and discourages me; a fly, buzzing past, alarms me; a word which I have to say, a gesture which I have to make, terrifies my idleness; fear and shame overpower me to such an extent that I would gladly hide myself from the sight of my fellow-creatures. If I have to act, I do not know what to do; if I have to speak, I do not know what to say; if anyone looks at me, I am put out of countenance. When I am strongly moved I sometimes know how to find the right words, but in ordinary conversation I can find absolutely nothing, and my condition is unbearable for the simple reason that I am obliged to speak.

Add to this, that none of my prevailing tastes centre in things that can be bought. I want nothing but unadulterated pleasures, and money poisons all. For instance, I am fond of the pleasures of the table; but, as I cannot endure either the constraint of good society or the drunkenness of the tavern, I can only enjoy them with a friend; alone, I cannot do so, for my imagination then occupies itself with other things, and eating affords me no pleasure. If my heated blood longs for women, my excited heart longs still more for affection. Women who could be bought for money would lose for me all their charms; I even doubt whether it would be in me to make use of them. I find it the same with all pleasures within my reach; unless they cost me nothing, I find them insipid. I only love those enjoyments which belong to no one but the first man who knows how to enjoy them.

. . . I worship freedom; I abhor restraint, trouble, dependence. As long as the money in my purse lasts, it assures my independence; it relieves me of the trouble of finding expedients to replenish it, a necessity which always inspired me with dread; but the fear of seeing it exhausted makes me hoard it carefully. The money which a man possesses is the instrument of freedom; that which we eagerly pursue is the instrument of slavery. Therefore I hold fast to that which I have, and desire nothing.

My disinterestedness is, therefore, nothing but idleness; the pleasure of possession is not worth the trouble of acquisition. In like manner, my extravagance is nothing but idleness; when the opportunity of spending agreeably presents itself, it cannot be too profitably employed. Money tempts me less than things, because between money and the possession of the desired object there is always an intermediary, whereas between the thing itself and the enjoyment of it there is none. If I see the thing, it tempts me; if I only see the means of gaining possession of it, it does not. For this reason I have committed thefts, and even now I sometimes pilfer trifles which tempt me, and which I prefer to take rather than to ask for; but neither when a child nor a grown-up man do I ever remember to have robbed anyone of a farthing, except on one occasion, fifteen years ago, when I stole seven *livres* ten *sous*.

Trans. anon. (New York: E. P. Dutton, n.d.)

The Sickness of the Century

[FROM *The Genius of Christianity*]

FRANÇOIS RENÉ,
VICOMTE DE CHATEAUBRIAND

1802

We still must speak of a state of the soul which, it seems to us, has not yet been described: it is that which precedes the development of great passions, when all the young, active, self-willed—yet restricted—faculties are exercised only upon themselves with neither goal nor aim. The more a race advances toward civilization, the more is augmented this condition of the vagueness of the passions. Finally there occurs a very sad situation: the great number of examples which one has before one's eyes, the multitude of books which deal with man and his feelings, make the individual clever without having experienced life. One becomes undeceived without having been deceived; some desires remain, but there are no more illusions. The imagination is rich, abundant, and wonderful; existence is poor, arid, and disenchanted. With a full heart one inhabits an empty world, and without having made use of anything, we are dissatisfied with everything.

The bitterness which this state of soul injects into life is incredible; the heart twists and turns in a hundred ways to employ those powers that it feels to be useless. The ancients little knew this secret anxiety, this sourness of stifled passions fermenting together. An active political existence, the games in the gymnasium and on the drill-field, activities in the forum and the public square filled up every moment and allowed no room for the heart to be bored.

Then again, they did not incline toward exaggerations, toward groundless hopes and fears, toward mobility of ideas and feelings, toward perpetual fickleness which is nothing but steadfast disgust—these dispositions that we acquire from intimate feminine society. Women, with us moderns, independent of the passion which they evoke, influence still more all the other sentiments. They have in their constitution a certain waywardness that they inject into us; they make our male character less resolute; and our passions, mollified by the mixture with theirs, take on a quality both wavering and tender. . . .

Trans. H. E. H.

Ode on Melancholy

JOHN KEATS

1819

No, no, go not to Lethe, neither twist
   Wolf's-bane, tight-rooted, for its poisonous wine;
Nor suffer thy pale forehead to be kissed
   By nightshade, ruby grape of Proserpine;
Make not your rosary of yew-berries,
   Nor let the beetle, nor the death-moth be
     Your mournful Psyche, nor the downy owl
A partner in your sorrow's mysteries;
   For shade to shade will come too drowsily,
     And drown the wakeful anguish of the soul.

But when the melancholy fit shall fall
   Sudden from heaven like a weeping cloud,

That fosters the droop-headed flowers all,
   And hides the green hill in an April shroud;
Then glut thy sorrow on a morning rose,
    Or on the rainbow of the salt sand-wave,
      Or on the wealth of globèd peonies;
Or if thy mistress some rich anger shows,
    Emprison her soft hand, and let her rave,
      And feed deep, deep upon her peerless eyes.

She dwells with Beauty—Beauty that must die;
   And Joy, whose hand is ever at his lips
Bidding adieu; and aching Pleasure nigh,
    Turning to Poison while the bee-mouth sips:
Ay, in the very temple of delight
    Veiled Melancholy has her sovran shrine,
      Though seen of none save him whose strenuous
        tongue
Can burst Joy's grape against his palate fine;
His soul shall taste the sadness of her might,
    And be among her cloudy trophies hung.

A Lost Generation

[FROM *The Confession of a Child of the Century*]

ALFRED DE MUSSET

1836

During the wars of the Empire, while the husbands
and brothers were in Germany, the anxious mothers
brought forth an ardent, pale, nervous generation. Conceived between two battles, educated amidst the noises
of war, thousands of children looked about them with

a somber eye while testing their puny muscles. From time to time their blood-stained fathers would appear, raise them on their gold-laced bosoms, then place them on the ground and remount their horses.

The life of Europe was centered in one man; all were trying to fill their lungs with the air which he had breathed. Every year France presented that man with three hundred thousand of her youth; it was the tax paid to Caesar, and, without that troop behind him, he could not follow his fortune. It was the escort he needed that he might traverse the world, and then perish in a little valley in a deserted island, under the weeping willow. . . . Nevertheless, the immortal emperor stood one day on a hill watching seven nations engaged in mutual slaughter; as he did not know whether he would be master of all the world or only half, Azrael passed along, touched him with the tip of his wing, and pushed him into the Ocean. At the noise of his fall, the dying powers sat up in their beds of pain; and stealthily advancing with furtive tread, all the royal spiders made the partition of Europe, and the purple of Caesar became the frock of Harlequin.

Then there seated itself on a world in ruins an anxious youth. All the children were drops of burning blood which had inundated the earth; they were born in the bosom of war, for war. For fifteen years they had dreamed of the snows of Moscow and of the sun of the pyramids. They had not gone beyond their native towns; but they were told that through each gate of these towns lay the road to a capital of Europe. They had in their heads all the world; they beheld the earth, the sky, the streets and the highways; all these were empty, and the bells of parish churches resounded faintly in the distance.

Pale phantoms, shrouded in black robes, slowly traversed the country; others knocked at the doors of houses, and when admitted, drew from their pockets large well-worn documents with which they drove out the tenants. From every direction came men still trembling with the fear which had seized them when they fled twenty years before. All began to urge their claims, disputing loudly and crying for help; it was strange that a single death should attract so many crows.

Three elements entered into the life which offered itself to these children: behind them a past forever destroyed, moving uneasily on its ruins with all the fossils of centuries of absolutism; before them the aurora of an immense horizon, the first gleams of the future; and between these two worlds—something like the Ocean which separates the old world from Young America, something vague and floating, a troubled sea filled with wreckage, traversed from time to time by some distant sail or some ship breathing out a heavy vapor; the present, in a word, which separates the past from the future, which is neither the one nor the other, which resemble both, and where one can not know whether, at each step, one is treading on a seed or a piece of refuse.

It was in this chaos that choice must be made; this was the aspect presented to children full of spirit and of audacity, sons of the Empire and grandsons of the Revolution.

A feeling of extreme uneasiness began to ferment in all young hearts. Condemned to inaction by the powers which governed the world, delivered to vulgar pedants of every kind, to idleness and to ennui, the youth saw the foaming billows which they had prepared to meet, subside. All these gladiators, glistening with oil, felt in the bottom of their souls an insupportable wretchedness. The richest became libertines; those of moderate fortune followed some profession and resigned themselves to the sword or to the robe. The poorest gave themselves up with cold enthusiasm to great thoughts, plunged into the frightful sea of aimless effort. As human weakness seeks association and as men are herds by nature, politics became mingled with it. There were struggles with the *garde du corps* on the steps of the legislative assembly; at the theater, Talma wore a peruke which made him resemble Caesar; every one flocked to the burial of a liberal deputy.

The customs of students and artists, those customs so free, so beautiful, so full of youth, began to experience the universal change. Men in taking leave of women whispered the word which wounds to the death: contempt. They plunged into the dissipation of wine and courtesans. Students and artists did the same; love was treated as glory and religion: it was an old illusion. The grisette, that class so dreamy, so romantic, so tender, and so sweet in love, abandoned herself to the counting-house and to the shop.

Then they formed into two camps; on the one side the exalted spirits, sufferers, all the expansive souls who had need of the infinite, bowed their heads and wept; they wrapped themselves in unhealthy dreams and there could be seen nothing but broken reeds on an ocean of bitterness. On the other side the men of the flesh remained standing, inflexible in the midst of positive joys, and cared for nothing except to count the money they had acquired. It was only a sob and a burst of laughter, the one coming from the soul, the other from the body.

This is what the soul said:

"Alas! Alas! religion has departed; the clouds of heaven fall in rain; we have no longer either hope or expectation, not even two little pieces of black wood in the shape of a cross before which to clasp our hands.

The star of the future is loath to rise; it cannot get above the horizon; it is enveloped in clouds, and like the sun in winter its disk is the color of blood, as in '93. There is no more love, no more glory. What heavy darkness over all the earth! And we shall be dead when the day breaks."

This is what the body said:

"Man is here below to satisfy his senses, he has more or less of white or yellow metal to which he owes more or less esteem. To eat, to drink, and to sleep, that is life. As for the bonds which exist between men, friendship consists in loaning money; but one rarely has a friend whom he loves enough for that. Kinship determines inheritance; love is an exercise of the body; the only intellectual joy is vanity."

Like the Asiatic plague exhaled from the vapors of the Ganges, frightful despair stalked over the earth. Already Chateaubriand, prince of poesy, wrapping the horrible idol in his pilgrim's mantle, had placed it on a marble altar in the midst of perfumes and holy incense. Already the children were tightening their idle hands and drinking in their bitter cup the poisoned brewage of doubt. Already things were drifting toward the abyss, when the jackals suddenly emerged from the earth. A cadaverous and infected literature which had no form but that of ugliness, began to sprinkle with fetid blood all the monsters of nature.

Who will dare to recount what was passing in the colleges? Men doubted everything: the young men denied everything. The poets sang of despair; the youth came from the schools with serene brow, their faces glowing with health and blasphemy in their mouths. Moreover, the French character, being by nature gay and open, readily assimilated English and German ideas; but hearts too light to struggle and to suffer withered like crushed flowers. Thus the principle of death descended slowly and without shock from the head to the bowels. Instead of having the enthusiasm of evil we had only the negation of the good; instead of despair, insensibility. Children of fifteen, seated listlessly under flowering shrubs, conversed for pastime on subjects which would have caused the motionless groves of Versailles to shudder with terror. The Communion of Christ, the host, those wafers that stand as the eternal symbol of divine love, were used to seal letters; the children spat upon the bread of God.

Happy they who escaped those times! Happy they who passed over the abyss while looking up to Heaven. There are such, doubtless, and they will pity us.

It is unfortunately true that there is in blasphemy a certain discharge of power which solaces the burdened heart. When an atheist, drawing his watch, gave God a quarter of an hour in which to strike him dead, it is certain that it was a quarter of an hour of wrath and of atrocious joy. It was the paroxysm of despair, a nameless appeal to all celestial powers; it was a poor wretched creature squirming under the foot that was crushing him; it was a loud cry of pain. And who knows? In the eyes of Him who sees all things, it was perhaps a prayer.

Thus these youth found employment for their idle powers in a fondness of despair. To scoff at glory, at religion, at love, at all the world, is a great consolation for those who do not know what to do; they mock at themselves and in doing so prove the correctness of their view. And then it is pleasant to believe oneself unhappy when one is only idle and tired. Debauchery, moreover, the first conclusion of the principle of death, is a terrible millstone for grinding the energies.

The rich said: "There is nothing real but riches, all else is a dream; let us enjoy and then let us die." Those of moderate fortune said: "There is nothing real but oblivion, all else is a dream; let us forget and let us die."

And the poor said: "There is nothing real but unhappiness, all else is a dream; let us blaspheme and die."

All the evils of the present come from two causes: the people who have passed through 1793 and 1814 nurse wounds in their hearts. That which was is no more; what will be is not yet. Do not seek elsewhere the cause of our malady.

Trans. anon. (New York: Bigelow & Smith, 1905).

Spleen

[FROM THE *Memoirs*]

HECTOR BERLIOZ

1832

It was during this period of my academic life that I once more fell a prey to the miserable disease (mental, nervous, imaginary, if you like) which I shall call the *bane of isolation*. I had my first attack of it when I was sixteen, and it came about in this wise. One beautiful May morning, at the Côte St. André, I was sitting in a meadow under the shade of some wide-spreading oak trees, reading one of Montjoie's novels, called *Manuscrit trouvé au Mont Pausillipe*. Although absorbed in my book, I was perfectly conscious of a soft, sad kind of air which was wafted over the plain at regular intervals. The Rogation processions were being celebrated, and the sound I heard arose from the chanting of the litanies by the peasants. There is something touching and poetical in this idea of wandering through the hills and dales in the springtime and invoking God's blessing on the fruits of the earth, and I was unspeakably affected by it. The procession halted at a wooden cross covered with creepers. I watched the people kneeling while the priest blessed the meadows, and then they wended their way onwards, singing their mournful song. I could occasionally distinguish our old priest's feeble voice, and some fragments of the words as the pious band drifted farther and farther away:

	. . . *Conservare digneris.*
The Peasants.	*Te rogamus audi nos!*
Decrescendo.	*Sancte Barnaba*
	Ora pro nobis!
Perdendo.	*Sancta Magdalena*
	Ora pro . . .
	Sancta Maria,
	Ora . . .
	Sancta . . .
	. . . nobis.

Silence . . . the faint rustling of the wheat, stirred by the soft morning air . . . the loving cry of the quail to his mate . . . the cheerful ortolan singing on the top of the poplars . . . the utter calm . . . the slow fall of a leaf from the oak . . . the dull throbbing of my own heart. . . . Life was so far, far away from me. . . . On the remote horizon the Alpine glaciers flashed like giant gems in the light of the mounting sun . . . below me Meylan . . . and beyond the Alps, Italy, Naples, Posilippo . . . the beings of whom I was reading . . . burning passions . . . an unfathomable and secret joy. . . . Oh for wings across space! I want life and love and enthusiasm and burning kisses, I want more and fuller life! But I am only an inert frame chained to the earth! Those beings are either fictitious, or they are dead. . . . What is love? . . . what is fame? . . . what are hearts? . . . Where is my star? . . . *the Stella montis?* Vanished possibly for ever. . . . When shall I see Italy?

And the paroxysm possessed me in full force. I suffered agonies, and, casting myself down on the ground, groaned and clutched the earth wildly, tore up the grass and the innocent daisies, with their upturned wondering eyes, in my passionate struggles against the horrible feeling of loneliness and sense of absence.

And yet what was this anguish, compared to the tortures I have endured since, which go on increasing day by day?

I do not know how to convey any adequate conception of this unutterable anguish. A physical experiment alone can give any idea of it. If you put a cup of water and a cup of sulphuric acid side by side, under the bell of an air-pump, and exhaust the air, you will see the water bubble, boil, and finally evaporate. The sulphuric acid absorbs the vapour as it evaporates, and, owing to the property possessed by the steam of carrying off the caloric, the water which is left in the cup freezes into a little lump of ice.

The same sort of thing happens when I become possessed by this feeling of loneliness and absence. There is a vacuum all round my beating breast, and I feel as if under the influence of some irresistible power my heart were evaporating and tending towards dissolution. My skin begins to pain and burn; I get hot all over; I feel an irresistible desire to call my friends and even strangers to help me, to protect me, to console me and preserve me from destruction, and to restrain the life which is being drawn out of me to the four quarters of the globe.

These crises are accompanied by no longing for death; the idea of suicide is intolerable; it is no wish to die— far from it, it is a yearning for more life, life fuller and more complete; one feels an infinite capacity for happiness which is outraged by the want of an adequate object, and which can only be satisfied by infinite, overpowering, *furious* delights proportioned to the unutterable amount of feeling which one longs to spend upon them.

This state is not *spleen,* but precedes it. It is the ebullition and evaporation of heart, senses, brain, and nervous fluid. The spleen follows, and is the congealing of all this—the lump of ice which remains in the bell of the air-pump.

Even in my calmer moods I feel a little of this *isolation*—for instance, on Sunday evenings, when the towns are still and everyone goes away to the country —because there is *happiness in the distance* and people are *absent.* The *adagios* of Beethoven's symphonies, some of the scenes in Gluck's *Alceste* and *Armide,* a song in his opera *Telemaco,* the Elysian fields in his *Orfée,* bring on fierce fits of the same pain; but these master-pieces contribute their own antidotes; they create tears, and tears bring relief. The *adagios* of some of Beetho-ven's sonatas, on the other hand, and Gluck's *Iphigénie en Tauride* pertain wholly to the state of spleen, and induce it; the atmosphere is cold and dark, the sky is gray and cloudy, and the north wind whistles drearily.

There are, moreover, two kinds of spleen—one ironi-cal, scoffing, passionate, violent, and malignant; the other taciturn and gloomy, requiring rest, silence, solitude, and sleep. Those who are possessed by this become utterly indifferent to everything, and would look unmoved on the ruin of the world. At such times I have wished that the earth were a shell filled with gunpowder, that I might set fire to it for my amusement.

Trans. Rachel and Eleanor Holmes (London: Macmillan, 1884).

THE ROMANTIC IN LOVE

> Every beloved object is the center of
> a Paradise.
>> —Novalis
>> (Friedrich von Hardenberg)

Werther in Love

[FROM *The Sorrows of Young Werther*]

JOHANN WOLFGANG VON
GOETHE

1774

July 13, 1771

No, I am not deceived. In her black eyes I read a
genuine interest in me and in my life. Yes, I feel it; and
I can believe my own heart which tells me—dare I say
it?—dare I pronounce the divine words?—that she
loves me!

That she loves me! How the idea exalts me in my own
eyes! And—as you can understand my feelings, I may
say it to you—how I worship myself since she loves me!

Is this presumption, or is it an awareness of the truth?
I do not know the man able to supplant me in the heart
of Charlotte; and yet when she speaks of her betrothed
with so much warmth and affection, I feel like the

soldier who has been stripped of his honors and titles, and deprived of his sword.

July 16, 1771

How my heart beats when by accident I touch her finger, or my feet meet hers under the table! I draw back as from a flame; but a secret force impels me forward again, and I become disordered. Her innocent, pure heart never knows what agony these little famili- arities inflict upon me. Sometimes when we are talking she lays her hand upon mine, and in the eagerness of conversation comes closer to me, and her divine breath comes to my lips—I feel as if lightning had struck me, and I could sink into the earth. And yet, Wilhelm, with all this heavenly confidence—if I should ever dare— you understand. No! my heart is not so depraved; it is weak, weak enough—but is that not a kind of depravity?

She is sacred to me. All passion is silenced in her presence; I do not know what I feel when I am near her. It is as if my soul beat in every nerve of my body. There is a melody which she plays on the piano with the touch of an angel—so simple is it, and yet so lofty! It is her favorite air; and when she strikes the first note, all worry and sorrow disappear in a moment.

I believe every word that is said of the ancient magic of music. How her simple song enchants me! And how she knows when to play it! Sometimes, when I feel like shooting a bullet into my head, she sings that air; the gloom and madness are dispersed, and I breathe freely again.

Trans. Victor Lange (New York: Rinehart & Co., 1949).

Love Is a Powerful Attraction

["On Love"]

PERCY BYSSHE SHELLEY

1815

What is love? Ask him who lives, what is life? ask him who adores, what is God?

I know not the internal constitution of other men, nor even thine, whom I now address. I see that in some external attributes they resemble me, but when, misled by that appearance, I have thought to appeal to something in common, and unburthen my inmost soul to them, I have found my language misunderstood, like one in a distant and savage land. The more opportunities they have afforded me for experience, the wider has appeared the interval between us, and to a greater distance have the points of sympathy been withdrawn. With a spirit ill fitted to sustain such proof, trembling and feeble through its tenderness, I have everywhere sought sympathy and have found only repulse and disappointment.

Thou demandest what is love? It is that powerful attraction towards all that we conceive, or fear, or hope beyond ourselves, when we find within our own thoughts the chasm of an insufficient void, and seek to awaken in all things that are, a community with what we experience within ourselves. If we reason, we would be understood; if we imagine, we would that the airy children of our brain were born anew within another's; if we feel, we would that another's nerves should vibrate to our own, that the beams of their eyes should kindle at once

and mix and melt into our own, that lips of motionless
ice should not reply to lips quivering and burning with
the heart's best blood. This is Love. This is the bond
and the sanction which connects not only man with
man, but with everything which exists. We are born
into the world, and there is something within us, from
the instant that we live, that more and more thirsts after
its likeness. It is probably in correspondence with this law
that the infant drains milk from the bosom of its mother;
this propensity develops itself with the development of
our nature. We dimly see within our intellectual nature
a minimum as it were of our entire self, yet deprived of
all that we condemn or despise, the ideal prototype of
everything excellent or lovely that we are capable
of conceiving as belonging to the nature of man. Not
only the portrait of our external being, but an assem-
blage of the minutest particles of which our nature is
composed; a mirror whose surface reflects only the
forms of purity and brightness; a soul within our soul
that describes a circle around its proper paradise, which
pain, and sorrow, and evil dare not overleap. To this we
eagerly refer all sensations, thirsting that they should
resemble or correspond with it. The discovery of its
antitype; the meeting with an understanding capable of
clearly estimating our own; and imagination which
should enter into and seize upon the subtle and delicate
peculiarities which we have delighted to cherish and
unfold in secret; with a frame whose nerves, like the
chords of two exquisite lyres, strung to the accompaniment of one delightful voice, vibrate with the vibrations
of our own; and of a combination of all these in such
proportion as the type within demands; this is the invisible and unattainable point to which Love tends; and
to attain which, it urges forth the powers of man to
arrest the faintest shadow of that, without the possession of which there is no rest nor respite to the heart
over which it rules. Hence in solitude, or in that

deserted state when we are surrounded by human
beings, and yet they sympathize not with us, we love
the flowers, the grass, and the waters, and the sky. In
the motion of the very leaves of spring, in the blue air,
there is then found a secret correspondence with our
heart. There is eloquence in the tongueless wind, and a
melody in the flowing brooks and the rustling of the
reeds beside them, which by their inconceivable relation
to something within the soul, awaken the spirits to a
dance of breathless rapture, and bring tears of mysterious tenderness to the eyes, like the enthusiasm of
patriotic success, or the voice of one beloved singing
to you alone. Sterne says that, if he were in a desert, he
would love some cypress. So soon as this want or power
is dead, man becomes the living sepulchre of himself,
and what yet survives is the mere husk of what once
he was.

"Emily, I Love Thee"

[FROM *Epipsychidion*]

PERCY BYSSHE SHELLEY

1821

Sweet Spirit! Sister of that orphan one,
Whose empire is the name thou weepest on,
In my heart's temple I suspend to thee
These votive wreaths of withered memory.

Poor captive bird! who, from thy narrow cage,
Pourest such music, that it might assuage
The rugged hearts of those who prisoned thee,
Were they not deaf to all sweet melody;

This song shall be thy rose: its petals pale
Are dead, indeed, my adored Nightingale!
But soft and fragrant is the faded blossom,
And it has no thorn left to wound thy bosom.

High, spirit-wingèd Heart! who dost for ever
Beat thine unfeeling bars with vain endeavour,
Till those bright plumes of thought, in which arrayed
It over-soared this low and worldly shade,
Lie shattered; and thy panting, wounded breast
Stains with dear blood its unmaternal nest!
I weep vain tears: blood would less bitter be,
Yet poured forth gladlier, could it profit thee.

Seraph of Heaven! too gentle to be human,
Veiling beneath that radiant form of Woman
All that is insupportable in thee
Of light, and love, and immortality!
Sweet Benediction in the eternal Curse!
Veiled Glory of this lampless Universe!
Thou Moon beyond the clouds! Thou living Form
Among the Dead! Thou Star above the Storm!
Thou Wonder, and thou Beauty, and thou Terror!
Thou Harmony of Nature's art! Thou Mirror
In whom, as in the splendour of the Sun,
All shapes look glorious which thou gazest on!
Ay, even the dim words which obscure thee now
Flash, lightning-like, with unaccustomed glow;
I pray thee that thou blot from this sad song
All of its much mortality and wrong,
With those clear drops, which start like sacred dew
From the twin lights thy sweet soul darkens through,
Weeping, till sorrow becomes ecstasy:
Then smile on it, so that it may not die.

I never thought before my death to see
Youth's vision thus made perfect. Emily,

I love thee; though the world by no thin name
Will hide that love from its unvalued shame.
Would we two had been twins of the same mother!
Or, that the name my heart lent to another
Could be a sister's bond for her and thee,
Blending two beams of one eternity!
Yet were one lawful or the other true,
These names, though dear, could paint not, as is due,
How beyond refuge I am thine. Ah me!
I am not thine: I am a part of *thee*.

Sweet Lamp! my moth-like Muse has burned its wings
Or, like a dying swan who soars and sings,
Young Love should teach Time, in his own gray style,
All that thou art. Art thou not void of guile,
A lovely soul formed to be blessed and bless?
A well of sealed and secret happiness,
Whose waters like blithe light and music are,
Vanquishing dissonance and gloom? A Star
Which moves not in the moving heavens, alone?
A Smile amid dark frowns? a gentle tone
Amid rude voices? a belovèd light?
A Solitude, a Refuge, a Delight?
A Lute, which those whom Love has taught to play
Make music on, to soothe the roughest day
And lull fond Grief asleep? a buried treasure?
A cradle of young thoughts of wingless pleasure?
A violet-shrouded grave of Woe?—I measure
The world of fancies, seeking one like thee,
And find—alas! mine own infirmity.

Blossoms of One Plant

[FROM *Lucinda*]

FRIEDRICH VON SCHLEGEL

DITHYRAMBIC FANTASY
ON THE LOVELIEST OF SITUATIONS

1799

A big tear falls upon the holy sheet which I found
here instead of you. How faithfully and how simply you
have sketched it, the old and daring idea of my dearest
and most intimate purpose! In you it has grown up, and
in this mirror I do not shrink from loving and admiring
myself. Only here I see myself in harmonious complete-
ness. For your spirit, too, stands distinct and perfect
before me, not as an apparition which appears and
fades away again, but as one of the forms that endure
forever. It looks at me joyously out of its deep eyes and
opens its arms to embrace my spirit. The holiest and
most evanescent of those delicate traits and utterances
of the soul, which to one who does not know the highest
seem like bliss itself, are merely the common atmosphere
of our spiritual breath and life.

The words are weak and vague. Furthermore, in this
throng of impressions I could only repeat anew the one
inexhaustible feeling of our original harmony. A great
future beckons me on into the immeasurable; each idea
develops a countless progeny. The extremes of unbridled
gayety and of quiet presentiment live together within
me. I remember everything, even the griefs, and all my

thoughts that have been and are to be bestir themselves and arise before me. The blood rushes wildly through my swollen veins, my mouth thirsts for the contact of your lips, and my fancy seeks vainly among the many forms of joy for one which might at last gratify my desire and give it rest. And then again I suddenly and sadly bethink me of the gloomy time when I was always waiting without hope, and madly loving without knowing it; when my innermost being overflowed with a vague longing, which it breathed forth but rarely in half-suppressed sighs.

Oh, I should have thought it all a fairy tale that there could be such joy, such love as I now feel, and such a woman, who could be my most tender Beloved, my best companion, and at the same time a perfect friend. For it was in friendship especially that I sought for what I wanted, and for what I never hoped to find in any woman. In you I found it all, and more than I could wish for; but you are so unlike the rest. Of what custom or caprice calls womanly, you know nothing. The womanliness of your soul, aside from minor peculiarities, consists in its regarding life and love as the same thing. For you all feeling is infinite and eternal; you recognize no separations, your being is an indivisible unity. That is why you are so serious and so joyous, why you regard everything in such a large and indifferent way; that is why you love me, all of me, and will surrender no part of me to the state, to posterity, or to manly pleasures. I am all yours; we are closest to each other and we understand each other. You accompany me through all the stages of manhood, from the utmost wantonness to the most refined spirituality. In you alone I first saw true pride and true feminine humility.

The most extreme suffering, if it is only surrounded, without separating us, would seem to me nothing but a charming antithesis to the sublime frivolity of our marriage. Why should we not take the harshest whim of chance for an excellent jest and a most frolicsome caprice, since we, like our love, are immortal? I can no longer say *my* love and *your* love; they are both alike in their perfect mutuality. Marriage is the everlasting unity and alliance of our spirits, not only for what we call this world and that world, but for the one, true, indivisible, nameless, endless world of our entire being, so long as we live. Therefore, if it seemed the proper time, I would drain with you a cup of poison, just as gladly and just as easily as that last glass of champagne we drank together, when I said, "And so let us drink out the rest of our lives." With these words I hurriedly quaffed the wine, before its noble spirit ceased to sparkle. And so I say again, let us live and love. I know you would not wish to survive me; you would rather follow your dying husband into his coffin. Gladly and lovingly would you descend into the burning abyss, even as the women of India do, impelled by a mad law, the cruel, constraining purpose of which desecrates and destroys the most delicate sanctities of the will.

On the other side, perhaps, longing will be more completely realized. I often wonder over it; every thought, and whatever else is fashioned within us, seems to be complete in itself, as single and indivisible as a person. One thing crowds out another, and that which just now was near and present soon sinks back into obscurity. And then again come moments of sudden and universal clarity, when several such spirits of the inner world completely fuse together into a wonderful wedlock, and many a forgotten bit of our ego shines forth in a new light and even illuminates the darkness of the future with its bright lustre. As it is in a small way, so is it also, I think, in a large way. That which we call a life is for the complete, inner, immortal man only a single idea, an indivisible feeling. And for him there

come, too, moments of the profoundest and fullest consciousness, when all lives fall together and mingle and
separate in a different way. The time is coming when
we two shall behold in one spirit that we are blossoms
of one plant, or petals of one flower. We shall then
know with a smile that what we now call merely hope
was really memory.

Do you know how the first seed of this idea germinated in my soul before you and took root in yours?
Thus does the religion of love weave our love ever and
ever more closely and firmly together, just as a child,
like an echo, doubles the happiness of its gentle parents.

Nothing can part us; and certainly any separation
would only draw me more powerfully to you. I bethink
me how at our last embrace, you vehemently resisting,
I burst into simultaneous tears and laughter. I tried to
calm myself, and in a sort of bewilderment I would not
believe that I was separated from you until the surrounding objects convinced me of it against my will.
But then my longing grew again irresistible, until on its
wings I sank back into your arms. Suppose words or a
human being to create a misunderstanding between us!
The piognant grief would be transient and quickly
resolve itself into complete harmony. How could separation separate us, when presence itself is to us, as it
were, too present? We have to cool and mitigate the
consuming fire with jests, and thus for us the most witty
of the forms and situations of joy is also the most beautiful. One among all is at once the wittiest and the
loveliest: when we exchange roles and with childish
delight try to see who can best imitate the other;
whether you succeed best with the tender vehemence
of a man, or I with the yielding devotion of a woman.
But, do you know, this sweet game has for me quite
other charms than its own. It is not merely the delight
of exhaustion or the anticipation of revenge. I see in

it a wonderful and profoundly significant allegory of the development of man and woman into complete humanity.

Trans. Paul Bernhard Thomas, in *The German Classics*, ed. Kuno Francke (New York: The German Publication Society, 1913).

Love Blooms and Dies

[FROM *The Lyrical Intermezzo*]

HEINRICH HEINE

1822-23

1

In May-month, wonderfully fair,
When buds burst forth in glee,
Then, deep within my heart,
Love too awoke for me.

In May-month, wonderfully fair,
When birds' songs filled the air,
To her I then confessed
My longing and despair.

2

All of my tears engender
Flowers that bloom in throngs,
And nightingales render
My sighs in lovely songs.

And sweetheart, if you love me,
Yours are the buds below
That window, whence lovely
Nightingales' songs shall flow.

18

Rage I'll yet scorn, although my heart is torn,
Oh love now gone for good! Rage I'll yet scorn.
Despite the way you shine, so diamond-bright,
No single beam falls in your heart's black night.

I've known it long. I saw you while I slept,
I saw your heart so black by darkness kept,
And saw the snake, while at your heart it ate,
I saw how miserable you are, my sweet.

42

My dearest, we sat close together,
Snug in our little bark,
The night was still, and the river
Loomed broad as we lay in the dark.

The phantom island in beauty,
Lay half-lit in moonlight haze;
Whence came forth sounds so pretty,
Set dancing the mist and the waves.

They rang ever sweeter and sweeter,
All surged rhythmically;
While we drifted ever so quiet,
Disconsolate, on the broad sea.

59

A single star drops swiftly
Down through the sparkling sky!
This is the star of lovers
That drops before my eye.

An apple-tree drops blossoms
And leaves to the waiting ground!

The playful breezes gaily
Whirl the leaves around.

A dying swan in the fish-pond
Sings as it glides on the wave,
And finally, weakly singing,
It sinks to its watery grave.

It is so still in the darkness!
The blossoms have blown from the tree,
The star has sputtered and vanished,
And faded the swan's melody.

65

The ancient, wicked verses,
The dreams so sore and bad,
We now shall bury deeply
In the biggest coffin made.

What I put within it,
Is not yet yours to ask;
But the coffin must be bigger
Than Heidelberg's great cask.

For this we need a bier,
Thick and huge each board;
Much longer than the big bridge
That Mainz once could afford.

Go get one dozen giants,
And stronger must be mine
Than even good Saint Christopher
In Köln's church, on the Rhine.

These ought to bear the coffin
And sink it 'neath the wave,

For such a great big catafalque
Requires a great big grave.

You wonder why the coffin
Must be so long and wide?
I put my love within it,
My sorrow lies beside.

Trans. H. E. H.

Love's Certainty

[FROM THE *Letters*]

JOHN KEATS

TO FANNY BRAWNE

[*Wentworth Place, February 1820?*]

My dear Fanny,

Do not let your mother suppose that you hurt me by writing at night. For some reason or other your last night's note was not so treasurable as former ones. I would fain that you call me *Love* still. To see you happy and in high spirits is a great consolation to me—still let me believe that you are not half so happy as my restoration would make you. I am nervous, I own, and may think myself worse than I really am; if so you must indulge me, and pamper with that sort of tenderness you have manifested towards me in different Letters. My sweet creature when I look back upon the pains and torments I have suffer'd for you from the day I left you to go to the Isle of Wight; the extasies in which I have pass'd some days and the miseries in their turn, I wonder the more at the Beauty which has kept up the spell so fervently. When I send this round I shall be in the front parlour watching to see you show yourself for a minute in the garden. How illness stands as a barrier betwixt me and you! Even if I was well—I must make myself as good a Philosopher as possible. Now I have had opportunities of passing nights anxious and awake I have found other thoughts intrude upon me. "If I should die," said I to myself, "I have left no immortal work behind me—nothing to make my friends proud of my memory—but I have lov'd the principle of beauty in all things, and if I had had time I would have made myself remember'd." Thoughts like these came very feebly whilst I was in health and every pulse beat for you— now you divide with this (may *I* say it?) "last infirmity of noble minds" all my reflection.

God bless you, Love.

J. Keats

[*Wentworth Place, March 1820?*]

My dearest Fanny,

I slept well last night and am no worse this morning for it. Day by day if I am not deceived I get a more unrestrain'd use of my Chest. The nearer a racer gets to the Goal the more his anxiety becomes; so I lingering upon the borders of health feel my impatience increase. Perhaps on your account I have imagined my illness more serious than it is: how horrid was the chance of slipping into the ground instead of into your arms—the difference is amazing Love. Death must come at last; Man must die, as Shallow says; but before that is my fate I fain would try what more pleasures than you have given, so sweet a creature as you can give. Let me have another op[p]ortunity of years before me and I will not die without being remember'd. Take care of yourself dear that we may both be well in the Summer. I do not at all fatigue myself with writing, having merely to put a line or two here and there, a Task which would worry a stout state of the body and mind, but which just suits me as I can do no more.

Your affectionate

J. K.

Tuesday Morn. [Kentish Town, May 1820]
My dearest Girl,

I wrote a Letter for you yesterday expecting to have seen your mother. I shall be selfish enough to send it though I know it may give you a little pain, because I wish you to see how unhappy I am for love of you, and endeavour as much as I can to entice you to give up your whole heart to me whose whole existence hangs upon you. You could not step or move an eyelid but it would shoot to my heart—I am greedy of you. Do not think of any thing but me. Do not live as if I was not existing. Do not forget me—but have I any right to say you forget me? Perhaps you think of me all day. Have I any right to wish you to be unhappy for me? You would forgive me for wishing it if you knew the extreme passion I have that you should love me—and for you to love me as I do you, you must think of no one but me, much less write that sentence. Yesterday and this morning I have been haunted with a sweet vision—I have seen you the whole time in your shepherdess dress. How my senses have ached at it! How my heart has been devoted to it! How my eyes have been full of Tears at it! I[n]deed I think a real Love is enough to occupy the widest heart. Your going to town alone, when I heard of it was a shock to me—yet I expected it—*promise me you will not for some time till I get better*. Promise me this and fill the paper full of the most endearing names. If you cannot do so with good will, do my Love tell me—say what you think—confess if your heart is too much fasten'd on the world. Perhaps then I may see you at a greater distance, I may not be able to appropriate you so closely to myself. Were you to loose a favorite bird from the cage, how would your eyes ache after it as long as it was in sight; when out of sight you would recover a little. Perhaps if you would, if so it is, confess to me how many things are necessary to you besides me, I might be happier; by being less tantaliz'd. Well may you exclaim, how selfish, how cruel not to let me enjoy my youth! to wish me to be unhappy! You must be so if you love me. Upon my Soul I can be contented with nothing else. If you would really what is call'd enjoy yourself at a Party—if you can smile in people's faces, and wish them to admire you *now*—you never have nor ever will love me. I see *life* in nothing but the certainty of your Love—convince me of it my sweetest. If I am not somehow convinc'd I shall die of agony. If we love we must not live as other men and women do—I cannot brook the wolfsbane of fashion and foppery and tattle—You must be mine to die upon the rack if I want you. I do not pretend to say I have more feeling than my fellows, but I wish you seriously to look over my letters kind and unkind and consider whether the Person who wrote them can be able to endure much longer the agonies and uncertainties which you are so peculiarly made to create. My recovery of bodily health will be of no benefit to me if you are not mine when I am well. For God's sake save me—or tell me my passion is of too awful a nature for you. Again God bless you

                                                    J. K.

No—my sweet Fanny—I am wrong—I do not want you to be unhappy—and yet I do, I must while there is so sweet a Beauty—my loveliest, my darling! good bye! I Kiss you—O the torments!

A Long, Long Kiss

[FROM *Don Juan*]

GEORGE GORDON,
LORD BYRON

1819

It was the cooling hour, just when the rounded
  Red sun sinks down behind the azure hill,
Which then seems as if the whole earth it bounded,
  Circling all nature, hush'd, and dim, and still,
With the far mountain-crescent half surrounded
  On one side, and the deep sea calm and chill,
Upon the other, and the rosy sky,
With one star sparkling through it like an eye.

And thus they wander'd forth, and hand in hand,
  Over the shining pebbles and the shells,
Glided along the smooth and harden'd sand,
  And in the worn and wild receptacles
Work'd by the storms, yet work'd as it were plann'd,
  In hollow halls, with sparry roofs and cells,
They turn'd to rest; and, each clasp'd by an arm,
Yielded to the deep twilight's purple charm.

They look'd up to the sky, whose floating glow
  Spread like a rosy ocean, vast and bright;
They gazed upon the glittering sea below,
  Whence the broad moon rose circling into sight;
They heard the waves splash, and the wind so low,
  And saw each other's dark eyes darting light

Into each other—and, beholding this,
Their lips drew near, and clung into a kiss;

A long, long kiss, a kiss of youth, and love,
   And beauty, all concentrating like rays
Into one focus, kindled from above;
   Such kisses as belong to early days,
Where heart, and soul, and sense, in concert move,
   And the blood's lava, and the pulse a blaze,
Each kiss a heart-quake,—for a kiss's strength,
I think it must be reckon'd by its length.

By length I mean duration; theirs endured
   Heaven knows how long—no doubt they never reck-
      on'd;
And if they had, they could not have secured
   The sum of their sensations to a second:
They had not spoken; but they felt allured,
   As if their souls and lips each other beckon'd,
Which, being join'd, like swarming bees they clung—
Their hearts the flowers from whence the honey sprung.

They were alone, but not alone as they
   Who shut in chambers think it loneliness;
The silent ocean, and the starlight bay,
   The twilight glow, which momently grew less,
The voiceless sands, and dropping caves, that lay
   Around them, made them to each other press,
As if there were no life beneath the sky
Save theirs, and that their life could never die.

They fear'd no eyes nor ears on that lone beach,
   They felt no terrors from the night; they were
All in all to each other; though their speech
   Was broken words, they *thought* a language there,—
And all the burning tongues the passions teach

Found in one sigh the best interpreter
Of nature's oracle—first love,—that all
Which Eve has left her daughters since her fall.

Haidée spoke not of scruples, ask'd no vows,
    Nor offer'd any; she had never heard
Of plight and promises to be a spouse,
    Or perils by a loving maid incurr'd;
She was all which pure ignorance allows,
    And flew to her young mate like a young bird,
And never having dreamt of falsehood, she
Had not one word to say of constancy.

She loved, and was beloved—she adored,
    And she was worshipp'd; after nature's fashion,
Their intense souls, into each other pour'd,
    If souls could die, had perish'd in that passion,—
But by degrees their senses were restored,
    Again to be o'ercome, again to dash on;
And, beating 'gainst *his* bosom, Haidée's heart
Felt as if never more to beat apart.

Alas! they were so young, so beautiful,
    So lonely, loving, helpless, and the hour
Was that in which the heart is always full,
    And, having o'er itself no further power,
Prompts deeds eternity cannot annul,
    But pays off moments in an endless shower
Of hell-fire—all prepared for people giving
Pleasure or pain to one another living.

Alas! for Juan and Haidée! they were
    So loving and so lovely—till then never,
Excepting our first parents, such a pair
    Had run the risk of being damn'd for ever;
And Haidée, being devout as well as fair,

Had, doubtless, heard about the Stygian river,
And hell and purgatory—but forgot
Just in the very crisis she should not.

They look upon each other, and their eyes
   Gleam in the moonlight; and her white arm clasps
Round Juan's head, and his around her lies
   Half buried in the tresses which it grasps;
She sits upon his knee, and drinks his sighs,
   He hers, until they end in broken gasps;
And thus they form a group that's quite antique,
Half naked, loving, natural, and Greek.

And when those deep and burning moments pass'd,
   And Juan sunk to sleep within her arms,
She slept not, but all tenderly, though fast,
   Sustain'd his head upon her bosom's charms;
And now and then her eye to heaven is cast,
   And then on the pale cheek her breast now warms,
Pillow'd on her o'erflowing heart, which pants
With all it granted, and with all it grants.

An infant when it gazes on a light,
   A child the moment when it drains the breast,
A devotee when soars the Host in sight,
   An Arab with a stranger for a guest,
A sailor when the prize has struck in fight,
   A miser filling his most hoarded chest,
Feel rapture; but not such true joy are reaping
As they who watch o'er what they love while sleeping.

For there it lies so tranquil, so beloved,
   All that it hath of life with us is living;
So gentle, stirless, helpless, and unmoved,
   And all unconscious of the joy 'tis giving;
All it hath felt, inflicted, pass'd, and proved,

Hush'd into depths beyond the watcher's diving;
There lies the thing we love with all its errors
And all its charms, like death without its terrors.

The lady watch'd her lover—and that hour
　　Of Love's, and Night's, and Ocean's solitude,
O'erflow'd her soul with their united power;
　　Amidst the barren sand and rocks so rude
She and her wave-worn love had made their bower,
　　Where nought upon their passion could intrude,
And all the stars that crowded the blue space
Saw nothing happier than her glowing face.

Alas! the love of women! it is known
　　To be a lovely and a fearful thing;
For all of theirs upon that die is thrown,
　　And if 'tis lost, life hath no more to bring
To them but mockeries of the past alone,
　　And their revenge is as the tiger's spring,
Deadly, and quick, and crushing; yet, as real
Torture is theirs, what they inflict they feel.

They are right; for man, to man so oft unjust,
　　Is always so to women; one sole bond
Awaits them, treachery is all their trust;
　　Taught to conceal, their bursting hearts despond
Over their idol, till some wealthier lust
　　Buys them in marriage—and what rests beyond?
A thankless husband, next a faithless lover,
Then dressing, nursing, praying, and all's over.

Some take a lover, some take drams or prayers,
　　Some mind their household, others dissipation,
Some run away, and but exchange their cares,
　　Losing the advantage of a virtuous station;
Few changes e'er can better their affairs,

Theirs being an unnatural situation,
From the dull palace to the dirty hovel:
Some play the devil, and then write a novel.

Haidée was Nature's bride, and knew not this:
    Haidée was Passion's child, born where the sun
Showers triple light, and scorches even the kiss
    Of his gazelle-eyed daughters; she was one
Made but to love, to feel that she was his
    Who was her chosen: what was said or done
Elsewhere was nothing. She had nought to fear,
Hope, care, nor love beyond,—her heart beat *here*.

And oh! that quickening of the heart, that beat!
    How much it costs us! yet each rising throb
Is in its cause as its effect so sweet,
    That Wisdom, ever on the watch to rob
Joy of its alchemy, and to repeat
    Fine truths; even Conscience, too, has a tough job
To make us understand each good old maxim,
So good—I wonder Castlereagh don't tax 'em.

And now 'twas done—on the lone shore were plighted
    Their hearts; the stars, their nuptial torches, shed
Beauty upon the beautiful they lighted:
    Ocean their witness, and the cave their bed,
By their own feelings hallow'd and united,
    Their priest was Solitude, and they were wed:
And they were happy, for to their young eyes
Each was an angel, and earth paradise.

    Canto II, stanzas 183-204.

Love's Analysis

STENDHAL
(Henri Beyle)
[from *On Love*]

1822

Let us recapitulate the seven stages of love. These are:
1. Admiration;
2. One says to one's self, "What pleasure," etc.;
3. Hope;
4. Love is born;
5. The first crystallization;
6. Doubt is born;
7. Second crystallization.

A year may elapse between 1 and 2, a month between 2 and 3; if hope does not come quickly, one renounces 2 imperceptibly, as causing too much unhappiness.

Between 3 and 4 there is but the twinkling of an eye.

There is no interval between 4 and 5. Only the degree of intimacy separates them.

A few days, more or less, in accordance with the degree of impetuosity and the boldness of the individual, may elapse between 5 and 6, and there is no interval between 6 and 7.

All love and all imagination partake of the quality of one of six temperaments, according to the individual:

The sanguine, or French, that of Monsieur de Francueil (*Memoirs* of Madame d'Épinay);

The choleric, or Spanish, that of Lauzun (Peguilhen in the *Memoirs* of Saint-Simon);

The melancholy, or German, that of Schiller's Don Carlos;

The phlegmatic, or Dutch;

The nervous, that of Voltaire;

The athletic, that of Milo of Crotona.

If the influence of temperament makes itself felt in ambition, avarice, friendship, and so on, what must it be in love, in which the physical also comes unavoidably into play?

Let us suppose that all forms of love can be reduced to the four varieties we have noted:

Passion-love, that of Julie d'Étanges;

Sympathy-love or gallantry;

Sensual love;

Vanity-love (a duchess is never more than thirty years old to a snob).

We must consider each of these four kinds of love in relation to their dependence on the different habits given to the imagination by each of the six different temperaments enumerated above. Tiberius had not the crazy imagination of Henry VIII.

We must consider all the combinations we obtain in this way in relation to the difference of habit dependent on governments or national characteristics:

1. Asiatic Despotism as it is seen in Constantinople.

2. Absolute Monarchy like that of Louis XIV.

3. Aristocracy disguised by a charter, or the government of a country for the benefit of the rich, as in England, all following the rules of so-called Biblical morality;

4. Federal Republicanism, or government for the benefit of all, as in the United States of America;

5. Constitutional Monarchy, or . . .

6. A State in Revolution, like Spain, Portugal, France. This condition of a country, by giving every one a strong passion, makes for naturalness of morals; it does away with trifles, conventional virtues and stupid

ceremonial; it steadies young men and makes them despise vanity-love and avoid gallantry.

A free government is a government which does no harm to its citizens, but which, on the contrary, gives them security and tranquillity. But it is a far cry from this to happiness; man must make his own happiness, for he would be a very callous man who considered himself perfectly happy merely because he enjoyed security and tranquillity. We confuse these things in Europe, and especially in Italy; being accustomed to governments that do us harm, we imagine that the supreme happiness would be to get rid of them, like sick men in the throes of great agony. The example of America clearly shows the contrary. There the government does its work very well and does no one any harm. But, as though destiny wished to confound and belie all our philosophy, or rather to accuse it of not dealing with every side of human nature, we who have been estranged for so many centuries from any actual experience of this kind by the wretched state of Europe, see that when the Americans fail to experience the misery which is usually brought about by governments, they seem to fail in themselves as well. It is as though the source of sensitiveness were dried up in them. They are just and they are rational, but they are anything but happy.

Is the Bible, or rather, are the ridiculous consequences and rules of conduct which warped intelligences deduct from this collection of poems and songs, sufficient to cause all this wretchedness? The effect seems to me to be very considerable for the cause.

Monsieur de Volney used to tell how, whilst he was seated at table in the country at the house of a worthy American, a well-to-do man surrounded by grown-up children, a young man entered the dining-room. "How do you do, William," said the father, "sit down." The traveller asked who the young man was. "He is my second son." "Where has he come from?" "From Canton."

The return of a son from the ends of the earth created no more excitement than that.

Their whole attention seems to be taken up with ordering their lives in a rational way and in avoiding discomfort; when at last they reach the moment of gathering the fruit of so much care and of such long-sustained habits of orderliness they have no life left for enjoyment.

One would think that the children of Penn have never read that line which seems to contain their history:

Et propter vitam, vivendi perdere causas.

In the winter, which as in Russia is the festive season of the country, young people of both sexes drive about night and day over the snow in sleighs, gaily travelling distances of fifteen or twenty miles without any one to look after them; and nothing untoward ever occurs.

There is the physical gaiety of youth which soon passes with the warmth of the blood and which is over at the age of twenty-five; but they lack the passions that make one enjoy life. Reasoning has become such a habit in the United States that crystallization is made impossible there.

I admire this happiness but I do not envy it: it is like the happiness of creatures of another and lower species. I cherish far greater hopes of Florida and of South America.

One thing which confirms my conjecture about North America is the complete lack of artists and writers. The United States have not yet supplied us with one act of a tragedy, one picture or one life of Washington.

Trans. H. B. V. (New York: Boni & Liveright, 1927).

[FROM *The Red and the Black*]

1831

When he saw Madame de Rênal again, the next morning, there was a strange look in his eyes; he watched her like an enemy with whom he would presently be engaged. This expression, so different from his expression overnight, made Madame de Rênal lose her head; she had been kind to him, and he appeared vexed. She could not take her eyes from his.

Madame Derville's presence excused Julien from his share of the conversation, and enabled him to concentrate his attention upon what he had in mind. His sole occupation, throughout the day, was that of fortifying himself by reading the inspired text which refreshed his soul.

He greatly curtailed the children's lessons, and when, later on, the presence of Madame de Rênal recalled him to the service of his own vanity, decided that it was absolutely essential that this evening she should allow her hand to remain in his.

The sun as it set and so brought nearer the decisive moment made Julien's heart beat with a strange excitement. Night fell. He observed, with a joy that lifted a huge weight from his breast, that it was very dark. A sky packed with big clouds, kept in motion by a hot breeze, seemed to forebode a tempest. The two women continued strolling until a late hour. Everything that they did this evening seemed strange to Julien. They were enjoying this weather, which, in certain delicate natures, seems to enhance the pleasure of love.

At last they sat down, Madame de Rênal next to Julien, and Madame Derville on the other side of her friend. Preoccupied with the attempt he must shortly make, Julien could think of nothing to say. The conversation languished.

"Shall I tremble like this and feel as uncomfortable the first time I have to fight a duel?" Julien wondered; for he had too little confidence either in himself or in others not to observe the state he was in.

In this agonising uncertainty, any danger would have seemed to him preferable. How often did he long to see Madame de Rênal called by some duty which would oblige her to return to the house and so leave the garden! The violence of the effort which Julien had to make to control himself was such that his voice was entirely altered; presently Madame de Rênal's voice became tremulous also, but Julien never noticed this. The ruthless warfare which his sense of duty was waging with his natural timidity was too exhausting for him to be in a condition to observe anything outside himself. The quarter before ten had sounded from the tower clock, without his having yet ventured on anything. Julien, ashamed of his cowardice, told himself: "At the precise moment when ten o'clock strikes, I shall carry out the intention which, all day long, I have been promising myself that I would fulfil this evening, or I shall go up to my room and blow my brains out."

After a final interval of tension and anxiety, during which the excess of his emotion carried Julien almost out of his senses, the strokes of ten sounded from the clock overhead. Each stroke of that fatal bell stirred an echo in his bosom, causing him almost a physical revulsion.

Finally, while the air was still throbbing with the last stroke of ten, he put out his hand and took that of Madame de Rênal, who at once withdrew it. Julien, without exactly knowing what he was doing, grasped her hand again. Although greatly moved himself, he was struck by the icy coldness of the hand he was clasping; he pressed it with convulsive force; a last attempt was made to remove it from him, but finally the hand was left in his grasp.

His heart was flooded with joy, not because he loved

Madame de Rênal, but because a fearful torment was now at an end. So that Madame Derville should not notice anything, he felt himself obliged to speak; his voice, now, was loud and ringing. Madame de Rênal's, on the other hand, betrayed such emotion that her friend thought she must be ill and suggested to her that they should go indoors. Julien saw the danger: "If Madame de Rênal returns to the drawing-room, I am going to fall back into the horrible position I have been in all day. I have not held this hand long enough to be able to reckon it as a definite conquest."

When Madame Derville repeated her suggestion that they should go into the drawing-room, Julien pressed the hand that lay in his.

Madame de Rênal, who was preparing to rise, resumed her seat, saying in a faint tone, "I do, as a matter of fact, feel a little unwell, but the fresh air is doing me good."

These words confirmed Julien's happiness, which, at this moment, was extreme: he talked, forgot to dissimulate, appeared the most charming of men to his two hearers. And yet there was still a slight want of courage in this eloquence which had suddenly come to him. He was in a deadly fear lest Madame Derville, exhausted by the wind which was beginning to rise, and heralded the storm, might decide to go in by herself to the drawing-room. Then he would be left alone with Madame de Rênal. He had found almost by accident the blind courage which was sufficient for action; but he felt that it lay beyond his power to utter the simplest of words to Madame de Rênal. However mild her reproaches might be, he was going to be defeated, and the advantage which he had just gained wiped out.

Fortunately for him, this evening, his touching and emphatic speeches found favour with Madame Derville, who as a rule found him as awkward as a schoolboy, and by no means amusing. As for Madame de Rênal,

her hand lying clasped in Julien's, she had no thought
of anything; she was allowing herself to live. The hours
they spent beneath this huge lime, which, local tradition
maintained, had been planted by Charles the Bold, were
for her a time of happiness. She listened with rapture to
the moaning of the wind in the thick foliage of the
lime, and the sound of the first few drops that were
beginning to fall upon its lowest leaves. Julien did not
notice a detail which would have greatly reassured
him; Madame de Rênal, who had been obliged to remove her hand from his, on rising to help her cousin
to pick up a pot of flowers which the wind had over-
turned at their feet, had no sooner sat down again
than she gave him back her hand almost without difficulty, and as though it had been an understood thing
between them.

Midnight had long since struck; at length it was time
to leave the garden: the party broke up. Madame de
Rênal, transported by the joy of being in love, was so
ignorant that she hardly reproached herself at all. Happiness robbed her of sleep. A sleep like lead carried off
Julien, utterly worn out by the battle that had been
raging all day in his heart between timidity and pride.

Next morning he was called at five o'clock; and (what
would have been a cruel blow to Madame de Rênal had
she known of it) he barely gave her a thought. He had
done *his duty, and a heroic duty.* Filled with joy by
this sentiment, he turned the key in the door of his bedroom and gave himself up with an entirely new pleasure
to reading about the exploits of his hero.

Trans. C. K. Scott-Moncrieff (New York: Modern Library, n.d.).

ROMANTIC SUICIDE

I have been half in love with easeful
Death.

—John Keats

Ode to a Nightingale

JOHN KEATS

1819

My heart aches, and a drowsy numbness pains
  My sense, as though of hemlock I had drunk,
Or emptied some dull opiate to the drains
  One minute past, and Lethe-wards had sunk:
'Tis not through envy of thy happy lot,
  But being too happy in thine happiness,—
    That thou, light-wingèd Dryad of the trees,
    In some melodious plot
  Of beechen green, and shadows numberless,
  Singest of summer in full-throated ease.

O, for a draught of vintage! that hath been
  Cooled a long age in the deep-delvèd earth,
Tasting of Flora and the country green,
  Dance, and Provençal song, and sunburnt mirth!
O for a beaker full of the warm South,
  Full of the true, the blushful Hippocrene,
    With beaded bubbles winking at the brim,

135

And purple-stainèd mouth;
That I might drink, and leave the world unseen,
    And with thee fade away into the forest dim:

Fade far away, dissolve, and quite forget
    What thou among the leaves hast never known,
The weariness, the fever, and the fret
    Here, where men sit and hear each other groan;
Where palsy shakes a few, sad, last gray hairs,
    Where youth grows pale, and spectre-thin, and dies;
        Where but to think is to be full of sorrow
            And leaden-eyed despairs,
    Where Beauty cannot keep her lustrous eyes,
        Or new Love pine at them beyond to-morrow.

Away! away! for I will fly to thee,
    Not charioted by Bacchus and his pards,
But on the viewless wings of Poesy,
    Though the dull brain perplexes and retards:
Already with thee! tender is the night,
    And haply the Queen-Moon is on her throne,
        Cluster'd around by all her starry Fays;
            But here there is no light,
    Save what from heaven is with the breezes blown
        Through verdurous glooms and winding mossy
            ways.

I cannot see what flowers are at my feet,
    Nor what soft incense hangs upon the boughs,
But, in embalmèd darkness, guess each sweet
    Wherewith the seasonable month endows
The grass, the thicket, and the fruit-tree wild;
    White hawthorn, and the pastoral eglantine;
        Fast fading violets cover'd up in leaves;
            And mid-May's eldest child,
    The coming musk-rose, full of dewy wine,
        The murmurous haunt of flies on summer eves.

Darkling I listen; and, for many a time
    I have been half in love with easeful Death,
Call'd him soft names in many a musèd rhyme,
    To take into the air my quiet breath;
Now more than ever seems it rich to die,
    To cease upon the midnight with no pain,
        While thou art pouring forth thy soul abroad
           In such an ecstasy!
    Still wouldst thou sing, and I have ears in vain—
      To thy high requiem become a sod.

Thou wast not born for death, immortal Bird!
    No hungry generations tread thee down;
The voice I hear this passing night was heard
    In ancient days by emperor and clown:
Perhaps the self-same song that found a path
    Through the sad heart of Ruth, when, sick for home,
      She stood in tears amid the alien corn;
        The same that oft-times hath
Charm'd magic casements, opening on the foam
    Of perilous seas, in faery lands forlorn.

Forlorn! the very word is like a bell
    To toll me back from thee to my sole self!
Adieu! the fancy cannot cheat so well
    As she is fam'd to do, deceiving elf.
Adieu! adieu! thy plaintive anthem fades
    Past the near meadows, over the still stream,
      Up the hillside; and now 'tis buried deep
        In the next valley-glades:
    Was it a vision, or a waking dream?
      Fled is that music:—Do I wake or sleep?

Case Histories

[FROM *Biographies of Suicides*]

CHRISTIAN HEINRICH SPIESS

1786

PREFACE

. . . I wish to warn the young man, in order that he not play lightheartedly with a young maiden's virtue and then through his faithlessness be her murderer. I wish to make the inexperienced maiden more cognizant of her danger by using terrible examples, thus to increase her concern for her virtue. I wish to show benevolent and sensitive hearts that a man's life is often saved by small but loving help; and show the wealthy miser that he deliberately murders when he hears the cry of the person in distress and remains unmoved, and gives no help when he should help, can help, and must help. Finally, I wish to give the most useful and the greatest comfort to those in despair, by proving to them through real examples that even in the most extreme need, and under the most frightful conditions, salvation and succor are still possible; that caution never abandons him who still has hope, and it certainly saves those who are harassed.

SUICIDE FROM LOVE

Princess Sophie von . . . . She arose at midnight, sought for something in her writing-desk, lay down on her bed once more, and was found dead the next morning.

Suicide from Poverty

Lieutenant von . . . . The Marquis received this important letter along with two other letters from his family. Unconcerned about the contents of the first missive, he ripped open the other two with whose handwriting he was familiar. Once more he discovered negative and threatening answers. He shot himself in the head with an already loaded pistol, without ever reading the first letter.

Suicide from Ambition

Major L. . . . At this point he pulled a pistol from his saddle-bag and fired it behind him in the air. "This belongs to Your Excellency!" Then he took out another pistol. "This one is for me!" And he put a bullet right through his head and fell from his horse without uttering another word.

Martin Hause: A Villain and a Suicide

He stole the wooden spoon with which he ate his hot soup once a week, stuck this in his throat and pushed it down so far that he choked himself.

A Sacrifice to Voluptuousness

"Here," said she to the brothel madame, "is where the Count saw me . . . But, by God, may he answer to God Almighty for my death!" With these words she jumped into the river; and despite the crowd that immediately hastened to the spot, her corpse was only found some three days later.

Trans. H. E. H.

Exquisite Forms of Dying

[FROM *Germany's Youngest Literary and
Cultural Epoch*]

HERMANN MARGGRAFF

1839

We have lived to see nine-year-old boys saving
their pocket money to buy powder and pistol in order
to execute an act of noisy self-annihilation. . . . Suicides such as that of the worthy Charlotte Stieglitz, who
did away with herself (as far as we can gather) out of
self-sacrificial motives—these tower with a kind of holiness over the mob of common self-destruction: that is,
if suicide can ever attain any kind of glorious holiness.

What one loves, one must be able to kill, as Johannes
Falk has said somewhere. Consequently any prevalence
of suicides may well be explained by this age of egotism
and selfishness. The healthier the age, the rarer the
suicides and the nobler the motive—indeed the manner
of killing: the sicker, more decadent, complicated, and
refined the age, all the more frequent are suicides. Simi-
larly, the more unworthy the motive, the more refined
and various are the ways of doing away with oneself.
. . . With us there was a time when the pistol was a
commonplace. Now people are much more refined. They
no longer find satisfaction in shooting, hanging, drown-
ing, and poisoning; they must employ more exquisite
forms of dying. A norm no longer exists: the utmost
caprice rules, even as it does in literature. Several mys-
tics have had themselves nailed to crosses. Unlucky

lovers or young poets who have met with defeat in their melodramas, in our day have suffocated themselves with coal gas or with steam. Napoleonists have jumped off the column at the *Vendôme;* a young girl ate sewing-needles with her honey-buns until her intestines developed incurable abscesses; a man in Birmingham crawled into a glowing oven and carbonized himself. Others chew and swallow glass. One ingenious suicide threw himself under the crushing wheels of a heavily loaded wagon—a new discovery which has found imitators. An Englishman hanged himself after decorating himself with candles, and thus he served as a chandelier for the guests he had invited. You can see that we are not lacking in talent as far as innovation is concerned, and humor has played no small role in this terrible situation. When that brilliant lover Sappho leaped from the Leucadian cliffs into the waves of the sea, this act contained some poetic ingredient. One pictures her inspired, illuminated face and her burning eyes; her sublime countenance on the rocks, her lyre beneath her arms as if she were some goddess and seer. Now she leaps away: her wide-waving garments spread, the waves of her loose hair blow in the wind; the yearning sea stretches its damp arms toward her. She touches them with her sandals; the waves tower lofty and murmur darkly while they cover up her face. They preserve her glowing heart in their cool deeps. But when some little Luise Brachmann, who has never sung Sappho's fiery love songs, goes out to the dingy river bank of an obscure stream amid night and fog—clad in a modern nightgown, with a rock placed with careful calculation about her neck—then we must shudder in ordinary, modern fashion, somewhat sinister. There is nothing good about this, nor does it kindle the faintest spark of poetry.

Trans. H. E. H.

Most Wretched of Men

[FROM *The Sorrows of Young Werther*]

JOHANN WOLFGANG VON
GOETHE

1774

November 21, 1771

She does not see, she does not feel that she is preparing a poison which will destroy us both; and I drink deeply of the draught that is to prove my destruction. What mean those looks of kindness with which she often—often? no, not often, but sometimes—looks at me, that politeness with which she hears an involuntary expression of my feeling, the tender pity for my suffering which she sometimes seems to show?

Yesterday, when I took leave, she took my hand and said, "Adieu, dear Werther." Dear Werther! It was the first time she ever called me "dear": it went through me. I have repeated it a hundred times; and last night, as I was going to bed and talked to myself about nothing in particular, I suddenly said, "Good night, dear Werther!" and I could not help laughing at myself.

November 22, 1771

I cannot pray, "Let her be mine!" Yet she often seems to belong to me. I cannot pray, "Give her to me!" for she is another's. I try to quiet my suffering by all sorts of cool arguments. If I let myself go, I could compose a whole litany of antitheses.

November 24, 1771

She feels what I suffer. This morning her look pierced
my very soul. I found her alone, and said nothing; she
looked at me. I no longer saw in her face the charms of
beauty or the spark of her mind; these had disappeared.
But I was struck by an expression much more touching
—a look of the deepest sympathy and of the gentlest
pity. Why was I afraid to throw myself at her feet?
Why did I not dare to take her in my arms, and answer
her with a thousand kisses? She turned to her piano for
relief, and in a low and sweet voice accompanied the
music with delicious sounds. Her lips never appeared
lovelier; they seemed but just to open, that they might
drink the sweet tones which came from the instrument,
and return the delicate echo from her sweet mouth. Oh,
if only I could convey all this to you! I was quite overcome, and bending down, pronounced this vow: "Never
will I dare to kiss you, beautiful lips which the spirits
of Heaven guard." And yet I will—but it stands like a
barrier before my soul—this bliss—and then die to
expiate the sin! Is it sin?

November 26, 1771

I often say to myself, "You alone are wretched; all
others are happy; none are distressed like you." Then I
read a passage of an ancient poet, and it is as if I looked
into my own heart. I have so much to endure! Have men
before me ever been so wretched?

"After eleven," December 25, 1771

"All is silent around me, and my soul is calm. I thank
Thee, God, that Thou hast given me strength and courage in these last moments! I step to the window, my
dearest, and can see a few stars through the passing
storm clouds. No, you will not fall. The Almighty sustains you, and me. I see the brightest lights of the Great

Bear, my favorite constellation. When I left you, Charlotte, and went out from your gate, it always was in front of me. With what rapture have I so often looked at it! How many times have I implored it with raised hands to witness my happiness! and still— But what is there, Charlotte, that does not remind me of you? Are you not everywhere about me? and have I not, like a child, treasured up every trifle which your saintly hands have touched?

"Beloved silhouette! I now return it to you; and I pray you to preserve it. Thousands of kisses have I pressed upon it, and a thousand times did it gladden my heart when I have left the house or returned.

"I have asked your father in a note to protect my body. At one corner of the churchyard, looking towards the fields, there are two linden trees—there I wish to lie. Your father can, and doubtless will, do this for his friend. You ask him, too! I will not expect it of pious Christians that their bodies should be buried near the corpse of a poor, unhappy wretch like me. I could wish to lie in some remote valley by the wayside, where priest and Levite may bless themselves as they pass by my tomb, and the Samaritan shed a tear.

"See, Charlotte, I do not shudder to take the cold and fatal cup, from which I shall drink the draught of death. Your hand gave it to me, and I do not tremble. All, all the wishes and the hopes of my life are fulfilled. Cold and stiff I knock at the brazen gates of Death.

"Oh that I might have enjoyed the bliss of dying for you! how gladly would I have sacrificed myself for you, Charlotte! And could I but restore your peace and happiness, with what resolution, with what joy, would I not meet my fate! But it is given to but a chosen few to shed their blood for those they loved, and by their death to kindle a hundredfold the happiness of those by whom they are beloved.

"Charlotte, I wish to be buried in the clothes I wear

at present; you have touched them, blessed them. I have begged this same favor of your father. My spirit soars above my coffin. I do not wish my pockets to be searched. This pink bow which you wore the first time I saw you, surrounded by the children— Oh, kiss them a thousand times for me, and tell them the fate of their unhappy friend! I think I see them playing around me. The darling children! How they swarm about me! How I attached myself to you, Charlotte! From the first hour I saw you, I knew I could not leave you! Let this ribbon be buried with me; it was a present from you on my birthday. How eagerly I accepted it all! I did not think that it would all lead to this! Be calm! I beg you, be calm!

"They are loaded—the clock strikes twelve. So be it! Charlotte! Charlotte, farewell, farewell!"

A neighbor saw the flash, and heard the shot; but, as everything remained quiet, he thought no more of it.

At six in the morning, the servant entered Werther's room with a candle. He found his master stretched on the floor, blood about him, and the pistol at his side. He called to him, took him in his arms, but there was no answer, only a rattling in the throat. The servant ran for a surgeon, for Albert. Charlotte heard the bell; a shudder seized her. She awakened her husband; both arose. The servant, in tears, stammered the dreadful news. Charlotte fell senseless at Albert's feet.

When the surgeon arrived, Werther was lying on the floor; his pulse beat, but his limbs were paralyzed. The bullet had entered the forehead over the right eye; his brains were protruding. He was bled in the arm; the blood came, and he breathed.

From the blood on the chair, it could be inferred that he had committed the deed sitting at his desk, and that he had afterwards fallen on the floor and had twisted convulsively around the chair. He was found lying on his back near the window. He was fully dressed in his boots, blue coat and yellow waistcoat.

The house, the neighbors, and the whole town were in commotion. Albert arrived. They had laid Werther on the bed. His head was bandaged, and the pallor of death was upon his face. His limbs were motionless; a terrible rattling noise came from his lungs, now strongly, now weaker. His death was expected at any moment.

He had drunk only one glass of the wine. "Emilia Galotti" lay open on his desk.

Let me say nothing of Albert's distress or of Charlotte's grief.

The old judge hastened to the house upon hearing the news; he kissed his dying friend amid a flood of tears. His eldest boys soon followed him on foot. In speechless sorrow they threw themselves on their knees by the bedside, and kissed his hands and face. The eldest, who was his favorite, clung to his lips till he was gone; even then the boy had to be taken away by force. At noon Werther died. The presence of the judge, and the arrangements he had made prevented a disturbance; that night, at the hour of eleven he had the body buried in the place that Werther had chosen.

The old man and his sons followed the body to the grave. Albert could not. Charlotte's life was in danger. The body was carried by workmen. No clergyman attended.

Trans. Victor Lange (New York: Rinehart & Co., 1949).

PART TWO

*The Romantic Hero and
the Fatal Woman*

THE HISTORICAL HERO: NAPOLEON

I belong to that generation born when the century began; which, nourished with the Emperor's bulletins, always had an unsheathed sword before its eyes.

—Alfred de Vigny

"The New Successor to Alexander and Caesar"

[FROM *The Charterhouse of Parma*]

STENDHAL
(HENRI BEYLE)

1839

On May 15th, 1796, General Bonaparte entered Milan at the head of that young army which had just before crossed the Bridge of Lodi to teach the world that after all these centuries Caesar and Alexander had a successor. The miracles of bravery and genius to which Italy was a witness, in the space of a few months awakened a slumbering people; only one week before the French arrived, the Milanese still regarded them

149

simply as a mob of brigands who were always accustomed to flee before the troops of His Imperial and Royal Majesty; at least that is what they were told three times each week by a little newspaper no larger than one's hand, printed on dirty paper.

In the Middle Ages the Republicans of Lombardy had attested to a bravery equal to that of the French, and hence they deserved to watch their city being completely razed to the ground by the German Emperors. Since then they had become *loyal subjects.* Their chief occupation was to print sonnets on little rose-colored taffeta handkerchiefs whenever the marriage of some young girl, belonging to a noble or rich family, took place. Two or three years after that great event in her life, this young girl would engage a *cavalier servant;* sometimes the name of the *cicisbeo* selected by her husband's family occupied an honorable place in the marriage contract. It was a far cry from these effeminate customs to the deep emotions aroused by the unexpected arrival of the French army. Presently a new and a passionate way of life sprang up. On May 15th, 1796, a whole people discovered that all they had respected up to then was now supremely ridiculous, indeed hateful. The departure of the last Austrian regiment marked the collapse of the old ideas: to risk one's life became all the rage and fashion. People discovered that in order really to be happy after centuries of insipid emotions, they had to love their country with a genuine love and seek out heroic deeds. The continuation of the jealous despotism of Charles V and Phillip II had plunged everyone into the darkest of nights; these statues were overturned, and immediately all was flooded with daylight. For the last half-century, even as the *Encyclopedia* and Voltaire blazed out in France, the monks had been crying out to the good people of Milan that learning to read or learning anything at all was a totally useless task; and that by paying one's exact tithe to the local parish priest, faithfully telling him all the little sins, a person was practically assured of getting a good seat in Paradise. To complete the disabling of this race who at one time were so formidable and so rational, Austria had sold them cheaply the right of not having to provide recruits for her army.

In 1796, the Milanese army was composed of twenty-four scoundrels dressed in red, who guarded the city with the aid of four magnificent regiments of Hungarian Grenadiers. Moral licence was extreme, passion was very rare. Otherwise, apart from the inconvenience of having to confess everything to one's priest, on pain of ruin in this world itself, the good people of Milan were still subjected to certain small monarchical obstacles which could not be anything but vexing. For example there was the Archduke, who lived in Milan and governed in the name of the Emperor his cousin, and who had the lucrative idea of trading in corn. Consequently there was a law preventing the peasants from selling their grain until His Highness had filled up his granaries.

In May 1796, three days after the French entered, a young artist and miniaturist—slightly crazy, named Gros (later famous), who had come with the army, having overheard about the Archduke's exploits in the great *Caffè dei Servi* (then very fashionable), the Archduke being at that time rather overweight—happened to pick up a list of ices printed on a sheet of rough yellow paper. On the back of this foolscap he sketched a fat Archduke, and a French soldier bayonetting him in the belly, where an unbelievable amount of grain poured out in the place of blood. What we regard as a lampoon or a caricature was unthought-of in this land of slippery despotism. The sketch that Gros left on the table in the *Caffè dei Servi* seemed like a miracle from Heaven; they engraved and printed it during that same

night, and the following day some twenty thousand
copies were sold.

Trans. H. E. H.

"Great Historical Individuals"

[FROM *The Philosophy of History*]

GEORG WILHELM FRIEDRICH HEGEL

1822-31

It is the same with all great historical individuals:
their own particular purposes contain the substantial will
of the World Spirit. They must be called "heroes," insofar as they have derived their purpose and vocation
not from the calm, regular course of things, sanctioned
by the existing order, but from a secret source whose
content is still hidden and has not yet broken through
into existence. The source of their actions is the inner
spirit, still hidden beneath the surface but already
knocking against the outer world as against a shell, in
order, finally, to burst forth and break it into pieces;
for it is a kernel different from that which belongs to
the shell. They are men, therefore, who appear to draw
the impulses of their lives from themselves. Their deeds
have produced a condition of things and a complex of
historical relations that appear to be their own interest
and their own work.

Such individuals have no consciousness of the Idea as
such. They are practical and political men. But at the
same time they are thinkers with insight into what is
needed and timely. They see the very truth of their
age and their world, the next genus, so to speak, which

is already formed in the womb of time. It is theirs to know this new universal, the necessary next stage of their world, to make it their own aim and put all their energy into it. The world-historical persons, the heroes of their age, must therefore be recognized as its seers—their words and deeds are the best of the age. Great men have worked for their own satisfaction and not that of others. Whatever prudent designs and well-meant counsels they might have gotten from others would have been limited and inappropriate under the circumstances. For it is they who knew best and from whom the others eventually learned and with whom they agreed or, at least, complied. For Spirit, in taking this new historical step, is the innermost soul of all individuals—but in a state of unconsciousness, which the great men arouse to consciousness. For this reason their fellow men follow these soul-leaders. . . . For they feel the irresistible power of their own spirit embodied in them.

Let us now cast a look at the fate of these world-historical individuals. . . . Thus they attained no calm enjoyment. Their whole life was labor and trouble, their whole being was in their passion. Once their objective is attained, they fall off like empty hulls from the kernel. They die early like Alexander, they are murdered like Caesar, transported to Saint Helena like Napoleon. This awful fact, that historical men were not what is called happy—for only private life in its manifold external circumstances can be "happy"—may serve as a consolation for those people who need it, the envious ones who cannot tolerate greatness and eminence. They strive to criticize the great and belittle greatness. Thus in modern times it has been demonstrated *ad nauseam* that princes are generally unhappy on their thrones. For this reason one does not begrudge them their position and finds it tolerable that *they* rather than oneself sit on the throne. The free man, however, is not envious, but gladly recognizes what is great and exalted and rejoices in its existence. . . .

A world-historical individual is not so sober as to adjust his ambition to circumstances; nor is he very considerate. He is devoted, come what may, to one purpose. Therefore such men may treat other great and even sacred interests inconsiderately—a conduct which indeed subjects them to moral reprehension. But so mighty a figure must trample down many an innocent flower, crush to pieces many things in its path.

Reason in History. Trans. Robert S. Hartman (New York: Liberal Arts Press, 1953).

Napoleon in 1799

[FROM Considerations Concerning . . . the French Revolution: "The Eighteenth Brumaire"]

MADAME DE STAËL

1818

On the 18th Brumaire [1799] the Council of Elders ordered that the legislative body be moved to Saint-Cloud on the next day, the 19th, because there they might more easily make use of military force. On the evening of the 18th the entire city was excited by the expectation of the events of the morrow; and there is no doubt at all that the majority of respectable persons, fearful for the return of the Jacobins, hoped at that time that General Bonaparte would have the advantage. I confess my own feelings to have been extremely confused. Once the struggle commenced, a momentary victory for the Jacobins might bring about bloodshed;

nevertheless at the thought of Bonaparte's triumph, I felt a sadness that I might call prophetic.

One of my friends, present at the meeting at Saint-Cloud, sent me messages every hour: at one time he advised me that the Jacobins were winning, and I once more prepared to leave France; but a moment later I learned that General Bonaparte had triumphed, the soldiers having dispersed the national representatives; and I wept—not for liberty, for it never existed in France—but for the hope of that same liberty, without which this land enjoys nothing but shame and misery. At this moment I felt it difficult to breathe; that sickness which has since become, I think, endemic for all who have lived under Bonaparte's authority.

They talk variously about the way this revolution of 18th Brumaire was accomplished. What most matters is to note on this occasion the characteristic traits of the man who has been master of the European continent for almost fifteen years. He presented himself before the bench at the Council of Elders, and wanted to persuade them by speaking to them with warmth and nobility; but he did not know how to explain himself in a sustained style; only in ordinary conversation does his biting and powerful wit show itself to advantage; on the other hand, since he doesn't have any real enthusiasm about any subject, he is eloquent only when he is abusive, and nothing was more difficult for him than to convince, while improvising in a respectful fashion, the assembly that he wished to win over. He tried to say to the Council of Elders: "I am the god of war and of fortune: follow me." But out of embarrassment he made use of the following pompous words, in place of those he would have liked to say: "You are all wretches, and I'll have you shot if you don't obey me."

On the 19th Brumaire he arrived at the Chamber of the Five Hundred, his arms crossed and with a very serious expression, followed by two huge grenadiers who guarded his tiny frame. The Jacobin deputies let out howls when they saw him come into the room; his brother Lucien, fortunately for him, was then President; in vain he rang the bell to re-establish order; cries of "Traitor" and "Usurper" came from all quarters; and one of the deputies, Bonaparte's compatriot, the Corsican Aréna, came up to the general and shook him violently by the collar of his coat. People have suggested, but without much proof, that he had a knife to kill him. In any case his act frightened Bonaparte; and he told the grenadiers beside him, as he let his head fall on one of their shoulders, "Get me out of here." The grenadiers carried him out of the crowd of surrounding deputies, and brought him from the chamber into the open; where, as soon as he was there, his presence of mind returned. He immediately mounted his horse; and, riding between the ranks of his grenadiers, he soon told them what he wanted of them. . . .

Immediately after General Bonaparte left the Chamber of the Five Hundred, the deputies opposed to him vehemently demanded that he be declared an outlaw; and it was then that his brother Lucien, President of the Assembly, did him an invaluable service by refusing to put this proposition to a voice vote despite the pressure put upon him. If he had consented, the decree would have passed; and no one could know the impression that such a decree might have had on his soldiers: they had continually deserted during the past ten years those of their generals whom legislative decrees had prescribed. True, the 18th Fructidor lost for the national representatives their character of legality, but the familiar words of the decree might have carried over the dissimilarity of situations. General Bonaparte hurriedly sent armed troops to take Lucien to safety outside the chamber; and as soon as he left, the grenadiers entered the Orangerie where the deputies had reassembled, and chased them out by marching from one end of the room to the other as if no one were there at all. The deputies, pushed against the wall, were forced to flee by the windows into the gardens of Saint-Cloud, clad in their senatorial togas. Representatives of the people had previously been proscribed in France; but this was the first time since the Revolution that anybody had made the civilian body ridiculous in the presence of the military; and Bonaparte, who wished to found his power on the degradation of the group as well as the individual, was delighted from the very first to know that he had destroyed the esteem of the deputies of the people. From this moment the moral force of the national representative was annihilated. . . .

General Bonaparte gave a speech in the committee room of the Five Hundred, in the presence of the officers of his staff and a few friends of the Directors, which was printed by the newspapers. This speech contained an interesting statement, and one that history might well note. "What have they done," he said, speaking of the Directory, "with that so lustrous France I bequeathed to them? I left them peace, and I returned to find war; I left them with victories, and I returned to find military reverses. Finally, what have they done with those hundred thousand Frenchmen I knew, my companions at arms, who are now dead?" Then (concluding his harangue suddenly in a calmer tone) he added: "This state of things cannot last; it will lead us in three years to despotism." Bonaparte has taken care to hasten the accomplishment of his prediction.

Trans. H. E H.

Byron on Bonaparte

[FROM "Ode to Napoleon Bonaparte"]

GEORGE GORDON,
LORD BYRON

1814

'Tis done—but yesterday a King!
  And arm'd with Kings to strive—
And now thou art a nameless thing
  So abject—yet alive!
Is this the man of thousand thrones,
Who strew'd our earth with hostile bones,
  And can he thus survive?
Since he, miscall'd the Morning Star,
Nor man nor fiend hath fallen so far.

Ill-minded man! why scourge thy kind
  Who bow'd so low the knee?
By gazing on thyself grown blind,
  Thou taught'st the rest to see.
With might unquestion'd,—power to save—
Thine only gift hath been the grave
  To those that worshipp'd thee;
Nor till thy fall could mortals guess
Ambition's less than littleness!

Thanks for the lesson—it will teach
  To after-warriors more
Than high Philosophy can preach,
  And vainly preach'd before.
That spell upon the minds of men

Breaks never to unite again,
    That led them to adore
Those Pagod things of sabre-sway,
With fronts of brass, and feet of clay.

The triumph and the vanity,
    The rapture of the strife—
The earthquake voice of Victory,
    To thee the breath of life;
The sword, the sceptre, and that sway
Which man seem'd made but to obey,
    Wherewith renown was rife—
All quell'd—Dark Spirit! what must be
The madness of thy memory!

The Desolator desolate!
    The Victor overthrown!
The Arbiter of others' fate
    A Suppliant for his own!
Is it some yet imperial hope
That with such change can calmly cope?
    Or dread of death alone?
To die a prince—or live a slave—
Thy choice is most ignobly brave! . . .

Thine evil deeds are writ in gore,
    Nor written thus in vain—
Thy triumphs tell of fame no more,
    Or deepen every stain—
If thou hadst died as honour dies,
Some new Napoleon might arise,
    To shame the world again—
But who would soar the solar height,
To set in such a starless night?

Weigh'd in the balance, hero dust
    Is vile as vulgar clay;

Thy scales, Mortality! are just
    To all that pass away;
But yet me thought the living great
Some higher sparks should animate,
    To dazzle and dismay;
Nor deem'd Contempt could thus make mirth
Of these, the Conquerors of the earth.

"The Glitter of His Genius"

[FROM *Autobiography and Memoirs*]

BENJAMIN ROBERT HAYDON

1814-46

June 12th, 1814. Went to Gérard the painter's, and was much affected at the portraits I saw there.

Buonaparte ten years ago: a horrid yellow for complexion; the tip of his nose tinged with red; his eyes fixed and stern, with a liquorish wateriness; his lips red dirt; his mouth cool, collected and resolute. All the other heads in the room looked like children beside him. Wilkie said, and so they did. I never was so horribly touched by a human expression.

June 24th, 1815 [after hearing the news of Waterloo]. How this victory pursues one's imagination! I read the *Gazette* four times without stopping.

June 25th, 1815. Read the *Gazette* again, till I know it actually by heart. Dined with [Leigh] Hunt. I give myself great credit for not worrying him to death at this news; he was quiet for some time, but knowing it must come by and by and putting on an air of indifference, he said: "Terrible battle this, Haydon." "A glorious one, Hunt." "Oh, yes, certainly," and to it we went.

Yet Hunt took a just and liberal view of the situation. As for Hazlitt, it is not to be believed how the destruction of Napoleon affected him; he seemed prostrated in mind and body: he walked about unwashed, unshaved, hardly sober by day, and always intoxicated by night, literally, without exaggeration, for weeks; until at length wakening as it were from his stupor, he at once left off stimulating liquors, and never touched them after.

Hazlitt's principle was, that crimes, want of honour, want of faith, or want of every virtue on earth, were nothing on the part of an individual raised from the middle classes to the throne, if they forwarded the victory of the popular principle while he remained there. I used to maintain that the basis of such a victory should be the very reverse of the vices, and cruelties, and weaknesses of decayed dynasties, and that in proportion as a man elevated as Napoleon was in such a cause deviated from the abstract virtue required he injured the cause itself and excused the very dynasties he wished to supplant and surpass.

July 12th, 1821. Wilkie drank tea with me tonight, and brought me news Napoleon was dead! Good God! I remember in 1806, as we were walking to the Academy, just after the battle of Jena, we were both groaning at the slowness of our means of acquiring fame in comparison with his. He is now dead in captivity, and we have gone quietly on, *"parvis componere magna,"* rising in daily respect, and have no cause to lament our silent progress. Ah, Napoleon, what an opportunity you lost! His death affects me to deep musing. I remember his rise in 1796, his glory, and his fall. Posterity can never estimate the sensations of those living at the time.

April 14th, 1845. Higginson lunched with me. He sailed with Napoleon on the *Bellerophon*. He said his influence on the men was fascinating, and he really feared they would have let him go if an enemy's ship had hove in sight. He used to borrow sixpences of the men, pinch the ears of the officers, and bewitch them without the least familiarity, in a manner that was unaccountable. Even Sir George [Cockburn] was affected by the end of the voyage. Higginson said, when he was caught watching you, he put on an expression of silliness to disguise his thoughts. (So too said Madame de Staël.)

June 22nd, 1846 [written shortly before Haydon cut his throat].

Last Thoughts of B. R. Haydon, half-past ten.

No man should use certain evil for probable good, however great the object. Evil is the prerogative of the Deity.

I create good, I create, I the Lord do these things. Wellington never used evil if the good was not certain. Napoleon had no such scruples, and I fear the glitter of his genius rather dazzled me; but had I been encouraged nothing but good would have come from me, because when encouraged I paid everybody. God forgive the evil for the sake of the good. Amen.

Cool Appraisal

[FROM THE *Letters*]

ARTHUR WELLESLEY,
DUKE OF WELLINGTON

Apethorpe, December 29, 1835

My dear Croker,

I have received **your** letter of the 26th November.
I have not got here any means of refreshing my memory
with such details as would be necessary in order to be of
much use to you. Buonaparte's whole life, civil, political,
and military, was a fraud. There was not a transaction,
great or small, in which lying and fraud were not introduced; but one must have a perfect recollection of facts,
and must be enabled to correct one's memory by reference to documents, in order to be able to write of them
with authority.

Of flagrant lies, the two most important in the military
branch of his life that I can now recollect are—first, the
expedition from Egypt into Syria, which totally failed,
and yet on his return to Egypt was represented to the
army there as a victory; there were illuminations, &c.

The next was the battle of Preussisch Eylau. This he
represented as a great victory. It is true that the allied
army retired after the battle. So did Buonaparte. You
will find the details of the Syrian affair in Bourienne,
where you likewise find Buonaparte's lies about the
defeat of the fleet.

I cannot here tell you where you will find the details

of the affair of Preussisch Eylau. I should think that Spain would afford you instances of fraud in his political schemes and negotiations. Cevallos will give you the detail of the frauds by which King Ferdinand was coaxed into a departure from Madrid, and afterwards from one town to another by a fresh lie, till he arrived at Bayonne, where he was seized as a traitor towards the Government of his father. In the meantime St. Sebastian, Pampeluna, Figueras, Barcelona, Spanish fortresses, were seized, each by some military trick of fraud, and held by the French troops till deprived by us.

Buonaparte's foreign policy was force and menace, aided by fraud and corruption. If the fraud was discovered, force and menace succeeded; and in most cases the unfortunate victim did not dare to avow that he perceived the fraud.

He tricked the King of Spain, Charles IV, by the concession of the kingdom of Etruria to his son-in-law. He afterwards forcibly deprived the said King in order to put in his brother-in-law. In short, there is no end of the violence and fraud of his proceedings.

Believe me, ever yours most sincerely,

Wellington

"I don't give a twopenny damn what's become of the ashes of Napoleon."

—Wellington

THE OUTSIDER

My joys, my griefs, my passions, and
  my powers,
Made me a stranger.

—Lord Byron

A Bad Essence

[FROM "The Editor's Preface to the New Edition
of *Wuthering Heights*"]

CHARLOTTE BRONTË

1850

Heathcliff, indeed, stands unredeemed; never once
swerving in his arrow-straight course to perdition, from
the time when "the little black-haired swarthy thing, as
dark as if it came from the Devil," was first unrolled out
of the bundle and set on its feet in the farmhouse
kitchen, to the hour when Nelly Dean found the grim,
stalwart corpse laid on its back in the panel-enclosed
bed, with wide-gazing eyes that seemed "to sneer at her
attempt to close them, and parted lips and sharp white
teeth that sneered too."

Heathcliff betrays one solitary human feeling, and
that is *not* his love for Catherine; which is a sentiment
fierce and inhuman; a passion such as might boil and

glow in the bad essence of some evil genius; a fire that might form the tormented centre—the eversuffering soul of a magnate of the infernal world: and by its quenchless and ceaseless ravage effect the execution of the decree which dooms him to carry Hell with him wherever he wanders. No; the single link that connects Heathcliff with humanity is his rudely-confessed regard for Hareton Earnshaw—the young man whom he has ruined; and then his half-implied esteem for Nelly Dean. These solitary traits omitted, we should say he was child neither of Lascar nor gipsy, but a man's shape animated by demon life—a Ghoul—an Afreet.

Whether it is right or advisable to create beings like Heathcliff, I do not know: I scarcely think it is. But this I know: the writer who possesses the creative gift owns something of which he is not always master—something that, at times, strangely wills and works for itself. He may lay down rules and devise principles, and to rules and principles it will perhaps for years lie in subjection; and then, haply without any warning of revolt, there comes a time when it will no longer consent to "harrow the valleys, or be bound with a band in the furrow"— when it "laughs at the multitude of the city, and regards not the crying of the driver"—when, refusing absolutely to make ropes out of sea-sand any longer, it sets to work on statue-hewing, and you have a Pluto or a Jove, a Tisiphone or a Psyche, a Mermaid or a Madonna, as Fate or Inspiration direct. Be the work grim or glorious, dread or divine, you have little choice left but quiescent adoption. As for you—the nominal artist—your share in it has been to work passively under dictates you neither delivered nor could question—that would not be uttered at your prayer, nor suppressed nor changed at your caprice. If the result be attractive, the World will praise you, who little deserve praise; if it be repulsive, the same World will blame you, who almost as little deserve blame.

Wuthering Heights was hewn in a wild workshop, with simple tools, out of homely materials. The statuary found a granite block on a solitary moor; gazing thereon, he saw how from the crag might be elicited a head, savage, swart, sinister; a form moulded with at least one element of grandeur—power. He wrought with a rude chisel, and from no model but the vision of his meditations. With time and labour, the crag took human shape; and there it stands colossal, dark, and frowning, half statue, half rock: in the former sense, terrible and goblin-like; in the latter, almost beautiful, for its colouring is of mellow grey, and moorland moss clothes it; and heath, with its blooming bells and balmy fragrance, grows faithfully close to the giant's foot.

He Loves and Hates Equally

[FROM *Wuthering Heights*]

EMILY BRONTË

1847

I descended and found Heathcliff waiting under the porch, evidently anticipating an invitation to enter. He followed my guidance without waste of words, and I ushered him into the presence of the master and mistress, whose flushed cheeks betrayed signs of warm talking. But the lady's glowed with another feeling when her friend appeared at the door: she sprang forward, took both his hands, and led him to Linton; and then she seized Linton's reluctant fingers and crushed them into his. Now fully revealed by the fire and candlelight, I was amazed, more than ever, to behold the transformation of Heathcliff. He had grown a tall, athletic, well-formed man; beside whom, my master seemed quite slender and youthlike. His upright carriage suggested the idea of his having been in the army. His countenance was much older in expression and decision of feature than Mr. Linton's; it looked intelligent, and retained no marks of former degradation. A half-civilised ferocity lurked yet in the depressed brows and eyes full of black fire, but it was subdued; and his manner was even dignified: quite divested of roughness, though too stern for grace. My master's surprise equalled or exceeded mine: he remained for a minute at a loss how to address the ploughboy, as he had called him. Heathcliff dropped his slight hand, and stood looking at him coolly till he chose to speak.

Mr. Heathcliff forms a singular contrast to his abode and style of living. He is a dark-skinned gipsy in aspect, in dress and manners a gentleman: that is, as much a gentleman as many a country squire: rather slovenly, perhaps, yet not looking amiss with his negligence, because he has an erect and handsome figure; and rather morose. Possibly, some people might suspect him of a degree of underbred pride; I have a sympathetic chord within that tells me it is nothing of the sort: I know, by instinct, his reserve springs from an aversion to showy displays of feeling—to manifestations of mutual kindliness. He'll love and hate equally under cover, and esteem it a species of impertinence to be loved or hated again. . . .

"Have you been listening at the door, Edgar?" asked the mistress, in a tone particularly calculated to provoke her husband, implying both carelessness and contempt of his irritation. Heathcliff, who had raised his eyes at the former speech, gave a sneering laugh at the latter; on purpose, it seemed, to draw Mr. Linton's attention to him. He succeeded; but Edgar did not mean to entertain him with any high flights of passion.

"I have been so far forbearing with you, sir," he said quietly; "not that I was ignorant of your miserable, degraded character, but I felt you were only partly responsible for that; and Catherine wishing to keep up your acquaintance, I acquiesced—foolishly. Your presence is a moral poison that would contaminate the most virtuous: for that cause, and to prevent worse consequences, I shall deny you hereafter admission into this house, and give notice now that I require your instant departure. Three minutes' delay will render it involuntary and ignominious."

Heathcliff measured the height and breadth of the speaker with an eye full of derision.

"Cathy, this lamb of yours threatens like a bull!" he said. "It is in danger of splitting its skull against my knuckles. By God! Mr. Linton, I'm mortally sorry that you are not worth knocking down!"

My master glanced towards the passage, and signed me to fetch the men: he had no intention of hazarding a personal encounter. I obeyed the hint; but Mrs. Linton, suspecting something, followed; and when I attempted to call them, she pulled me back, slammed the door to, and locked it.

"Fair means!" she said, in answer to her husband's look of angry surprise. "If you have not courage to attack him, make an apology, or allow yourself to be beaten. It will correct you of feigning more valour than you possess. No, I'll swallow the key before you shall get it! I'm delightfully rewarded for my kindness to each! After constant indulgence of one's weak nature, and the other's bad one, I earn for thanks two samples of blind ingratitude, stupid to absurdity! Edgar, I was defending you and yours; and I wish Heathcliff may flog you sick, for daring to think an evil thought of me!"

It did not need the medium of a flogging to produce that effect on the master. He tried to wrest the key from Catherine's grasp, and for safety she flung it into the hottest part of the fire; whereupon Mr. Edgar was taken with a nervous trembling, and his countenance grew deadly pale. For his life he could not avert that excess of emotion, mingled anguish and humiliation overcame him completely. He leant on the back of a chair, and covered his face.

"Oh, heavens! In old days, this would win you knighthood!" exclaimed Mrs. Linton. "We are vanquished! we are vanquished! Heathcliff would as soon lift a finger at you as a king would march his army against a colony of mice. Cheer up! you shan't be hurt! Your type is not a lamb, it's a suckling leveret."

"I wish you joy of the milk-blooded coward, Cathy!" said her friend. "I compliment you on your taste. And that is the slavering, shivering thing you preferred to me! I would not strike him with my fist, but I'd kick him with my foot, and experience considerable satisfaction. Is he weeping, or is he going to faint for fear?"

The fellow approached and gave the chair on which Linton rested a push. He'd better have kept his distance; my master quickly sprang erect, and struck him full on the throat a blow that would have levelled a slighter man. It took his breath for a minute; and while he choked, Mr. Linton walked out by the back door into the yard, and from thence to the front entrance.

"There! you've done with coming here," cried Catherine. "Get away, now; he'll return with a brace of pistols, and half-a-dozen assistants. If he did overhear us, of course he'd never forgive you. You've played him an ill turn, Heathcliff! But go—make haste! I'd rather see Edgar at bay than you."

"Do you suppose I'm going with that blow burning in my gullet?" he thundered. "By hell, no! I'll crush his ribs in like a rotten hazel-nut before I cross the threshold!

If I don't floor him now, I shall murder him sometime; so, as you value his existence, let me get at him!"

"My young lady is looking sadly the worse for her change of condition," I remarked. "Somebody's love comes short in her case, obviously: whose, I may guess; but, perhaps, I shouldn't say."

"I should guess it was her own," said Heathcliff. "She degenerates into a mere slut! She is tired of trying to please me uncommonly early. You'd hardly credit it, but the very morrow of our wedding, she was weeping to go home. However, she'll suit this house so much the better for not being over nice, and I'll take care she does not disgrace me by rambling abroad."

"Well, sir," returned I, "I hope you'll consider that Mrs. Heathcliff is accustomed to be looked after and waited on; and that she has been brought up like an only daughter, whom every one was ready to serve. You must let her have a maid to keep things tidy about her, and you must treat her kindly. Whatever be your notion of Mr. Edgar, you cannot doubt that she has a capacity for strong attachments, or she wouldn't have abandoned the elegances, and comforts, and friends of her former home, to fix contentedly, in such a wilderness as this, with you."

"She abandoned them under a delusion," he answered; "picturing in me a hero of romance, and expecting unlimited indulgences from my chivalrous devotion. I can hardly regard her in the light of a rational creature, so obstinately has she persisted in forming a fabulous notion of my character and acting on the false impressions she cherished. But, at last, I think she begins to know me: I don't perceive the silly smiles and grimaces that provoked me at first; and the senseless incapability of discerning that I was in earnest when I gave her my opinion of her infatuation and herself. It was a marvellous effort of perspicacity to discover that I did not love her. I believed, at one time, no lessons could teach her that! And yet it is poorly learnt; for this morning she announced, as a piece of appalling intelligence, that I had actually succeeded in making her hate me! A positive labour of Hercules, I assure you! If it be achieved, I have cause to return thanks. Can I trust your assertion, Isabella? Are you sure you hate me? If I let you alone for half a day, won't you come sighing and wheedling to me again? I dare say she would rather I had seemed all tenderness before you: it wounds her vanity to have the truth exposed. But I don't care who knows that the passion was wholly on one side; and I never told her a lie about it. She cannot accurse me of showing one bit of deceitful softness. The first thing she saw me do, on coming out of the Grange, was to hang up her little dog; and when she pleaded for it, the first words I uttered were a wish that I had the hanging of every being belonging to her, except one: possibly she took that exception for herself. But no brutality disgusted her: I suppose she has an innate admiration of it, if only her precious person were secure from injury! Now, was it not the depth of absurdity—of genuine idiocy, for that pitiful, slavish, mean-minded brach to dream that I could love her? Tell your master, Nelly, that I never, in all my life, met with such an abject thing as she is. She even disgraces the name of Linton; and I've sometimes relented, from pure lack of invention, in my experiments on what she could endure, and still creep shamefully cringing back! But tell him, also, to set his fraternal and magisterial heart at ease: that I keep strictly within the limits of the law. I have avoided, up to this period, giving her the slightest right to claim a separation; and, what's more, she'd thank nobody for dividing us. If she desired to go, she might: the nuisance of her presence outweighs the gratification to be derived from tormenting her!"

"Mr. Heathcliff," said I, "this is the talk of a madman; your wife, most likely, is convinced you are mad; and, for that reason, she has borne with you hitherto: but now that you say she may go, she'll doubtless avail herself of the permission. You are not so bewitched, ma'am, are you, as to remain with him of your own accord?"

"Take care, Ellen!" answered Isabella, her eyes sparkling irefully; there was no misdoubting by their expression the full success of her partner's endeavours to make himself detested. "Don't put faith in a single word he speaks. He's a lying fiend! a monster, and not a human being! I've been told I might leave him before; and I've made the attempt, but I dare not repeat it! Only, Ellen, promise you'll not mention a syllable of his infamous conversation to my brother or Catherine. Whatever he may pretend, he wishes to provoke Edgar to desperation: he says he has married me on purpose to obtain power over him; and he shan't obtain it—I'll die first! I just hope, I pray, that he may forget his diabolical prudence and kill me! The single pleasure I can imagine is to die or see him dead!"

"There—that will do for the present!" said Heathcliff. "If you are called upon in a court of law, you'll remember her language, Nelly! And take a good look at that countenance: she's near the point which would suit me. No; you're not fit to be your own guardian, Isabella, now; and I, being your legal protector, must detain you in my custody, however distasteful the obligation may be. Go upstairs; I have something to say to Ellen Dean in private. That's not the way: upstairs, I tell you! Why, this is the road upstairs, child!"

He seized, and thrust her from the room: and returned muttering:

"I have no pity! I have no pity! The more the worms writhe, the more I yearn to crush out their entrails! It is a moral teething; and I grind with greater energy, in proportion to the increase of pain."

As I spoke, I observed a large dog lying on the sunny grass beneath raise its ears as if about to bark, and then smoothing them back, announce, by a wag of the tail, that some one approached whom it did not consider a stranger. Mrs. Linton bent forward, and listened breathlessly. The minute after a step traversed the hall; the open house was too tempting for Heathcliff to resist walking in: most likely he supposed that I was inclined to shirk my promise, and so resolved to trust to his own audacity. With straining eagerness Catherine gazed towards the entrance of her chamber. He did not hit the right room directly, she motioned me to admit him, but he found it out ere I could reach the door, and in a stride or two was at her side, and had her grasped in his arms.

He neither spoke nor loosed his hold for some five minutes, during which period he bestowed more kisses than ever he gave in his life before, I dare say: but then my mistress had kissed him first, and I plainly saw that he could hardly bear, for downright agony, to look into her face! The same conviction had stricken him as me, from the instant he beheld her, that there was no prospect of ultimate recovery there—she was fated, sure to die.

"Oh, Cathy! Oh, my life! how can I bear it?" was the first sentence he uttered, in a tone that did not seek to disguise his despair. And now he stared at her so earnestly that I thought the very intensity of his gaze would bring tears into his eyes; but they burned with anguish: they did not melt.

"What now?" said Catherine, leaning back, and returning his look with a suddenly clouded brow: her humour was a mere vane for constantly varying caprices. "You and Edgar have broken my heart, Heathcliff! And you both came to bewail the deed to me, as if *you* were the people to be pitied! I shall not pity you, not I. You have killed me—and thriven on it, I think. How strong you are! How many years do you mean to live after I am gone?"

Heathcliff had knelt on one knee to embrace her; he attempted to rise, but she seized his hair, and kept him down.

"I wish I could hold you," she continued bitterly, "till we were both dead! I shouldn't care what you suffered. I care nothing for your sufferings. Why shouldn't *you* suffer? I do! Will you forget me? Will you be happy when I am in the earth? Will you say twenty years hence, 'That's the grave of Catherine Earnshaw. I loved her long ago, and was wretched to lose her; but it is past. I've loved many others since: my children are dearer to me than she was; and at death, I shall not rejoice that I am going to her; I shall be sorry that I must leave them!' Will you say so, Heathcliff?"

"Don't torture me till I am as mad as yourself," cried he, wrenching his head free, and grinding his teeth.

The two, to a cool spectator, made a strange and fearful picture. Well might Catherine deem that heaven would be a land of exile to her, unless with her mortal body she cast away her moral character also. Her present countenance had a wild vindictiveness in its white cheek, and a bloodless lip and scintillating eye; and she retained in her closed fingers a portion of the locks she had been grasping. As to her companion, while raising himself with one hand, he had taken her arm with the other; and so inadequate was his stock of gentleness to the requirements of her condition, that on his letting go I saw four distinct impressions left blue in the colourless skin.

"Are you possessed with a devil," he pursued savagely, "to talk in that manner to me when you are dying? Do you reflect that all those words will be branded on my memory, and eating deeper eternally after you have left me? You know you lie to say I have killed you: and, Catherine, you know that I could as soon forget you as my existence! Is it not sufficient for your infernal selfishness, that while you are at peace I shall writhe in the torments of hell?"

"I shall not be at peace," moaned Catherine, recalled to a sense of physical weakness by the violent, unequal throbbing of her heart, which beat visibly and audibly under this excess of agitation.

A movement of Catherine's relieved me a little presently: she put up her hand to clasp his neck, and bring her cheek to his as he held her; while he, in return, covering her with frantic caresses, said wildly—

"You teach me now how cruel you've been—cruel and false. *Why* did you despise me? *Why* did you betray your own heart, Cathy? I have not one word of comfort. You deserve this. You have killed yourself. Yes, you may kiss me, and cry; and wring out my kisses and tears: they'll blight you—they'll damn you. You loved me—then what *right* had you to leave me? What right—answer me—for the poor fancy you felt for Linton? Because misery and degradation, and death, and nothing that God or Satan could inflict would have parted us, *you*, of your own will, did it. I have not broken your heart—*you* have broken it; and in breaking it, you have broken mine. So much the worse for me, that I am strong. Do I want to live? What kind of living will it be when you—oh, God! would *you* like to live with your soul in the grave?"

"Let me alone. Let me alone," sobbed Catherine. "If I have done wrong, I'm dying for it. It is enough! You left me too: but I won't upbraid you! I forgive you. Forgive me!"

"It is hard to forgive, and to look at those eyes, and feel those wasted hands," he answered. "Kiss me again;

and don't let me see your eyes! I forgive what you have done to me. I love *my* murderer—but *yours!* How can I?"

"Yes, she's dead!" I answered, checking my sobs and drying my cheeks. "Gone to heaven, I hope; where we may, every one, join her, if we take due warning and leave our evil ways to follow good!"

"Did *she* take due warning, then?" asked Heathcliff, attempting a sneer. "Did she die like a saint? Come, give me a true history of the event. How did—"

He endeavored to pronounce the name, but could not manage it; and compressing his mouth he held a silent combat with his inward agony, defying, meanwhile, my sympathy with an unflinching ferocious stare. "How did she die?" he resumed at last—fain, notwithstanding his hardihood, to have a support behind him; for, after the struggle, he trembled, in spite of himself, to his very finger-ends.

"Poor wretch!" I thought; "you have a heart and nerves the same as your brother men! Why should you be anxious to conceal them? Your pride cannot blind God! You tempt Him to wring them, till He forces a cry of humiliation.

"Quietly as a lamb!" I answered aloud. "She drew a sigh, and stretched herself, like a child reviving, and sinking again to sleep; and five minutes after I felt one little pulse at her heart, and nothing more!"

"And—did she ever mention me?" he asked, hesitating, as if he dreaded the answer to his question would introduce details that he could not bear to hear.

"Her senses never returned; she recognized nobody from the time you left her," I said. "She lies with a sweet smile on her face; and her latest ideas wandered back to pleasant early days. Her life closed in a gentle dream—may she wake as kindly in the other world!"

"May she wake in torment!" he cried, with frightful

vehemence, stamping his foot, and groaning in a sudden paroxysm of ungovernable passion. "Why, she's a liar to the end! Where is she? Not *there*—not in heaven—not perished—where? Oh, you said you care nothing for my sufferings! And I pray one prayer—I repeat it till my tongue stiffens—Catherine Earnshaw, may you not rest as long as I am living! You said I killed you—haunt me, then! The murdered *do* haunt their murderers, I believe. I know that ghosts *have* wandered on earth. Be with me always—take any form—drive me mad! only *do* not leave me in this abyss, where I cannot find you! Oh, God! it is unutterable! I *cannot* live without my life! I *cannot* live without my soul!"

He dashed his head against the knotted trunk; and, lifting up his eyes, howled, not like a man, but like a savage beast being goaded to death with knives and spears. I observed several splashes of blood about the bark of the tree, and his hand and forehead were both stained; probably the scene I witnessed was a repetition of others acted during the night. It hardly moved my compassion—it appalled me: still, I felt reluctant to quit him so. But the moment he recollected himself enough to notice me watching, he thundered a command for me to go, and I obeyed. He was beyond my skill to quiet or console!

"Five minutes ago, Hareton seemed a personification of my youth, not a human being: I felt to him in such a variety of ways, that it would have been impossible to have accosted him rationally. In the first place, his startling likeness to Catherine connected him fearfully with her. That, however, which you may suppose the most potent to arrest my imagination, is actually the least: for what is not connected with her to me? and what does not recall her? I cannot look down to this floor, but her features are shaped in the flags! In every cloud, in every tree—filling the air at night, and caught by glimpses in every object by day—I am surrounded with her image! The most ordinary faces of men and women—my own features—mock me with a resemblance. The entire world is a dreadful collection of memoranda that she did exist, and that I have lost her! Well, Hareton's aspect was the ghost of my immortal love; of my wild endeavours to hold my right; my degradation, my pride, my happiness, and my anguish:

"But it is frenzy to repeat these thoughts to you: only it will let you know why, with a reluctance to be always alone, his society is no benefit; rather an aggravation of the constant torment I suffer; and it partly contributes to render me regardless how he and his cousin go on together. I can give them no attention, any more."

"You have no feelings of illness, have you?" I asked.

"No, Nelly, I have not," he answered.

"Then you are not afraid of death?" I pursued.

"Afraid? No!" he replied. "I have neither a fear, nor a presentiment, nor a hope of death. Why should I? With my hard constitution and temperate mode of living, and unperilous occupations, I ought to, and probably *shall*, remain above ground till there is scarcely a black hair on my head. And yet, I cannot continue in this condition! I have to remind myself to breathe— almost to remind my heart to beat! And it is like bending back a stiff spring: it is by compulsion that I do the slightest act not prompted by one thought; and by compulsion that I notice anything alive or dead, which is not associated with one universal idea. I have a single wish, and my whole being and faculties are yearning to attain it. They have yearned towards it so long, and so unwaveringly, that I'm convinced it *will* be reached— and *soon*—because it has devoured my existence: I am swallowed up in the anticipation of its fulfillment. My confessions have not relieved me; but they may account for some otherwise unaccountable phases of humour which I show. O God! It is a long fight, I wish it were over!"

He solicited the society of no one more. At dusk, he went into his chamber. Through the whole night, and far into the morning, we heard him groaning and murmuring to himself. Hareton was anxious to enter; but I bade him fetch Dr. Kenneth, and he should go in and see him. When he came, and I requested admittance and tried to open the door, I found it locked; and Heathcliff bid us be damned. He was better, and would be left alone; so the doctor went away.

The following evening was very wet: indeed it poured down till day-dawn; and, as I took my morning walk round the house, I observed the master's window swinging open, and the rain driving straight in. He cannot be in bed, I thought: those showers would drench him through. He must either be up or out. But I'll make no more ado, I'll go boldly and look.

Having succeeded in obtaining entrance with another key, I ran to unclose the panels, for the chamber was vacant; quickly pushing them aside, I peeped in. Mr. Heathcliff was there—laid on his back. His eyes met mine so keen and fierce, I started; and then he seemed to smile. I could not think him dead: but his face and throat were washed with rain; the bed-clothes dripped, and he was perfectly still. The lattice, flapping to and fro, had grazed one hand that rested on the sill; no blood trickled from the broken skin, and when I put my fingers to it, I could doubt no more: he was dead and stark!

I hasped the window; I combed his black long hair from his forehead; I tried to close his eyes: to extinguish, if possible, that frightful, life-like gaze of exultation before any one else beheld it. They would not shut: they seemed to sneer at my attempts: and his parted lips and sharp white teeth sneered too! Taken with another fit of cowardice, I cried out for Joseph. Joseph shuffled up and made a noise; but resolutely refused to meddle with him. "Th' divil's harried off his soul," he cried, "and he may hev his carcass into t' bargain, for aught I care! Ech! what a wicked un he looks girning at death!" and the old sinner grinned in mockery. I thought he intended to cut a caper round the bed; but, suddenly composing himself, he fell on his knees, and raised his hands, and returned thanks that the lawful master and the ancient stock were restored to their rights.

I felt stunned by the awful event; and my memory unavoidably recurred to former times with a sore of oppressive sadness. But poor Hareton, the most wronged, was the only one who really suffered much. He sat by the corpse all night, weeping in bitter earnest. He pressed its hand, and kissed the sarcastic savage face that every one else shrank from contemplating; and bemoaned him with that strong grief which springs naturally from a generous heart, though it be tough as tempered steel.

Dr. Kenneth was perplexed to pronounce of what disorder the master died. I concealed the fact of his having swallowed nothing for four days, fearing it might lead to trouble, and then, I am persuaded, he did not abstain on purpose: it was the consequence of his strange illness, not the cause.

We buried him, to the scandal of the whole neighbourhood, as he wished. Earnshaw and I, the sexton, and six men to carry the coffin, comprehended the whole attendance. The six men departed when they had let it down into the grave: we stayed to see it covered. Hareton, with a streaming face, dug green sods, and laid them over the brown mound himself: at present it is as smooth and verdant as its companion mounds—and I hope its tenant sleeps as soundly. But the country folk, if you ask them, would swear on the Bible that he *walks:* there are those who speak of having met him near the church, and on the moor, and even in this house. Idle tales, you'll say, and so say I. Yet that old man by the kitchen fire affirms he has seen two on 'em, looking out of his chamber window, on every rainy night since his death: and an odd thing happened to me about a month ago. I was going to the Grange one evening—a dark evening, threatening thunder—and, just at the turn of the Heights, I encountered a little boy with a sheep and two lambs before him; he was crying terribly; and I supposed the lambs were skittish, and would not be guided.

"What's the matter, my little man?" I asked.

"There's Heathcliff and a woman, yonder, under t' nab," he blubbered, "un I darnut pass 'em."

I saw nothing; but neither the sheep nor he would go on; so I bid him take the road lower down. He probably raised the phantoms from thinking, as he traversed the moors alone, on the nonsense he had heard his parents and companions repeat. Yet, still, I don't like being out in the dark now; and I don't like being left by myself in this grim house: I cannot help it; I shall be glad when they leave it, and shift to the Grange.

"They are going to the Grange, then," I said.

"Yes," answered Mrs. Dean, "as soon as they are married, and that will be on New Year's day."

"And who will live here, then?"

"Why, Joseph will take care of the house, and, perhaps, a lad to keep him company. They will live in the kitchen, and the rest will be shut up."

"For the use of such ghosts as choose to inhabit it," I observed.

"No, Mr. Lockwood," said Nelly, shaking her head. "I believe the dead are at peace: but it is not right to speak of them with levity."

At that moment the garden gate swung to; the ramblers were returning.

"*They* are afraid of nothing," I grumbled, watching

their approach through the window. "Together they would brave Satan and all his legions."

As they stepped on to the door-stones, and halted to take a last look at the moon—or, more correctly, at each other by her light—I felt irresistibly impelled to escape them again; and, pressing a remembrance into the hand of Mrs. Dean, and disregarding her expostulations at my rudeness, I vanished through the kitchen as they opened the house door; and so should have confirmed Joseph in his opinion of his fellow-servant's gay indiscretions, had he not fortunately recognised me for a respectable character by the sweet ring of a sovereign at his feet.

My walk home was lengthened by a diversion in the direction of the kirk. When beneath its walls, I perceived decay had made progress, even in seven months: many a window showed black gaps deprived of glass; and slates jutted off, here and there, beyond the right line of the roof, to be gradually worked off in coming autumn storms.

I sought, and soon discovered, the three head-stones on the slope next the moor: the middle one grey, and half buried in heath: Edgar Linton's only harmonised by the turf and moss creeping up its foot: Heathcliff's still bare.

I lingered round them, under that benign sky; watched the moths fluttering among the heath and harebells, listened to the soft wind breathing through the grass, and wondered how any one could ever imagine unquiet slumbers for the sleepers in that quiet earth.

Why Accept Society's Laws?

[FROM *Antony*]

ALEXANDRE DUMAS
(THE ELDER)

1831

ADÈLE (*returning*): Antony!

ANTONY: Do you wish me to tell you my secret, now? . . .

ADÈLE: Oh! I know it, now I know it. How that woman has made me suffer!

ANTONY: Suffer, bah! That's madness; the whole thing is nothing but prejudice; and I now begin to find myself quite foolish.

ADÈLE: You?

ANTONY: Certainly! When I might have lived with people of my own class, I had the impudence to believe that with a soul that feels, a mind that thinks, a heart that beats . . . one might have everything that one needed to reclaim a position as a man in society, with a social rank in the world. What vanity!

ADÈLE: Oh! Now I understand everything that was puzzling to me . . . your somber character, that I found so fantastic . . . everything, everything . . . even your departure, which I hadn't realized! Poor Antony!

ANTONY (*depressed*): Yes, poor Antony! For who could tell you, you could describe what I suffered when I had to leave you? In your love I had lost my unhappiness: days and months went by like seconds, like dreams; near you I forgot almost everything. . . . Then came a man, and reminded me of everything. He offered you rank, a name in the world . . . and reminded me, me, that I had neither rank nor name to give her to whom I would have offered my blood.

ADÈLE: Then why . . . then why didn't you say that? (*She looks at the clock*) Ten thirty; oh, you miserable, miserable man!

ANTONY: Say that! Yes, perhaps at that time you thought you loved me, but would you have forgotten for one instant what I was to you when you thought about it later. But your parents insisted on a name . . . and what probability was there that they would have preferred poor Antony over the honorable Baron d'Hervey! . . . Then it was that I asked you for two weeks; one last hope remained for me. There is a man who is ordered, I do not know by whom, every year to throw me the wherewithal on which to live for a year; I ran to find him, I threw myself at his feet; I begged him in the name of all he held the most sacred, God, his soul, his mother—even he had a mother!—to tell me who were my parents, and what I might look forward to or expect from them! Curse him! And may his mother die! I could get nothing out of him. I left him, I went out as if I were a madman, a desperate man, ready to ask every woman I met, "Are you my mother?"

ADÈLE: Dear friend!

ANTONY: Other men at least have a brother, a father, a mother when something dashes all their hopes! . . . arms to open for them, that there they might grieve. I! I! I don't even have a tombstone where I might read one name, and weep.

ADÈLE: Calm yourself, for Heaven's sake! Calm yourself!

ANTONY: Other men have a country; I alone, I have none! For what is a country? The place where one is born, the family that one leaves behind, the friends one longs for . . . I, I don't even know where first I opened my eyes. I have no family whatsoever, I have no country whatsoever, all I had was found in one name, that was yours, and you forbid me to say it.

ADÈLE: Antony, the world has its laws, society has its own demands; whatever duties and precedents may be, men have made them what they are; and even if I had the wish to get away from these things, I would still have to accept them.

ANTONY: But why should I, I accept them? Not one of those who have made them can boast of having saved any pity for me or of doing me a service; no, thank God, from them I have received nothing but injustice, and I owe them nothing but my hatred. I would detest myself on that day when any man made me like him. Those to whom I have entrusted my secret have thrown my mother's sin in my face. My poor mother! They say, "Unhappy you, who have no parents!" Those from whom I have hidden it have vilified my life. They say, "Shame on you, who cannot admit openly to society where you get your fortune! These two words, unhappiness and shame, have become attached to me like two evil demons. I wanted to vanquish prejudice by education. Arts, languages, sciences, I've studied them all, learned them all. Mad I was to increase my sensibility so that despair might dwell there! Natural gifts or acquired learning, all fade away before the blemish of my birth; careers open to the most mediocre men are closed to me; I would have to give my name, and I have no name. Oh! Had only I have been born poor and remained ignorant! Lost in the crowd, I would not have been pursued by prejudices; the closer they get to the ground, the fewer they become, until finally three feet under, they disappear completely.

ADÈLE: Yes, yes, I understand. Oh! Pity yourself! Pity yourself! It is only with me that you can pity yourself!

ANTONY: I saw you, I loved you; the dream of love succeeded those of ambition and knowledge; I clung to life, I threw myself into the future, anxious as I was to forget the past. I was happy . . . a few days . . . the only happy days in my life! Thank you, my angel! Because to you I owe this burst of happiness, which I would not have known without you. But then Colonel d'Hervey— Curses! Oh! If only you know how unhappiness makes a man bad! How many times, when I thought about that man, I went to sleep with my hand on my dagger! And I dreamed of the Place de Grève and of the scaffold!

ADÈLE: Antony! You make me tremble . . .

ANTONY: I left, I returned; between those two words is a space of three years. I don't know how I spent those three years; I am not even sure I lived through them, except that I have the memory of a vague and constant sadness. I no longer feared the insults and injuries of other men; all I felt was my heart, and that belonged completely to you. I said to myself, "I shall see her again. It is impossible that she has forgotten me. I shall confess my secret to her . . . perhaps then she'll scorn me, hate me."

ADÈLE: Antony, oh! How could you have thought that?

ANTONY: And I, in my turn, I shall hate her as much as I do the others; or rather, because she will know what I have suffered, what I am suffering . . . perhaps she will let me stay near her . . . live in the same city as she does!

ADÈLE: Impossible.

ANTONY: Oh! Yet I must either hate or love, Adèle! I want one or the other. I believed for a moment that I might go away again. What madness! I would tell you this, but you needn't believe it; Adèle, I love you, do you understand? If you want ordinary love, you'll have to be loved by a happy man! Duty and virtue! . . . silly words! A murder can make you a widow. I could take this murder on myself; whether my blood flows from my own hand or from that of the executioner, who cares! It won't gush over anybody, it will only sprinkle the ground. Ah! You believed that you could love me, tell me so, open Heaven to me . . . and then everything collapsed when the priest uttered a few words. Leave, fly away, stay here, you belong to me, Adèle! To me, do you understand? I want you, I shall have you. Shall it be a crime for both of us? Let it be, I shall do it. Adèle, Adèle! I swear it by the same God I blaspheme! By my mother, whom I do not know!

ADÈLE: Calm yourself, you unhappy man! You are threatening me! You are threatening a woman.

ANTONY (*throwing himself at her feet*): Ah! Ah! . . . Mercy, mercy, pity, help me! Do I know what I am saying? My head is whirling, my words are foolish words without sense. Oh! I am so unhappy! If I could weep . . . If I could weep like a woman . . . Oh! laugh! laugh! . . . a man who weeps . . . I laugh at it myself . . . ah! ah!

ADÈLE: You are mad and you are driving me mad.

ANTONY: Adèle! Adèle!

Trans. H. E. H.

The Social Contract's Deep Deceptions

[FROM *Père Goriot*]

HONORÉ DE BALZAC

1834

[*Vautrin, arch-criminal, otherwise known as Jacques Collin, has just been betrayed to the police.*]

That head and face, in harmony with his torso, were assisted by his short and brick-red hair which lent them a frightful character of blended cunning and strength; and they were clearly illuminated as if glowing with the fires of Hell. Everyone understood all about Vautrin —his past, his present, his inexorable doctrines, his religion of egotistical pleasure, the cynicism of his thoughts and acts which granted him his royalty, and the power of his secret organization fit to do anything. The blood rose to his face and his eyes glowed like those of a wild-cat. He jumped up into the air with a movement so filled with ferocious energy, he roared so loudly, that all the boarders shrieked with terror. At this leonine gesture, the police agents took advantage of the general confusion to seize their pistols. Collin understood his danger when he saw each weapon cocked and glittering, and suddenly exhibited the greatest human strength. What a horrible and majestic spectacle! His countenance presented a phenomenon that might only be compared to a boiler full of thick steam, powerful enough to blast mountains, but which a single drop of cold water might dissipate in a moment. The drop of water that cooled his rage was the lightning-like speed of his thought. He smiled and looked at his wig.

"This is not one of your days to be polite," said he to the Chief of Police.

He stretched out his hands to the guards, calling them up with a nod of his head. "Officers, put on your manacles or hand-cuffs. I ask those present to witness that I offer no resistance."

The dining room resounded with murmurs of admiration, extorted by the promptness with which the lava and flames burst forth from this human volcano, only to subside.

"That's something you didn't bargain for, you house-breaker," continued the convict, looking at the famous Director of the Police Detectives.

"Come on, undress him!" ordered the gentleman from the Petite Rue Sainte-Anne scornfully.

"Why?" asked Collin. "There are ladies present. I deny nothing, and I am giving myself up."

He paused and surveyed the assembly like an orator about to make startling statements.

"Write this down, Papa Lachapelle," he said to a little white-haired old man, who was sitting at the end of the table and who had taken from his portfolio a sheet on which to record the proceedings." I confess to being Jacques Collin, called Trompe-la-Mort, who was condemned to twenty years' imprisonment in irons; and I have just proved to you that I didn't steal my surname. Had I but raised my hand," said he to the boarders," these three police-informers would have covered Mama Vauquer's pretty floor with my grape jelly. These fools have gotten me mixed up in a nice trap!"

The manners and customs of the galleys, their abrupt shifts from the pleasant to the horrible, their frightening greatness, the good fellowship and baseness, all were suddenly caught up in this episode and by this man;

who was no longer an individual man, but rather the exemplar of a degenerate nation, of a savage, logical, brutal, and docile race. In one second Collin had become a poet from Hell, who represented every human sentiment save one—repentance. He looked like some fallen angel who wanted perpetual war. Rastignac lowered his eyes, accepting this kinship in crime as expiation for his own evil thoughts.

"Who betrayed me?" asked Collin, letting his terrible eyes wander over the group.

And, pausing at Mademoiselle Michonneau: "It was you," he said, "you old dog-fish! You brought on that pretended heart attack, you snooper! If I said two words, I could have your throat cut within the week. But I forgive you; I am a Christian. Anyway, it wasn't you who sold me. But who did? Ah! Ah! You're searching around upstairs, are you?" he exclaimed as he heard the police officers opening his closets and seizing his effects." The nests are empty; the birds flew away yesterday. And you shall never know anything. I keep my books here," he said tapping his forehead. "Now I know who sold me. It can only be that rogue, Fil-de-Soie. Right, Papa Custodian?" he asked the Chief of Police. "It fits in too well with the time I had the banknotes upstairs. All right, little spies, nothing more to be found. As for Fil-de-Soie, he'll be dead and buried within two weeks, even if you have him guarded by your entire police force. How much did you give to Michonnette here?" he asked the policemen. "A thousand crowns! I was worth much more than that, you decrepit Ninon, you tattered Pompadour, you Venus of Père-Lachaise. If you had warned me, you could have had six thousand francs. Ah! But you didn't guess that, you old purveyor of human flesh, or you would have given me the preference. Yes, I would have given them gladly to avoid a trip that is inconvenient to me and makes me lose money," he continued as they put on the handcuffs.

"These fellows enjoy dragging me around forever to torment me. If only they would send me right off to the galleys, I'd soon be back at my business, in spite of those little ninnies on the Quai des Orfèvres. Down on the galleys they'll all put themselves out to help their general, good old Trompe-la-Mort, to escape. Is there any one of you who has, as do I, more than ten thousand brothers ready to do anything for you?" he asked proudly. "There is still some virtue here," he said, striking his heart. "I have never betrayed anyone. Look here, you old dog-fish," he said, speaking to the old maid. "They look at me with terror; but you, you make them retch with disgust. Take your loot."

He paused as he looked at the boarders.

"What fools you are!" he said. "Have you never seen a convict? A convict of the stamp of Collin, standing here, is less cowardly than other men, and one who protests against the deep deceptions of the social contract, as Jean-Jacques Rousseau calls it, he whose disciple I am proud to be. In brief, I stand alone against the government with its pile of courts, its policemen, its budgets; and I take them all in."

Trans. H. E. H.

A Spiritual Exile

[*The Heiligenstadt Testament*]

LUDWIG VAN BEETHOVEN

· 1802

FOR MY BROTHERS CARL AND JOHANN VAN BEETHOVEN

Oh you men who regard or declare me to be malignant, stubborn, or cynical, how unjust are you toward

me! You do not know the secret cause of my seeming
so. From childhood onward, my heart and mind
prompted me to be kind and tender, and I was ever
inclined to accomplish great deeds. But only think that,
during the last six years, I have been in a wretched
condition, rendered worse by unintelligent physicians,
deceived from year to year with hopes of improvement,
and then finally forced to the prospect of *lasting infirmity* (which may last for years, or even be totally incurable). Born with a fiery, active temperament, even
susceptive of the diversions of society, I had soon to
retire from the world, to live a solitary life. At times,
even, I endeavored to forget all this, but how harshly
was I driven back by the redoubled experience of my
bad hearing! Yet it was not possible for me to say to
men: Speak louder, shout, for I am deaf. Alas! how
could I declare the weakness of a sense which in me
ought to be more acute than in others—a sense which
formerly I possessed in highest perfection, a perfection such as few in my profession enjoy or ever have
enjoyed; no, I cannot do it. Forgive, therefore, if you
see me withdraw, when I would willingly mix with you.
My misfortune pains me doubly in that I am certain to
be misunderstood. For me there can be no recreation in
the society of my fellow creatures, no refined conversations, no interchange of thought. Almost alone, and
mixing in society only when absolutely necessary, I
am compelled to live as an exile. If I approach near to
people, a feeling of hot anxiety comes over me lest my
condition should be noticed—for so it was during
these past six months which I spent in the country.
Ordered by my intelligent physician to spare my hearing as much as possible, he almost fell in with my
present frame of mind, although many a time I was carried away by my sociable inclinations. But how humiliating was it, when some one standing close to me heard
a distant flute, and I heard *nothing*, or a *shepherd*

singing, and again I heard nothing. Such incidents almost drove me to despair; at times I was on the point
of putting an end to my life—*art* alone restrained my
hand. Oh! it seemed as if I could not quit this earth
until I had produced all I felt within me, and so I
continued this wretched life—wretched, indeed, and
with so sensitive a body that a somewhat sudden change
can throw me from the best into the worst state.
Patience, I am told, I must choose as my guide. I have
done so—lasting, I hope, will be my resolution to bear
up until it pleases the inexorable Parcae to break the
thread. Forced already, in my 28th year, to become a
philosopher, it is not easy—for an artist more difficult
than for any one else.

O Divine Being, Thou who lookest down into my
inmost soul, Thou understandest; Thou knowest that
love for mankind and a desire to do good dwell therein!
Oh, my fellow men, when one day you read this, remember that you were unjust to me and let the unfortunate one console himself if he can find one like himself,
who, in spite of all obstacles which nature has thrown in
his way, has still done everything in his power to be
received into the ranks of worthy artists and men.—
You, my brothers Carl and [Johann], as soon as I am
dead, beg Professor Schmidt, if he be still living, to
describe my malady; and annex this written account to
that of my illness, so that at least the world, so far as is
possible, may become reconciled to me after my death.
—And now I declare you both heirs to my small fortune
(if such it may be called). Divide it honorably and
dwell in peace, and help each other. What you have
done against me has, as you know, long been forgiven.
And you, brother Carl, I especially thank you for the
attachment you have shown toward me of late. My
prayer is that your life may be better, less troubled by
cares, than mine. Recommend to your children *virtue;*

it alone can bring happiness, not money. I speak from experience. It was virtue which bore me up in time of trouble; to her, next to my art, I owe thanks for my not having laid violent hands on myself.—Farewell, and love one another!—My thanks to all friends, especially *Prince Lichnowsky* and *Professor Schmidt.*—I should much like one of you to keep as an heirloom the instruments given to me by Prince Lichnowsky, but let no strife arise between you concerning them; if money should be of more service to you, just sell them. How happy I feel, that, even when lying in my grave, I may be useful to you!—

So let it be.—I joyfully hasten to meet death.—If it come before I have had opportunity to develop all *my* artistic faculties, it will come, my hard fate notwithstanding, too soon, and I should probably wish it later— yet even then I shall be happy, for will it not deliver me from a state of endless suffering? Come when thou wilt, I shall face thee courageously.—Farewell, and when I am dead do not entirely forget me. This I deserve from you, for during my lifetime I often thought of you, and how to make you happy. Be ye so!—

Ludwig von Beethoven
Heiligenstadt, October 6, 1802.

Thus I take my leave of you—and indeed with sadness.—Yes, that wonderful hope—that until now I had, at least that I might be cured to a small degree, must be abandoned. Like those fallen leaves in autumn, it is withered for me. Even as I came, now must I go— and even that strong courage—that so often strengthened me on summer days—has disappeared. Oh Divine Providence! let me have one pure day of happiness!— or so long now has any inner response to happiness been alien to me.—Oh when, when, my God—shall I be able to feel happiness in the temple of nature and man-

kind!—Never?—no—oh, that would be too cruel!—
Heiligenstadt, October 10, 1802

Trans. J. S. Shedlock (*German Classics*, ed. Kuno Francke. New York: German Publication Society, 1913). Postscript trans. H. E. H.

The Torture of the Self

["Egotism; or, The Bosom Serpent"]

NATHANIEL HAWTHORNE

1843

"Here he comes!" shouted the boys along the street. "Here comes the man with a snake in his bosom!"

This outcry, saluting Herkimer's ears as he was about to enter the iron gate of the Elliston mansion, made him pause. It was not without a shudder that he found himself on the point of meeting his former acquaintance, whom he had known in the glory of youth, and whom now after an interval of five years, he was to find the victim either of a diseased fancy or a horrible physical misfortune.

"A snake in his bosom!" repeated the young sculptor to himself. "It must be he. No second man on earth has such a bosom friend. And now, my poor Rosina, Heaven grant me wisdom to discharge my errand aright! Woman's faith must be strong indeed since thine has not yet failed."

Thus musing, he took his stand at the entrance of the gate and waited until the personage so singularly announced should make his appearance. After an instant or two he beheld the figure of a lean man, of unwholesome look, with glittering eyes and long black hair, who

seemed to imitate the motion of a snake; for, instead of
walking straight forward with open front, he undulated
along the pavement in a curved line. It may be too fanciful to say something, either in his moral or material
aspect, suggested the idea that a miracle had been
wrought by transforming a serpent into a man, but so
imperfectly that the snaky nature was yet hidden, and
scarcely hidden, under the mere outward guise of
humanity. Herkimer remarked that his complexion had
a greenish tinge over its sickly white, reminding him
of a species of marble out of which he had once wrought
a head of Envy, with her snaky locks.

The wretched being approached the gate, but, instead
of entering, stopped short and fixed the glitter of his
eye full upon the compassionate yet steady countenance
of the sculptor.

"It gnaws me! It gnaws me!" he exclaimed.

And then there was an audible hiss, but whether it
came from the apparent lunatic's own lips, or was the
real hiss of a serpent, might admit of a discussion. At all
events, it made Herkimer shudder to his heart's core.

"Do you know me, George Herkimer?" asked the
snake-possessed.

Herkimer did know him; but it demanded all the intimate and practical acquaintance with the human face,
acquired by modelling actual likenesses in clay, to
recognize the features of Roderick Elliston in the visage
that now met the sculptor's gaze. Yet it was he. It added
nothing to the wonder to reflect that the once brilliant
young man had undergone this odious and fearful
change during the no more than five brief years of Herkimer's abode at Florence. The possibility of such a
transformation being granted, it was as easy to conceive
it effected in a moment as in an age. Inexpressibly
shocked and startled, it was still the keenest pang when
Herkimer remembered that the fate of his cousin Rosina,

the ideal of gentle womanhood, was indissolubly interwoven with that of a being whom Providence seemed
to have unhumanized.

"Elliston! Roderick!" cried he, "I had heard of this;
but my conception came far short of the truth. What has
befallen you? Why do I find you thus?"

"Oh, 'tis a mere nothing! A snake! A snake! The com-
monest thing in the world. A snake in the bosom—that's
all," answered Roderick Elliston. "But how is your own
breast?" continued he, looking the sculptor in the eye
with the most acute and penetrating glance that it had
ever been his fortune to encounter. "All pure and wholesome? No reptile there? By my faith and conscience,
and by the devil within me, here is a wonder! A man
without a serpent in his bosom!"

"Be calm, Elliston," whispered George Herkimer, lay-
ing his hand upon the shoulder of the snake-possessed.
"I have crossed the ocean to meet you. Listen! Let us
be private. I bring a message from Rosina—from your
wife!"

"It gnaws me! It gnaws me!" muttered Roderick.

With this exclamation, the most frequent in his
mouth, the unfortunate man clutched both hands upon
his breast as if an intolerable sting or torture impelled
him to rend it open and let out the living mischief, even
should it be intertwined with his own life. He then
freed himself from Herkimer's grasp by a subtle motion, and, gliding through the gate, took refuge in his
antiquated family residence. The sculptor did not pursue him. He saw that no available intercourse could be
expected at such a moment, and was desirous, before
another meeting, to inquire closely into the nature of
Roderick's disease and the circumstances that had reduced him to so lamentable a condition. He succeeded
in obtaining the necessary information from an eminent
medical gentleman.

Shortly after Elliston's separation from his wife—now

nearly four years ago—his associates had observed a singular gloom spreading over his daily life, like those chill, gray mists that sometimes steal away the sunshine from a summer's morning. The symptoms caused them endless perplexity. They knew not whether ill health were robbing his spirits of elasticity, or whether a canker of the mind was gradually eating, as such cankers do, from his moral system into the physical frame, which is but the shadow of the former. They looked for the root of this trouble in his shattered schemes of domestic bliss,—wilfully shattered by himself,—but could not be satisfied of its existence there. Some thought that their once brilliant friend was in an incipient stage of insanity, of which his passionate impulses had perhaps been the forerunners; others prognosticated a general blight and gradual decline. From Roderick's own lips they could learn nothing. More than once, it is true, he had been heard to say, clutching his hands convulsively upon his breast,—"It gnaws me! It gnaws me!"—but, by different auditors, a great diversity of explanation was assigned to this ominous expression. What could it be that gnawed the breast of Roderick Elliston? Was it sorrow? Was it merely the tooth of physical disease? Or, in his reckless course, often verging upon profligacy, if not plunging into its depths, had he been guilty of some deed which made his bosom a prey to the deadlier fangs of remorse? There was plausible ground for each of these conjectures; but it must not be concealed that more than one elderly gentleman, the victim of good cheer and slothful habits, magisterially pronounced the secret of the whole matter to be Dyspepsia!

Meanwhile, Roderick seemed aware how generally he had become the subject of curiosity and conjecture, and, with a morbid repugnance to such notice, or to any notice whatsoever, estranged himself from all companionship. Not merely the eye of man was a horror to him; not merely the light of a friend's countenance; but even the blessed sunshine, likewise, which in its universal beneficence typifies the radiance of the Creator's face, expressing his love for all the creatures of his hand. The dusky twilight was now too transparent for Roderick Elliston; the blackest midnight was his chosen hour to steal abroad; and if ever he were seen, it was when the watchman's lantern gleamed upon his figure, gliding along the street, with his hands clutched upon his bosom, still muttering, "It gnaws me! It gnaws me!" What could it be that gnawed him?

After a time, it became known that Elliston was in the habit of resorting to all the noted quacks that infested the city, or whom money would tempt to journey thither from a distance. By one of these persons, in the exultation of a supposed cure, it was proclaimed far and wide, by dint of handbills and little pamphlets on dingy paper, that a distinguished gentleman, Roderick Elliston, Esq., had been relieved of a SNAKE in his stomach! So here was the monstrous secret, ejected from its lurking place into public view, in all its horrible deformity. The mystery was out, but not so the bosom serpent. He, if it were anything but a delusion, still lay coiled in his living den. The empiric's cure had been a sham, the effect, it was supposed, of some stupefying drug which more nearly caused the death of the patient than of the odious reptile that possessed him. When Roderick Elliston regained entire sensibility, it was to find his misfortune the town talk—the more than nine days' wonder and horror—while, at his bosom, he felt the sickening motion of a thing alive, and the gnawing of that restless fang which seemed to gratify at once a physical appetite and a fiendish spite.

He summoned the old black servant, who had been bred up in his father's house, and was a middle-aged man while Roderick lay in his cradle.

"Scipio!" he began; and then paused, with his arms

folded over his heart. "What do people say of me, Scipio?"

"Sir! my poor master! that you had a serpent in your bosom," answered the servant with hesitation.

"And what else?" asked Roderick, with a ghastly look at the man.

"Nothing else, dear master," replied Scipio, "only that the doctor gave you a powder, and that the snake leaped out upon the floor."

"No, no!" muttered Roderick to himself, as he shook his head, and pressed his hands with a more convulsive force upon his breast, "I feel him still. It gnaws me! It gnaws me!"

From this time the miserable sufferer ceased to shun the world, but rather solicited and forced himself upon the notice of acquaintances and strangers. It was partly the result of desperation on finding that the cavern of his own bosom had not proved deep and dark enough to hide the secret, even while it was so secure a fortress for the loathsome fiend that had crept into it. But still more, this craving for notoriety was a symptom of the intense morbidness which now pervaded his nature. All persons chronically diseased are egotists, whether the disease be of the mind or body; whether it be sin, sorrow, or merely the more tolerable calamity of some endless pain, or mischief among the cords of mortal life. Such individuals are made acutely conscious of a self, by the torture in which it dwells. Self, therefore, grows to be so prominent an object with them that they cannot but present it to the face of every casual passer-by. There is a pleasure—perhaps the greatest of which the sufferer is susceptible—in displaying the wasted or ulcerated limb, or the cancer in the breast; and the fouler the crime, with so much the more difficulty does the perpetrator prevent it from thrusting up its snake-like head to frighten the world; for it is that cancer, or that crime, which constitutes their respective individuality. Roderick Elliston, who, a little while before, had held himself so scornfully above the common lot of men, now paid full allegiance to this humiliating law. The snake in his bosom seemed the symbol of a monstrous egotism to which everything was referred, and which he pampered, night and day, with a continual and exclusive sacrifice of devil worship.

He soon exhibited what most people considered indubitable tokens of insanity. In some of his moods, strange to say, he prided and gloried himself on being marked out from the ordinary experience of mankind, by the possession of a double nature, and a life within a life. He appeared to imagine that the snake was a divinity, —not celestial, it is true, but darkly infernal,—and that he thence derived an eminence and a sanctity, horrid, indeed, yet more desirable than whatever ambition aims at. Thus he drew his misery around him like a regal mantle, and looked down triumphantly upon those whose vitals nourished no deadly monster. Oftener, however, his human nature asserted its empire over him in the shape of a yearning for fellowship. It grew to be his custom to spend the whole day in wandering about the streets, aimlessly, unless it might be called an aim to establish a species of brotherhood between himself and the world. With cankered ingenuity, he sought out his own disease in every breast. Whether insane or not, he showed so keen a perception of frailty, error, and vice, that many persons gave him credit for being possessed not merely with a serpent, but with an actual fiend, who imparted this evil faculty of recognizing whatever was ugliest in man's heart.

For instance, he met an individual, who, for thirty years, had cherished a hatred against his own brother. Roderick, amidst the throng of the street, laid his hand on this man's chest, and looking full into his forbidding face,—

"How is the snake to-day?" he inquired, with a mock expression of sympathy.

"The snake!" exclaimed the brother hater—"what do you mean?"

"The snake! The snake! Does he gnaw you?" persisted Roderick. "Did you take counsel with him this morning when you should have been saying your prayers? Did he sting, when you thought of your brother's health, wealth, and good repute? Did he caper for joy, when you remembered the profligacy of his only son? And whether he stung, or whether he frolicked, did you feel his poison throughout your body and soul, converting everything to sourness and bitterness? That is the way of such serpents. I have learned the whole nature of them from my own!"

"Where is the police?" roared the object of Roderick's persecution, at the same time giving an instinctive clutch to his breast. "Why is this lunatic allowed to go at large?"

"Ha, ha!" chuckled Roderick, releasing his grasp of the man. "His bosom serpent has stung him then!"

Often it pleased the unfortunate young man to vex people with a lighter satire, yet still characterized by somewhat of snakelike virulence. One day he encountered an ambitious statesman, and gravely inquired after the welfare of his boa constrictor; for of that species, Roderick affirmed, this gentleman's serpent must needs be, since its appetite was enormous enough to devour the whole country and constitution. At another time, he stopped a close-fisted old fellow, of great wealth, but who skulked about the city in the guise of a scarecrow, with a patched blue surtout, brown hat, and mouldy boots, scraping pence together, and picking up rusty nails. Pretending to look earnestly at this respectable person's stomach, Roderick assured him that his snake was a copper-head, and had been generated by the immense quantities of that base metal, with which he daily defiled his fingers. Again, he assaulted a man of rubicund visage, and told him that few bosom serpents had more of the devil in them than those that breed in the vats of a distillery. The next whom Roderick honored with his attention was a distinguished clergyman, who happened just then to be engaged in a theological controversy, where human wrath was more perceptible than divine inspiration.

"You have swallowed a snake in a cup of sacramental wine," quoth he.

"Profane wretch!" exclaimed the divine; but, nevertheless, his hand stole to his breast.

He met a person of sickly sensibility, who, on some early disappointment, had retired from the world, and thereafter held no intercourse with his fellow-men, but brooded sullenly or passionately over the irrevocable past. This man's very heart, if Roderick might be believed, had been changed into a serpent, which would finally torment both him and itself to death. Observing a married couple, whose domestic troubles were matter of notoriety, he condoled with both on having mutually taken a house adder to their bosoms. To an envious author, who depreciated works which he could never equal, he said that his snake was the slimiest and filthiest of all the reptile tribe, but was fortunately without a sting. A man of impure life, and a brazen face, asking Roderick if there were any serpent in his breast, he told him that there was, and of the same species that once tortured Don Rodrigo, the Goth. He took a fair young girl by the hand, and gazing sadly into her eyes, warned her that she cherished a serpent of the deadliest kind within her gentle breast; and the world found the truth of those ominous words, when, a few months afterwards, the poor girl died of love and shame. Two ladies, rivals in fashionable life, who tormented one another with a thousand little stings of womanish spite, were given to understand that each of their hearts was a nest of diminutive snakes, which did quite as much mischief as one great one.

But nothing seemed to please Roderick better than to lay hold of a person infected with jealousy, which he represented as an enormous green reptile, with an ice-cold length of body, and the sharpest sting of any snake save one.

"And what one is that?" asked a by-stander, overhearing him.

It was a dark-browed man who put the question; he had an evasive eye, which in the course of a dozen years had looked no mortal directly in the face. There was an ambiguity about this person's character,—a stain upon his reputation,—yet none could tell precisely of what nature, although the city gossips, male and female, whispered the most atrocious surmises. Until a recent period he had followed the sea, and was, in fact, the very ship-master whom George Herkimer had encountered, under such singular circumstances, in the Grecian Archipelago.

"What bosom serpent has the sharpest sting?" repeated this man; but he put the question as if by a reluctant necessity, and grew pale while he was uttering it.

"Why need you ask?" replied Roderick, with a look of dark intelligence. "Look into your own breast. Hark! my serpent bestirs himself! He acknowledges the presence of a master field!"

And then, as the by-standers afterwards affirmed, a hissing sound was heard, apparently in Roderick Elliston's breast. It was said, too, that an answering hiss came from the vitals of the shipmaster, as if a snake were actually lurking there and had been aroused by the call of its brother reptile. If there were in fact any such sound, it might have been caused by a malicious exercise of ventriloquism on the part of Roderick.

Thus making his own actual serpent—if a serpent there actually was in his bosom—the type of each man's fatal error, or hoarded sin, on unquiet conscience, and striking his sting so unremorsefully into the sorest spot, we may well imagine that Roderick became the pest of the city. Nobody could elude him—none could withstand him. He grappled with the ugliest truth that he could lay his hand on, and compelled his adversary to do the same. Strange spectacle in human life where it is the instinctive effort of one and all to hide those sad realities, and leave them undisturbed beneath a heap of superficial topics which constitute the materials of intercourse between man and man! It was not to be tolerated that Roderick Elliston should break through the tacit compact by which the world has done its best to secure repose without relinquishing evil. The victims of his malicious remarks, it is true, had brothers enough to keep them in countenance; for, by Roderick's theory, every mortal bosom harbored either a brood of small serpents or one overgrown monster that had devoured all the rest. Still the city could not bear this new apostle. It was demanded by nearly all, and particularly by the most respectable inhabitants, that Roderick should no longer be permitted to violate the received rules of decorum by obtruding his own bosom serpent to the public gaze, and dragging those of decent people from their lurking places.

Accordingly, his relatives interfered and placed him in a private asylum for the insane. When the news was noised abroad, it was observed that many persons walked the streets with freer countenances and covered their breasts less carefully with their hands.

His confinement, however, although it contributed not a little to the peace of the town, operated unfavorably upon Roderick himself. In solitude his melancholy grew more black and sullen. He spent whole days— indeed, it was his sole occupation—in communing with the serpent. A conversation was sustained, in which, as it seemed, the hidden monster bore a part, though unintelligibly to the listeners, and inaudible except in a hiss. Singular as it may appear, the sufferer had now contracted a sort of affection for his tormentor, mingled, however, with the intensest loathing and horror. Nor were such discordant emotions incompatible. Each, on the contrary, imparted strength and poignancy to its opposite. Horrible love—horrible antipathy—embracing one another in his bosom, and both concentrating themselves upon a being that had crept into his vitals or been engendered there, and which was nourished with his food, and lived upon his life, and was as intimate with him as his own heart, and yet was the foulest of all created things! But not the less was it the true type of a morbid nature.

Sometimes, in his moments of rage and bitter hatred against the snake and himself, Roderick determined to be the death of him, even at the expense of his own life. Once he attempted it by starvation; but, while the wretched man was on the point of famishing, the monster seemed to feed upon his heart, and to thrive and wax gamesome, as if it were his sweetest and most congenial diet. Then he privily took a dose of active poison, imagining that it would not fail to kill either himself or the devil that possessed him, or both together. Another mistake; for if Roderick had not yet been destroyed by his own poisoned heart nor the snake by gnawing it, they had little to fear from arsenic or corrosive sublimate. Indeed, the venomous pest appeared to operate as an antidote against all other poisons. The physicians tried to suffocate the fiend with tobacco smoke. He breathed it as freely as if it were his native atmosphere. Again, they drugged their patient with opium and drenched him with intoxicating liquors, hoping that the snake might thus be reduced to stupor and perhaps be ejected from the stomach. They succeeded in rendering Roderick insensible; but, placing their hands upon his breast, they were inexpressibly horror stricken to feel the monster wriggling, twining, and darting to and fro within his narrow limits, evidently enlivened by the opium or alcohol, and incited to unusual feats of activity. Thenceforth they gave up all attempts at cure or palliation. The doomed sufferer submitted to his fate, resumed his former loathsome affection for the bosom fiend, and spent whole miserable days before a looking-glass, with his mouth wide open, watching, in hope and horror, to catch a glimpse of the snake's head far down within his throat. It is supposed that he succeeded; for the attendants once heard a frenzied shout, and, rushing into the room, found Roderick lifeless upon the floor. He was kept but little longer under restraint. After minute investigation, the medical directors of the asylum decided that his mental disease did not amount to insanity, nor would warrant his confinement, especially as its influence upon his spirits was unfavorable, and might produce the evil which it was meant to remedy. His eccentricities were doubtless great; he had habitually violated many of the customs and prejudices of society; but the world was not, without surer ground, entitled to treat him as a madman. On this decision of such competent authority Roderick was released, and had returned to his native city the very day before his encounter with George Herkimer.

As soon as possible after learning these particulars the sculptor, together with a sad and tremulous companion, sought Elliston at his own house. It was a large, sombre edifice of wood, with pilasters and a balcony, and was divided from one of the principal streets by a terrace of three elevations, which was ascended by successive flights of stone steps. Some immense old elms almost concealed the front of the mansion. This spacious and once magnificent family residence was built by a grandee of the race early in the past century, at which epoch, land being of small comparative value, the garden and other grounds had formed quite an extensive domain.

Although a portion of the ancestral heritage had been alienated, there was still a shadowy enclosure in the rear of the mansion where a student, or a dreamer, or a man of stricken heart might lie all day upon the grass, amid the solitude of murmuring boughs, and forget that a city had grown up around him.

Into this retirement the sculptor and his companion were ushered by Scipio, the old black servant, whose wrinkled visage grew almost sunny with intelligence and joy as he paid his humble greetings to one of the two visitors.

"Remain in the arbor," whispered the sculptor to the figure that leaned upon his arm. "You will know whether, and when, to make your appearance."

"God will teach me," was the reply. "May He support me too!"

Roderick was reclining on the margin of a fountain which gushed into the fleckered sunshine with the same clear sparkle and the same voice of airy quietude as when trees of primeval growth flung their shadows across its bosom. How strange is the life of a fountain! —born at every moment, yet of an age coeval with the rocks, and far surpassing the venerable antiquity of a forest.

"You are come! I have expected you," said Elliston, when he became aware of the sculptor's presence.

His manner was very different from that of the preceding day—quiet, courteous, and, as Herkimer thought, watchful both over his guest and himself. This unnatural restraint was almost the only trait that betokened anything amiss. He had just thrown a book upon the grass, where it lay half opened, thus disclosing itself to be a natural history of the serpent tribe, illustrated by life-like plates. Near it lay that bulky volume, the Ductor Dubitantium of Jeremy Taylor, full of cases of conscience, and in which most men, possessed of a conscience, may find something applicable to their purpose.

"You see," observed Elliston, pointing to the book of
serpents, while a smile gleamed upon his lips, "I am
making an effort to become better acquainted with my
bosom friend; but I find nothing satisfactory in this
volume. If I mistake not, he will prove to be *sui generis,*
and akin to no other reptile in creation."

"Whence came this strange calamity?" inquired the
sculptor.

"My sable friend Scipio has a story," replied Roderick,
"of a snake that had lurked in this fountain—pure and
innocent as it looks—ever since it was known to the
first settlers. This insinuating personage once crept into
the vitals of my great grandfather and dwelt there many
years, tormenting the old gentleman beyond mortal
endurance. In short it is a family peculiarity. But, to tell
you the truth, I have no faith in this idea of the snake's
being an heirloom. He is my own snake, and no man's
else."

"But what was his origin?" demanded Herkimer.

"Oh, there is poisonous stuff in any man's heart
sufficient to generate a brood of serpents," said Elliston
with a hollow laugh. "You should have heard my homi-
lies to the good town's-people. Positively, I deem myself fortunate in having bred but a single serpent. You,
however, have none in your bosom, and therefore cannot sympathize with the rest of the world. It gnaws me!
It gnaws me!"

With this exclamation Roderick lost his self-control
and threw himself upon the grass, testifying his agony
by intricate writhings, in which Herkimer could not but
fancy a resemblance to the motions of a snake. Then,
likewise, was heard that frightful hiss, which often ran
through the sufferer's speech, and crept between the
words and syllables without interrupting their succession.

"This is awful indeed!" exclaimed the sculptor—"an
awful infliction, whether it be actual or imaginary. Tell

me, Roderick Elliston, is there any remedy for this loathsome evil?"

"Yes, but an impossible one," muttered Roderick, as he lay wallowing with his face in the grass. "Could I for one instant forget myself, the serpent might not abide within me. It is my diseased self-contemplation that has engendered and nourished him."

"Then forget yourself, my husband," said a gentle voice above him; "forget yourself in the idea of another!"

Rosina had emerged from the arbor, and was bending over him with the shadow of his anguish reflected in her countenance, yet so mingled with hope and unselfish love that all anguish seemed but an earthly shadow and a dream. She touched Roderick with her hand. A tremor shivered through his frame. At that moment, if report be trustworthy, the sculptor beheld a waving motion through the grass, and heard a tinkling sound, as if something had plunged into the fountain. Be the truth as it might, it is certain that Roderick Elliston sat up like a man renewed, restored to his right mind, and rescued from the fiend which had so miserably overcome him in the battle-field of his own breast.

"Rosina!" cried he, in broken and passionate tones, but with nothing of the wild wail that had haunted his voice so long, "forgive! forgive!"

Her happy tears bedewed his face.

"The punishment has been severe," observed the sculptor. "Even Justice might now forgive; how much more a woman's tenderness! Roderick Elliston, whether the serpent was a physical reptile, or whether the morbidness of your nature suggested that symbol to your fancy, the moral of the story is not the less true and strong. A tremendous Egotism, manifesting itself in your case in the form of jealousy, is as fearful a fiend as ever stole into the human heart. Can a breast, where it has dwelt so long, be purified?"

"Oh yes," said Rosina with a heavenly smile. "The

serpent was but a dark fantasy, and what it typified was as shadowy as itself. The past, dismal as it seems, shall fling no gloom upon the future. To give it its due importance we must think of it but as an anecdote in our Eternity."

"Neither Trust, nor Truth, nor Love"

[FROM *The Red and the Black*]

STENDHAL
(HENRI BEYLE)

1831

[*Julien Sorel has been condemned to death for an attempt on the life of Mme. de Rênal; but on visiting him in prison she has again become his mistress.*]

One evening Julien thought seriously of taking his life. His spirit was exhausted by the profound dejection into which the departure of Madame de Rênal had cast him. Nothing pleased him any more, either in real life or in imagination. Want of exercise was beginning to affect his health and to give him the weak and excitable character of a young German student. He was losing that manly pride which repels with a forcible oath certain degrading ideas by which the miserable are assailed.

"I have loved the Truth. . . . Where is it to be found? . . . Everywhere hypocrisy, or at least charlatanism, even among the most virtuous, even among the greatest"; and his lips curled in disgust. . . . "No, man cannot place any trust in man.

"Madame de ——, when she was making a collection

for her poor orphans, told me that some Prince had just given her ten louis; a lie. But what am I saying? Napoleon at Saint-Helena! . . . Pure charlatanism, a proclamation in favour of the King of Rome.

"Great God! If such a man as he, at a time, too, when misfortune ought to recall him sternly to a sense of duty, stoops to charlatanism, what is one to expect of the rest of the species?

"Where is Truth? In religion. . . . Yes," he added with a bitter smile of the most intense scorn, "in the mouths of the Maslons, the Frilairs, the Castanèdes. . . . Perhaps in true Christianity, whose priests would be no more paid than were the Apostles? But Saint Paul was paid with the pleasure of commanding, of speaking, of hearing himself spoken of. . . .

"Ah! If there were a true religion. . . . Idiot that I am! I see a gothic cathedral, storied windows; my feeble heart imagines the priest from those windows. . . . My soul would understand him, my soul has need of him. I find only a fop with greasy hair . . . little different, in fact, from the Chevalier de Beauvoisis.

"But a true priest, a Massillon, a Fénelon. . . . Massillon consecrated Dubois. The *Mémoires de Saint-Simon* have spoiled Fénelon for me; but still, a true priest. . . . Then the tender hearts would have a meeting-place in this world. . . . We should not remain isolated. . . . This good priest would speak to us of God. But what God? Not the God of the Bible, a petty despot, cruel and filled with a thirst for vengeance . . . but the God of Voltaire, just, good, infinite. . . ."

He was disturbed by all his memories of that Bible which he knew by heart. . . . "But how, whenever *three are gathered together,* how is one to believe in that great name of God, after the frightful abuse that our priests make of it?

"To live in isolation! . . . What torture! . . .

"I am becoming foolish and unjust," said Julien, beating his brow. I am isolated here in this cell; but I have not *lived in isolation* on this earth; I had always the compelling idea of *duty*. The duty that I had laid down for myself, rightly or wrongly, was like the trunk of a strong tree against which I leaned during the storm; I tottered, I was shaken. After all, I was only a man . . . but I was not carried away.

"It is the damp air of this cell that makes me think of isolation. . . .

"And why be a hypocrite still when I am cursing hypocrisy? It is not death, nor the cell, nor the damp air, it is the absence of Madame de Rênal that is crushing me. If I were at Verrières, and, in order to see her, were obliged to live for weeks on end hidden in the cellars of her house, should I complain?

"The influence of my contemporaries is too strong for me," he said aloud and with a bitter laugh. "Talking alone to myself, within an inch of death, I am still a hypocrite. . . . Oh, nineteenth century!"

Except during the moments usurped by the presence of Mathilde, Julien was living upon love and with hardly a thought of the future. A curious effect of this passion, in its extreme form and free from all pretence, was that Madame de Rênal almost shared his indifference and mild gaiety.

"In the past," Julien said to her, "when I might have been so happy during our walks in the woods of Vergy, a burning ambition led my soul into imaginary tracts. Instead of my pressing to my heart this lovely arm which was so near to my lips, the thought of my future tore me away from you; I was occupied with the countless battles which I should have to fight in order to build up a colossal fortune. . . . No, I should have died without knowing what happiness meant, had you not come to visit me in this prison."

Two incidents occurred to disturb this tranquil existence. Julien's confessor, for all that he was a Jansenist, was not immune from an intrigue by the Jesuits, and quite unawares became their instrument.

He came one day to inform him that if he were not to fall into the mortal sin of suicide, he must take every possible step to obtain a reprieve. Now, the clergy having considerable influence at the Ministry of Justice in Paris, an easy method offered itself: he must undergo a sensational conversion. . . .

"Sensational!" Julien repeated. "Ah! I have caught you at the same game, Father, play-acting like any missionary. . . ."

"Your tender age," the Jansenist went on gravely, "the interesting appearance with which Providence has blessed you, the motive itself of your crime, which remains inexplicable, the heroic measures of which Mademoiselle de La Mole is unsparing on your behalf, everything, in short, including the astonishing affection that your victim shews for you, all these have combined to make you the hero of the young women of Besançon. They have forgotten everything for you, even politics. . . .

"Your conversion would strike an echo in their hearts, and would leave a profound impression there. You can be of the greatest service to religion, and am I to hesitate for the frivolous reason that the Jesuits would adopt the same course in similar circumstances! And so, even in this particular case which has escaped their rapacity, they would still be doing harm! Let such a thing never be said. . . . The tears which will flow at your conversion will annul the corrosive effect of ten editions of the impious works of Voltaire."

"And what shall I have left," replied Julien coldly, "if I despise myself? I have been ambitious, I have no wish to reproach myself; I acted then according to the expediency of the moment. Now, I am living from day to day. But, generally speaking, I should be making myself extremely unhappy, if I gave way to any cowardly temptation. . . ."

The other incident, which affected Julien far more keenly, arose from Madame de Rênal. Some intriguing friend or other had managed to persuade this simple, timid soul that it was her duty to go to Saint-Cloud, and to throw herself at the feet of King Charles X.

She had made the sacrifice of parting from Julien, and after such an effort, the unpleasantness of making a public spectacle of herself, which at any other time would have seemed to her worse than death, was no longer anything in her eyes.

"I shall go to the King, I shall confess proudly that you are my lover: the life of a man, and of such a man as Julien, must outweigh all other considerations. I shall say that it was out of jealousy that you attempted my life. There are endless examples of poor young men who have been saved in such cases by the humanity of a jury, or by that of the King. . . ."

"I shall cease to see you, I shall bar the door of my prison against you," cried Julien, "and most certainly I shall kill myself in despair, the day after, unless you swear to me that you will take no step that will make us both a public spectacle. This idea of going to Paris is not yours. Tell me the name of the intriguing woman who suggested it to you. . . .

"Let us be happy throughout the few remaining days of this brief life. Let us conceal our existence; my crime is only too plain. Mademoiselle de La Mole has unbounded influence in Paris, you may be sure that she is doing all that is humanly possible. Here in the provinces, I have all the wealthy and respectable people against me. Your action would embitter still further these wealthy and above all moderate men, for whom life is such an easy matter. . . . Let us not give food for laughter to the Maslons, the Valenods, and a thousand people better worth than they."

The bad air of the cell became insupportable to Julien. Fortunately on the day on which he was told that he must die, a bright sun was gladdening the earth, and he himself was in a courageous mood. To walk in the open air was a delicious sensation to him, as is treading solid earth to a mariner who has long been at sea. "There, all is well," he said to himself, "I am not lacking in courage."

Never had that head been so poetic as at the moment when it was about to fall. The most precious moments that he had known in the past in the woods of Vergy came crowding into his mind with an extreme vividness.

Everything passed simply, decorously, and without affectation on his part.

Two days earlier, he had said to Fouqué: "For my emotions I cannot answer; this damp and hideous cell gives me moments of fever in which I am not myself; but fear, no; no one shall see me blench."

He had made arrangements in advance that on the morning of the last day, Fouqué should carry off Mathilde and Madame de Rênal.

"Take them in the same carriage," he had told him. "Arrange that the post-horses shall gallop all the time. They will fall into one another's arms, or else will shew a deadly hatred for one another. In either case, the poor women will have some slight distraction from their terrible grief."

Julien had made Madame de Rênal swear that she would live to look after Mathilde's child.

"Who knows? Perhaps we continue to have sensation after our death," he said one day to Fouqué. "I should dearly like to repose, since repose is the word, in that little cave in the high mountain that overlooks Verrières. Many a time, as I have told you, retiring by night to that cave, and casting my gaze afar over the richest provinces of France, I have felt my heart ablaze with ambition: it was my passion then. . . . Anyhow, that cave is

precious to me, and no one can deny that it is situated
in a spot that a philosopher's heart might envy. . . .
Very well! These worthy members of the Congregation
of Besançon make money out of everything; if you know
how to set about it, they will sell you my mortal remains. . . ."

Fouqué was successful in this grim transaction. He
was spending the night alone in his room, by the body
of his friend, when to his great surprise, he saw Mathilde
appear. A few hours earlier, he had left her ten leagues
from Besançon. There was a wild look in her eyes.

"I wish to see him," she said to him.

Fouqué had not the courage to speak or to rise. He
pointed with his finger to a great blue cloak on the floor;
in it was wrapped all that remained of Julien.

She fell upon her knees. The memory of Boniface de
La Mole and of Marguerite de Navarre gave her, no
doubt, a superhuman courage. Her trembling hands un-
folded the cloak. Fouqué turned away his eyes.

He heard Mathilde walking rapidly about the room.
She lighted a number of candles. When Fouqué had
summoned up the strength to look at her, she had placed
Julien's head upon a little marble table, in front of her,
and was kissing his brow. . . .

Mathilde followed her lover to the tomb which he had
chosen for himself. A great number of priests escorted
the coffin and, unknown to all, alone in her draped carriage, she carried upon her knees the head of the man
whom she had so dearly loved.

Coming thus near to the summit of one of the high
mountains of the Jura, in the middle of the night, in that
little cave magnificently illuminated with countless
candles, a score of priests celebrated the Office of the
Dead. All the inhabitants of the little mountain villages,
through which the procession passed, had followed it,
drawn by the singularity of this strange ceremony.

Mathilde appeared in their midst in a flowing garb of

mourning, and, at the end of the service, had several thousands of five franc pieces scattered among them.

Left alone with Fouqué, she insisted upon burying her lover's head with her own hands. Fouqué almost went mad with grief.

By Mathilde's orders, this savage grot was adorned with marbles sculptured at great cost, in Italy.

Madame de Rênal was faithful to her promise. She did not seek in any way to take her own life; but, three days after Julien, died while embracing her children.

Trans. C. K. Scott-Moncrieff (New York: Modern Library, n.d.).

THE HERO'S CONSORT:
THE FATAL WOMAN

"*Her* lips were red, *her* looks were free,
Her locks were yellow as gold:
Her skin was as white as leprosy,
The Night-mare LIFE-IN-DEATH was she,
Who thicks man's blood with cold."

—Samuel Taylor Coleridge

The Lorelei

[FROM *The Return Home*]

HEINRICH HEINE

1823-24

I cannot explain the sadness
That's fallen on my breast.
An old, old fable haunts me,
And will not let me rest.

The air grows cool in the twilight,
And softly the Rhine flows on;
The peak of a mountain sparkles
Beneath the setting sun.

220

More lovely than a vision,
A girl sits high up there;
Her golden jewelry glistens,
She combs her golden hair.

With a comb of gold she combs it,
And sings an evensong;
The wonderful melody reaches
A boat, as it sails along.

The boatman hears, with an anguish
More wild than was ever known;
He's blind to the rocks around him;
His eyes are for her alone.

—At last the waves devoured
The boat, and the boatman's cry;
And this she did with her singing,
The golden Loreley.

Trans. Aaron Kramer (from *The Poetry and Prose of Heinrich Heine*, ed. Frederic Ewen. New York: Citadel Press, 1948).

Heaven No Home

[FROM *Wuthering Heights*]

EMILY BRONTË

1847

"Nelly, do you never dream queer dreams?" she said, suddenly, after some minutes' reflection.

"Yes, now and then," I answered.

"And so do I. I've dreamt in my life dreams that have

stayed with me ever after, and changed my ideas: they've gone through and through me, like wine through water, and altered the colour of my mind. And this is one; I'm going to tell it—but take care not to smile at any part of it."

"Oh! don't, Miss Catherine!" I cried. "We're dismal enough without conjuring up ghosts and visions to perplex us. Come, come, be merry and like yourself! Look at little Hareton! *he's* dreaming nothing dreary. How sweetly he smiles in his sleep!"

"Yes; and how sweetly his father curses in his solitude! You remember him, I dare say, when he was just such another as that chubby thing: nearly as young and innocent. However, Nelly, I shall oblige you to listen: it's not long; and I've no power to be merry to-night."

"I won't hear it, I won't hear it!" I repeated hastily.

I was superstitious about dreams then, and am still; and Catherine had an unusual gloom in her aspect, that made me dread something from which I might shape a prophecy, and foresee a fearful catastrophe. She was vexed, but she did not proceed. Apparently taking up another subject, she recommenced in a short time.

"If I were in heaven, Nelly, I should be extremely miserable."

"Because you are not fit to go there," I answered. "All sinners would be miserable in heaven."

"But it is not for that. I dreamt once that I was there."

"I tell you I won't hearken to your dreams, Miss Catherine! I'll go to bed," I interrupted again.

She laughed, and held me down; for I made a motion to leave my chair.

"This is nothing," cried she. "I was only going to say that heaven did not seem to be my home; and I broke my heart with weeping to come back to earth; and the angels were so angry that they flung me out into the middle of the heath on the top of Wuthering Heights; where I woke sobbing for joy. That will do to explain

my secret, as well as the other. I've no more business to
marry Edgar Linton than I have to be in heaven; and if
the wicked man in there had not brought Heathcliff so
low, I shouldn't have thought of it. It would degrade
me to marry Heathcliff now; so he shall never know how
I love him: and that, not because he's handsome, Nelly,
but because he's more myself than I am. Whatever our
souls are made of, his and mine are the same; and Linton's is as different as a moonbeam from lightning, or
frost from fire."

"Nelly, I see now, you think me a selfish wretch; but
did it never strike you that if Heathcliff and I married,
we should be beggars? whereas, if I marry Linton, I can
aid Heathcliff to rise, and place him out of my brother's
power."

"With your husband's money, Miss Catherine?" I
asked. "You'll find him not so pliable as you calculate
upon: and, though I'm hardly a judge, I think that's
the worst motive you've given yet for being the wife of
young Linton."

"It is not," retorted she; "it is the best! The others
were the satisfaction of my whims: and for Edgar's sake,
too, to satisfy him. This is for the sake of one who comprehends in his person my feelings to Edgar and myself. I cannot express it; but surely you and everybody
have a notion that there is or should be an existence of
yours beyond you. What were the use of my creation, if
I were entirely contained here? My great miseries in
this world have been Heathcliff's miseries, and I
watched and felt each from the beginning: my great
thought in living is himself. If all else perished, and *he*
remained, *I* should still continue to be; and if all else
remained, and he were annihilated, the universe would
turn to a mighty stranger: I should not seem a part of it.
My love for Linton is like the foliage in the woods: time
will change it, I'm well aware, as winter changes the

trees. My love for Heathcliff resembles the eternal rocks beneath: a source of little visible delight, but necessary. Nelly, I *am* Heathcliff! He's always, always in my mind: not as a pleasure, any more than I am always a pleasure to myself, but as my own being. So don't talk of our separation again: it is impracticable; and——"

She paused, and hid her face in the folds of my gown; but I jerked it forcibly away. I was out of patience with her folly!

Cold Enchantress

["La Belle Dame sans Merci," first version]

JOHN KEATS

1819

O what can ail thee Knight at arms
    Alone and palely loitering?
The sedge is withered from the Lake
    And no birds sing!

O what can ail thee Knight at arms
    So haggard, and so woe begone?
The squirrel's granary is full
    And the harvest's done.

I see a lily on thy brow
    With anguish moist and fever dew,
And on thy cheeks a fading rose
    Fast withereth too—

I met a Lady in the Meads
    Full beautiful, a faery's child;

Her hair was long, her foot was light
   And her eyes were wild—

I made a Garland for her head,
   And bracelets too, and fragrant Zone:
She looked at me as she did love
   And made sweet moan—

I set her on my pacing steed
   And nothing else saw all day long
For sidelong would she bend and sing
   A faery's song—

She found me roots of relish sweet
   And honey wild and manna dew
And sure in language strange she said
   I love thee true—

She took me to her elfin grot
   And there she wept and sighed full sore,
And there I shut her wild wild eyes
   With kisses four.

And there she lulled me asleep,
   And there I dreamed Ah Woe betide!
The latest dream I ever dreamt
   On the cold hill side.

I saw pale Kings, and Princes too,
   Pale warriors, death pale were they all,
Who cried, Le belle dame sans merci
   Thee hath in thrall.

I saw their starved lips in the gloam
   With horrid warning gaped wide,
And I awoke, and found me here
   On the cold hill's side.

And this is why I sojourn here
  Alone and palely loitering;
Though the sedge is withered from the Lake
  And no birds sing— . . .

A Strange Child

[FROM *Undine*]

FRIEDRICH DE LA MOTTE FOUQUE

1811

Huldbrand and the fisherman sprang from their seats and were on the point of following the angry girl. Before they reached the cottage door, however, Undine had long vanished in the shadowy darkness without, and not even the sound of her light footstep betrayed the direction of her flight. Huldbrand looked enquiringly at his host; it almost seemed to him as if the whole sweet apparition which had suddenly merged again into the night, were nothing else than one of that band of the wonderful forms which had, but a short time since, carried on their pranks with him in the forest. But the old man murmured between his teeth, "This is not the first time she has treated us in this way. Now we have aching hearts and sleepless eyes the whole night through; for who knows that she may not some day come to harm, if she is thus out alone in the dark until daylight." "Then let us for God's sake follow her," cried Huldbrand anxiously. "What would be the good of it?" replied the old man. "It would be a sin were I to allow you, all alone, to follow the foolish girl in the solitary night, and my old limbs would not overtake the wild runaway, even if we knew in what direction she had gone." "We had better at any rate call after her, and beg her to come back," said Huldbrand; and he began to call in the most earnest manner, "Undine! Undine! Pray come back!" The old man shook his head, saying that all that shouting would help but little, for the knight had no idea how self-willed the little truant was. But still he could not forbear often calling out with him in the dark night, "Undine! Ah! dear Undine, I beg you to come back—only this once!"

It turned out, however, as the fisherman had said. No Undine was to be heard or seen, and as the old man would on no account consent that Huldbrand should go in search of the fugitive, they were at last both obliged to return to the cottage. Here they found the fire on the hearth almost gone out, and the old wife, who took Undine's flight and danger far less to heart than her husband, had already retired to rest. The old man blew up the fire, laid some dry wood on it, and by the light of the flame sought out a tankard of wine, which he placed between himself and his guest. "You, Sir Knight," said he, "are also anxious about that silly girl, and we would both rather chatter and drink away a part of the night than keep turning round on our rush mats trying in vain to sleep. Is it not so?" Huldbrand was well satisfied with the plan, the fisherman obliged him to take the seat of honour vacated by the good old housewife, and both drank and talked together in a manner becoming two honest and trusting men. It is true, as often as the slightest thing moved before the windows, or even at times when nothing was moving, one of the two would look up and say, "She is coming!" Then they would be silent for a moment or two, and as nothing appeared, they would shake their heads and sigh and go on with their talk.

As, however, neither could think of anything but of Undine, they knew of nothing better to do, than that

the old fisherman should tell the story, and the knight
should hear, in what manner Undine had first come to
the cottage. He therefore began as follows:

"It is now about fifteen years ago that I was one day
crossing the wild forest with my goods, on my way to
the city. My wife had stayed at home, as her wont is,
and at this particular time for a very good reason, for
God had given us in our tolerably advanced age, a
wonderfully beautiful child. It was a little girl; and a
question already arose between us, whether for the sake
of the new comer, we would not leave our lovely home
that we might better bring up this dear gift of heaven
in some more habitable place. Poor people indeed cannot do in such cases as you may think they ought, Sir
Knight, but, with God's blessing, every one must do
what he can. Well, the matter was tolerably in my head
as I went along. This slip of land was so dear to me, and
I shuddered when amidst the noise and brawls of the
city, I thought to myself, 'In such scenes as these, or in
one not much more quiet, thou wilt also soon make thy
abode!' But at the same time I did not murmur against
the good God, on the contrary, I thanked Him in secret
for the new-born babe; I should be telling a lie, too,
were I to say, that on my journey through the wood,
going or returning, any thing befell me out of the
common way, and at that time I had never seen any of
its fearful wonders. The Lord was ever with me in those
mysterious shades."

As he spoke he took his little cap from his bald head,
and remained for a time occupied with prayerful
thoughts; he then covered himself again, and continued:

"On this side the forest, alas! a sorrow awaited. My
wife came to meet me with tearful eyes and clad in
mourning. 'Oh! Good God!' I groaned, 'where is our dear
child? speak!' 'With Him on whom you have called, dear
husband,' she replied; and we now entered the cottage
together weeping silently. I looked around for the little

corpse, and it was then only that I learned how it had all happened.

"My wife had been sitting with the child on the edge of the lake, and as she was playing with it, free of all fear and full of happiness, the little one suddenly bent forward, as if attracted by something very beautiful in the water. My wife saw her laugh, the dear angel, and stretch out her little hands; but in a moment she had sprung out of her mother's arms, and had sunk beneath the watery mirror. I sought long for our little lost one; but it was all in vain; there was no trace of her to be found.

"The same evening we, childless parents, were sitting silently together in the cottage; neither of us had any desire to talk, even had our tears allowed us. We sat gazing into the fire on the hearth. Presently, we heard something rustling outside the door; it flew open, and a beautiful little girl three or four years old, richly dressed, stood on the threshold smiling at us. We were quite dumb with astonishment, and I knew not at first whether it were a vision or a reality. But I saw the water dripping from her golden hair and rich garments, and I perceived that the pretty child had been lying in the water, and needed help. 'Wife,' said I, 'no one has been able to save our dear child; yet let us at any rate do for others, what would have made us so blessed.' We undressed the little one, put her to bed, and gave her something warm; at all this she spoke not a word and only fixed her eyes, that reflected the blue of the lake and of the sky, smilingly upon us.

"Next morning we quickly perceived that she had taken no harm from her wetting, and I now enquired about her parents, and how she had come here.

"But she gave a confused and strange account. She must have been born far from here, not only because for these fifteen years I have not been able to find out anything of her parentage, but because she then spoke, and at times still speaks, of such singular things, that such as we are, cannot tell but that she may have dropped upon us from the moon. She talks of golden castles, of crystal domes, and heaven knows what besides. The story that she told with most distinctness was, that she was out in a boat with her mother on the great lake, and fell into the water, and that she only recovered her senses here under the trees where she felt herself quite happy on the merry shore.

"We had still a great misgiving and perplexity weighing on our hearts. We had indeed soon decided to keep the child we had found and to bring her up in the place of our lost darling; but who could tell us whether she had been baptised or not? She herself could give us no information on the matter. She generally answered our questions by saying that she well knew she was created for God's praise and glory, and that she was ready to let us do with her whatever would tend to His honour and glory.

"My wife and I thought that if she were not baptised, there was no time for delay, and that if she were, a good thing could not be repeated too often. And in pursuance of this idea, we reflected upon a good name for the child, for we now were often at a loss to know what to call her. We agreed at last that Dorothea would be most suitable for her, for I had once heard that it meant, a *gift of God*, and she had surely been sent to us by God as a gift and comfort in our misery. She, on the other hand, would not hear of this, and told us that she thought she had been called Undine by her parents, and that Undine she wished still to be called. Now this appeared to me a heathenish name, not to be found in any calendar, and I took counsel therefore of a priest in the city. He also would not hear of the name of Undine, but at my earnest request he came with me through the mysterious forest in order to perform the rite of baptism here in my cottage. The little one stood before us so prettily

arrayed and looked so charming, that the priest's heart
was at once moved within him, and she flattered him so
prettily, and braved him so merrily that at last he could
no longer remember the objections he had had ready
against the name of Undine. She was therefore baptised
'Undine,' and during the sacred ceremony she behaved
with great propriety and sweetness, wild and restless as
she invariably was at other times. For my wife was
quite right when she said that it has been hard to put
up with her. If I were to tell you—"

The knight interrupted the fisherman to draw his
attention to a noise, as of a rushing flood of waters,
which had caught his ear during the old man's talk, and
which now burst against the cottage window with redoubled fury. Both sprang to the door. There they saw,
by the light of the now risen moon, the brook which
issued from the wood, wildly overflowing its banks, and
whirling away stones and branches of trees in its sweeping course. The storm, as if awakened by the tumult,
burst forth from the mighty clouds which passed rapidly
across the moon; the lake roared under the furious
lashing of the wind; the trees of the little peninsula
groaned from root to topmost bough, and bent, as if
reeling, over the surging waters. "Undine! for Heaven's
sake, Undine!" cried the two men in alarm. No answer
was returned, and regardless of every other consideration, they ran out of the cottage, one in this direction,
and the other in that, searching and calling.

Trans. unknown (London: Macmillan, 1897).

Fatal Kisses

CHARLES BAUDELAIRE

THE VAMPIRE

[FROM *Flowers of Evil*]

1855-61

You, who like a dagger ploughed
Into my heart with deadly thrills:
You who, stronger than a crowd
Of demons, mad, and dressed to kill,

Of my dejected soul have made
Your bed, your lodging, and domains:
To whom I'm linked (Unseemly Jade!)
As is a convict to his chain,

Or as the gamester to his dice,
Or as the drunkard to his dram,
Or as the carrion to its lice—
I curse you. Would my curse could damn!

I have besought the sudden blade
To win for me my freedom back.
Perfidious poison have I prayed
To help my cowardice. Alack!

Both poison and the sword disdained
My cowardice, and seemed to say,

"You are not fit to be unchained
From your damned servitude. Away,

You imbecile! since if from her empire
We were to liberate the slave,
You'd raise the carrion of your vampire,
By your own kisses, from the grave."

LETHE

[FROM *Flotsam* (*Les Épaves*, 1866), the poems
suppressed in the first edition of
Flowers of Evil]

1857-64

Rest on my heart, deaf, cruel soul, adored
Tigress, and monster with the lazy air.
I long, in the black jungles of your hair,
To force each finger thrilling like a sword:

Within wide skirts, filled with your scent, to hide
My bruised and battered forehead hour by hour,
And breathe, like dampness from a withered flower,
The pleasant mildew of a love that died.

Rather than live, I wish to sleep, alas!
Lulled in a slumber soft and dark as death,
In ruthless kisses lavishing my breath
Upon your body smooth as burnished brass.

To swallow up my sorrows in eclipse,
Nothing can match your couch's deep abysses;
The stream of Lethe issues from your kisses
And powerful oblivion from your lips.

Like a predestined victim I submit:
My doom, to me, henceforth, is my delight,

A willing martyr in my own despite
Whose fervour fans the faggots it has lit.

To drown my rancour and to heal its smart,
Nepenthe and sweet hemlock, peace and rest,
I'd drink from the twin summits of a breast
That never lodged the semblance of a heart.

The Metamorphoses of the Vampire

[FROM *Flotsam*]

1852-64

The crimson-fruited mouth that I desired—
While, like a snake on coals, she twinged and twired,
Kneading her breasts against her creaking bust—
Let fall those words impregnated with musk,
—"My lips are humid: by my learned science,
All conscience, in my bed, becomes compliance.
My breasts, triumphant, staunch all tears; for me
Old men, like little children, laugh with glee.
For those who see me naked, I replace
Sun, moon, the sky, and all the stars in space.
I am so skilled, dear sage, in arts of pleasure,
That, when a man my deadly arms I measure,
Or to his teeth and kisses yield my bust,
Timid yet lustful, fragile, yet robust,
On sheets that swoon with passion—you might see
Impotent angels damn themselves for me."

When of my marrow she had sucked each bone
And, languishing, I turned with loving moan
To kiss her in return, with overplus,—
She seemed a swollen wineskin, full of pus.
I shut my eyes with horror at the sight,
But when I opened them, in the clear light,
I saw, instead of the great swollen doll
That, bloated with my lifeblood, used to loll,

The debris of a skeleton, assembling
With shrill squawks of a weathercock, lie trembling,
Or sounds, with which the howling winds commingle,
Of an old Inn-sign on a rusty tringle.

Trans. Roy Campbell (*Poems of Baudelaire*. New York: Pantheon
Books, 1952).

THE
METAPHYSICAL QUESTER

Strike through the mask!
—Herman Melville

Aspiration without Limit

[FROM *Faust, Part I*]

JOHANN WOLFGANG VON
GOETHE

1808

NIGHT

(*In a high-vaulted narrow Gothic room Faust, restless,
in a chair at his desk.*)

FAUST

Here stand I, ach, Philosophy
Behind me and Law and Medicine too
And, to my cost, Theology—
All these I have sweated through and through
And now you see me a poor fool
As wise as when I entered school!
They call me Master, they call me Doctor,
Ten years now I have dragged my college

Along by the nose through zig and zag
Through up and down and round and round
And this is all that I have found—
The impossibility of knowledge!
It is this that burns away my heart;
Of course I am cleverer than the quacks,
Than master and doctor, than clerk and priest,
I suffer no scruple or doubt in the least,
I have no qualms about devil or burning,
Which is just why all joy is torn from me,
I cannot presume to make use of my learning,
I cannot presume I could open my mind
To proselytize and improve mankind.

Besides, I have neither goods nor gold,
Neither reputation nor rank in the world;
No dog would choose to continue so!
Which is why I have given myself to Magic
To see if the Spirit may grant me to know
Through its force and its voice full many a secret,
May spare the sour sweat that I used to pour out
In talking of what I know nothing about,
May grant me to learn what it is that girds
The world together in its inmost being,
That the seeing its whole germination, the seeing
Its workings, may end my traffic in words.

O couldst thou, light of the full moon,
Look now thy last upon my pain,
Thou for whom I have sat belated
So many midnights here and waited
Till, over books and papers, thou
Didst shine, sad friend, upon my brow!
O could I but walk to and fro
On mountain heights in thy dear glow
Or float with spirits round mountain eyries
Or weave through fields thy glances glean

And freed from all miasmal theories
Bathe in thy dew and wash me clean!

Oh! Am I still stuck in this jail?
This God-damned dreary hole in the wall
Where even the lovely light of heaven
Breaks wanly through the painted panes!
Cooped up among these heaps of books
Gnawed by worms, coated with dust,
Round which to the top of the Gothic vault
A smoke-stained paper forms a crust.
Retorts and canisters lie pell-mell
And pyramids of instruments,
The junk of centuries, dense and mat—
Your world, man! World? They call it that!

And yet you ask why your poor heart
Cramped in your breast should feel such fear,
Why an unspecified misery
Should throw your life so out of gear?
Instead of the living natural world
For which God made all men his sons
You hold a reeking mouldering court
Among assorted skeletons.

Away! There is a world outside!
And this one book of mystic art
Which Nostradamus wrote himself,
Is this not adequate guard and guide?
By this you can tell the course of the stars,
By this, once Nature gives the word,
The soul begins to stir and dawn,
A spirit by a spirit heard.
In vain your barren studies here
Construe the signs of sanctity.
You Spirits, you are hovering near;
If you can hear me, answer me!

(*He opens the book and perceives the sign of the Macrocosm.*)

Ha! What a river of wonder at this vision
Bursts upon all my senses in one flood!
And I feel young, the holy joy of life
Glows new, flows fresh, through nerve and blood!
Was it a god designed this hieroglyph to calm
The storm which but now raged inside me,
To pour upon my heart such balm,
And by some secret urge to guide me
Where all the powers of Nature stand unveiled around
     me?
Am I a God? It grows so light!
And through the clear-cut symbol on this page
My soul comes face to face with all creating Nature.
At last I understand the dictum of the sage:
"The spiritual world is always open,
Your mind is closed, your heart is dead;
Rise, young man, and plunge undaunted
Your earthly breast in the morning red."

(*He contemplates the sign.*)

Into one Whole how all things blend,
Function and live within each other!
Passing gold buckets to each other
How heavenly powers ascend, descend!
The odour of grace upon their wings,
They thrust from heaven through earthly **things**
And as all sing so *the* All sings!
What a fine show! Aye, but only a show!
Infinite Nature, where can I tap thy veins?
Where are thy breasts, those well-springs of all life
On which hang heaven and earth,
Towards which my dry breast strains?
They well up, they give drink, but I feel drought and
     dearth.

(He turns the pages and perceives the sign of the Earth Spirit.)

How differently this new sign works upon me!
Thy sign, thou Spirit of the Earth, 'tis thine
And thou art nearer to me.
At once I feel my powers unfurled,
At once I glow as from new wine
And feel inspired to venture into the world,
To cope with the fortunes of earth benign or malign,
To enter the ring with the storm, to grapple and clinch,
To enter the jaws of the shipwreck and never flinch.
Over me comes a mist,
The moon muffles her light,
The lamp goes dark.
The air goes damp. Red beams flash
Around my head. There blows
A kind of a shudder down from the vault
And seizes on me.
It is thou must be hovering round me, come at my
     prayers!
Spirit, unveil thyself!
My heart, oh my heart, how it tears!
And how each and all of my senses
Seem burrowing upwards towards new light, new breath!
I feel my heart has surrendered, I have no more defences.
Come then! Come! Even if it prove my death!

(He seizes the book and solemnly pronounces the sign of the Earth Spirit. There is a flash of red flame and the Spirit appears in it.)

SPIRIT

Who calls upon me?

FAUST

Appalling vision!

SPIRIT

You have long been sucking at my sphere,
Now by main force you have drawn me here
And now—

FAUST

No! Not to be endured!

SPIRIT

With prayers and with pantings you have procured
The sight of my face and the sound of my voice—
Now I am here. What a pitiable shivering
Seizes the Superman. Where is the call of your soul?
Where the breast which created a world in itself
And carried and fostered it, swelling up, joyfully quiver-
ing,
Raising itself to a level with Us, the Spirits?
Where are you, Faust, whose voice rang out to me,
Who with every nerve so thrust yourself upon me?
Are you the thing that at a whiff of my breath
Trembles throughout its living frame,
A poor worm crawling off, askance, askew?

FAUST

Shall I yield to Thee, Thou shape of flame?
I am Faust, I can hold my own with Thee.

SPIRIT

In the floods of life, in the storm of work,
In ebb and flow,
In warp and weft,
Cradle and grave,
An eternal sea,
A changing patchwork,
A glowing life,

At the whirring loom of Time I weave
The living clothes of the Deity.

FAUST

Thou who dost rove the wide world round,
Busy Spirit, how near I feel to Thee!

SPIRIT

You are like that Spirit which you can grasp,
Not me!

(*The Spirit vanishes.*)

FAUST

Not Thee!
Whom then?
I who am Godhead's image,
Am I not even like Thee!

(*A knocking on the door.*)

Death! I know who that is. My assistant!
So ends my happiest, fairest hour.
The crawling pedant must interrupt
My visions at their fullest flower!

(*Wagner enters in dressing-gown and nightcap, a lamp in his hand.*)

. . . .

MEPHISTOPHELES

. . . I will bind myself to your service in this world,
To be at your beck and never rest nor slack;
When we meet again on the other side,
In the same coin you shall pay me back.

FAUST

The other side gives me little trouble;
First batter this present world to rubble,

Then the other may rise—if that's the plan.
This earth is where my springs of joy have started,
And this sun shines on me when broken-hearted;
If I can first from them be parted,
Then let happen what will and can!
I wish to hear no more about it—
Whether there too men hate and love
Or whether in those spheres too, in the future,
There is a Below or an Above.

MEPHISTOPHELES

With such an outlook you can risk it.
Sign on the line! In these next days you will get
Ravishing samples of my arts;
I am giving you what never man saw yet.

FAUST

Poor devil, can *you* give anything ever?
Was a human spirit in its high endeavour
Even once understood by one of your breed?
Have you got food which fails to feed?
Or red gold which, never at rest,
Like mercury runs away through the hand?
A game at which one never wins?
A girl who, even when on my breast,
Pledges herself to my neighbour with her eyes?
The divine and lovely delight of honour
Which falls like a falling star and dies?
Show me the fruits which, before they are plucked,
    decay,
And the trees which day after day renew their green!

MEPHISTOPHELES

Such a commission doesn't alarm me,
I have such treasures to purvey.
But, my good friend, the time draws on when we
Should be glad to feast at our ease on something good.

FAUST

If ever I stretch myself on a bed of ease,
Then I am finished! Is that understood?
If ever your flatteries can coax me
To be pleased with myself, if ever you cast
A spell of pleasure that can hoax me—
Then let *that* day be my last!
That's my wager!

MEPHISTOPHELES

Done!

FAUST

Let's shake!
If ever I say to the passing moment
'Linger a while! Thou art so fair!'
Then you may cast me into fetters,
I will gladly perish then and there!
Then you may set the death-bell tolling,
Then from my service you are free,
The clock may stop, its hand may fall,
And that be the end of time for me!

MEPHISTOPHELES

Think what you're saying, we shall not forget it.

FAUST

And you are fully within your rights;
I have made no mad or outrageous claim.
If I stay as I am, I am a slave—
Whether yours or another's, it's all the same.

MEPHISTOPHELES

I shall this very day at the College Banquet
Enter your service with no more ado,

But just one point—As a life-and-death insurance
I must trouble you for a line or two.

FAUST

So you, you pedant, you too like things in writing?
Have you never known a man? Or a man's word?
  Never?
Is it not enough that my word of mouth
Puts all my days in bond for ever?
Does not the world rage on in all its streams
And shall a promise hamper *me*?
Yet this illusion reigns within our hearts
And from it who would be gladly free?
Happy the man who can inwardly keep his word;
Whatever the cost, he will not be loath to pay!
But a parchment, duly inscribed and sealed,
Is a bogey from which all wince away.
The word dies on the tip of the pen
And wax and leather lord it then.
What do you, evil spirit, require?
Bronze, marble, parchment, paper?
Quill or chisel or pencil of slate?
You may choose whichever you desire.

MEPHISTOPHELES

How can you so exaggerate
With such a hectic rhetoric?
Any little snippet is quite good—
And you sign it with one little drop of blood.

FAUST

If that is enough and is some use,
One may as well pander to your fad.

MEPHISTOPHELES

Blood is a very special juice.

FAUST

Only do not fear that I shall break this contract.
What I promise is nothing more
Than what all my powers are striving for.
I have puffed myself up too much, it is only
Your sort that really fits my case.
The great Earth Spirit has despised me
And Nature shuts the door in my face.
The thread of thought is snapped asunder,
I have long loathed knowledge in all its fashions.
In the depths of sensuality
Let us now quench our glowing passions!
And at once make ready every wonder
Of unpenetrated sorcery!
Let us cast ourselves into the torrent of time,
In the whirl of eventfulness,
Where disappointment and success,
Pleasure and pain may chop and change
As chop and change they will and can;
It is restless action makes the man.

MEPHISTOPHELES

No limit is fixed for you, no bound;
If you'd like to nibble at everything
Or to seize upon something flying round—
Well, may you have a run for your money!
But seize your chance and don't be funny!

FAUST

I've told you, it is no question of happiness.
The most painful joy, enamoured hate, enlivening
Disgust—I devote myself to all excess.
My breast, now cured of its appetite for knowledge,
From now is open to all and every smart,
And what is allotted to the whole of mankind
That will I sample in my inmost heart,

Grasping the highest and lowest with my spirit,
Piling men's weal and woe upon my neck,
To extend myself to embrace all human selves
And to founder in the end, like them, a wreck.

Trans. Louis MacNeice (New York: Oxford Press, 1951).

Pardonable Audacity for Faust

[FROM *Observations on Goethe's Faust*]

GÉRARD DE NERVAL
(GÉRARD LABRUNIE)

1828

Where else has the sublime character of Faust been better set forth than in this work, in these lofty meditations whose brilliance my weak prose could never grasp? Every generous mind has experienced something of this condition of the human spirit, aiming without respite toward some divine revelation—tugging, so to speak, at the whole length of its chain until that moment when cold reality comes to disenchant the audacity of its illusions and its hopes; and, like the voice of God, dashes it back to the world of dust.

This passion for knowledge and for immortality, Faust possesses to the highest degree. Often this raises him to the level of a god or to the concept we have of deity. Yet everything about him is natural and probable. If his is all the grandeur and strength of the human race, his are also all its weaknesses. When he asked Hell for the help that Heaven denied him, doubtlessly his first thought was for these seeming and apparent boons, and for universal wisdom. By good deeds he hoped to sanctify such diabolic treasures; and via knowledge he hoped to receive absolution from God for his audacity. All that was necessary to upset these dreams, was his love for a young girl. Here was that apple from the Garden of Eden which, in lieu of knowledge and life, gave him the satisfaction of the moment and an eternity of torture.

Manfred and Don Juan are the two dramatic characters who come closest to Faust. But what a difference! Manfred is remorse personified. Still, he has a fantastic quality about him hard for us to accept on rational grounds. Everything about him, both his strength and his weaknesses, is raised to a superhuman plane. He inspires astonishment within us at the same time that he arouses no interest. No one has participated in either his joys or his sorrows. This observation is still more applicable to Don Juan. If Faust and Manfred have given us certain delineations of a type of human perfection, then Don Juan can be nothing more than a type of demoralization, dedicated in the long run to the spirit of evil. We feel that both these qualities are worthy of each other. Yet the result is the same for all three of these heroes. Love for women finally defeats them! . . .

What a parallel is to be drawn between these three different, yet so great, creations! . . . I dare not allow myself to be forced to continue it! Given that Faust is quite superior to the other two; again, how much Margareta surpasses Don Juan's vulgar conquests and that imagined Astarte of Manfred!

Trans. H. E. H.

The Germans Are Doctor Faust

[FROM *The Romantic School*]

HEINRICH HEINE

1833

During the middle ages the populace attributed all extraordinary intellectual powers to a compact with the devil, and Albertus Magnus, Raimond Lullus, Theophrastus Paracelsus, Agrippa von Nettesheim, and Roger Bacon in England, were held to be magicians, sorcerers, and conjurers. But the ballads and romances tell much stranger stories concerning Doctor Faustus, who is reputed to have demanded from the devil not only a knowledge of the profoundest secrets of nature, but also the most realistic physical pleasures. This is the self-same Faust who invented printing, and who lived at a time when people began to inveigh against the strictness of church authority, and to make independent researches. With Faust the mediaeval epoch of faith ends, and the modern era of critical, scientific investigation begins. It is, in fact, of the greatest significance that Faust should have lived, according to popular tradition, at the very beginning of the Reformation, and that he himself should have invented printing, the art which gave science the victory over faith; an art, however, which has also robbed us of the catholic peace of mind, and plunged us into doubts and revolutions—another than I would perhaps say: and had finally delivered us into the power of Satan. But no! knowledge, science, the comprehension of nature through reason, eventually give us the enjoyments of which faith, that is, Catholic

Christianity, has so long defrauded us; we now recognize the truth that mankind is destined to an earthly, as well as to a heavenly, equality. The political brotherhood which philosophy inculcates is more beneficial to us than the purely spiritual brotherhood, for which we are indebted to Christianity. The thought becomes transformed into words, the words become deeds, and we may yet be happy during our life on this earth. If, in addition to this, we also attain after death that heavenly felicity which Christianity promises so assuredly, so much the better.

The German people had, for a long time, felt a profound presentiment of this, for the Germans themselves are that learned Doctor Faust; they themselves are that spiritualist, who, having at last comprehended the inadequateness of the spiritual life alone, reinstates the flesh in its rights. But still biased by the symbolism of Catholic poetry, in which God is pictured as the representative of the spirit, and the devil as that of the flesh, the rehabilitation of the flesh was characterized as an apostasy from God, and a compact with the devil.

But some time must yet elapse ere the deeply significant prophecy of that poem will be fulfilled as regards the German people, and the spirit itself, comprehending the usurpation of spiritualism, become the champion of the rights of the flesh. That will be the revolution, the great daughter of the Reformation.

Trans. S. L. Fleischman (New York: Henry Holt, 1882).

Seeking Things beyond Mortality

[FROM *Manfred*]

GEORGE GORDON,
LORD BYRON

1817

WITCH

Son of Earth!
I know thee, and the powers which give thee power;
I know thee for a man of many thoughts,
And deeds of good and ill, extreme in both,
Fatal and fated in thy sufferings.
I have expected this—what wouldst thou with me?

MANFRED

To look upon thy beauty—nothing further.
The face of the earth hath madden'd me, and I
Take refuge in her mysteries, and pierce
To the abodes of those who govern her—
But they can nothing aid me. I have sought
From them what they could not bestow, and now
I search no further.

WITCH

What could be the quest
Which is not in the power of the most powerful,
The rulers of the invisible?

MANFRED

A boon;
But why should I repeat it? 'twere in vain.

WITCH

I would not that; let thy lips utter it.

MANFRED

Well, though it torture me, 'tis but the same;
My pang shall find a voice. From my youth upwards
My spirit walk'd not with the souls of men,
Nor look'd upon the earth with human eyes;
The thirst of their ambition was not mine,
The aim of their existence was not mine;
My joys, my griefs, my passions, and my powers,
Made me a stranger; though I wore the form,
I had no sympathy with breathing flesh,
Nor midst the creatures of clay that girded me
Was there but one who—but of her anon.
I said with men, and with the thoughts of men,
I held but slight communion; but instead,
My joy was in the wilderness,—to breathe
The difficult air of the iced mountain's top,
Where the birds dare not build, nor insect's wing
Flit o'er the herbless granite; or to plunge
Into the torrent, and to roll along
On the swift whirl of the new breaking wave
Of river-stream, or ocean, in their flow.
In these my early strength exulted; or
To follow through the night the moving moon,
The stars and their development; or catch
The dazzling lightnings till my eyes grew dim;
Or to look, list'ning, on the scatter'd leaves,
While Autumn winds were at their evening song.
These were my pastimes, and to be alone;
For if the beings, of whom I was one,—
Hating to be so,—cross'd me in my path,
I felt myself degraded back to them,
And all was clay again. And then I dived,
In my lone wanderings, to the caves of death,

Searching its cause in its effect; and drew
From wither'd bones, and skulls, and heap'd up dust,
Conclusions most forbidden. Then I pass'd
The nights of years in sciences untaught,
Save in the old time; and with time and toil,
And terrible ordeal, and such penance
As in itself hath power upon the air,
And spirits that do compass air and earth,
Space, and the peopled infinite, I made
Mine eyes familiar with Eternity,
Such as, before me, did the Magi, and
He who from out their fountain dwellings raised
Eros and Anteros, at Gadara,
As I do thee;—and with my knowledge grew
The thirst of knowledge, and the power and joy
Of this most bright intelligence, until—

WITCH

Proceed.

MANFRED

     Oh! I but thus prolong'd my words,
Boasting these idle attributes, because
As I approach the core of my heart's grief—
But to my task. I have not named to thee
Father or mother, mistress, friend, or being,
With whom I wore the chain of human ties;
If I had such, they seem'd not such to me;
Yet there was one—

WITCH

    Spare not thyself—proceed.

MANFRED

She was like me in lineaments; her eyes,
Her hair, her features, all, to the very tone
Even of her voice, they said were like to mine;
But soften'd all, and temper'd into beauty:

She had the same lone thoughts and wanderings,
The quest of hidden knowledge, and a mind
To comprehend the universe: nor these
Alone, but with them gentler powers than mine,
Pity, and smiles, and tears—which I had not;
And tenderness—but that I had for her;
Humility—and that I never had.
Her faults were mine—her virtues were her own—
I loved her, and destroy'd her!

WITCH

       With thy hand?

MANFRED

Not with my hand, but heart, which broke her heart;
It gazed on mine, and wither'd. I have shed
Blood, but not hers—and yet her blood was shed;
I saw—and could not stanch it.

WITCH

          And for this—
A being of the race thou dost despise,
The order, which thine own would rise above,
mingling with us and ours,—thou dost forgo
The gifts of our great knowledge, and shrink'st back
To recreant mortality—Away!

MANFRED

Daughter of Air! I tell thee, since that hour—
But words are breath—look on me in my sleep,
Or watch my watchings—Come and sit by me!
My solitude is solitude no more,
But peoples with the Furies;—I have gnash'd
My teeth in darkness till returning morn,
Then cursed myself till sunset;—I have pray'd
For madness as a blessing—'tis denied me.

I have affronted death—but in the war
Of elements the waters shrunk from me,
And fatal things pass'd harmless; the cold hand
Of an all-pitiless demon held me back,
Back by a single hair, which would not break.
In fantasy, imagination, all
The affluence of my soul—which one day was
A Croesus in creation—I plunged deep,
But, like an ebbing wave, it dash'd me back
Into the gulf of my unfathom'd thought.
I plunged amidst mankind—Forgetfulness
I sought in all, save where 'tis to be found.
And that I have to learn; my sciences,
My long-pursued and superhuman art,
Is mortal here: I dwell in my despair—
And live—and live for ever.

WITCH

                    It may be
That I can aid thee.

MANFRED

                    To do this thy power
Must wake the dead, or lay me low with them.
Do so—in any shape—in any hour—
With any torture—so it be the last.

WITCH

That is not in my province; but if thou
Wilt swear obedience to my will, and do
My bidding, it may help thee to thy wishes.

MANFRED

I will not swear—Obey! and whom? the spirits
Whose presence I command, and be the slave
Of those who served me—Never!

WITCH

Is this all?
Hast thou no gentler answer?—Yet bethink thee,
And pause ere thou rejectest.

MANFRED

I have said it.

WITCH

Enough! I may retire then—say!

MANFRED

Retire!

(*The Witch disappears.*)

. . . .

NEMESIS

What doth he here then?

FIRST DESTINY

Let him answer that.

MANFRED

Ye know what I have known; and without power
I could not be amongst ye: but there are
Powers deeper still beyond—I come in quest
Of such, to answer unto what I seek.

NEMESIS

What wouldst thou?

MANFRED

Thou canst not reply to me.
Call up the dead—my question is for them.

NEMESIS

Great Arimanes, doth thy will avouch
The wishes of this mortal?

ARIMANES

Yea.

NEMESIS

Whom wouldst thou
Uncharnel?

MANFRED

One without a tomb—call up Astarte.

NEMESIS

Shadow! or Spirit!
    Whatever thou art,
Which still doth inherit
    The whole or a part
Of the form of thy birth,
    Of the mould of thy clay,
Which return'd to the earth,
    Re-appear to the day!
Bear what thou borest,
    The heart and the form,
And the aspect thou worest
    Redeem from the worm.
Appear!—Appear!—Appear!
Who sent thee there requires thee here!

(*The Phantom of Astarte rises and stands in the midst.*)

MANFRED

Can this be death? there's bloom upon her cheek;
But now I see it is no living hue,
But a strange hectic—like the unnatural red

Which Autumn plants upon the perish'd leaf.
It is the same! Oh, God! that I should dread
To look upon the same—Astarte!—No,
I cannot speak to her—but bid her speak—
Forgive me or condemn me.

NEMESIS

By the power which hath broken
    The grave which enthrall'd thee,
Speak to him, who hath spoken,
    Or those who have call'd thee!

MANFRED

                        She is silent,
And in that silence I am more than answer'd.

NEMESIS

My power extends no further. Prince of Air!
It rests with thee alone—command her voice.

ARIMANES

Spirit—obey this sceptre!

NEMESIS

                Silent still!
She is not of our order, but belongs
To the other powers. Mortal! thy quest is vain,
And we are baffled also.

MANFRED

              Hear me, hear me—
Astarte! my beloved! speak to me:
I have so much endured—so much endure—
Look on me! the grave hath not changed thee more
Than I am changed for thee. Thou lovedst me
Too much, as I loved thee: we were not made
To torture thus each other, though it were

The deadliest sin to love as we have loved.
Say that thou loath'st me not—that I do bear
This punishment for both—that thou wilt be
One of the blessed—and that I shall die;
For hitherto all hateful things conspire
To bind me in existence—in a life
Which makes me shrink from immortality—
A future like the past. I cannot rest.
I know not what I ask, nor what I seek:
I feel but what thou art, and what I am;
And I would hear yet once before I perish
The voice which was my music—Speak to me!
For I have call'd on thee in the still night,
Startled the slumbering birds from the hush'd boughs,
And woke the mountain wolves, and made the caves
Acquainted with thy vainly echoed name,
Which answer'd me—many things answer'd me—
Spirits and men—but thou wert silent all.
Yet speak to me! I have outwatch'd the stars,
And gazed o'er heaven in vain in search of thee.
Speak to me! I have wander'd o'er the earth,
And never found thy likeness—Speak to me!
Look on the fiends around—they feel for me:
I fear them not, and feel for thee alone—
Speak to me! though it be in wrath;—but say—
I reck not what—but let me hear thee once—
This once—once more!

PHANTOM OF ASTARTE

Manfred!

MANFRED

    Say on, say on—
I live but in the sound—it is thy voice!

PHANTOM

Manfred! To-morrow ends thine earthly ills.
Farewell!

MANFRED

Yet one word more—am I forgiven?

PHANTOM

Farewell!

MANFRED

Say, shall we meet again?

PHANTOM

Farewell!

MANFRED

One word for mercy! Say, thou lovest me.

PHANTOM

Manfred!

(*The Spirit of Astarte disappears.*)

NEMESIS

She's gone, and will not be recall'd;
Her words will be fulfill'd. Return to the earth.

A SPIRIT

He is convulsed.—This is to be a mortal
And seek the things beyond mortality.

ANOTHER SPIRIT

Yet, see, he mastereth himself, and makes
His torture tributary to his will.
Had he been one of us, he would have made
An awful spirit.

NEMESIS

Hast thou further question
Of our great sovereign, or his worshipers?

MANFRED

None.

NEMESIS

Then, for a time, farewell.

MANFRED

We meet then! Where? On the earth?—
Even as thou wilt: and for the grace accorded
I now depart a debtor. Fare ye well!

(*Exit Manfred.*)

.   .   .   .

SPIRIT

Mortal! thine hour is come—Away! I say.

MANFRED

I knew, and know my hour is come, but not
To render up my soul to such as thee:
Away! I'll die as I have lived—alone.

SPIRIT

Then I must summon up my brethren.—Rise!

(*Other Spirits rise up.*)

ABBOT

Avaunt! ye evil ones!—Avaunt! I say;
Ye have no power where piety hath power,
And I do charge ye in the name——

SPIRIT

                              Old man!
We know ourselves, our mission, and thine order;
Waste not thy holy words on idle uses,
It were in vain: this man is forfeited.
Once more I summon him—Away! Away!

MANFRED

I do defy ye,—though I feel my soul
Is ebbing from me, yet I do defy ye;
Nor will I hence, while I have earthly breath
To breathe my scorn upon ye—earthly strength
To wrestle, though with spirits; what ye take
Shall be ta'en limb by limb.

SPIRIT

      Reluctant mortal!
Is this the Magian who would so pervade
The world invisible, and make himself
Almost our equal? Can it be that thou
Art thus in love with life? the very life
Which made thee wretched!

MANFRED

         Thou false fiend, thou liest!
My life is in its last hour,—*that* I know,
Nor would redeem a moment of that hour;
I do not combat against death, but thee
And thy surrounding angels; my past power,
Was purchased by no compact with thy crew,
But by superior science—penance, daring,
And length of watching, strength of mind, and skill
In knowledge of our fathers—when the earth
Saw men and spirits walking side by side,
And gave ye no supremacy: I stand
Upon my strength—I do defy—deny—
Spurn back, and scorn ye!—

SPIRIT

        But thy many crimes
Have made thee—

MANFRED

What are they to such as thee?
Must crimes be punish'd but by other crimes,
And greater criminals?—Back to thy hell!
Thou hast no power upon me, *that* I feel;
Thou never shalt possess me, *that* I know:
What I have done is done; I bear within
A torture which could nothing gain from thine:
The mind which is immortal makes itself
Requital for its good or evil thoughts,—
Is its own origin of ill and end—
And its own place and time: its innate sense,
When stripp'd of this mortality, derives
No colour from the fleeting things without,
But is absorb'd in sufferance or in joy,
Born from the knowledge of its own desert.
Thou didst not tempt me, and thou couldst not tempt
    me;
I have not been thy dupe, nor am thy prey—
But was my own destroyer, and will be
My own hereafter.—Back, ye baffled fiends!—
The hand of death is on me—but not yours!
(*The Demons disappear.*)

ABBOT

Alas! how pale thou art—thy lips are white—
And thy breast heaves—and in thy gasping throat
The accents rattle: Give thy prayers to heaven—
Pray—albeit but in thought,—but die not thus.

MANFRED

'Tis over—my dull eyes can fix thee not;
But all things swim around me, and the earth
Heaves as it were beneath me. Fare thee well!
Give me thy hand.

ABBOT

Cold—cold—even to the heart—
But yet one prayer—Alas! how fares it with thee?

MANFRED

Old man! 'tis not so difficult to die.

(Manfred expires.)

ABBOT

He's gone—his soul hath ta'en its earthless flight;
Whither? I dread to think—but he is gone.

A Dark and Doubtful Voyage

[FROM Melmoth the Wanderer]

CHARLES MATURIN

1820

As the Wanderer advanced still nearer till his figure
touched the table, Monçada and Melmoth started up in
irrepressible horror, and stood in attitudes of defence,
though conscious at the moment that all defence was
hopeless against a being that withered and mocked at
human power. The Wanderer waved his arm with an
action that spoke defiance without hostility—and the
strange and solemn accents of the only human voice that
had respired mortal air beyond the period of mortal
life, and never spoken but to the ear of guilt or suffering,
and never uttered to that ear aught but despair, rolled
slowly on their hearing like a peal of distant thunder.

"Mortals—you are here to talk of my destiny and of the events which it has involved. That destiny is accomplished, I believe, and with it terminate those events that have stimulated your wild and wretched curiosity. I am here to tell you of both!—I—I—of whom you speak, am here!—Who can tell so well of Melmoth the Wanderer as himself, now that he is about to resign that existence which has been the object of terror and wonder to the world?—Melmoth, you behold your ancestor—the being on whose portrait is inscribed the date of a century and a half, is before you.—Monçada, you see an acquaintance of a later date." (A grim smile of recognition wandered over his features as he spoke.) "Fear nothing," he added, observing the agony and terror of his involuntary hearers. "What have you to fear!" he continued, while a flash of derisive malignity once more lit up the sockets of his dead eyes. "You, Senhor, are armed with your beads—and you, Melmoth, are fortified by that vain and desperate inquisitiveness, which might, at a former period, have made you my victim" (and his features underwent a short but horrible convulsion), "but now makes you only my mockery."

"Have you aught to quench my thirst?" he added, seating himself. The senses of Monçada and his companion reeled in delirious terror, and the former, in a kind of wild confidence, filled a glass of water, and offered it to the Wanderer with a hand as steady, but somewhat colder, as he would have presented it to one who sat beside him in human companionship. The Wanderer raised it to his lips, and tasted a few drops, then replacing it on the table, said with a laugh, wild indeed, but no longer ferocious, "Have you seen," said he to Monçada and Melmoth, who gazed with dim and troubled sight on this vision, and wist not what to think—"Have you seen the fate of Don Juan, not as he is pantomimed on your paltry stage, but as he is represented in the real horrors of his destiny by the Spanish writers? There the spectre returns the hospitality of his inviter, and summons him in turn to a feast. The banquet-hall is a church—he arrives—it is illuminated with a mysterious light—invisible hands hold lamps fed by no earthly substance, to light the apostate to his doom! He enters the church, and is greeted by a numerous company—the spirits of those whom he has wronged and murdered, uprisen from their charnel, and swathed in shrouds, stand there to welcome him! As he passes among them, they call on him in hollow sounds to pledge them in goblets of blood which they present to him—and beneath the altar, by which stands the spirit of him whom the parricide has murdered, the gulf of perdition is yawning to receive him! Through such a band I must soon prepare to pass! Isidora! thy form will be the last I must encounter—and the most terrible! Now for the last drop I must taste of earth's produce—the last that shall wet my mortal lips!" He slowly finished the draught of water. Neither of his companions had the power to speak. He sat down in a posture of heavy musing, and neither ventured to interrupt him.

They kept silence till the morning was dawning, and a faint light streamed through the closed shutters. Then the Wanderer raised his heavy eyes, and fixed them on Melmoth. "Your ancestor has come home," he said; "his wanderings are over! What has been told or believed of me is now of light avail to me. The secret of my destiny rests with myself. If all that fear has invented, and credulity believed of me be true, to what does it amount? That if my crimes have exceeded those of mortality, so will my punishment. I have been on earth a terror, but not an evil to its inhabitants. None can participate in my destiny but with his own consent— *none have consented*—none can be involved in its tremendous penalties, but by participation. I alone must sustain the penalty. If I have put forth my hand, and eaten of the fruit of the interdicted tree, am I not driven from the presence of God and the region of paradise, and sent to wander amid worlds of barrenness and curse for ever and ever?

"It has been reported of me, that I obtained from the enemy of souls a range of existence beyond the period allotted to mortality—a power to pass over space without disturbance or delay, and visit remote regions with the swiftness of thought—to encounter tempests without the *hope* of their blasting me, and penetrate into dungeons, whose bolts were as flax and tow at my touch. It has been said that this power was accorded to me, that I might be enabled to tempt wretches in their fearful hour of extremity, with the promise of deliverance and immunity, on condition of their exchanging situations with me. If this be true, it bears attestation to a truth uttered by the lips of one I may not name, and echoed by every human heart in the habitable world.

"No one has ever exchanged destinies with Melmoth the Wanderer. *I have traversed the world in the search, and no one, to gain that world, would lose his own soul!* Not Stanton in his cell—nor you, Monçada, in the prison of the Inquisition—nor Walberg, who saw his children perishing with want—nor another."

He paused, and though on the verge of his dark and doubtful voyage, he seemed to cast one look of bitter and retrospective anguish on the receding shore of life, and see, through the mists of memory, one form that stood there to bid him farewell. He rose. "Let me, if possible, obtain an hour's repose. Aye, repose—sleep!" he repeated, answering the silent astonishment of his hearers' looks, "my existence is still human!"—and a ghastly and derisive smile wandered over his features for the last time, as he spoke. How often had that smile frozen the blood of his victims! Melmoth and

Monçada quitted the apartment; and the Wanderer, sinking back in his chair, slept profoundly. He slept, but what were the visions of his last earthly slumber?

Where the Mother of All Things Lives
[FROM *The Disciples at Saïs*]

NOVALIS
(FRIEDRICH VON HARDENBERG)

1798

A merry playfellow, his temples decked with roses and convolvulus came running by and saw the Disciple sitting absorbed in himself. "Dreamer!" he cried, "thou art quite on the wrong road. In such a way thou wilt make no great progress. The mood's the best of all things. Is that indeed a mood of Nature? Thou art still young, and dost thou not feel the dictates of youth in every vein? Do not Love and Longing fill thy breast? How canst thou sit in solitude? Does Nature sit solitary? Joy and desire flee from the solitary; and what use is nature to thee without desire? Only with men is she at home, this Spirit who crowds all the senses with a thousand different colours, who surrounds thee like an invisible Lover. At our Feasts her tongue is loosed; she sits aloft and carols songs of gladdest life. Thou hast never yet loved, poor fellow; at the first kiss a new world will open to thee and life will penetrate thy ravished heart with its thousand rays. I will tell thee a tale. Listen! There lived once upon a time in the land of the setting sun a young man. He was very good, but above the ordinary, extraordinary. He fretted himself inces-

santly about nothing and yet again nothing, went quietly
about on his own account when others played together
and were merry, and indulged in strange things. Caves
and woods were his favorite haunts; he talked continually with quadrupeds and birds, with trees and
rocks; of course in no sensible words, but only in such
foolish twaddle as would make one die of laughing. But
he ever remained morose and solemn notwithstanding
that the squirrels and monkeys, the parrots and bull-
finches gave themselves all the trouble in the world to
distract him and put him in the right path again. The
goose told him tales, the stream rippled a roundelay, a
great heavy stone made comic leaps and a rose crept
round him amicably and twined herself in his locks,
while the ivy caressed his thoughtful brow. But his
solemnity and depression were stubborn. His parents
were very grieved; they knew not what they ought to
do. He was healthy and eat well; they had never crossed
him. Only a few years back he was cheerful and blithe
as anyone, first in all games, and approved by every
maiden. He was really beautiful, looked like a picture
and danced like an angel. Amongst the maidens there
was one, a precious, exquisite child; she seemed to be
of wax, her hair was like gold silk, her lips were cherry
red like a doll's, her eyes burning black. Who saw her
might have thought to perish of it, so lovely was she. At
that time Rosenblütchen, for so she was called, was dear
to the beautiful Hyacinth, for that was his name, and in
fact he loved her to the point of death. The other children knew nothing about it. The violet had whispered
it to them first. The house kittens had noticed it, for the
houses of their parents lay close together. When at night
Hyacinth stood at his window and Rosenblütchen at
hers, and the little cats passed by on their mouse-hunt
and saw the two there they laughed and giggled so loud
that it made the lovers quite cross. The violet had told
it in confidence to the strawberry, who told it to her

friend the gooseberry, who did not omit to scratch
Hyacinth as he came along. So very soon the whole garden and wood knew all about it, and when Hyacinth
went out there rang from all sides: "Little Rosenblütchen
is my darling!" Then Hyacinth was annoyed, but he had
to laugh with all his heart when a little lizard came
gliding past, sat himself on a warm stone, and waving
his little tail, sang:

> Rosenblütchen, little pet,
> Once upon a time went blind,
> So when Hyacinth she met
> She embraced him. Being blind
> She just thought he was her mother,
> When she found it was another
> Did she mind? no not a bit,
> Only kissed him as before.
> Was she frightened? not a whit,
> Merely kissed him more and more.

Alas, how soon this glorious time was over. There
came a man from foreign parts who had travelled as-
tonishingly far, who had a long beard, deep eyes, fear-
some eyebrows, and who wore a marvellous robe of
many folds with strange figures woven into it. He sat
himself down before the house belonging to Hyacinth's
parents. Hyacinth was filled with curiosity, and went
out to him and brought him bread and wine. He
parted his white beard, and told his story far on into the
night. Hyacinth kept awake and did not fidget nor grow
tired of listening. From what transpired afterwards he
told a great deal about strange lands, of unexplored
regions, of amazing extraordinary things. He stayed
there three days and descended with Hyacinth into
profound depths. Rosenblütchen heartily cursed the old
warlock, for Hyacinth became quite possessed by his
discourse, and concerned himself with nothing else. He
would scarcely take his food. At last the old man went
away, but he left with Hyacinth a little book in which
no one could read. Hyacinth gave him more fruit, bread

and wine, and accompanied him far upon his way. He returned pensive and from thenceforward began a new way of life. Rosenblütchen certainly had a right to be pitied, for from that time he made little enough of her, and was always self-engrossed. Now it happened that one day he came home, and was as though new born. He fell on the necks of his parents and wept. "I must away into strange lands," he said; "the old Sibyl in the forest has told me how I am to become whole; she threw the book into the fire, and bade me come to you and ask your blessing. Perhaps I may return soon, perhaps never. Greet little Rosenblütchen; I would willingly have spoken with her. I know not how it is with me; something urges me away. If I try to think of the old days, mightier thoughts intervene. Peace is fled together with heart and love. I must go seek them. I would like to tell you whither, but I do not know. Thither where the Mother of All Things lives, the Veiled Virgin. My desire is aflame for Her. Farewell." He tore himself away from them and departed. His parents lamented and shed tears. Rosenblütchen stayed in her chamber and wept bitterly. Hyacinth hastened through valleys and deserts, over mountains and streams, towards the Mysterious Land. He questioned men and animals, rocks and trees concerning Isis, the sacred Goddess. Many laughed, many kept silence, from none did he receive the information he sought. At first he passed through a rude wild country; mists and clouds intercepted his passage and never-ceasing storms. Then he passed through interminable deserts of sand and fiery dust, and as he wandered his humour also was changed. The time seemed long to him; the inward tumult was appeased, he grew more gentle and the mighty urgence was gradually reduced to a quiet but intense aspiration in which his whole spirit was melted. It was as though many years had passed over him. The country became at the same time richer and more varied, the air warm and azure, the road more level. Green bushes allured him with pleasant shade. But he did not understand their speech. Besides they did not seem to speak while yet they filled his heart with green colours and a cool still perfume. That sweet longing waxed higher and higher in him, and the leaves expanded with sap; birds and beasts were noisier and more joyous, the fruits more aromatic, the heavens a deeper blue, the air milder, his love warmer, time went faster as if it saw itself nearing the goal. One day he lighted on a crystal brook, and on a cloud of flowers that came tripping down the valley between black mountain peaks as high as heaven. They greeted him kindly, with familiar words. "Dear country folk," he said, "where can I really find the sacred dwelling-place of Isis? It must needs be somewhere near here, and you are perhaps more at home than I." "We are only passing through," answered the flowers; "a family of spirits is travelling abroad, and we prepare their way and resting-place. Yet we have but just come through a place where we heard your name. Only go upwards whence we came, and you will learn more." The flowers and the brook laughed as they said this, offered him a refreshing draught, and went on their way. He followed their advice, asked again and again, and finally came to that long-sought dwelling that lay hidden beneath palms and other rare trees. His heart beat with an infinite yearning, and the sweetest shyness overcame him in this habitation of the eternal centuries. He slumbered enveloped by heavenly perfumes, for it was only a dream that could lead him to the Holy of Holies. Mysteriously his dream led him to the sound of loud, delicious music and alternating harmonies through endless halls full of curious things. It all seemed to him so familiar, and yet of an hitherto unrecognised splendour. Then the last vestiges of earthliness disappeared as though consumed in air, and he stood before the Celestial Virgin. He raised the diaphanous glistening veil, and Rosenblütchen sank into his arms. A distant music encompassed the secrets of the lovers' meeting, and the effusions of their love, and shut away everything inharmonious from this abode of rapture. Hyacinth lived ever after with Rosenblütchen, among his glad parents and his playfellows, and innumerable grandchildren thanked the old Sibyl for her counsel and her fire, for at that time people had as many children as they wished for.

Trans. Una Birch (London: Methuen, 1903).

The Devil Buys a Shadow

[FROM *Peter Schlemihl*]

ADALBERT VON CHAMISSO

1814

I had hastily glided through the rose-grove, descended the hill, and found myself on a wide grassplot, when, alarmed with the apprehension of being discovered wandering from the beaten path, I looked around me with enquiring apprehension. How was I startled when I saw the old man in the grey coat behind, and advancing towards me! He immediately took off his hat, and bowed to me more profoundly than any one had ever done before. It was clear he wished to address me, and without extreme rudeness I could not avoid him. I, in my turn, uncovered myself, made my obeisance, and stood still with bare head, in the sunshine, as if rooted there. I shook with terror while I saw him approach; I felt like a bird fascinated by a rattlesnake. He appeared sadly perplexed, kept his eye on the ground, made several bows, approached nearer, and with a low and trembling voice, as if he were asking alms, thus accosted me:

"Will the gentleman forgive the intrusion of one who has stopt him in this unusual way? I have a request to make, but pray pardon . . ." "In the name of heaven, Sir!" I cried out in my anguish, "what can I do for one who—" We both started back, and methought both blushed deeply.

After a momentary silence he again began: "During the short time when I enjoyed the happiness of being near you, I observed, Sir—will you allow me to say so— I observed, with unutterable admiration, the beautiful beautiful shadow in the sun, which with a certain noble contempt, and perhaps without being aware of it, you threw off from your feet; forgive me this, I confess, too daring intrusion, but should you be inclined to transfer it to me?"

He was silent, and my head turned round like a water-wheel. What could I make of this singular proposal for disposing of my shadow? He is crazy! thought I; and with an altered tone, yet more forcible, as contrasted with the humility of his own, I replied, "How is this, good friend? Is not your own shadow enough for you? This seems to me a whimsical sort of bargain indeed."

He began again, "I have in my pocket many matters which might not be quite unacceptable to the gentleman; for this invaluable shadow I deem any price too little."

A chill came over me: I remembered what I had seen, and knew not how to address him whom I had just ventured to call my good friend. I spoke again, and assumed an extraordinary courtesy to set matters in order.

"Pardon, Sir, pardon your most humble servant, I do not quite understand your meaning; how can my shadow—" He interrupted me: "I only beg your permission to be allowed to lift up your noble shadow, and put it in my pocket: how to do it is my own affair. As a proof of my gratitude for the gentleman, I leave him the choice of all the jewels which my pocket affords; the genuine divining rods, mandrake roots, change pennies, money extractors, the napkins of Rolando's Squire, and divers other miracle-workers—a choice assortment; but all this is not fit for you—better that you should have Fortunatus's wishing-cap, restored spick and span new; and also a fortune-bag which belonged to him." "Fortunatus's fortune-bag!" I exclaimed; and, great as had been my terror, all my senses were now enraptured by the sound. I became dizzy—and nothing but double ducats seemed sparkling before my eyes.

"Condescend, Sir, to inspect and make a trial of this bag." He put his hand into his pocket, and drew from it a moderately sized, firmly-stitched purse of thick cordovan, with two convenient leather cords hanging to it, which he presented to me. I instantly dipped into it, drew from it ten pieces of gold, and ten more, and ten more, and yet ten more; I stretched out my hand. "Done! the bargain is made; I give you my shadow for your purse." He grasped my hand, and knelt down behind me, and with wonderful dexterity I perceived him loosening my shadow from the ground from head to foot; he lifted it up; he rolled it together and folded it, and at last put it into his pocket. He then stood erect, bowed to me again, and returned back to the rose grove. I thought I heard him laughing softly to himself. I held, however, the purse tight by its strings—the earth was sun-bright all around me—and my senses were still wholly confused.

Trans. Sir John Bowring (New York: A. Dunham, 1874).

"I Am the Fallen Angel"

[FROM *Frankenstein; or The Modern Prometheus*]

MARY WOLLSTONECRAFT SHELLEY

1818

It was nearly noon when I arrived at the top of the ascent. For some time I sat upon the rock that overlooks the sea of ice. A mist covered both that and the surrounding mountains. Presently a breeze dissipated the cloud, and I descended upon the glacier. The surface is very uneven, rising like the waves of a troubled sea, descending low, and interspersed by rifts that sink deep. The field of ice is almost a league in width, but I spent nearly two hours in crossing it. The opposite mountain is a bare perpendicular rock. From the side where I now stood Montanvert was exactly opposite, at the distance of a league; and above it rose Mount Blanc, in awful majesty. I remained in a recess of the rock, gazing on this wonderful and stupendous scene. The sea, or rather the vast river of ice, wound among its depenent mountains, whose aerial summits hung over its recesses. Their icy and glittering peaks shone in the sunlight over the clouds. My heart, which was before sorrowful, now swelled with something like joy; I exclaimed—"Wandering spirits, if indeed ye wander, and do not rest in your narrow beds, allow me this faint happiness, or take me, as your companion, away from the joys of life."

As I said this, I suddenly beheld the figure of a man, at some distance, advancing towards me with superhuman speed. He bounded over the crevices in the ice, among which I had walked with caution; his stature, also, as he approached, seemed to exceed that of man. I was troubled: a mist came over my eyes, and I felt a faintness seize me; but I was quickly restored by the cold gale of the mountains. I perceived, as the shape came nearer (sight tremendous and abhorred!) that it was the wretch whom I had created. I trembled with rage and horror, resolving to wait his approach, and then close with him in mortal combat. He approached; his countenance bespoke bitter anguish, combined with disdain and malignity, while its unearthly ugliness rendered it almost too horrible for human eyes. But I scarcely observed this; rage and hatred had at first deprived me of utterance, and I recovered only to overwhelm him with words expressive of furious detestation and contempt.

"Devil," I exclaimed, "do you dare approach me? and do not you fear the fierce vengeance of my arm wreaked on your miserable head? Begone, vile insect! or rather, stay, that I may trample you to dust! and, oh! that I could, with the extinction of your miserable existence, restore those victims whom you have so diabolically murdered!"

"I expected this reception," said the daemon. "All men hate the wretched; how, then, must I be hated, who am miserable beyond all living things! Yet you, my creator, detest and spurn me, thy creature, to whom thou art bound by ties only dissoluble by the annihilation of one of us. You purpose to kill me. How dare you sport thus with life? Do your duty towards me, and I will do mine towards you and the rest of mankind. If you will comply with my conditions, I will leave them and you at peace; but if you refuse, I will glut the maw of death, until it be satiated with the blood of your remaining friends."

"Abhorred monster! fiend that thou art! the tortures

of hell are too mild a vengeance for thy crimes. Wretched devil! you reproach me with your creation; come on, then, that I may extinguish the spark which I so negligently bestowed."

My rage was without bounds; I sprang on him, impelled by all the feelings which can arm one being against the existence of another.

He easily eluded me, and said—

"Be calm! I entreat you to hear me, before you give vent to your hatred on my devoted head. Have I not suffered enough that you seek to increase my misery? Life, although it may only be an accumulation of anguish, is dear to me, and I will defend it. Remember, thou hast made me more powerful than thyself; my height is superior to thine; my joints more supple. But I will not be tempted to set myself in opposition to thee. I am thy creature, and I will be even mild and docile to my natural lord and king, if thou wilt also perform thy part, the which thou owest me. Oh, Frankenstein, be not equitable to every other, and trample upon me alone, to whom thy justice, and even thy clemency and affection, is most due. Remember, that I am thy creature; I ought to be thy Adam; but I am rather the fallen angel, whom thou drivest from joy for no misdeed. Everywhere I see bliss, from which I alone am irrevocably excluded. I was benevolent and good; misery made me a fiend. Make me happy, and I shall again be virtuous."

"Begone! I will not hear you. There can be no community between you and me; we are enemies. Begone, or let us try our strength in a fight, in which one must fall."

"How can I move thee? Will no entreaties cause thee to turn a favourable eye upon thy creature, who implores thy goodness and compassion? Believe me, Frankenstein: I was benevolent; my soul glowed with love and humanity: but am I not alone, miserably alone? You, my creator, abhor me; what hope can I gather from your fellow-creatures, who owe me nothing? they spurn and hate me. The desert mountains and dreary glaciers are my refuge. I have wandered here many days; the caves of ice, which I only do not fear, are a dwelling to me, and the only one which man does not grudge. These bleak skies I hail, for they are kinder to me than your fellow-beings. If the multitude of mankind knew of my existence, they would do as you do, and arm themselves for my destruction. Shall I not then hate them who abhor me? I will keep no terms with my enemies. I am miserable, and they shall share my wretchedness. Yet it is in your power to recompense me, and deliver them from an evil which it only remains for you to make so great that not only you and your family, but thousands of others, shall be swallowed up in the whirlwinds of its rage. Let your compassion be moved, and do not disdain me. Listen to my tale: when you have heard that, abandon or commiserate me, as you shall judge that I deserve. But hear me. The guilty are allowed, by human laws, bloody as they are, to speak in their own defence before they are condemned. Listen to me, Frankenstein. You accuse me of murder; and yet you would, with a satisfied conscience, destroy your own creature. Oh, praise the eternal justice of man! Yet I ask you not to spare me: listen to me; and then, if you can, and if you will, destroy the work of your hands."

"Why do you call to my remembrance," I rejoined, "circumstances, of which I shudder to reflect, that I have been the miserable origin and author? Cursed be the day, abhorred devil, in which you first saw light! Cursed (although I curse myself) be the hands that formed you! You have made me wretched beyond expression. You have left me no power to consider whether I am just to you or not. Begone! relieve me from the sight of your detested form."

"Thus I relieve thee, my creator," he said, and placed

his hated hands before my eyes which I flung from me with violence; "thus I take from thee a sight which you abhor. Still thou canst listen to me, and grant me thy compassion. By the virtues that I once possessed, I demand this from you. Hear my tale; it is long and strange, and the temperature of this place is not fitting to your fine sensations; come to the hut upon the mountain. The sun is yet high in the heavens; before it descends to hide itself behind yon snowy precipices, and illuminate another world, you will have heard my story, and can decide. On you it rests whether I quit for ever the neighbourhood of man, and lead a harmless life, or become the scourge of your fellow-creatures, and the author of your own speedy ruin."

The End of the Quest

[FROM *Moby Dick*]

HERMAN MELVILLE

1851

With matted beard, and swathed in a bristling sharkskin apron, about mid-day, Perth was standing between his forge and anvil, the latter placed upon an iron-wood log, with one hand holding a pike-head in the coals, and with the other at his forge's lungs, when Captain Ahab came along, carrying in his hand a small rusty-looking leathern bag. While yet a little distance from the forge, moody Ahab paused; till at last, Perth, withdrawing his iron from the fire, began hammering it upon the anvil—the red mass sending off the sparks in thick hovering flights, some of which flew close to Ahab.

"Are these thy Mother Carey's chickens, Perth? they are always flying in thy wake; birds of good omen, too, but not to all!—look here, they burn; but thou—thou liv'st among them without a scorch."

"Because I am scorched all over, Captain Ahab," answered Perth, resting for a moment on his hammer; "I am past scorching; not easily can'st thou scorch a scar."

"Well, well; no more. Thy shrunk voice sounds too calmly, sanely woful to me. In no Paradise myself, I am impatient of all misery in others that is not mad. Thou should'st go mad, blacksmith; say, why dost thou not go mad? How can'st thou endure without being mad? Do the heavens yet hate thee, that thou can'st not go mad?—What wert thou making there?"

"Welding an old pike-head, sir; there were seams and dents in it."

"And can'st thou make it all smooth again, blacksmith, after such hard usage as it had?"

"I think so, Sir."

"And I suppose thou can'st smoothe almost any seams and dents; never mind how hard the metal, blacksmith?"

"Aye, Sir, I think I can; all seams and dents but one."

"Look ye here, then," cried Ahab, passionately advancing, and leaning with both hands on Perth's shoulders; "look ye here—*here*—can ye smoothe out a seam like this, blacksmith," sweeping one hand across his ribbed brow; "if thou could'st, blacksmith, glad enough would I lay my head upon thy anvil, and feel thy heaviest hammer between my eyes. Answer! Can'st thou smoothe this seam?"

"Oh! that is the one, Sir! Said I not all seams and dents but one?"

"Aye, blacksmith, it is the one; aye, man, it is unsmoothable; for though thou only see'st it here in my flesh, it has worked down into the bone of my skull— *that* is all wrinkles! But, away with child's play; no

more gaffs and pikes to-day. Look ye here!" jingling
the leathern bag, as if it were full of gold coins. "I,
too, want a harpoon made; one that a thousand yoke
of fiends could not part, Perth; something that will
stick in a whale like his own fin-bone. There's the stuff,"
flinging the pouch upon the anvil. "Look ye, blacksmith, these are the gathered nail-stubs of the steel
shoes of racing horses."

"Horse-shoe stubs, Sir? Why, Captain Ahab, thou
hast here, then, the best and stubbornest stuff we
blacksmiths ever work."

"I know it, old man; these stubs will weld together
like glue from the melted bones of murderers. Quick!
forge me the harpoon. And forge me first, twelve rods
for its shank; then wind, and twist, and hammer these
twelve together like the yarns and strands of a tow-
line. Quick! I'll blow the fire."

When at last the twelve rods were made, Ahab tried
them one by one, by spiralling them, with his own
hand, round a long, heavy iron bolt. "A flaw!" rejecting
the last one. "Work that over again, Perth."

This done, Perth was about to begin welding the
twelve into one, when Ahab stayed his hand, and said
he would weld his own iron. As, then, with regular,
gasping hems, he hammered on the anvil, Perth passing
to him the glowing rods, one after the other, and the
hard pressed forge shooting up its intense straight
flame, the Parsee passed silently, and bowing over his
head towards the fire, seemed invoking some curse or
some blessing on the toil. But, as Ahab looked up, he
slid aside.

"What's that bunch of lucifers dodging about there
for?" muttered Stubb, looking on from the forecastle.
"That Parsee smells fire like a fusee; and smells of it
himself, like a hot musket's powder-pan."

At last the shank, in one complete rod, received its
final heat; and as Perth, to temper it, plunged it all

hissing into the cask of water near by, the scalding steam shot up into Ahab's bent face.

"Would'st thou brand me, Perth?" wincing for a moment with the pain; "have I been but forging my own branding-iron, then?"

"Pray God, not that; yet I fear something, Captain Ahab. Is not this harpoon for the White Whale?"

"For the white fiend! But now for the barbs; thou must make them thyself, man. Here are my razors— the best of steel; here, and make the barbs sharp as the needle-sleet of the Icy Sea."

For a moment, the old blacksmith eyed the razors as though he would fain not use them.

"Take them, man, I have no need for them; for I now neither shave, sup, nor pray till—but here—to work!"

Fashioned at last into an arrowy shape, and welded by Perth to the shank, the steel soon pointed the end of the iron; and as the blacksmith was about giving the barbs their final heat, prior to tempering them, he cried to Ahab to place the water-cask near.

"No, no—no water for that; I want it of the true death-temper. Ahoy, there! Tashtego, Queequeg, Daggoo! What say ye, pagans! Will ye give me as much blood as will cover this barb?" holding it high up. A cluster of dark nods replied, Yes. Three punctures were made in the heathen flesh, and the White Whale's barbs were then tempered.

"Ego non baptizo te in nomine patris, sed in nomine diaboli!" deliriously howled Ahab, as the malignant iron scorchingly devoured the baptismal blood.

Now, mustering the spare poles from below, and selecting one of hickory, with the bark still investing it, Ahab fitted the end to the socket of the iron. A coil of new tow-line was then unwound, and some fathoms of it taken to the windlass, and stretched to a great tension. Pressing his foot upon it, till the rope hummed like a harp-string, then eagerly bending over it, and seeing no strandings, Ahab exclaimed, "Good! and now for the seizings."

At one extremity the rope was unstranded, and the separate spread yarns were all braided and woven round the socket of the harpoon; the pole was then driven hard up into the socket; from the lower end the rope was traced half way along the pole's length, and firmly secured so, with intertwistings of twine. This done, pole, iron, and rope—like the Three Fates—remained inseparable, and Ahab moodily stalked away with the weapons; the sound of his ivory leg, and the sound of the hickory pole, both hollowly ringing along every plank. But ere he entered his cabin, a light, unnatural, half-bantering, yet most piteous sound was heard. Oh, Pip! thy wretched laugh, thy idle but unresting eye; all thy strange mummeries not unmeaningly blended with the black tragedy of the melancholy ship, and mocked it!

The morning of the third day dawned fair and fresh, and once more the solitary night-man at the fore-mast-head was relieved by crowds of the daylight look-outs, who dotted every mast and almost every spar.

"D'ye see him?" cried Ahab; but the whale was not yet in sight.

"In his infallible wake, though; but follow that wake, that's all. Helm there; steady, as thou goest, and hast been going. What a lovely day again! were it a new-made world, and made for a summer-house to the angels, and this morning the first of its throwing open to them, a fairer day could not dawn upon that world. Here's food for thought, had Ahab time to think; but Ahab never thinks; he only feels, feels, feels; *that's* tingling enough for mortal man! to think's audacity. God only has that right and privilege. Thinking is, or ought to be, a coolness and a calmness; and our poor

hearts throb, and our poor brains beat too much for
that. And yet, I've sometimes thought my brain was
very calm—frozen calm, this old skull cracks so, like
a glass in which the contents turned to ice, and shiver
it. And still this hair is growing now; this moment
growing, and heat must breed it; but no, it's like that
sort of common grass that will grow anywhere, between
the earthy clefts of Greenland ice or in Vesuvius lava.
How the wild winds blow it; they whip it about me as
the torn shreds of split sails lash the tossed ship they
cling to. A vile wind that has no doubt blown ere this
through prison corridors and cells, and wards of hospi-
tals, and ventilated them, and now comes blowing
hither as innocent as fleeces. Out upon it!—it's tainted.
Were I the wind, I'd blow no more on such a wicked,
miserable world. I'd crawl somewhere to a cave, and
slink there. And yet, 'tis a noble and heroic thing, the
wind! who ever conquered it? In every fight it has the
last and bitterest blow. Run tilting at it, and you but
run through it. Ha! a coward wind that strikes stark
naked men, but will not stand to receive a single blow.
Even Ahab is a braver thing—a nobler thing than
that. Would now the wind but had a body; but all the
things that most exasperate and outrage mortal man,
all these things are bodiless, but only bodiless as objects, not as agents. There's a most special, a most cunning, oh, a most malicious difference! And yet, I say
again, and swear it now, that there's something all
glorious and gracious in the wind. These warm Trade
Winds, at least, that in the clear heavens blow straight
on, in strong and steadfast, vigorous mildness; and veer
not from their mark, however the baser currents of
the sea may turn and tack, and mightiest Mississippies
of the land swift and swerve about, uncertain where
to go at last. And by the eternal Poles! these same
Trades that so directly blow my good ship on; these

Trades, or something like them—something so unchangeable, and full as strong, blow my keeled soul
along! To it! Aloft there! Where d'ye see?"

"Nothing, Sir."

"Nothing! and noon at hand! The doubloon goes
a-begging! See the sun! Aye, aye, it must be so. I've
oversailed him. How, got the start? Aye, he's chasing
me now; not I, *him*—that's bad; I might have known
it, too. Fool! the lines—the harpoons he's towing. Aye,
aye. I have run him by last night. About! about! Come
down, all of ye, but the regular look outs! Man the
braces!"

Steering as she had done, the wind had been somewhat on the Pequod's quarter, so that now being
pointed in the reverse direction, the braced ship sailed
hard upon the breeze as she re-churned the cream in
her own white wake.

"Against the wind he now steers for the open jaw,"
murmured Starbuck to himself, as he coiled the new
hauled mainbrace upon the rail. "God keep us, but
already my bones feel damp within me, and from the
inside wet my flesh. I misdoubt me that I disobey my
God in obeying him!"

"Stand by to sway me up!" cried Ahab, advancing
to the hempen basket. "We should meet him soon."

"Aye, aye, Sir," and straightway Starbuck did Ahab's
bidding, and once more Ahab swung on high.

A whole hour now passed; gold-beaten out to ages.
Time itself now held long breaths with keen suspense.
But at last, some three points off the weather bow,
Ahab described the spout again, and instantly from the
three mast-heads three shrieks went up as if the tongues
of fire had voiced it.

"Forehead to forehead I meet thee, this third time,
Moby Dick! On deck there!—brace sharper up; crowd
her into the wind's eye. He's too far off to lower yet,
Mr. Starbuck. The sails shake! Stand over that helms-

man with a top-maul! So, so; he travels fast, and I must
down. But let me have one more good round look aloft
here at the sea; there's time for that. An old, old sight,
and yet somehow so young; aye, and not changed a
wink since I first saw it, a boy, from the sand-hills of
Nantucket! The same!—the same!—the same to Noah
as to me. There's a soft shower to leeward. Such lovely
leewardings! They must lead somewhere—to something
else than common land, more palmy than the palms.
Leeward! the White Whale goes that way; look to
windward, then; the better if the bitterer quarter. But
good bye, good bye, old mast-head! What's this?—
green? aye, tiny mosses in these warped cracks. No
such green weather stains on Ahab's head! There's the
difference now between man's old age and matter's.
But aye, old mast, we both grow old together; sound
in our hulls, though, are we not, my ship? Aye, minus
a leg, that's all. By heaven this dead wood has the
better of my live flesh every way. I can't compare with
it; and I've known some ships made of dead trees out-
last the lives of men made of the most vital stuff of
vital fathers. What's that he said? he should still go
before me, my pilot; and yet to be seen again? But
where? Will I have eyes at the bottom of the sea, sup-
posing I descend those endless stairs? and all night
I've been sailing from him, wherever he did sink to.
Aye, aye, like many more thou told'st direful truth as
touching thyself, O Parsee; but, Ahab, there thy shot
fell short. Good by, mast-head—keep a good eye upon
the whale, the while I'm gone. We'll talk to-morrow,
nay, to-night, when the White Whale lies down there,
tied by head and tail."

He gave the word; and still gazing round him, was
steadily lowered through the cloven blue air to the
deck.

In due time the boats were lowered; but as standing
in his shallop's stern, Ahab just hovered upon the point

of the descent, he waved to the mate,—who held one of the tackle-ropes on deck—and bade him pause.

"Starbuck!"

"Sir?"

"For the third time my soul's ship starts upon this voyage, Starbuck."

"Aye, Sir, thou wilt have it so."

"Some ships sail from their ports, and ever afterwards are missing, Starbuck!"

"Truth, Sir: saddest truth."

"Some men die at ebb tide; some at low water; some at the full of the flood;—and I feel now like a billow that's all one crested comb, Starbuck. I am old;—shake hands with me, man."

Their hands met; their eyes fastened; Starbuck's tears the glue.

"Oh, my captain, my captain!—noble heart—go not —go not!—see, it's a brave man that weeps; how great the agony of the persuasion then!"

"Lower away!"—cried Ahab, tossing the mate's arm from him. "Stand by the crew!"

In an instant the boat was pulling round close under the stern.

"The sharks! the sharks!" cried a voice from the low cabin-window there; "O master, my master, come back!"

But Ahab heard nothing; for his own voice was high-lifted then; and the boat leaped on.

Yet the voice spake true; for scarce had he pushed from the ship, when numbers of sharks, seemingly rising from out the dark waters beneath the hull, maliciously snapped at the blades of the oars, every time they dipped in the water; and in this way accompanied the boat with their bites. It is a thing not uncommonly happening to the whale-boats in those swarming seas; the sharks at times apparently following them in the same prescient way that vultures hover over the ban-ners of marching regiments in the east. But these were the first sharks that had been observed by the Pequod since the White Whale had been descried; and whether it was that Ahab's crew were all such tiger-yellow barbarians, and therefore their flesh more musky to the senses of the sharks—a matter sometimes well known to affect them,—however it was, they seemed to follow that one boat without molesting the others.

"Heart of wrought steel!" murmured Starbuck gazing over the side, and following with his eyes the receding boat—"canst thou yet ring boldly to that sight? —lowering thy keel among ravening sharks, and followed by them, open-mouthed to the chase; and this the critical third day?—For when three days flow together in one continuous intense pursuit; be sure the first is the morning, the second the noon, and the third the evening and the end of that thing—be that end what it may. Oh! my God! what is this that shoots through me, and leaves me so deadly calm, yet expectant,—fixed at the top of a shudder! Future things swim before me, as in empty outlines and skeletons; all the past is somehow grown dim. Mary, girl! thou fadest in pale glories behind me; boy! I seem to see but thy eyes grown wondrous blue. Strangest problems of life seem clearing; but clouds sweep between—Is my journey's end coming? My legs feel faint; like his who has footed it all day. Feel thy heart,—beats it yet?—Stir thyself, Starbuck!—stave it off—move, move! speak aloud!— Mast-head there! See ye my boy's hand on the hill?— Crazed;—aloft there!—keep thy keenest eye upon the boats:—mark well the whale!—Ho! again!—drive off that hawk! see! he pecks—he tears the vane"—pointing to the red flag flying at the main-truck—"Ha! he soars away with it!—Where's the old man now? see'st though that sight, oh Ahab!—shudder, shudder!"

The boats had not gone very far, when by a signal from the mast-heads—a downward pointed arm, Ahab knew that the whale had sounded; but intending to be near him at the next rising, he held on his way a little sideways from the vessel; the becharmed crew maintaining the profoundest silence, as the head-beat waves hammered and hammered against the opposing bow.

"Drive, drive in your nails, oh ye waves! to their uttermost heads drive them in! ye but strike a thing without a lid; and no coffin and no hearse can be mine: —and hemp only can kill me! Ha! ha!"

Suddenly the waters around them slowly swelled in broad circles; then quickly upheaved, as if sideways sliding from a submerged berg of ice, swiftly rising to the surface. A low rumbling sound was heard; a subterraneous hum; and then all held their breaths; as bedraggled with trailing ropes, and harpoons, and lances, a vast form shot lengthwise, but obliquely from the sea. Shrouded in a thin drooping veil of mist, it hovered for a moment in the rainbowed air; and then fell swamping back into the deep. Crushed thirty feet upwards, the waters flashed for an instant like heaps of fountains, then brokenly sank in a shower of flakes, leaving the circling surface creamed like new milk round the marble trunk of the whale.

"Give way!" cried Ahab to the oarsmen, and the boats darted forward to the attack; but maddened by yesterday's fresh irons that corroded in him, Moby Dick seemed combinedly possessed by all the angels that fell from heaven. The wide tiers of welded tendons overspreading his broad white forehead, beneath the transparent skin, looked knitted together; as head on, he came churning his tail among the boats; and once more flailed them apart; spilling out the irons and lances from the two mates' boats, and dashing in one side of the upper part of their bows, but leaving Ahab's almost without a scar.

While Daggoo and Queequeg were stopping the

strained planks; and as the whale swimming out from
them, turned, and showed one entire flank as he shot
by them again; at that moment a quick cry went up.
Lashed round and round to the fish's back; pinioned
in the turns upon turns in which, during the past night,
the whale had reeled the involutions of the lines around
him, the half torn body of the Parsee was seen; his
sable raiment frayed to shreds; his distended eyes
turned full upon old Ahab.

The harpoon dropped from his hand.

"Befooled, befooled!"—drawing in a long lean breath
—"Aye, Parsee! I see thee again.—Aye, and thou goest
before; and this, *this* then is the hearse that thou didst
promise. But I hold thee to the last letter of thy word.
Where is the second hearse? Away, mates, to the ship!
those boats are useless now; repair them if ye can in
time, and return to me; if not, Ahab is enough to die
—Down, men! the first thing that but offers to jump
from this boat I stand in, that thing I harpoon. Ye are
not other men, but my arms and my legs; and so obey
me.—Where's the whale? gone down again?"

But he looked too nigh the boat; for as if bent upon
escaping with the corpse he bore, and as if the particular place of the last encounter had been but a stage
in his leeward voyage, Moby Dick was now again
steadily swimming forward; and had almost passed the
ship,—which thus far had been sailing in the contrary
direction to him, though for the present her headway
had been stopped. He seemed swimming with his utmost velocity, and now only intent upon pursuing his
own straight path in the sea.

"Oh! Ahab," cried Starbuck, "not too late is it, even
now, the third day, to desist. See! Moby Dick seeks
thee not. It is thou, thou, that madly seekest him!"

Setting sail to the rising wind, the lonely boat was
swiftly impelled to leeward, by both oars and canvas.
And at last when Ahab was sliding by the vessel, so

near as plainly to distinguish Starbuck's face as he leaned over the rail, he hailed him to turn the vessel about, and follow him, not too swiftly, at a judicious interval. Glancing upwards, he saw Tashtego, Queequeg, and Daggoo, eagerly mounting to the three mastheads; while the oarsmen were rocking in the two staved boats which had but just been hoisted to the side, and were busily at work in repairing them. One after the other, through the portholes, as he sped, he also caught flying glimpses of Stubb and Flask, busying themselves on deck among bundles of new irons and lances. As he saw all this; as he heard the hammers in the broken boats; far other hammers seemed driving a nail into his heart. But he rallied. And now marking that the vane or flag was gone from the main-masthead, he shouted to Tashtego, who had just gained that perch, to descend again for another flag, and a hammer and nails, and so nail it to the mast.

Whether fagged by the three days' running chase, and the resistance to his swimming in the knotted hamper he bore; or whether it was some latent deceitfulness and malice in him: whichever was true, the White Whale's way now began to abate, as it seemed, from the boat so rapidly nearing him once more; though indeed the whale's last start had not been so long a one as before. And still as Ahab glided over the waves the unpitying sharks accompanied him; and so pertinaciously stuck to the boat; and so continually bit at the plying oars, that the blades became jagged and crunched, and left small splinters in the sea, at almost every dip.

"Heed them not! those teeth but give new rowlocks to your oars. Pull on! 'tis the better rest, the shark's jaw than the yielding water."

"But at every bite, Sir, the thin blades grow smaller and smaller!"

"They will last long enough! pull on!—But who can

tell"—he muttered—"whether these sharks swim to feast on the whale or on Ahab?—But pull on! Aye, all alive, now—we near him. The helm! take the helm; let me pass,"—and so saying, two of the oarsmen helped him forward to the bows of the still flying boat.

At length as the craft was cast to one side, and ran ranging along with the White Whale's flank, he seemed strangely oblivious of its advance—as the whale sometimes will—and Ahab was fairly within the smoky mountain mist, which, thrown off from the whale's spout, curled round his great, Monadnock hump; he was even thus close to him; when, with body arched back, and both arms lengthwise high-lifted to the poise, he darted his fierce iron, and his far fiercer curse into the hated whale. As both steel and curse sank to the socket, as if sucked into a morass, Moby Dick sideways writhed; spasmodically rolled his nigh flank against the bow, and, without staving a hole in it, so suddenly canted the boat over, that had it not been for the elevated part of the gunwale to which he then clung, Ahab would once more have been tossed into the sea. As it was, three of the oarsmen—who foreknew not the precise instant of the dart, and were therefore unprepared for its effects—these were flung out; but so fell, that, in an instant two of them clutched the gunwale again, and rising to its level on a combing wave, hurled themselves bodily inboard again; the third man helplessly dropping astern, but still afloat and swimming.

Almost simultaneously, with a mighty volition of ungraduated, instantaneous swiftness, the White Whale darted through the weltering sea. But when Ahab cried out to the steersman to take new turns with the line, and hold it so; and commanded the crew to turn round on their seats, and tow the boat up to the mark; the moment the treacherous line felt that double strain and tug, it snapped in the empty air!

"What breaks in me? Some sinew cracks!—'tis whole again; oars! oars! Burst in upon him!"

Hearing the tremendous rush of the sea-crashing boat, the whale wheeled round to present his blank forehead at bay; but in that evolution, catching sight of the nearing black hull of the ship; seemingly seeing in it the source of all his persecutions; bethinking it—it may be—a larger and nobler foe; of a sudden, he bore down upon its advancing prow, smiting his jaws amid fiery showers of foam.

Ahab staggered; his hand smote his forehead. "I grow blind; hands! stretch out before me that I may yet grope my way. Is't night?"

"The whale! The ship!" cried the cringing oarsmen.

"Oars! oars! Slope downwards to thy depths, O sea, that ere it be for ever too late, Ahab may slide this last, last time upon his mark! I see: the ship! the ship! Dash on, my men! Will ye not save my ship?"

But as the oarsmen violently forced their boat through the sledge-hammering seas, the before whale-smitten bow-ends of two planks burst through, and in an instant almost, the temporarily disabled boat lay nearly level with the waves; its half-wading, splashing crew, trying hard to stop the gap and bale out the pouring water.

Meantime, for that one beholding instant, Tashtego's mast-head hammer remained suspended in his hand; and the red flag, half-wrapping him as with a plaid, then streamed itself straight out from him, as his own forward-flowing heart; while Starbuck and Stubb, standing upon the bowsprit beneath, caught sight of the down-coming monster just as soon as he.

"The whale, the whale! Up helm, up helm! Oh, all ye sweet powers of air, now hug me close! Let not Starbuck die, if die he must, in a woman's fainting fit. Up helm, I say—ye fools, the jaw! the jaw! Is this the end of all my bursting prayers? all my life-long fidelities? Oh, Ahab, Ahab, lo, thy work. Steady! helmsman, steady. Nay, nay! Up helm again! He turns to meet us! Oh, his unappeasable brow drives on towards one, whose duty tells him he cannot depart. My God, stand by me now!"

"Stand not by me, but stand under me, whoever you are that will now help Stubb; for Stubb, too, sticks here. I grin at thee, thou grinning whale! Who ever helped Stubb, or kept Stubb awake, but Stubb's own unwinking eye? And now poor Stubb goes to bed upon a mattress that is all too soft; would it were stuffed with brushwood! I grin at thee, thou grinning whale! Look ye, sun, moon, and stars! I call ye assassins of as good a fellow as ever spouted up his ghost. For all that, I would yet ring glasses with ye, would ye but hand the cup! Oh, oh! oh, oh! thou grinning whale, but there'll be plenty of gulping soon! Why fly ye not, O Ahab! For me, off shoes and jacket to it; let Stubb die in his drawers! A most mouldy and over salted death, though;—cherries! cherries! cherries! Oh, Flask, for one red cherry ere we die!"

"Cherries? I only wish that we were where they grow. Oh, Stubb, I hope my poor mother's drawn my part-pay ere this; if not, few coppers will now come to her, for the voyage is up."

From the ship's bows, nearly all the seamen now hung inactive; hammers, bits of plank, lances, and harpoons, mechanically retained in their hands, just as they had darted from their various employments; all their enchanted eyes intent upon the whale, which from side to side strangely vibrating his predestinating head, sent a broad band of overspreading semicircular foam before him as he rushed. Retribution, swift vengeance, eternal malice were in his whole aspect, and spite of all that mortal man could do, the solid white buttress of his forehead smote the ship's starboard bow, till men and timbers reeled. Some fell flat upon their

faces. Like dislodged trucks, the heads of the harpooners aloft shook on their bull-like necks. Through the
breach, they heard the waters pour, as mountain torrents down a flume.

"The ship! The hearse!—the second hearse!" cried
Ahab from the boat; "its wood could only be American!"

Diving beneath the settling ship, the whale ran quivering along its keel; but turning under water, swiftly
shot to the surface again, far off the other bow, but
within a few yards of Ahab's boat, where, for a time,
he lay quiescent.

"I turn my body from the sun. What ho, Tashtego!
let me hear thy hammer. Oh! ye three unsurrendered
spires of mine; thou uncracked keel; and only god-
bullied hull; thou firm deck, and haughty helm, and
Pole-pointed prow,—death-glorious ship! must ye then
perish, and without me? Am I cut off from the last
fond pride of meanest shipwrecked captains? Oh, lonely
death on lonely life! Oh, now I feel my topmost greatness lies in my topmost grief. Ho, ho! from all your
furthest bounds, pour ye now in, ye bold billows of
my whole foregone life, and top this one piled comber
of my death! Towards thee I roll, thou all-destroying
but unconquering whale; to the last I grapple with
thee; from hell's heart I stab at thee; for hate's sake I
spit my last breath at thee. Sink all coffins and all
hearses to one common pool! and since neither can be
mine, let me then tow to pieces, while still chasing thee,
though tied to thee, thou damned whale! *Thus,* I give
up the spear!"

The harpoon was darted; the stricken whale flew
forward; with igniting velocity the line ran through the
groove;—ran foul. Ahab stooped to clear it; he did clear
it; but the flying turn caught him round the neck, and
voicelessly as Turkish mutes bowstring their victim,
he was shot out of the boat, ere the crew knew he was

gone. Next instant, the heavy eye-splice in the rope's final end flew out of the stark-empty tub, knocked down an oarsman, and smiting the sea, disappeared in its depths.

For an instant, the tranced boat's crew stood still; then turned, "The ship? Great God, where is the ship?" Soon they through dim, bewildering mediums saw her sidelong fading phantom, as in the gaseous Fata Morgana; only the uppermost masts out of water; while fixed by infatuation, or fidelity, or fate, to their once lofty perches, the pagan harpooners still maintained their sinking look-outs on the sea. And now, concentric circles seized the lone boat itself, and all its crew, and each floating oar, and every lance-pole, and spinning, animate and inanimate, all round and round in one vortex, carried the smallest chip of the Pequod out of sight.

But as the last whelmings intermixingly poured themselves over the sunken head of the Indian at the mainmast, leaving a few inches of the erect spar yet visible, together with long streaming yards of the flag, which calmly undulated, with ironical coincidings, over the destroying billows they almost touched;—at that instant, a red arm and a hammer hovered backwardly uplifted in the open air, in the act of nailing the flag faster and yet faster to the subsiding spar. A sky-hawk that tauntingly had followed the main-truck downwards from its natural home among the stars, pecking at the flag, and incommoding Tashtego there; this bird now chanced to intercept its broad fluttering wing between the hammer and the wood; and simultaneously feeling that ethereal thrill, the submerged savage beneath, in his death-gasp, kept his hammer frozen there; and so the bird of heaven, with archangelic shrieks, and his imperial beak thrust upwards, and his whole captive form folded in the flag of Ahab, went down with his ship, which, like Satan would not sink to hell till she had dragged a living part of heaven along with her, and helmeted herself with it.

Now small fowls flew screaming over the yet yawning gulf; a sullen white surf beat against its steep sides; then all collapsed, and the great shroud of the sea rolled on as it rolled five thousand years ago.

PART THREE

The Romance of the Past

ROMANTIC HELLENISM

. . . doze
Upon the flowers thro' which Ilissus
flows.

—Walter Savage Landor

Beautiful Nature, Beautiful Greeks

[FROM *On Simple and Sentimental Poetry*]

FRIEDRICH SCHILLER

1795

If we think of that beautiful nature which surrounded the ancient Greeks, if we remember how intimately that people, under its blessed sky, could live with that free nature; how their mode of imagining, and of feeling, and their manners, approached far nearer than ours to the simplicity of nature, how faithfully the works of their poets express this; we must necessarily remark, as a strange fact, that so few traces are met among them of that *sentimental* interest that we moderns ever take in the scenes of nature and in natural characters. I admit that the Greeks are superiorly exact and faithful in their descriptions of nature. They reproduce their details with care, but we see that they take no more interest in them and no more heart in them than in describing a vestment, a shield, armour, a piece of furniture, or any production of the mechanical arts. In their love for the object it seems that they make no difference between what exists in itself and what owes its existence to art, to the human will. It seems that nature interests their minds and their curiosity more than moral feeling. They do not attach themselves to it with that depth of feeling, with that gentle melancholy, that characterise the moderns. Nay, more, by personifying nature in its particular phenomena, by deifying it, by representing its effects as the acts of free being, they take from it that character of calm necessity which is precisely what makes it so attractive to us. Their impatient imagination only traverses nature to pass beyond it to the drama of human life. It only takes pleasure in the spectacle of what is living and free; it requires characters, acts, the accidents of fortune and of manners; and whilst it happens with *us*, at least in certain moral dispositions, to curse our prerogative, this free will, which exposes us to so many combats with ourselves, to so many anxieties and errors, and to wish to exchange it for the condition of beings destitute of reason, for that fatal existence that no longer admits of any choice, but which is so calm in its uniformity,—while we do this, the Greeks, on the contrary, only have their imagination occupied in retracing human nature in the inanimate world, and in giving to the will an influence where blind necessity rules.

Whence can arise this difference between the spirit of the ancients and the modern spirit? How comes it that, being, for all that relates to nature, incomparably below the ancients, we are superior to them precisely on this point, that we render a more complete homage to nature; that we have a closer attachment to it; and that we are capable of embracing even the inanimate world with the most ardent sensibility? It is because nature, in our time, is no longer in man, and that we no longer encounter it in its primitive truth, except out of humanity, in the inanimate world. It is not because we are more *conformable to nature*—quite the contrary; it is because in our social relations, in our mode of existence, in our manners, we are in *opposition with nature*. This is what leads us, when the instinct of truth and of simplicity is awakened—this instinct which, like the moral aptitude from which it proceeds, lives incorruptible and indelible in every human heart—to procure for it in the physical world the satisfaction which there is no hope of finding in the moral order. This is the reason why the feeling that attaches us to nature is connected so closely with that which makes us regret our infancy, for ever flown, and our primitive innocence. Our childhood is all that remains of nature in humanity, such as civilisation has made it, of untouched, unmutilated nature. It is, therefore, not wonderful, when we meet out of us the impress of nature, that we are always brought back to the idea of our childhood. . . .

It is in the fundamental idea of poetry that the poet is everywhere the *guardian* of nature. When he can no longer entirely fill this part, and has already in himself suffered the deleterious influence of arbitrary and factitious forms, or has had to struggle against this influence, he presents himself as the *witness* of nature and as its avenger. The poet will, therefore, be the *expression* of nature itself, or his part will be to *seek* it, if men have lost sight of it. Hence arise two kinds of poetry, which embrace and exhaust the entire field of poetry. All poets—I mean those who are really so—will belong, according to the time when they flourish, according to the accidental circumstances that have influenced their education generally, and the different dispositions of mind through which they pass, will belong, I say, to the order of the *sentimental* poetry or to *simple* poetry.

As long as man dwells in a state of pure nature (I mean pure and not coarse nature), all his being acts at once like a simple sensuous unity, like a harmonious whole. The senses and reason, the receptive faculty and the spontaneously active faculty, have not been as yet separated in their respective faculty and the spontaneously active faculty, have not been as yet separated in their respective functions: *à fortiori* they are not yet in contradiction with each other. Then the feelings of man are not the formless play of chance; nor are his thoughts an empty play of the imagination, without any value. His feelings proceed from the law of necessity; his *thoughts* from *reality*. But when man enters the state of civilisation, and art has fashioned him, this *sensuous* harmony which was in him disappears, and henceforth he can only manifest himself as a *moral unity*, that is, as aspiring to unity. The harmony that existed as a *fact* in the former state, the harmony of feeling and thought, only exists now in an *ideal* state. It is no longer in him, but out of him; it is a conception of thought which he must begin by realising in himself; it is no longer a fact, a reality of his life. Well, now let us take the idea of poetry, which is nothing else than *expressing humanity as completely as possible,* and let us apply this idea to these two states. We shall be brought to infer that, on the one hand, in the state of natural simplicity, when all the faculties of man are exerted together, his being still manifests itself in a harmonious unity, where, consequently, the *totality* of his nature expresses itself in reality itself, the part of the *poet* is necessarily to imitate the real as completely as is possible. In the state of civilisation, on the contrary, when this harmonious competition of the whole of human nature is no longer anything but an idea, the part of the poet is necessarily to raise reality to the ideal, or what amounts to the same thing, *to represent the ideal.* And, actually, these are the only two ways in which, in general, the poetic genius can manifest itself. Their great difference is quite evident, but though there be great opposition between them, a higher idea exists that embraces both, and there is no cause to be astonished if this idea coincides with the very idea of humanity.

This is not the place to pursue this thought any further, as it would require a separate discussion to place it in its full light. But if we only compare the modern and ancient poets together, not according to the accidental forms which they may have employed, but according to their spirit, we shall be easily convinced of the truth of this thought. The thing that touches us in the ancient poets is nature; it is the truth of sense, it is a present and a living reality: modern poets touch us through the medium of ideas.

Trans. anon. (London: Bohn Library, 1875).

Venus in the House

[FROM *Crotchet Castle*]

THOMAS LOVE PEACOCK

1831

MR. CROTCHET: Sir, ancient sculpture is the true school of modesty. But where the Greeks had modesty, we have cant; where they had poetry, we have cant; where they had patriotism, we have cant; where they had any thing that exalts, delights, or adorns humanity, we have nothing but cant, cant, cant. And, sir, to show my contempt for cant in all its shapes, I have adorned my house with the Greek Venus, in all her shapes, and am ready to fight her battle, against all the societies that ever were instituted for the suppression of truth and beauty.

THE REVEREND DOCTOR FOLLIOTT: My dear sir, I am afraid you are growing warm. Pray be cool. Nothing contributed so much to good digestion as to be perfectly cool after dinner.

CROTCHET: Sir, the Lacedaemonian virgins wrestled naked with young men; and they grew up, as the wise Lycurgus had foreseen, into the most modest of women, and the most exemplary of wives and mothers.

FOLLIOTT: Very likely, sir; but the Athenian virgins did no such thing, and they grew up into wives who stayed at home,—stayed at home, sir; and looked after the husband's dinner,—his dinner, sir, you will please to observe.

CROTCHET: And what was the consequence of that, sir? that they were such very insipid persons that the husband would not go home to eat his dinner, but preferred the company of some Aspasia, or Lais.

FOLLIOTT: Two very different persons, sir, give me leave to remark.

CROTCHET: Very likely, sir; but both too good to be married in Athens.

FOLLIOTT: Sir, Lais was a Corinthian.

CROTCHET: 'Od's vengeance, sir, some Aspasia and any other Athenian name of the same sort of person you like—

FOLLIOTT: I do not like the sort of person at all: the sort of person I like, as I have already implied, is a modest woman, who stays at home and looks after her husband's dinner.

CROTCHET: Well, sir, that was not the taste of the Athenians. They preferred the society of women who would not have made any scruple about sitting as models to Praxiteles; as you know, sir, very modest women in Italy did to Canova: one of whom, an Italian countess, being asked by an English lady, "how she could bear it?" answered, "Very well; there was a good fire in the room."

FOLLIOTT: Sir, the English lady should have asked how the Italian lady's husband could bear it. The phials of my wrath would overflow if poor dear Mrs. Folliott—sir, in return for your story, I will tell you a story of my ancestor, Gilbert Folliott. The devil haunted him, as he did Saint Francis, in the likeness of a beautiful damsel; but all he could get from the exemplary Gilbert was an admonition to wear a stomacher and longer petticoats.

CROTCHET: Sir, your story makes for my side of the question. It proves that the devil, in the likeness of a fair damsel, with short petticoats and no stomacher, was almost too much for Gilbert Folliott. The force of the spell was in the drapery.

FOLLIOTT: Bless my soul, sir!

CROTCHET: Give me leave, sir. Diderot—

FOLLIOTT: Who was he, sir?

CROTCHET: Who was he, sir? the sublime philosopher, the father of the encyclopaedia, of all the encyclopaedias that have ever been printed.

FOLLIOTT: Bless me, sir, a terrible progeny! they belong to the tribe of *Incubi*.

CROTCHET: The great philosopher, Diderot,—

FOLLIOTT: Sir, Diderot is not a man after my heart. Keep to the Greeks, if you please; albeit this Sleeping Venus is not an antique.

CROTCHET: Well, sir, the Greeks: why do we call the Elgin marbles inestimable? Simply because they are true to nature. And why are they so superior in that point to all modern works, with all our greater knowledge of anatomy? Why, sir, but because the Greeks, having no cant, had better opportunities of studying models?

FOLLIOTT: Sir, I deny our greater knowledge of anatomy. But I shall take the liberty to employ, on this oc-

casion, the *argumentum ad hominem.* Would you have allowed Miss Crotchet to sit for a model to Canova?
CROTCHET: Yes, sir.

"God bless my soul, sir!" exclaimed the Reverend Doctor Folliott, throwing himself back into a chair, and flinging up his heels, with the premeditated design of giving emphasis to his exclamation: but by miscalculating his *impetus,* he overbalanced his chair, and laid himself on the carpet in a right angle, of which his back was the base.

Mignon's Song

[FROM *Wilhelm Meister's Apprenticeship*]

JOHANN WOLFGANG VON GOETHE

1783

Know you that country where the lemons grow,
Where oranges among the dark leaves glow?
The blue sky breeds a wind both soft and bland,
There lofty bay-tree and the laurel stand.
Know you this well?
       There, oh there
Would I with you, my sweet beloved, fare!

Know you that house? On pillars rests the dome.
The hallway shines: we're dazzled by each room.
Statues of marble look us through and through:
My lonesome child, what have they done to you?
Know you this well?
       There, oh there
Would I with you, my sweet protector, fare!

Know you the mountain and its cloudy trail?
The mist-bound mule-driver seeks his path to scale.
Deep in the grotto dwells the dragon's brood.
The cliff falls sharp, and from it pours the flood.
Know you this well?
        There, oh there
Lies our goal. Here, father, must we fare!

Trans. H. E. H.

Hyperion's Song of Fate

FRIEDRICH HÖLDERLIN

1798

You wander above in the light
  On tender ground, O holiest of spirits!
    Glittering god-given breezes
     Move you lightly,
      As her fingers, the artist's,
       Pluck holy strings.

Fateless, sleeping like a
  Nurseling, breathe those heavenly ones;
    Chastely kept
     In modest buds,
      Their souls
       Are ever-blooming,
        And their blessed eyes
         Gaze out so quietly
         On clear eternity.

But we have the fortune
  Never to stay in one place,

We vanish, we topple,
   We, suffering mankind,
      Blindly, from one
         Hour to the next,
            Tossed like water from one cliff
               To yet another cliff,
                  Yearlong down to depths deep in
                     doubt.

Trans. H. E. H.

Ode on a Grecian Urn

JOHN KEATS

1819

Thou still unravish'd bride of quietness,
   Thou foster-child of silence and slow time,
Sylvan historian, who canst thus express
   A flowery tale more sweetly than our rhyme:
What leaf-fring'd legend haunts about thy shape
   Of deities or mortals, or of both,
      In Tempe or the dales of Arcady?
What men or gods are these? What maidens loth?
   What mad pursuit? What struggle to escape?
      What pipes and timbrels? What wild ecstasy?

Heard melodies are sweet, but those unheard
   Are sweeter; therefore, ye soft pipes, play on;
Not to the sensual ear, but, more endear'd,
   Pipe to the spirit ditties of no tone:
Fair youth, beneath the trees, thou canst not leave
   Thy song, nor ever can those trees be bare;
      Bold Lover, never, never canst thou kiss,

Though winning near the goal—yet, do not grieve;
　　She cannot fade, though thou hast not thy bliss,
　　　For ever wilt thou love, and she be fair!

Ah, happy, happy boughs! that cannot shed
　　Your leaves, nor ever bid the Spring adieu;
And, happy melodist, unwearied,
　　For ever piping songs for ever new;
More happy love! more happy, happy love!
　　For ever warm and still to be enjoy'd,
　　　For ever panting, and for ever young;
All breathing human passion far above,
　　That leaves a heart high-sorrowful and cloy'd,
　　　A burning forehead, and a parching tongue.

Who are these coming to the sacrifice?
　　To what green altar, O mysterious priest,
Lead'st thou that heifer lowing at the skies,
　　And all her silken flanks with garlands drest?
What little town by river or sea shore,
　　Or mountain-built with peaceful citadel,
　　　Is emptied of its folk, this pious morn?
And, little town, thy streets for evermore
　　Will silent be: and not a soul to tell
　　　Why thou are desolate, can e'er return.

O Attic shape! Fair attitude! with brede
　　Of marble men and maidens overwrought,
With forest branches and the trodden weed;
　　Thou, silent form, dost tease us out of thought
As doth eternity: Cold Pastoral!
　　When old age shall this generation waste,
　　　Thou shalt remain, in midst of other woe
Than ours, a friend to man, to whom thou say'st,
　　"Beauty is truth, truth beauty"—that is all
　　　Ye know on earth, and all ye need to know.

The Isles of Greece

[FROM *Don Juan*]

GEORGE GORDON,
LORD BYRON

1821

The isles of Greece! the isles of Greece
    Where burning Sappho loved and sung,
Where grew the arts of war and peace,
    Where Delos rose, and Phoebus sprung!
Eternal summer gilds them yet,
But all, except their sun, is set.

The Scian and the Teian muse,
    The hero's harp, the lover's lute,
Have found the fame your shores refuse
    Their place of birth alone is mute
To sounds which echo further west
Than your sires' "Islands of the Blest."

The mountains look on Marathon—
    And Marathon looks on the sea;
And musing there an hour alone,
    I dream'd that Greece might still be free;
For standing on the Persians' grave,
I could not deem myself a slave.

A king sate on the rocky brow
    Which looks o'er sea-born Salamis;
And ships, by thousands, lay below,
    And men in nations;—all were his!

He counted them at break of day—
And when the sun set, where were they?

And where are they? and where art thou,
    My country? On thy voiceless shore
The heroic lay is tuneless now—
    The heroic bosom beats no more!
And must thy lyre, so long divine,
Degenerate into hands like mine?

'Tis something in the dearth of fame,
    Though link'd among a fetter'd race,
To feel at least a patriot's shame,
    Even as I sing, suffuse my face;
For what is left the poet here?
For Greeks a blush—for Greece a tear.

Must *we* but weep o'er days more blest?
    Must *we* but blush?—Our fathers bled.
Earth! render back from out thy breast
    A remnant of our Spartan dead!
Of the three hundred grant but three,
Tc make a new Thermopylae!

What, silent still? and silent all?
    Ah! no;—the voices of the dead
Sound like a distant torrent's fall,
    And answer, "Let one living head,
    But one, arise,—we come, we come!"
'Tis but the living who are dumb.

In vain—in vain: strike other chords;
    Fill high the cup with Samian wine!
Leave battles to the Turkish hordes,
    And shed the blood of Scio's vine!
Hark! rising to the ignoble call—
How answers each bold Bacchanal!

You have the Pyrrhic dance as yet;
   Where is the Pyrrhic phalanx gone?
Of two such lessons, why forget
   The nobler and the manlier one?
You have the letters Cadmus gave—
Think ye he meant them for a slave?

Fill high the bowl with Samian wine!
   We will not think of themes like these!
It made Anacreon's song divine:
   He served—but served Polycrates—
A tyrant; but our masters then
Were still, at least, our countrymen.

The tyrant of the Chersonese
   Was freedom's best and bravest friend;
That tyrant was Miltiades!
   O that the present hour would lend
Another despot of the kind!
Such chains as his were sure to bind.

Fill high the bowl with Samian wine!
   On Suli's rock, and Parga's shore,
Exists the remnant of a line
   Such as the Doric mothers bore;
And there, perhaps, some seed is sown,
The Heracleidan blood might own.

Trust not for freedom to the Franks—
   They have a king who buys and sells;
In native swords and native ranks
   The only hope of courage dwells:
But Turkish force and Latin fraud
Would break your shield, however broad.

Fill high the bowl with Samian wine!
   Our virgins dance beneath the shade—

I see their glorious black eyes shine;
   But gazing on each glowing maid,
My own the burning tear-drop laves,
To think such breasts must suckle slaves.

Place me on Sunium's marbled steep,
   Where nothing, save the waves and I,
May hear our mutual murmurs sweep;
   There, swan-like, let me sing and die:
A land of slaves shall ne'er be mine—
Dash down yon cup of Samian wine!

The World's Great Age Begins Anew

[FROM *Hellas*]

PERCY BYSSHE SHELLEY

1821

CHORUS

The world's great age begins anew,
   The golden years return,
The earth doth like a snake renew
   Her winter weeds outworn:
Heaven smiles, and faiths and empires gleam,
Like wrecks of a dissolving dream.

A brighter Hellas rears its mountains
   From waves serener far;
A new Penëus rolls his fountains
   Against the morning star.
Where fairer Tempes bloom, there sleep
Young Cyclads on a sunnier deep.

A loftier Argo cleaves the main,
 Fraught with a later prize;
Another Orpheus sings again,
 And loves, and weeps, and dies.
A new Ulysses leaves once more
Calypso for his native shore.

Oh, write no more the tale of Troy,
 If earth Death's scroll must be!
Nor mix with Laian rage the joy
 Which dawns upon the free:
Although a subtler Sphinx renew
Riddles of death Thebes never knew.

Another Athens shall arise,
 And to remoter time
Bequeath, like sunset to the skies,
 The splendour of its prime;
And leave, if nought so bright may live,
All earth can take or Heaven can give.

Saturn and Love their long repose
 Shall burst, more bright and good
Than all who fell, than One who rose,
 Than many unsubdued:
Not gold, not blood, their altar dowers,
But votive tears and symbol flowers.

Oh, cease! must hate and death return?
 Cease! must men kill and die?
Cease! drain not to its dregs the urn
 Of bitter prophecy.
The world is weary of the past,
Oh, might it die or rest at last!

Hellenism:
The Ideal versus the Reality

[FROM *Recollections of the Last Days of Shelley and Byron*]

E. J. TRELAWNEY

[SHELLEY IN 1822]

When I was at Leghorn with Shelley, I drew him towards the docks, saying,

"As we have a spare hour let's see if we can't put a girdle round the earth in forty minutes. In these docks are living specimens of all the nationalities of the world; thus we can go round it, and visit and examine any particular nation we like, observing their peculiar habits, manners, dress, language, food, productions, arts, and naval architecture; for see how varied are the shapes, build, rigging, and decorations of the different vessels. There lies an English cutter, a French *chasse-marée*, an American clipper, a Spanish *tartan*, an Austrian *trabacolo*, a Genoese *felucca*, a Sardinian *zebeck*, a Neopolitan brig, a Sicilian *sparanza*, a Dutch *galleot*, a Danish *snow*, a Russian *hermaphrodite*, a Turkish *sackalever*, a Greek *bombard*. I don't see a Persian *dow*, an Arab *grab*, or a Chinese *junk*; but there are enough for our purpose and to spare. As you are writing a poem, 'Hellas,' about the modern Greeks, would it not be as well to take a look at them amidst all the din of the docks? I hear their shrill nasal voices, and should like to know if you can trace in the language or lineaments of these Greeks of the nineteenth century, A.D., the faintest resemblance to the lofty and sublime spirits who lived in the fourth century, B.C. An English merchant who has dealings with them, told me he thought these modern Greeks were, if judged by their actions, a cross between the Jews and gypsies; —but here comes the Capitano Zarita; I know him."

So dragging Shelley with me I introduced him, and asking to see the vessel, we crossed the plank from the quay and stood on the deck of the *San Spiridione* in the midst of her chattering irascible crew. They took little heed of the skipper, for in these trading vessels each individual of the crew is part owner, and has some share in the cargo; so they are all interested in the speculation—having no wages. They squatted about the decks in small knots, shrieking, gesticulating, smoking, eating, and gambling like savages.

"Does this realize your idea of Hellenism, Shelley?" I said.

"No! But it does of Hell," he replied.

The captain insisted on giving us pipes and coffee in his cabin, so I dragged Shelley down. Over the rudder-head facing us, there was a gilt box enshrining a flaming gaudy daub of a saint, with a lamp burning before it; this was *Il Padre Santo Spiridione*, the ship's godfather. The skipper crossed himself and squatted on the dirty divan. Shelley talked to him about the Greek revolution that was taking place, but from its interrupting trade the captain was opposed to it.

"Come away!" said Shelley. "There is not a drop of the old Hellenic blood here. These are not the men to rekindle the ancient Greek fire; their souls are extinguished by traffic and superstition. Come away!"—and away we went.

"It is but a step," I said, "from these ruins of worn-out Greece to the New World; let's board the American clipper."

"I had rather not have any more of my hopes and illusions mocked by sad realities," said Shelley.

THE
NORTHERN BARBARIANS

. . . the gravity and solemnity of a Celtic hero.

—Hugh Blair

The Descent of Odin

AN ODE. FROM THE NORSE TONGUE

THOMAS GRAY

1768

Uprose the king of men with speed,
And saddled straight his coal-black steed;
Down the yawning steep he rode,
That leads to Hela's drear abode.
Him the Dog of Darkness spied,
His shaggy throat he open'd wide,
While from his jaws, with carnage fill'd,
Foam and human gore distill'd:
Hoarse he bays with hideous din,
Eyes that glow, and fangs that grin;
And long pursues, with fruitless yell,
The father of the powerful spell.
Onward still his way he takes,
(The groaning earth beneath him shakes),

Till full before his fearless eyes
The portals nine of hell arise.
  Right against the eastern gate,
By the moss-grown pile he sate;
Where long of yore to sleep was laid
The dust of the prophetic maid.
Facing to the northern clime,
Thrice he trac'd the runic rhyme;
Thrice pronounc'd, in accents dread,
The thrilling verse that wakes the dead;
Till from out the hollow ground
Slowly breath'd a sullen sound.

PROPHETESS

What call unknown, what charms presume
To break the quiet of the tomb?
Who thus afflicts my troubled sprite,
And drags me from the realms of night?
Long on these mold'ring bones have beat
The winter's snow, the summer's heat,
The drenching dews, and driving rain!
Let me, let me sleep again.
Who is he, with voice unblest,
That calls me from the bed of rest?

ODIN

A traveller, to thee unknown,
Is he that calls, a warrior's son.
Thou the deeds of light shalt know;
Tell me what is done below,
For whom yon glitt'ring board is spread,
Drest for whom yon golden bed.

PROPHETESS

Mantling in the goblet see
The pure bev'rage of the bee,

O'er it hangs the shield of gold;
'Tis the drink of Balder bold:
Balder's head to death is giv'n.
Pain can reach the sons of Heav'n!
Unwilling I my lips unclose:
Leave me, leave me to repose.

ODIN

Once again my call obey.
Prophetess, arise, and say,
What dangers Odin's child await,
Who the author of his fate.

PROPHETESS

In Hoder's hand the hero's doom:
His brother sends him to the tomb.
Now my weary lips I close:
Leave me, leave me to repose.

ODIN

Prophetess, my spell obey,
Once again arise, and say,
Who th' avenger of his guilt,
By whom shall Hoder's blood be spilt.

PROPHETESS

In the caverns of the west,
By Odin's fierce embrace comprest,
A wondrous boy shall Rinda bear,
Who ne'er shall comb his raven hair,
Nor wash his visage in the stream,
Nor see the sun's departing beam;
Till he on Hoder's corse shall smile
Flaming on the fun'ral pile.
Now my weary lips I close:
Leave me, leave me to repose.

ODIN

Yet a while my call obey.
Prophetess, awake, and say,
What virgins these, in speechless woe,
That bend to earth their solemn brow,
That their flaxen tresses tear,
And snowy veils, that float in air.
Tell me, whence their sorrows rose:
Then I leave thee to repose.

PROPHETESS

Ha! no traveller art thou;
King of men, I know thee now,
Mightiest of a mighty line—

ODIN

No boding maid of skill divine
Art thou, nor prophetess of good;
But mother of 'the giant brood!

PROPHETESS

Hie thee hence, and boast at home,
That never shall enquirer come
To break my iron-sleep again;
Till Lok has burst his tenfold chain.
Never, till substantial Night
Has reassum'd her ancient right;
Till wrapp'd in flames, in ruin hurl'd,
Sinks the fabric of the world.

Melancholy Warriors

[FROM Ossian's *Fingal*]

JAMES MACPHERSON

1762

On Cromla's resounding side, Connal spoke to the chief of the noble car. "Why that gloom, son of Semo? Our friends are the mighty in fight. Renowned art thou, O warrior! many were the deaths of thy steel. Often has Bragela met, with blue-rolling eyes of joy, often has she met her hero, returning in the midst of the valiant; when his sword was red with slaughter; when his foes were silent in the fields of the tomb. Pleasant to her ears were thy bards, when thy deeds arose in song.

"But behold the king of Morven! He moves, below, like a pillar of fire. His strength is like the stream of Lubar, or the wind of the echoing Cromla; when the branchy forests of night are torn from all their rocks! Happy are thy people, O Fingal! thine arm shall finish their wars. Thou art the first in their dangers; the wisest in the days of their peace. Thou speakest, and thy thousands obey; armies tremble at the sound of thy steel. Happy are thy people, O Fingal! king of resounding Selma! Who is that so dark and terrible coming in the thunder of his course? who but Starno's son to meet the king of Morven? Behold the battle of the chiefs! It is the storm of the ocean, when two spirits meet far distant, and contend for the rolling of waves. The hunter hears the noise on his hill. He sees the high billows advancing to Ardven's shore!"

Such were the words of Connal when the heroes met in fight. There was the clang of arms! their every blow like the hundred hammers of the furnace! Terrible is the battle of the kings; dreadful the look of their eyes. Their dark-brown shields are cleft in twain. Their steel flies, broken, from their helms, They fling their weapons down. Each rushes to his hero's grasp: their sinewy arms bend round each other: they turn from side to side, and strain and stretch their large spreading limbs below. But when the pride of their strength arose, they shook the hill with their heels. Rocks tumble from their places on high; the green-headed bushes are over-turned. At length the strength of Swaran fell; the king of the groves is bound. Thus have I seen on Cona; but Cona I behold no more! thus have I seen two dark hills, removed from their place, by the strength of the bursting stream. They turn from side to side in their fall; their tall oaks meet one another on high. Then they tumble together with all their rocks and trees. The streams are turned by their side. The red ruin is seen afar.

"Sons of distant Morven," said Fingal, "guard the king of Lochlin! he is strong as his thousand waves. His hand is taught to war. His race is of the times of old. Gaul, thou first of my heroes; Ossian, king of songs, attend. He is the friend of Agandecca; raise to joy his grief. But, Oscar, Fillan, and Ryno, ye children of the race! pursue Lochlin over Lena; that no vessel may hereafter bound on the dark-rolling waves of Inistore!"

They flew sudden across the heath. He slowly moved, like a cloud of thunder, when the sultry plain of sum-mer is silent and dark; his sword is before him as a sunbeam; terrible as the streaming meteor of night. He came toward a chief of Lochlin. He spoke to the son of the wave. "Who is that so dark and sad, at the rock of the roaring stream? He cannot bound over its course. How stately is the chief! his bossy shield is on his side; his spear like the tree of the desert! Youth of the dark-red hair, art thou of the foes of Fingal?"

"I am a son of Lochlin," he cries; "strong is my arm in war. My spouse is weeping at home. Orla shall never return!" "Or fights or yields the hero?" said Fingal of the noble deeds. "Foes do not conquer in my presence: my friends are renowned in the hall. Son of the wave, follow me, partake the feast of my shells: pursue the deer of my desert: be thou the friend of Fingal." "No," said the hero; "I assist the feeble. My strength is with the weak in arms. My sword has been always unmatched, O warrior! let the king of Morven yield!" "I never yielded, Orla! Fingal never yielded to man. Draw thy sword and choose thy foe. Many are my heroes!"

"Does then the king refuse the fight?" said Orla of the dark-brown shield. "Fingal is a match for Orla; and he alone of all his race! But, king of Morven, if I shall fall; as one time the warrior must die; raise my tomb in the midst: let it be the greatest on Lena. Send, over the dark-blue wave, the sword of Orla to the spouse of his love; that she may show it to her son, with tears, to kindle his soul to war." "Son of the mournful tale," said Fingal, "why dost thou awaken my tears? One day the warriors must die, and the children see their useless arms in the hall. But, Orla! thy tomb shall rise. Thy white-bosomed spouse shall weep over thy sword."

They fought on the heath of Lena. Feeble was the arm of Orla. The sword of Fingal descended, and cleft his shield in twain. It fell and glittered on the ground, as the moon on the ruffled stream. "King of Morven," said the hero, "lift thy sword and pierce my breast. Wounded and faint from battle, my friends have left me here. The mournful tale shall come to my love on the banks of the streamy Lota; when she is alone in the wood; and the rustling blast in the leaves!"

"No!" said the king of Morven, "I will never wound

thee, Orla. On the banks of Lota let her see thee, escaped from the hands of war. Let thy grey-haired father, who, perhaps, is blind with age; let him hear the sound of thy voice, and brighten within his hall. With joy let the hero rise, and search for his son with his hands!" "But never will he find him, Fingal," said the youth of the streamy Lota. "On Lena's heath I must die; foreign bards shall talk of me. My broad belt covers my wound of death. I give it to the wind!"

The dark blood poured from his side; he fell pale on the heath of Lena. Fingal bent over him as he died, and called his younger chiefs. "Oscar and Fillan, my sons, raise high the memory of Orla. Here let the dark-haired hero rest, far from the spouse of his love. Here let him rest in his narrow house, far from the sound of Lota. The feeble will find his bow at home; but will not be able to bend it. His faithful dogs howl on his hills; his boars, which he used to pursue, rejoice. Fallen is the arms of battle! the mighty among the valiant is low! Exalt the voice, and blow the horn, ye sons of the king of Morven! Let us go back to Swaran, to send the night away on song. Fillan, Oscar, and Ryno, fly over the heath of Lena. Where, Ryno, art thou, young son of fame? Thou art not wont to be the last to answer thy father's voice!"

"Ryno," said Ullin, first of bards, "is with the awful forms of his fathers. With Trathal, king of shields; with Trenmor of mighty deeds. The youth is low, the youth is pale; he lies on Lena's heath!" "Fell the swiftest in the race," said the king, "the first to bend the bow? Thou scarce hast been known to me! why did young Ryno fall? But sleep thou softly on Lena; Fingal shall soon behold thee. Soon shall my voice be heard no more, and my footsteps cease to be seen. The bards will tell of Fingal's name. The stones will talk of me. But, Ryno, thou art low indeed! thou hast not received thy fame. Ullin, strike the harp for Ryno; tell what the chief would have been. Farewell, thou first in every field! No more shall I direct thy dart; Thou that hast been so fair! I behold thee not. Farewell." The tear is on the cheek of the king, for terrible was his son in war. His son! that was like a beam of fire by night on a hill; when the forests sink down in its course, and the traveller trembles at the sound! But the winds drive it beyond the steep. It sinks from sight, and darkness prevails.

"Whose fame is in that dark-green tomb?" begun the king of generous shells; "four stones with their heads of moss stand there! They mark the narrow house of death. Near it let Ryno rest. A neighbour to the brave let him lie. Some chief of fame is here, to fly, with my son, on clouds. O Ullin, raise the songs of old. Awake their memory in their tomb. If in the field they never fled, my son shall rest by their side. He shall rest, far distant from Morven, on Lena's resounding plains!"

Ossian Supersedes Homer

[FROM *The Sorrows of Young Werther*]

JOHANN WOLFGANG VON GOETHE

1774

October 12, 1771

Ossian has superseded Homer in my heart. What a world into which that magnificent poet carries me! To wander over the heath, blown about by the winds, which conjure up by the feeble light of the moon the spirits of our ancestors; to hear from the mountaintops, mid the roar of the rivers, their plaintive groans coming from deep caverns; and the laments of the maiden who sighs and perishes on the moss-covered, grass-grown tomb of the warrior who loved her. I meet the gray bard as he wanders on the heath seeking the footsteps of his fathers; alas! he finds only their tombstones. Then, turning to the pale moon, as it sinks beneath the waves of the rolling sea, the memory of past ages stirs in the soul of the hero—days when the friendly light shone upon the brave warriors and their bark laden with spoils, returning in triumph. When I read the deep sorrow in his countenance, see his dying glory sink exhausted into the grave, as he draws new and heart-thrilling delight from the impotent shades of his beloved ones, casting a look on the cold earth and the tall grass, exclaiming, "The traveler will come— will come who has seen my beauty, and will ask, 'Where is the bard—the illustrious son of Fingal?' He will pass over my tomb, and seek me in vain!"—O friend, I would, like a true and noble knight, draw my sword, and deliver my lord from the long and painful languor of a living death, and dismiss my own soul to follow the demigod whom my hand had set free!

December 25, 1771

"Have you brought nothing to read?" Charlotte enquired. He had nothing. "There in my drawer," she continued, "is your own translation of some of the songs of Ossian. I have not read them yet, I always hoped to hear you recite them; but it never seemed possible to arrange it." He smiled, and fetched the manuscript. A tremor ran through him as he took it in his hand, and his eyes were filled with tears as he looked at it. He sat down and read.

"Star of descending night! fair is thy light in the west! thou liftest thy unshorn head from thy cloud; thy steps are stately on thy hill. What dost thou behold in the plain? The stormy winds are laid. The murmur of the torrent comes from afar. Roaring waves climb the distant rock. The flies of evening are on their feeble wings; the hum of their course is on the field. What dost thou behold, fair light? But thou dost smile and depart. Thy waves come with joy around thee; they bathe thy lovely hair. Farewell, thou silent beam! Let the light of Ossian's soul arise!

"And it does arise in its strength! I behold my departed friends. Their gathering is on Lora, as in the days of other years. Fingal comes like a watery column of mist! his heroes are around; and see the bards of song—gray-haired Ullin! stately Ryno. Alpin with the tuneful voice! the soft complaint of Minona! How are ye changed, my friends, since the days of Selma's feast, when we contended, like gales of spring as they fly along the hill, and bend by turns the feebly whistling grass!

"Minona came forth in her beauty, with downcast look and tearful eye. Her hair flew slowly on the blast that rushed unfrequent from the hill. The souls of the heroes were sad when she raised the tuneful voice. Often had they seen the grave of Salgar, the dark dwelling of white-bosomed Colma. Colma left alone on the hill, with all her voice of song! Salgar promised to come; but the night descended around. Hear the voice of Colma, when she sat alone on the hill!

"*Colma:* It is night; I am alone, forlorn on the hill of storms. The wind is heard on the mountain. The torrent is howling down the rock. No hut receives me from the rain; forlorn on the hill of winds!

"Rise, moon, from behind thy clouds! Stars of the night, arise! Lead me, some light, to the place where my love rests from the chase alone! His bow near him unstrung, his dogs panting around him! But here I must sit alone by the rock of the mossy stream. The stream and the wind roar aloud. I hear not the voice of my love! Why delays my Salgar; why the chief of the hill his promise? Here is the rock, and here the tree; hère is the roaring stream! Thou didst promise with night to be here. Ah, whither is my Salgar gone? With thee I would fly from my father, with thee from my brother of pride. Our race have long been foes: we are not foes, O Salgar!

"Cease a little while, O wind! stream, be thou silent awhile! Let my voice be heard around; let my wanderer hear me! Salgar! it is Colma who calls. Here is the tree and the rock. Salgar, my love, I am here! Why delayest thou thy coming? Lo! the calm moon comes forth. The flood is bright in the vale; the rocks are gray on the steep. I see him not on the brow. His dogs come not before him with tidings of his near approach. Here I must sit alone!

"Who lie on the heath beside me? Are they my love and my brother? Speak to me, O my friends! To Colma they give no reply. Speak to me: I am alone! My soul is tormented with fears. Ah, they are dead! Their swords are red from the fight. Oh, my brother! my brother! why hast thou slain my Salgar? Why, O Salgar! hast thou slain my brother? Dear were ye both to me! what shall I say in your praise? Thou wert fair on the hill among thousands! he was terrible in fight! Speak to me! hear my voice! hear me, sons of my love! They are silent, silent forever! Cold, cold, are their breasts of clay! Oh, from the rock on the hill, from the top of the windy steep, speak, ye ghosts of the dead! Speak, I will not be afraid! Whither are ye gone to rest? In what cave of the hill shall I find the departed? No feeble voice is on the gale: no answer half drowned in the storm!

"I sit in my grief: I wait for morning in my tears! Rear the tomb, ye friends of the dead. Close it not till Colma comes. My life flies away like a dream. Why should I stay behind? Here shall I rest with my friends, by the stream of the sounding rock. When night comes

on the hill—when the loud winds arise, my ghost shall
stand in the blast, and mourn the death of my friends.
The hunter shall hear from his booth; he shall fear,
but love my voice! For sweet shall my voice be for my
friends: pleasant were her friends to Colma.

"Such was thy song, Minona, softly blushing daughter
of Torman. Our tears descended for Colma, and our
souls were sad! Ullin came with his harp; he gave the
song of Alpin. The voice of Alpin was pleasant; the
soul of Ryno was a beam of fire! But they had rested in
the narrow house; their voice had ceased in Selma!
Ullin had returned one day from the chase before the
heroes fell. He heard their strife on the hill; their song
was soft, but sad! They mourned the fall of Morar, first
of mortal men! His soul was like the soul of Fingal; his
sword like the sword of Oscar. But he fell, and his
father mourned; his sister's eyes were full of tears. Minona's eyes were full of tears, the sister of car-borne
Morar. She retired from the song of Ullin, like the moon
in the west, when she foresees the shower, and hides
her fair head in a cloud. I touched the harp with Ullin;
the song of mourning rose! . . ."

A torrent of tears which streamed from Charlotte's
eyes, and gave relief to her oppressed heart, stopped
Werther's reading. He threw down the sheets, seized
her hand, and wept bitterly. Charlotte leaned upon her
other arm, and buried her face in her handkerchief;
both were terribly agitated. They felt their own fate
in the misfortunes of Ossian's heroes—felt this together,
and merged their tears. Werther's eyes and lips
burned on Charlotte's arm; she trembled, she wished
to go, but grief and pity lay like a leaden weight upon
her. She took a deep breath, recovered herself, and
begged Werther, sobbing, to continue—implored him
with the very voice of Heaven! He trembled, his heart
ready to burst; then taking up the sheets again, he
read in a broken voice: "Why dost thou awake me, O

breath of Spring, thou dost woo me and say, 'I cover thee with the drops of heaven'? But the time of my fading is near, the blast that shall scatter my leaves. Tomorrow shall the traveller come; he that saw me in my beauty shall come. His eyes will search the field, but they will not find me."

The whole force of these words fell upon the unfortunate Werther. In deepest despair, he threw himself at Charlotte's feet, seized her hands, and pressed them to his eyes and to his forehead. An apprehension of his terrible plan seemed to strike her. Her thoughts were confused: she held his hands, pressed them to her bosom; and turning toward him with the tenderest expression, her burning cheek touched his. They lost sight of everything. The world vanished before them. He clasped her in his arms tightly, and covered her trembling, stammering lips with furious kisses. "Werther!" she cried with choking voice, turning away. "Werther!" and, with a feeble hand, pushed him from her. And again, more composed and from the depth of her heart, she repeated, "Werther!"

Trans. Victor Lange (New York: Rinehart & Co., 1949).

Mynstrelles Songe

THOMAS CHATTERTON

1777

O! synge untoe mie roundelaie,
O! droppe the brynie teare wythe mee,
Daunce ne moe atte hallie daie,
Lycke a reynynge ryver bee;
    Mie love ys dedde,

Gon to hys death-bedde,
Al under the wyllowe tree.

Blacke hys cryne as the wyntere nyghte,
Whyte hys rode as the sommer snowe,
Rodde hys face as the mornynge lyghte;
Cale he lyes ynne the grave belowe;
    Mie love ys dedde,
    Gon to hys deathe-bedde,
    Al under the wyllowe tree.

Swote hys tyngue as the throstles note,
Quycke ynn daunce as thoughte canne bee,
Defte hys taboure, codgelle stote;
O! hee lyes bie the wyllowe tree:
    Mie love ys dedde,
    Gon to hys deathe-bedde,
    Alle underre the wyllowe tree.

Harke! the ravenne flappes hys wygne,
In the briered delle belowe;
Harke! the dethe-owle loude dothe synge,
To the nyghte-mares as heie goe;
    Mie love ys dedde,
    Gon to hys deathe-bedde,
    Al under the wyllowe tree.

See! the whyte moone sheenes onne hie;
Whyterre ys mie true loves shroude;
Whyterre yanne the mornynge skie,
Whyterre yanne the evenynge cloude;
    Mie love ys dedde,
    Gon to hys deathe-bedde,
    Al under the wyllowe tree.

Heere, uponne mie true loves grave,
Schalle the baren fleurs be layde,

Nee one hallie Seyncte to save
Al the celness of a mayde.
    Mie love ys dedde,
    Gon to hys deathe-bedde,
    Alle under the wyllowe tree.

Wythe mie hondes I'lle dente the brieres
Rounde his hallie corse to gre,
Ouphante fairie, lyghte youre fyres,
Heere mie boddie stylle schalle bee.
    Mie love ys dedde,
    Gon to hys deathe-bedde,
    Al under the wyllowe tree.

Comme, wythe acorne-coppe and thorne,
Drayne mie hartys blodde awaie;
Lyfe and all yttes goode I scorne,
Daunce bie nete, or feaste by daie.
    Mie love ys dedde,
    Gon to hys deathe-bedde,
    Al under the wyllowe tree.

Waterre wytches, crownede wythe reytes,
Bere mee to yer leathalle tyde.
I die; I comme; mie true love waytes.
Thos the damselle spake, and dyed.

THE GOTHIC REVIVAL,
OR THE HAUNTED CASTLE

True views on Mediaevalism, Time
alone will bring.

—W. S. Gilbert

This Truly Christian Epoch

[FROM *Christendom or Europe: A Fragment*]

NOVALIS

(FRIEDRICH VON HARDENBERG)

1799

Fine, splendid times there were when Europe was
one Christian country, when one Christendom inhabited this civilized continent; a large, common interest
linked together the farthest provinces of this huge
spiritual empire. One sovereign guided and united the
great political forces without owning great secular possessions. An enormous guild to which all had access
lay immediately beneath him and strove eagerly to
consolidate his benevolent might. Every member of
this company was universally honored; and if the com-
moners sought comfort or help, protection or advice

336

from him while gladly, generously tendering to his assorted needs, such a man in turn earned protection, respect, and the right of audience from his superiors; and all men took care of these elect, wonderfully equipped and endowed souls as if they were children of heaven, whose very presence and affection bestowed manifold blessings. Men were bound to their utterances by a childish trust. Mankind could peacefully pursue its daily occupations on the earth, for these holy men guaranteed the future, forgave all sins, obliterated and transformed all life's discolorations. They were experienced pilots on huge uncharted seas in whose keeping mankind could count all storms but as naught and be certain of making a safe arrival and landing on the coasts of its true fatherland.

The wildest and most voracious desires paled before the respect and obedience preached by their words. From them peace flowed. They preached nothing save love for our holy, beautiful Lady of Christendom, who, endowed with divine power, was ready to redeem every believer from the most terrible of dangers. They spoke of holy men long dead who through their fidelity and devotion to the blessed Mother and her heavenly, lovely Child had resisted earthly temptation, had subsequently attained to divine honor, and were now protective, benevolent forces for their living brethren, willing helpers in their need, advocates for human transgressions and effective friends to mankind before the throne of Heaven. With what serenity did men then come forth from beautiful congregations in mystery-filled churches, decorated with heart-warming images, filled with sweet fragrance and enlivened by holy, exalted music. In them were gratefully preserved the consecrated remains of former God-fearing men, in precious containers. And through glorious signs and wonders, the divine beneficence and omnipotence, the gracious power of these blessed pure souls was revealed. Thus do lovers guard a lock of hair or letters from their dead sweethearts and nourish their sweet passion until death reunites them. With intense care, everything that had belonged to these beloved souls was collected together, and anyone who owned or even touched so comforting a relic held himself fortunate. Now and then divine grace seems to have descended upon some particular image or tomb. Thence from all over flocked men with beautiful offerings to carry away with them complimentary gifts: peace of mind and health of body. Assiduously did this powerful, peace-loving society seek to make all mankind partner to this beautiful faith, and it sent forth its ambassadors to all the continents on the globe to proclaim everywhere the Gospel of Life and to make the Kingdom of Heaven the sole kingdom in this world. The wise sovereign of the Church rightly resisted presumptuous developments of human potentialities at the price of religious sensibility, as well as any untimely and dangerous discoveries in the area of knowledge. Thus he forbade the public assertion by daring thinkers that the earth was merely an insignificant planet; for he well understood that if men lost respect for their residence and their earthly home, they would also lose respect for their heavenly abode and their own race; they would prefer finite knowledge to infinite faith and accustom themselves to despise everything great and awe-inspiring, seeing such things merely as the dead offshoots of scientific law. All the wise and revered men of Europe gathered at his court. Hither flowed all treasures, destroyed Jerusalem was avenged and Rome itself became Jerusalem, the sacred seat of divine government on earth. Princes submitted their quarrels to the father of Christendom, willingly laid they their crowns and their majesties at his feet; indeed they felt it to their glory to spend the evening of their lives as members of this lofty guild, meditating divinity within lonely monastery walls. How benevolent and how appropriate was this government and institution to man's inner nature is demonstrated by the powerful upsurge of all other human forces, the harmonious development of all capabilities, the vast height attained by single individuals in all areas of the arts and sciences in existence, and by the flourishing trade in spiritual and physical goods in all parts of Europe and as far as the distant Indies.

Such were the chief outlines of this truly Catholic and Christian epoch. But men were neither sufficiently mature nor educated for this magnificent kingdom. It was a first love that perished beneath the pressure of commercial life, a love whose recollection was driven away by self-centered cares, whose bond was later condemned as a fraud and an illusion to be sentenced in the light of subsequent experiences, then forever destroyed by a large multitude of Europeans. This great inner schism, accompanied as it was by devastating wars, was a noteworthy sign of what culture can do to spiritual sensitivity, or at least of the temporary injury of culture at a certain degree. This eternal awareness cannot be destroyed, but it can be dimmed, paralyzed, and put aside by other elements. An aged society diminishes men's inclinations, their pride in their race, and accustoms them to divert all their thoughts and deeds toward attaining their creature-comforts; their needs and their methods of satisfying them become more complicated; avaricious man has so much time to acquaint himself with these arts and to attain proficiency in their exercise, that no time remains for quiet recollection, for the attentive contemplation of the inner world. Present concerns seem to lie closer to him when cases of conflict arise, and thus the beautiful buds of his youth, faith and love, wilt and give way to tough fruits, knowledge and possession. In late autumn men recall spring as a childish dream and with childish simplicity hope that the full granaries will last so forever. A certain degree of loneliness seems necessary for the cultivation of deeper insight, and therefore many a sacred seed is suffocated by the mass of men, and the gods are frightened away, fleeing the restless tumult of worldly distractions and the negotiation of petty affairs. Furthermore, are we not surely dealing with periods and epochs that have been cyclic, where opposite tendencies have alternated? Is it not their very essence to wax and to wane, to be impermanent; and is not also a resurrection, a rejuvenation in novel and vital form surely to be expected from them? Progressive and ever-expanding evolutions on an ever-larger scale are the material of history.

Trans. H. E. H.

"Those Venerable Cathedrals"

[FROM *The Genius of Christianity*]

FRANÇOIS RENÉ,
VICOMTE DE CHATEAUBRIAND

1802

It is even curious to remark how readily the poets and novelists of this infidel age, by a natural return toward the manners of our ancestors, introduce dungeons, spectres, castles, and Gothic churches, into their fictions,—so great is the charm of recollections associated with religion and the history of our country. Nations do not throw aside their ancient customs as people do their

old clothes. Some part of them may be discarded; but
there will remain a portion, which with the new manners will form a very strange mixture.

In vain would you build Grecian temples, ever so
elegant and well lighted, for the purpose of assembling
the *good people* of St. Louis and Queen Blanche, and
making them adore a *metaphysical God;* they would
still regret those *Notre Dames* of Rheims and Paris—
those venerable cathedrals, overgrown with moss, full
of generations of the dead and the ashes of their forefathers; they would still regret the tombs of those
heroes, the Montmorencys, on which they loved to
kneel during mass; to say nothing of the sacred fonts
to which they were carried at their birth. The reason
is that all these things are essentially interwoven
with their manners; that a monument is not venerable,
unless a long history of the past be, as it were, inscribed beneath its vaulted canopy, black with age.
For this reason, also, there is nothing marvellous in a
temple whose erection we have witnessed, whose echoes
and whose domes were formed before our eyes. God
is the eternal law; his origin, and whatever relates
to his worship, ought to be enveloped in the night of
time.

You could not enter a Gothic church without feeling
a kind of awe and a vague sentiment of the Divinity.
You were all at once carried back to those times when
a fraternity of cenobites, after having meditated in
the woods of their monasteries, met to prostrate themselves before the altar and to chant the praises of the
Lord, amid the tranquillity and the silence of night.
Ancient France seemed to revive altogether; you beheld all those singular costumes, all that nation so different from what it is at present; you were reminded of
its revolutions, its productions, and its arts. The more
remote were these times the more magical they ap-

peared, the more they inspired ideas which always end with a reflection on the nothingness of man and the rapidity of life. . . .

Every thing in a Gothic church reminds you of the labyrinths of a wood; every thing excites a feeling of religious awe, of mystery, and of the Divinity.

The two lofty· towers erected at the entrance of the edifice overtop the elms and yew trees of the churchyard, and produce the most picturesque effect on the azure of heaven. Sometimes their twin heads are illumined by the first rays of dawn; at others they appear crowned with a capital of clouds or magnified in a foggy atmosphere. The birds themselves seem to make a mistake in regard to them, and to take them for the trees of the forests; they hover over their summits, and perch upon their pinnacles. But, lo! confused noises suddenly issue from the top of these towers and scare away the affrighted birds. The Christian architect, not content with building forests, has been desirous to retain their murmurs; and, by means of the organ and of bells, he has attached to the Gothic temple the very winds and thunders that roar in the recesses of the woods. Past ages, conjured up by these religious sounds, raise their venerable voices from the bosom of the stones, and are heard in every corner of the vast cathedral. The sanctuary re-echoes like the cavern of the ancient Sibyl; loud-tonged bells swing over your head, while the vaults of death under your feet are profoundly silent.

Trans. C. I. White (Baltimore: J. Murphy and Company, 1862).

A Terrifying Castle

HORACE WALPOLE

[FROM THE *Letters*]

TO WILLIAM COLE

March 9, 1765

I had time but to write a short note with the "Castle of Otranto," as your messenger called upon me at four o'clock, as I was going to dine abroad. Your partiality to me and Strawberry have, I hope, inclined you to excuse the wildness of the story . . . Shall I confess to you, what was the origin of this romance! I waked one morning, in the beginning of last June, from a dream, of which, all I could recover was, that I had thought myself in an ancient castle (a very natural dream for a head filled like mine with Gothic story), and that on the uppermost bannister of a great staircase I saw a gigantic hand in armour. In the evening I sat down, and began to write, without knowing in the least what I intended to say or relate. . . . I was so engrossed with my tale, which I completed in less than two months, that one evening, I wrote from the time I had drunk my tea, about six o'clock, till half an hour after one in the morning, when my hand and fingers were so weary, that I could not hold the pen to finish the sentence, but left Matilda and Isabella talking, in the middle of a paragraph . . .

[FROM *The Castle of Otranto*]

1764

[*The story concerns a curse on the house of Manfred, Prince of Otranto. Hippolita is his wife, whom he wishes to divorce to marry Isabella; Matilda is his daughter, whom he later unwittingly kills.*]

Matilda waited on her mother to enjoy the freshness of the evening on the ramparts of the castle.

Soon as the company were dispersed their several ways, *Frederic,* quitting his chamber, inquired if *Hippolita* was alone, and was told by one of her attendants, who had not noticed her going forth, that, at that hour, she generally withdrew to her oratory, where he probably would find her. The Marquis, during the repast, had beheld *Matilda* with increase of passion. He now wished to find *Hippolita* in the disposition her Lord had promised. The portents that had alarmed him were forgotten in his desires. Stealing softly and unobserved to the apartment of *Hippolita,* he entered it with a resolution to encourage her acquiescence to the divorce, having perceived that *Manfred* was resolved to make the possession of *Isabella* an unalterable condition, before he would grant *Matilda* to his wishes.

The Marquis was not surprized at the silence that reigned in the Princess's apartment. Concluding her, as he had been advertized, in her oratory, he passed on. The door was ajar; the evening gloomy and overcast. Pushing open the door gently, he saw a person kneeling before the altar. As he approached nearer, it seemed not a woman, but one in a long woolen weed, whose back was towards him. The person seemed absorbed in prayer. The Marquis was about to return, when the figure, rising, stood some moments fixed in meditation, without regarding him. The Marquis, expecting the holy person to come forth, and meaning to excuse his uncivil interruption, said, Reverend father, I sought the Lady *Hippolita.*—*Hippolita!* replied a hollow voice; camest thou to this castle to seek *Hippolita?* and then the figure, turning slowly round, discovered to *Frederic* the fleshless jaws and empty sockets of a skeleton, wrapt in a hermit's cowl. Angels of grace, protect me! cried *Frederic,* recoiling. Deserve their protection! said the Spectre. *Frederic,* falling on his knees, adjured the Phantom to take pity on him. Dost thou not remember me? said the apparition: Remember the wood of *Joppa!*—Art thou that holy Hermit? cried *Frederic,* trembling; Can I do aught for thy eternal peace?—Wast thou delivered from bondage, said the spectre, to pursue carnal delights?—Hast thou forgotten the buried sabre, and the behest of Heaven engraven on it?—I have not, I have not, said *Frederic;* but say, blest spirit, what is thy errand to me?—what remains to be done?—To forget *Matilda!* said the apparition—and vanished.

Frederic's blood froze in his veins. For some minutes he remained motionless. Then, falling prostrate on his face before the altar he besought the intercession of every saint for pardon. A flood of tears succeeded to this transport; and the image of the beauteous *Matilda,* rushing, in spite of him, on his thoughts, he lay on the ground in a conflict of penitence and passion. Ere he could recover from this agony of his spirits, the Princess *Hippolita,* with a taper in her hand, entered the oratory alone. Seeing a man, without motion, on the floor, she gave a shriek, concluding him dead. Her fright brought *Frederic* to himself. Rising suddenly, his face bedewed with tears, he would have rushed from her presence; but *Hippolita,* stopping him, conjured him, in the most plaintive accents, to explain the cause of his disorder, and by what strange chance she had found him there in that posture. Ah! virtuous Princess, said the Marquis, penetrated with grief—and stopped. For the love of Heaven, my Lord, said *Hippolita,* disclose the cause of this transport! what mean these doleful sounds, this alarming exclamation on my name? What woes has Heaven still in store for the wretched *Hippolita?*—Yet silent!—By every

pitying angel, I adjure thee, noble Prince, continued
she, falling at his feet, to disclose the purport of what
lies at thy heart—I see thou feelest for me; thou feelest
the sharp pangs that thou inflictest—speak, for pity!—
does aught thou knowest concern my child?—I cannot
speak, cried *Frederic,* bursting from her—Oh! *Matilda!*

More Terror

[FROM "Prefatory Memoir to the Novels of
Mrs. Ann Radcliffe"]

SIR WALTER SCOTT

1824

The species of romance which Mrs. Radcliffe introduced bears nearly the same relation to the novel that
the modern anomaly entitled a Melo-drame does to the
proper drama. It does not appeal to the judgment by
deep delineations of human feeling, or stir the passions
by scenes of deep pathos, or awaken the fancy by
tracing out, with spirit and vivacity, the lighter traces
of life and manners, or excite mirth by strong represen-
tations of the ludicrous or humorous. In other words, it
attains its interest neither by the path of comedy nor
of tragedy; and yet it has, notwithstanding, a deep,
decided, and powerful effect, gained by means independent of both—by an appeal, in one word, to the
passion of fear, whether excited by natural dangers, or
by the suggestions of superstition. The force, therefore, of the production, lies in the delineation of external incident, while the characters of the agents, like
the figures in many landscapes, are entirely subordinate to the scenes in which they are placed; and are

only distinguished by such outlines as make them seem appropriate to the rocks and trees, which have been the artist's principal objects. The persons introduced,— and here also the correspondence holds betwixt the melo-drame and such romances as *The Mysteries of Udolpho,*—bear the features, not of individuals, but of the class to which they belong. A dark and tyrannical count; an aged crone of a housekeeper, the depositary of many a family legend; a garrulous waiting-maid; a gay and light-hearted valet; a villain or two of all work; and a heroine, fulfilled with all perfections, and subjected to all manner of hazards, form the stock-in-trade of a romancer or a melo-dramatist; and if these personages be dressed in the proper costume, and converse in language sufficiently appropriate to their stations and qualities, it is not expected that the audience shall shake their sides at the humour of the dialogue, or weep over its pathos.

The materials of these celebrated romances, and the means employed in conducting the narrative, are all selected with a view to the author's primary object, of moving the reader by ideas of impending danger, hidden guilt, supernatural visitings,—by all that is terrible, in short, combined with much that is wonderful. For this purpose, her scenery is generally as gloomy as her tale, and her personages are those at whose frown that gloom grows darker. She has uniformly selected the south of Europe for her place of action, whose passions, like the weeds of the climate, are supposed to attain portentous growth under the fostering sun; which abounds with ruined monuments of antiquity, as well as the more massive remnants of the middle ages, and where feudal tyranny and catholic superstition still continue to exercise their sway over the slave and bigot, and to indulge to the haughty lord, or more haughty priest, that sort of despotic power, the exercise of which seldom fails to deprave the heart, and disorder the judgment. These circumstances are skilfully selected, to give probability to events which could not, without great violation of truth, be represented as having taken place in England. Yet, even with the allowances which we make for foreign minds and manners, the unterminating succession of misfortunes which press upon the heroine, strikes us as unnatural. She is continually struggling with the tide of adversity, and hurried downwards by its torrent; and if any more gay description is occasionally introduced, it is only as a contrast, not a relief, to the melancholy and gloomy tenor of the narrative.

In working upon the sensations of natural and superstitious fear, Mrs. Radcliffe has made much use of obscurity and suspense, the most fertile source, perhaps, of sublime emotion; for there are few dangers that do not become familiar to the firm mind, if they are presented to consideration as certainties, and in all their open and declared character, whilst, on the other hand, the bravest have shrunk from the dark and the doubtful. To break off the narrative, when it seemed at the point of becoming most interesting—to extinguish a lamp just when a parchment containing some hideous secret ought to have been read, to exhibit shadowy forms and half-heard sounds of woe, were resources which Mrs. Radcliffe has employed with more effect than any other writer of romance.

A Gothic Burial

[FROM *The Mysteries of Udolpho*]

ANN RADCLIFFE

1794

Emily, shuddering with emotions of horror and grief, assisted by Annette, prepared the corpse for interment; and having wrapped it in cerements and covered it with a winding-sheet, they watched beside it, till past midnight, when they heard the approaching footsteps of the men, who were to lay it in its earthly bed. It was with difficulty that Emily overcame her emotion, when, the door of the chamber being thrown open, their gloomy countenances were seen by the glare of the torch they carried, and two of them, without speaking, lifted the body on their shoulders, while the third preceding them with the light, descended through the castle towards the grave, which was in the lower vault of the chapel within the castle walls.

They had to cross two courts towards the east wing of the castle, which, adjoining the chapel, was, like it, in ruins: but the silence and gloom of these courts had now little power over Emily's mind, occupied as it was with more mournful ideas; and she scarcely heard the low and dismal hooting of the night-birds, that roosted among the ivied battlements of the ruin, or perceived the still flittings of the bat, which frequently crossed her way. But when, having entered the chapel and passed between the mouldering pillars of the aisles, the bearers stopped at a flight of steps, that led down to a low arched door, and, their comrade having descended to

unlock it, she saw imperfectly the gloomy abyss beyond;—saw the corpse of her aunt carried down these
steps, and the ruffian-like figure, that stood with a torch
at the bottom to receive it—all her fortitude was lost
in emotions of inexpressible grief and terror. She turned
to lean upon Annette, who was cold and trembling like
herself, and she lingered so long on the summit of the
flight, that the gleam of the torch began to die away
on the pillars of the chapel, and the men were almost
beyond her view. Then, the gloom around her awakening other fears, and a sense of what she considered to
be her duty overcoming her reluctance, she descended
to the vaults, following the echo of footsteps and the
faint ray that pierced the darkness, till the harsh grating
of a distant door, that was opened to receive the corpse,
again appalled her.

After the pause of a moment, she went on, and, as
she entered the vaults, saw between the arches, at some
distance, the men lay down the body near the edge of
an open grave, where stood another of Montoni's men
and a priest, whom she did not observe, till he began
the burial service; then, lifting her eyes from the
ground, she saw the venerable figure of the friar, and
heard him in a low voice, equally solemn and affecting,
perform the service for the dead. At the moment in
which they let down the body into the earth, the scene
was such as only the dark pencil of a Domenichino,
perhaps, could have done justice to. The fierce features
and wild dress of the *condottieri*, bending with their
torches over the grave, into which the corpse was descending, were contrasted by the venerable figure of
the monk, wrapt in long black garments, his cowl
thrown back from his pale face, on which the light
gleaming strongly showed the lines of affliction softened
by piety, and the few grey locks, which time had spared
on his temples: while, beside him, stood the softer
form of Emily, who leaned for support upon Annette;

her face half averted, and shaded by a thin veil, that
fell over her figure; and her mild and beautiful countenance fixed in grief so solemn as admitted not of
tears, while she thus saw committed untimely to the
earth her last relative and friend. The gleams, thrown
between the arches of the vaults, where, here and
there, the broken ground marked the spots in which
other bodies had been recently interred, and the general
obscurity beyond were circumstances, that alone would
have led on the imagination of a spectator to scenes
more horrible than even that, which was pictured at
the grave of the misguided and unfortunate Madame
Montoni.

The Death of the Monk

[FROM *The Monk*]

MATTHEW GREGORY LEWIS

1796

[*Ambrosio, a monk fallen into depravity, is finally cap-
tured and sentenced to death by the Inquisition. The
Devil saves him, only to damn him to a worse destruction.*]

He reflected on the conditions proposed with horror.
On the other hand, he believed himself doomed to perdition, and that, by refusing the demon's succor, he only
hastened tortures which he never could escape. The
fiend saw that his resolution was shaken. He renewed
his instances, and endeavoured to fix the abbot's inde-
cision. He described the agonies of death in the most
terrific colours; and he worked so powerfully upon Ambrosio's despair and fears, that he prevailed upon him

to receive the parchment. He then struck the iron pen which he held into a vein of the monk's left hand. It pierced deep, and was instantly filled with blood: yet Ambrosio felt no pain from the wound. The pen was put into his hand: it trembled. The wretch placed the parchment on the table before him, and prepared to sign it. Suddenly he held his hand: he started away hastily, and threw the pen upon the table.

"What am I doing?" he cried. Then turning to the fiend with a desperate air: "Leave me! Begone! I will not sign the parchment."

"Fool!" exclaimed the disappointed demon, darting looks so furious as penetrated the friar's soul with horror. "Thus am I trifled with? Go, then! Rave in agony, expire in tortures, and then learn the extent of the Eternal's mercy! But beware how you make me again your mock! Call me no more, till resolved to accept my offers. Summon me a second time to dismiss me thus idly, and these talons shall rend you into a thousand pieces. Speak yet again: will you sign the parchment?"

"I will not. Leave me. Away!"

Instantly the thunder was heard to roll horribly; once more the earth trembled with violence: the dungeon resounded with loud shrieks, and the demon fled with blasphemy and curses.

At first the monk rejoiced at having resisted the seducer's arts, and obtained a triumph over mankind's enemy; but as the hour of punishment drew near, his former terrors revived in his heart; their momentary repose seemed to have given them fresh vigour; the nearer that the time approached, the more did he dread appearing before the throne of God: he shuddered to think how soon he must be plunged into eternity— how soon meet the eyes of his Creator, whom he had so grievously offended. The bell announced midnight: it was the signal for being led to the stake. As he listened to the first stroke, the blood ceased to circulate in the abbot's veins; he heard death and torture murmured in each succeeding sound: he expected to see the archers entering his prison: and as the bell forbore to toll, he seized the magic volume in a fit of despair. He opened it, turned hastily to the seventh page, and as if fearing to allow himself a moment's thought, ran over the fatal lines with rapidity.

Accompanied by his former terrors, Lucifer again stood before the trembler.

"You have summoned me," said the fiend. "Are you determined to be wise? Will you accept my conditions? You know them already. Renounce your claim to salvation, make over to me your soul, and I bear you from this dungeon instantly. Yet is it time. Resolve, or it will be too late. Will you sign the parchment?"

"I must—Fate urges me—I accept your conditions."

"Sign the parchment," replied the demon, in an exulting tone.

The contract and the bloody pen still lay upon the table. Ambrosio drew near it. He prepared to sign his name. A moment's reflection made him hesitate.

"Hark!" cried the tempter; "they come—be quick. Sign the parchment, and I bear you from hence this moment."

In effect, the archers were heard approaching, appointed to lead Ambrosio to the stake. The sound encouraged the monk in his resolution. "What is the import of this writing?" said he.

"It makes your soul over to me for ever, and without reserve."

"What am I to receive in exchange?"

"My protection, and release from this dungeon. Sign it, and this instant I bear you away."

Ambrosio took up the pen. He set it to the parchment. Again his courage failed him; he felt a pang of terror at his heart, and once more threw the pen upon the table.

"Weak and puerile!" cried the exasperated fiend. "Away with this folly! Sign the writing this instant, or I sacrifice you to my rage."

At this moment the bolt of the outward door was drawn back. The prisoner heard the rattling of chains; the heavy bar fell; the archers were on the point of entering. Worked up to frenzy by the urgent danger, shrinking from the approach of death, terrified by the demon's threats, and seeing no other means to escape destruction, the wretched monk complied. He signed the fatal contract, and gave it hastily into the evil spirit's hands, whose eyes, as he received the gift, glared with malicious rapture.

"Take it!" said the God-abandoned man. "Now then, save me! snatch me from hence!"

"Hold! Do you freely and absolutely renounce your Creator and His Son?"

"I do! I do!"

"Do you make over your soul to me for ever?"

"For ever!"

"Without reserve or subterfuge? without future appeal to the Divine Mercy?"

The last chain fell from the door of the prison. The key was heard turning in the lock. Already the iron door grated heavily upon its rusty hinges.

"I am yours for ever, and irrevocably!" cried the monk, wild with terror; "I abandon all claim to salvation. I own no power but yours. Hark! hark! they come! Oh, save me! bear me away!"

"I have triumphed! You are mine past reprieve, and I fulfil my promise."

While he spoke, the door unclosed. Instantly the demon grasped one of Ambrosio's arms, spread his broad pinions, and sprang with him into the air. The roof opened as they soared upwards, and closed again when they had quitted the dungeon.

In the meanwhile, the gaoler was thrown into the

utmost surprise by the disappearance of his prisoner.
Though neither he nor the archers were in time to
witness the monk's escape, a sulphurous smell prevailing
through the prison sufficiently informed them by whose
aid he had been liberated. They hastened to make their
report to the grand inquisitor. The story, how a sorcerer
had been carried away by the Devil, was soon noised
about Madrid; and for some days the whole city was
employed in discussing the subject. Gradually it ceased
to be the topic of conversation. Other adventures arose,
whose novelty engaged universal attention, and Ambrosio was soon forgotten as totally as if he never had
existed. While this was passing, the monk, supported
by his infernal guide, traversed the air with the rapidity of an arrow, and a few moments placed him upon
a precipice's brink, the steepest in Sierra Morena.

Though rescued from the Inquisition, Ambrosio as
yet was insensible of the blessings of liberty. The damn-
ing contract weighed heavy upon his mind; and the
scenes in which he had been a principal actor had left
behind them such impressions as rendered his heart the
seat of anarchy and confusion. The objects now before
his eyes, and which the full moon sailing through clouds
permitted him to examine, were ill calculated to inspire
that calm of which he stood so much in need. The disorder of his imagination was increased by the wildness
of the surrounding scenery—by the gloomy caverns
and steep rocks, rising above each other, and dividing
the passing clouds; solitary clusters of trees, scattered
here and there, among whose thick-twined branches
the wind of night sighed hoarsely and mournfully; the
shrill cry of mountain eagles, who had built their nests
among these lonely deserts; the stunning roar of torrents, as swelled by late rains they rushed violently
down tremendous precipices, and the dark waters of a
silent sluggish stream, which faintly reflected the moon-
beams, and bathed the rock's base on which Ambrosio

stood. The abbot cast round him a look of terror. His infernal conductor was still by his side, and eyed him with a look of mingled malice, exultation, and contempt.

"Whither have you brought me?" said the monk at length, in a hollow, trembling voice. "Why am I placed in this melancholy scene? Bear me from it quickly! Carry me to Matilda!"

The fiend replied not, but continued to gaze upon him in silence. Ambrosio could not sustain his glance; he turned away his eyes, while thus spoke the demon:

"I have him then in my power! This model of piety! this being without reproach! this mortal who placed his puny virtues on a level with those of angels! He is mine—irrevocably, eternally mine! Companions of my sufferings! denizens of hell! how grateful will be my present!"

He paused—then addressed himself to the monk: "Carry you to Matilda!" he continued, repeating Ambrosio's words: "Wretch! you shall soon be with her! You will deserve a place near her, for hell boasts no miscreant more guilty than yourself. Hark, Ambrosio! while I unveil your crimes! You have shed the blood of two innocents; Antonia and Elvira perished by your hand. That Antonia whom you violated was your sister! that Elvira whom you murdered gave you birth! Tremble, abandoned hypocrite, inhuman parricide, incestuous ravisher! Tremble at the extent of your offences! And you it was who thought yourself proof against temptation, absolved from human frailties, and free from error and vice! Is pride, then, a virtue? Is inhumanity no fault? Know, vain man! that I long have marked you for my prey: I watched the movements of your heart; I saw that you were virtuous from vanity, not principle; and I seized the fit moment of seduction. I observed your blind idolatry of the Madonna's picture. I bade a subordinate but crafty spirit assume a similar form, and you eagerly yielded to the blandishments of Matilda. Your pride was gratified by her flattery; your lust only needed an opportunity to break forth; you ran into the snare blindly, and scrupled not to commit a crime which you blamed in another with unfeeling severity. It was I who threw Matilda in your way; it was I who gave you entrance to Antonia's chamber; it was I who caused the dagger to be given you which pierced your sister's bosom, and it was I who warned Elvira in dreams of your designs upon her daughter, and thus, by preventing your profiting by her sleep, compelled you to add rape as well as incest to the catalogue of your crimes. Hear, hear, Ambrosio! Had you resisted me one minute longer, you had saved your body and soul. The guards whom you heard at your prison-door came to signify your pardon. But I had already triumphed: my plots had already succeeded. Scarcely could I propose crimes so quick as you performed them. You are mine, and Heaven itself cannot rescue you from my power. Hope not that your penitence will make void our contract. Here is your bond signed with your blood; you have given up your claim to mercy, and nothing can restore to you the rights which you have foolishly resigned. Believe you that your secret thoughts escaped me? No, no—I read them all! You trusted that you should still have time for repentance. I saw your artifice, knew its falsity, and rejoiced in deceiving the deceiver! You are mine beyond reprieve: I burn to possess my right, and alive you quit not these mountains."

During the demon's speech, Ambrosio had been stupefied by terror and surprise. This last declaration roused him.

"Not quit these mountains alive!" he exclaimed. "Perfidious! what mean you? Have you forgotten our contract?"

The fiend answered by a malicious laugh.

"Our contract! Have I not performed my part? What more did I promise than to save you from your prison? Have I not done so? Are you not safe from the Inquisition—safe from all but from me? Fool that you were, to confide yourself to a devil! Why did you not stipulate for life, and power, and pleasure?—then all would have been granted: now, your reflections come too late. Miscreant! prepare for death; you have not many hours to live!"

On hearing this sentence, dreadful were the feelings of the devoted wretch! He sank upon his knees, and raised his hands towards heaven.

The fiend read his intention, and prevented it. "What!" he cried, darting at him a look of fury; "dare you still implore the Eternal's mercy? Would you feign penitence, and again act an hypocrite's part? Villain! resign your hopes of pardon. Thus I secure my prey."

As he said this, darting his talons into the monk's shaven crown, he sprang with him from the rock. The caves and mountains rang with Ambrosio's shrieks. The demon continued to soar aloft, till reaching a dreadful height, he released the sufferer. Headlong fell the monk through the airy waste: the sharp point of rock received him, and he rolled from precipice to precipice, till, bruised and mangled, he rested on the river's banks. Instantly a violent storm arose: the winds in fury rent up rocks and forests: the sky was now black with clouds, now sheeted with fire: the rain fell in torrents; it swelled the stream; the waves overflowed their banks; they reached the spot where Ambrosio lay, and, when they abated, carried with them into the river the corpse of the despairing monk.

Haughty lady, why shrunk you back when yon poor frail one drew near? Was the air infected by her errors? Was your purity soiled by her passing breath? Ah, lady! smooth that insulting brow: stifle the reproach just bursting from your scornful lip: wound not a soul that bleeds already! She has suffered, suffers still. Her air is gay, but her heart is broken; her dress sparkles, but her bosom groans.

Lady, to look with mercy on the conduct of others is a virtue no less than to look with severity on your own.

A Rationalist Heroine in a Gothic Novel

[FROM *Northanger Abbey*]

JANE AUSTEN

1818

The night was stormy; the wind had been rising at intervals the whole afternoon; and by the time the party broke up, it blew and rained violently. Catherine, as she crossed the hall, listened to the tempest with sensations of awe; and when she heard it rage round a corner of the ancient building, and close with sudden fury a distant door, felt for the first time that she was really in an Abbey. Yes, these were characteristic sounds: they brought to her recollection a countless variety of dreadful situations and horrid scenes which such buildings had witnessed, and such storms ushered in; and most heartily did she rejoice in the happier circumstances attending her entrance within walls so solemn! *She* had nothing to dread from midnight assassins or drunken gallants. Henry had certainly been only in jest in what he had told her that morning. In a house so furnished, and so guarded, she could have nothing to explore or to suffer, and might go to her bedroom as securely as if it had been her own chamber at Fullerton. Thus wisely fortifying her mind, as she proceeded upstairs, she was enabled, especially on perceiving that Miss Tilney slept only two doors from her, to enter her room with a tolerably stout heart; and her spirits were immediately assisted by the cheerful blaze of a wood fire. "How much better is this," said she, as she walked to the fender; "how much better to find a fire ready lit, than to have to wait shivering in the cold, till all the family are in bed, as so many poor girls have been obliged to do, and then to have a faithful old servant frightening one by coming in with a faggot! How glad I am that Northanger is what it is! If it had been like some other places, I do not know that, in such a night as this, I could have answered for my courage; but now, to be sure, there is nothing to alarm one."

She looked round the room. The window curtains seemed in motion. It could be nothing but the violence of the wind penetrating through the divisions of the shutters; and she stepped boldly forward, carelessly humming a tune, to assure herself of its being so, peeped courageously behind each curtain, saw nothing on either low window-seat to scare her, and on placing a hand against the shutter, felt the strongest conviction of the wind's force. A glance at the old chest, as she turned away from this examination, was not without its use; she scorned the causeless fears of an idle fancy, and began with a most happy indifference to prepare herself for bed. "She should take her time; she should not hurry herself; she did not care if she were the last person up in the house. But she would not make up her fire: *that* would seem cowardly, as if she wished for the protection of light after she were in bed." The fire, therefore, died away, and Catherine, having spent the best part of an hour in her arrangements, was beginning to think of stepping into bed, when, on giving a parting glance round the room, she was struck by the appearance of a high, old-fashioned black cabinet, which though in a situation conspicuous enough, had never caught her notice before. Henry's words, the description of the ebony cabinet which was to escape her observation at first, immediately rushed across her; and though there could be nothing really in it, there was something whimsical, it was certainly a very remarkable coincidence! She took her candle and looked closely at the cabinet. It was not absolutely ebony and gold; but it was Japan, black and yellow Japan of the handsomest kind; and as she held her candle, the yellow had very much the effect of gold.

The key was in the door, and she had a strange fancy to look into it; not, however, with the smallest expectation of finding anything, but it was so very odd, after what Henry had said. In short, she could not sleep till she had examined it. So, placing the candle with great caution on a chair, she seized the key with a very tremulous hand, and tried to turn it, but it resisted her utmost strength. Alarmed but not discouraged, she tried it another way; a bolt flew, and she believed herself successful; but how strangely mysterious! the door was still immovable. She paused a moment in breathless wonder. The wind roared down the chimney, the rain beat in torrents against the windows, and everything seemed to speak the awfulness of her situation. To retire to bed, however, unsatisfied on such a point, would be in vain, since sleep must be impossible with the consciousness of a cabinet so mysteriously closed in her immediate vicinity. Again, therefore, she applied herself to the key, and after moving it in every possible way, for some instants, with the determined celerity of hope's last effort, the door suddenly yielded to her hand: her heart leaped with exultation at such a victory, and having thrown open each folding door, the second being secured only by bolts of less wonder-

ful construction than the lock, though in that her eye
could not discern anything unusual, a double range of
small drawers appeared in view, with some larger
drawers above and below them, and in the centre, a
small door, closed also with lock and key, secured in
all probability a cavity of importance.

Catherine's heart beat quick, but her courage did not
fail her. With a cheek flushed by hope, and an eye
straining with curiosity, her fingers grasped the handle
of a drawer and drew it forth. It was entirely empty.
With less alarm and greater eagerness she seized a
second, a third, a fourth—each was equally empty.
Not one was left unsearched, and in not one was anything found. Well read in the art of concealing a treasure, the possibility of false linings to the drawers did
not escape her, and she felt round each with anxious
acuteness in vain. The place in the middle alone remained now unexplored; and though she had "never
from the first had the smallest idea of finding anything
in any part of the cabinet, and was not in the least
disappointed at her ill success thus far, it would be
foolish not to examine it thoroughly while she was
about it." It was some time, however, before she could
unfasten the door, the same difficulty occurring in the
management of this inner lock as of the outer; but at
length it did open; and not vain, as hitherto, was her
search; her quick eyes directly fell on a roll of paper
pushed back into the further part of the cavity, apparently for concealment, and her feelings at that moment were indescribable. Her heart fluttered, her knees
trembled, and her cheeks grew pale. She seized, with
an unsteady hand, the precious manuscript, for half a
glance sufficed to ascertain written characters; and
while she acknowledged with awful sensations this
striking exemplification of what Henry had foretold,
resolved instantly to peruse every line before she attempted to rest.

The dimness of the light her candle emitted made
her turn to it with alarm; but there was no danger of
its sudden extinction, it had yet some hours to burn;
and that she might not have any greater difficulty in
distinguishing the writing than what its ancient date
might occasion, she hastily snuffed it. Alas! it was
snuffed and extinguished in one. A lamp could not
have expired with more awful effect. Catherine, for a
few moments, was motionless with horror. It was done
completely; not a remnant of light in the wick could
give hope to the rekindling breath. Darkness impenetrable and immovable filled the room. A violent gust
of wind, rising with sudden fury, added fresh horror
to the moment. Catherine trembled from head to foot.
In the pause which succeeded, a sound like receding
footsteps and the closing of a distant door struck on
her affrighted ear. Human nature could support no
more. A cold sweat stood on her forehead, the manuscript fell from her hand, and groping her way to the
bed, she jumped hastily in, and sought some suspen-
sions of agony by creeping far underneath the clothes.
To close her eyes in sleep that night she felt must be
entirely out of the question. With a curiosity so justly
awakened, and feelings in every way so agitated, repose must be absolutely impossible. The storm, too,
abroad so dreadful! She had not been used to feel
alarm from wind, but now every blast seemed fraught
with awful intelligence. The manuscript so wonderfully
found, so wonderfully accomplishing the morning's prediction, how was it to be accounted for? What could
it contain? to whom could it relate? by what means
could it have been so long concealed? and how singularly strange that it should fall to her lot to discover it!
Till she had made herself mistress of its contents, however, she could have neither repose nor comfort; and
with the sun's first rays she was determined to peruse
it. But many were the tedious hours which must yet

intervene. She shuddered, tossed about in her bed, and envied every quiet sleeper. The storm still raged, and various were the noises, more terrific even than the wind, which struck at intervals on her startled ear. The very curtains of her bed seemed at one moment in motion, and at another the lock of her door was agitated, as if by the attempt of somebody to enter. Hollow murmurs seemed to creep along the gallery, and more than once her blood was chilled by the sound of distant moans. Hour after hour passed away, and the wearied Catherine had heard three proclaimed by all the clocks in the house, before the tempest subsided, or she unknowingly fell fast asleep.

"The Fantastic Richness of Gothic Ornament"

[FROM *Vivian Grey*]

BENJAMIN DISRAELI

1827

How shall we describe Château Desir, that place fit for all princes? In the midst of a park of great extent, and eminent for scenery as varied as might please nature's most capricious lover; in the midst of green lawns and deep winding glens, and cooling streams, and wild forest, and soft woodland, there was gradually formed an elevation, on which was situate a mansion of great size, and of that bastard, but picturesque style of architecture, called the Italian Gothic. The date of its erection was about the middle of the sixteenth century. You entered by a noble gateway, in which the pointed style still predominated; but in various parts of which, the Ionic column, and the prominent keystone, and other creations of Roman architecture, intermingled with the expiring Gothic, into a large quadrangle, to which the square casement windows, and the triangular pediments or gable ends supplying the place of battlements, gave a varied and Italian feature. In the centre of the court, from a vast marble basin, the rim of which was enriched by a splendidly sculptured lotus border, rose a marble group representing Amphitrite with her marine attendants, whose sounding shells and coral sceptres sent forth their subject element in sparkling showers. This work, the chef d'œuvre of a celebrated artist of Vicenza, had been purchased by Valerian, first Lord Carabas, who having spent the greater part of his life as the representative of his monarch at the Ducal Court of Venice, at length returned to his native country; and in the creation of Château Desir endeavoured to find some consolation for the loss of his beautiful villa on the banks of the Adige.

Over the gateway there rose a turreted tower, the small square window of which, notwithstanding its stout stanchions, illumined the muniment room of the House of Carabas. In the spandrils of the gateway and in many other parts of the building might be seen the arms of the family; while the tall twisted stacks of chimneys, which appeared to spring from all parts of the roof, were carved and built in such curious and quaint devices that they were rather an ornament than an excrescence. When you entered the quadrangle, you found one side solely occupied by the old hall, the huge carved rafters of whose oak roof rested on corbels of the family supporters against the walls. These walls were of stone, but covered half-way from the ground with a panelling of curiously-carved oak; whence were suspended, in massy frames, the family portraits, painted by Dutch and Italian artists. Near the dais, or upper part of the hall, there projected an oriel window, which as you beheld, you scarcely knew what most to admire, the radiancy of its painted panes or the fantastic richness of Gothic ornament, which was profusely lavished in every part of its masonry. Here too the Gothic pendent and the Gothic fan-work were intermingled with the Italian arabesques, which, at the time of the building of the Château, had been recently introduced into England by Hans Holbein and John of Padua.

How wild and fanciful are those ancient arabesques! Here at Château Desir, in the panelling of the old hall, might you see fantastic scrolls, separated by bodies ending in termini, and whose heads supported the Ionic volute, while the arch, which appeared to spring from these capitals, had, for a keystone, heads more monstrous than those of the fabled animals of Ctesias; or so ludicrous, that you forgot the classic griffin in the grotesque conception of the Italian artist. Here was a gibbering monkey, there a grinning pulcinello; now you viewed a chattering devil, which might have figured in the "Temptation of St. Anthony"; and now a mournful, mystic, bearded countenance, which might have flitted in the back scene of a "Witches' Sabbath."

A long gallery wound through the upper story of two other sides of the quadrangle, and beneath were the show suite of apartments with a sight of which the admiring eyes of curious tourists were occasionally delighted.

The grey stone walls of this antique edifice were, in many places, thickly covered with ivy and other parasitical plants, the deep green of whose verdure beautifully contrasted with the scarlet glories of the pyrus japonica, which gracefully clustered round the windows of the lower chambers. The mansion itself was immediately surrounded by numerous ancient forest trees. There was the elm with its rich branches bending down like

clustering grapes; there was the wide-spreading oak
with its roots fantastically gnarled; here was the ash,
with its smooth bark and elegant leaf; and the silver
beech, and the gracile birch; and the dark fir, affording
with its rough foliage a contrast to the trunks of its more
beautiful companions, or shooting far above their
branches, with the spirit of freedom worthy of a rough
child of the mountains.

Around the Castle were extensive pleasure-grounds,
which realised the romance of the "Gardens of Veru-
lam." And truly, as you wandered through their enchanting paths there seemed no end to their various
beauties, and no exhaustion of their perpetual novelty.
Green retreats succeeded to winding walks; from the
shady berceau you vaulted on the noble terrace; and
if, for an instant, you felt wearied by treading the
velvet lawn, you might rest in a mossy cell, while your
mind was soothed by the soft music of falling waters.
Now your curious eyes were greeted by Oriental animals, basking in a sunny paddock; and when you
turned from the white-footed antelope and the dark-
eyed gazelle, you viewed an aviary of such extent,
that within its trellised walls the imprisoned songsters
could build, in the free branches of a tree, their natural
nests.

"O fair scene!" thought Vivian Grey, as he approached on a fine summer's afternoon, the splendid
Château. "O fair scene! doubly fair to those who quit
for thee the thronged and agitated city. And can it be,
that those who rest within this enchanted domain, can
think of anything but sweet air, and do aught but
revel in the breath of perfumed flowers?" And here he
gained the garden-house: so he stopped his soliloquy,
and gave his horse to the groom.

Fifteenth-Century Paris Revisited

[FROM *Notre-Dame de Paris*]

VICTOR HUGO

1831

[FROM THE INTRODUCTION]

Some years ago, while visiting, or rather exploring, Notre-Dame, the author of this book discovered in an obscure corner of one of the towers this word, carved upon the wall:

'ΑΝΑΓΚΗ

These Greek characters, black with age and cut deep into the stone with the peculiarities of form and arrangement common to Gothic calligraphy that marked them the work of some hand in the Middle Ages, and above all the sad and mournful meaning which they expressed, forcibly impressed the author.

He questioned himself, he tried to divine what sad soul was loath to quit the earth without leaving behind this brand of crime or misery upon the brow of the old church.

Since then the wall has been whitewashed or scraped (I have forgotten which), and the inscription has vanished. For this is the way in which, for some two hundred years, we have treated the wonderful churches of the Middle Ages. They are mutilated in every part, inside as well as out. The priest whitewashes them, the archdeacon scrapes them; then come the people, who tear them down.

So, save for the frail memory which the author of this book here dedicates to it, nothing now remains of the

mysterious word engraved upon the dark tower of
Notre-Dame, nothing of the unknown fate which is
summed up so sadly. The man who wrote that word
upon the wall faded away; the word in its turn has
faded from the church wall; the church itself, perhaps,
will soon vanish from the earth.

Upon that word this book is based.

[From the Novel]

This procession, which our readers saw as it started
from the Palace, had taken shape as it marched, en-
listing all the available vagabonds and scamps and idle
thieves in Paris; so that it presented quite a respectable
appearance when it reached the Grève.

First came the barn-stormers, the chief cackling cove
at the head, on horseback, with his aids on foot, holding his stirrup and bridle. Behind walked the rest of
the barn-stormers, male and female, with their little
ones clamoring on their backs; all, men, women, and
children, in rags and tatters. Then came the thieves'
brotherhood; that is, all the robbers in France, ranged
according to their degree, the least expert coming first.
Thus they filed along four by four, armed with the
various insignia of their degrees. In this singular faculty,
most of them maimed, some halt, some with but one
arm, were shoplifters, mock pilgrims, tramps who pretended to have been bitten by wolves, dummy chuckers,
thimble-riggers, sham Abrams, Jeremy Diddlers, sham
cripples, mumpers, pallyards, showful pitchers, rogues
pretending to have been burned out, cadgers, old soldiers, high-flyers, swell mobsmen, gonnofs, flash coves
—a list long enough to weary Homer himself. In the
centre of the conclave of gonnofs and flash coves might
dimly be distinguished the head of the thieves' brotherhood, the "Grand Coëre," or king of rogues, squatting
in a small cart, drawn by two big dogs. After the

fraternity of thieves came the Empire of Galilee. Guil-
laume Rousseau, Emperor of the Galilees, marches
majestic in his purple robes stained with wine, preceded
by mountebanks fighting and dancing Pyrrhic dances,
surrounded by his mace-bearers, tools, and the clerks
of the Court of Exchequer. Last came the *basoche*
(the corporation of lawyers' clerks), with their sheaves
of maize crowned with flowers, their black gowns, their
music worthy of a Witches' Sabbath, and their huge
yellow wax candles. In the midst of this throng the
high officials of the fraternity of fools bore upon their
shoulders a barrow more heavily laden with tapers
than the shrine of St. Geneviève in time of plague;
and upon this barrow rode resplendent, with crosier,
cope, and mitre, the new Lord of Misrule, the bell-
ringer of Notre-Dame, Quasimodo the Humpback.

Each division of this grotesque procession had its
own peculiar music. The barn-stormers drew discordant
notes from their balafos and their African tabors. The
thieves, a far from musical race, were still using the
viol, the cowherd's horn, and the quaint rubeb of the
twelfth century. Nor was the Empire of Galilee much
more advanced; their music was almost wholly confined to some wretched rebec dating back to the infancy of the art, still imprisoned within the *re-la-mi*.
But it was upon the Lord of Misrule that all the musical
riches of the period were lavished in one magnificent
cacophony. There were treble rebecs, counter-tenor
rebecs, tenor rebecs, to say nothing of flutes and brass
instruments. Alas! our readers may remember that this
was Gringoire's orchestra.

It is difficult to convey any idea of the degree of
proud and sanctimonious rapture which Quasimodo's
hideous and painful face had assumed during the journey from the Palace to the Grève. This was the first
thrill of vanity which he had ever felt. Hitherto he had
known nothing but humiliation, disdain of his estate,

and disgust for his person. Therefore, deaf as he was, he enjoyed, like any genuine pope, the plaudits of that mob which he had hated because he felt that it hated him. What mattered it to him that his subjects were a collection of fools, cripples, thieves, and beggars! They were still subjects, and he a sovereign! And he took seriously all the mock applause, all the satirical respect with which, it must be confessed, there was a slight mixture of very real fear in the hearts of the throng. For the humped back was strong; for the bandy legs were nimble; for the deaf ears were malicious: three qualities which tempered the ridicule.

Moreover, we are far from fancying that the new Lord of Misrule realized clearly either his own feelings or those which he inspired. The spirit lodged in that imperfect body was necessarily something dull and incomplete. Therefore what he felt at this instant was absolutely vague, indistinct, and confused to him. Joy only pierced the cloud; pride prevailed. The sombre and unhappy face was radiant.

We shall now attempt to give some idea of the general view seen from the top of the towers of Notre-Dame.

To the spectator who reached this pinnacle in a breathless condition, all was at first a dazzling sea of roofs, chimneys, streets, bridges, squares, spires, and steeples. Everything burst upon his vision at once— the carved gable, the steep roof, the turret hanging from the angles of the walls, the eleventh-century stone pyramid, the fifteenth-century slate obelisk, the round bare tower of the donjon-keep, the square elaborately wrought tower of the church, the great, the small, the massive, and the light. The eye wandered for a time, plunging deep down into this labyrinth, where there was no one thing destitute of originality, purpose, genius, and beauty, nothing uninspired by art, from

the tiniest house with carved and painted front, outside timbers, surbased door, and overhanging stories, to
the royal Louvre, which then had a colonnade of
towers. But the principal masses to be seen when the
eye became wonted to this medley of buildings were as
follows:

First, the City. The island of the City, as says Sauval,
who, in spite of his nonsense, sometimes hits upon a
happy phrase—"the island of the City is shaped like a
huge ship buried in the mud and stranded in the current towards the middle of the Seine." We have just
explained that in the fifteenth century this ship was
moored to the shores of the stream by five bridges. This
likeness to a vessel also struck the heraldic scribes; for
it is thence, and not from the Norman siege, say Favyn
and Pasquier, that the ship blazoned on the ancient
shield of Paris is taken. To him who can decipher it,
the science of heraldry is another algebra, the science
of heraldry is a language. The whole history of the
second half of the Middle Ages is written out in heraldry, as is the history of the first half in the symbolism
of the Roman Church. The hieroglyphs of feudalism
follow those of theocracy.

The City, then, first fell upon the eye with its stern
to the east and its prow to the west. Facing the prow,
the spectator saw a countless collection of ancient roofs,
above which rose, broad and round, the leaden bolster
of the Sainte-Chapelle, like an elephant's back laden
with its tower. Only in this case the tower was the
most daring, the most daintily wrought, the most delicately carved spire that ever gave glimpses of the sky
through its lace-like cone. In front of Notre-Dame, close
at hand, three streets emptied into the space in front
of the cathedral—a beautiful square lined with old
houses. Over the southern side of this square hung the
wrinkled and frowning front of the Hospital, or Hôtel-
Dieu, and its roof, which seemed covered with warts

and pimples. Then to the left, to the right, to the east,
to the west, throughout the City limits, narrow as they
were, rose the steeples of its one-and-twenty churches
of every age, of every form and every size, from the low,
worm-eaten Roman campanile of Saint-Denis-du-Pas
(Carcer Glaucini) to the slender spires of Saint-Pierre-
aux-Boeufs and Saint-Laundry. Behind Notre-Dame
were revealed, on the north, the cloisters with their
Gothic galleries; on the south, the semi-Roman palace
of the bishop; on the east, the borders of the Terrain,
a plot of waste land. Amid this accumulation of houses,
by the tall mitres made of openwork stone, which
crowned the highest windows of the palace, then placed
even in the very roof, the eye could also distinguish
the hotel given by the town in the reign of Charles VI
to Juvénal des Ursins; a little farther away, the tarred
booths of the Palus Market; elsewhere, again, the new
chancel of Saint-Germain-le-Vieux, pieced out in 1458
with a bit of the Rue-aux-Febves; and then, at intervals, a square crowded with people; a pillory set up at
some street corner; a fine fragment of the pavement of
Philip Augustus, superb flagging laid in the middle of
the road, and furrowed to prevent horses from slipping,
which was so ill replaced in the sixteenth century by
the wretched flints and pebbles known as "the pavement of the League"; a deserted back yard with one
of those open turret staircases which were common in
the fifteenth century, and an example of which may
still be seen in the Rue des Bourdonnais. Finally, to
the right of the Sainte-Chapelle, towards the west, the
Palace of Justice reared its group of towers on the
water's edge. The tall trees of the king's gardens, which
covered the western end of the City, hid the Île du Pas-
seur. As for the water, from the top of the towers of
Notre-Dame it was barely visible on either side of the
City: the Seine was concealed by bridges, the bridges
by houses.

And if the spectator looked beyond those bridges, the roofs of which were of a greenish tint, mouldy before their time by the damp vapors rising from the water, if he turned to the left in the direction of the University, the first building which attracted him was a broad, low group of towers, the Petit-Châtelet, whose wide-mouthed porch swallowed up the end of the Petit-Pont; then, if his eye followed the shore from east to west, from the Tournelle to the Tour de Nesle, he saw a long line of houses with carved beams and stained-glass windows, overhanging the pavement story upon story, an endless zigzag of homely gables, often interrupted by the mouth of some street, and sometimes also by the front or the projecting corner of a huge stone mansion, spreading out its courtyards and gardens, its wings and its main buildings, quite at its ease amid this mob of narrow crowded houses, like a great lord in a rabble of rustic clowns. There were five or six of these mansions on the quay, from the house of Lorraine, which shared the great monastery enclosure next the Tournelle with the Bernardines, to the family mansion of the De Nesles, the main tower of which bounded Paris on that side, and whose painted roofs for three months in the year silvered the scarlet disk of the setting sun with their dark triangles.

This side of the Seine, moreover, was the less commercial of the two; students were noisier and more numerous than laborers, and, properly speaking, the quay extended only from the Pont Saint-Michel to the Tour de Nesle. The rest of the river bank was now a bare beach, as beyond the Bernardine monastery, and then again a mass of houses washed by the water, as between the two bridges.

There was a vast clamor of washerwomen; they shouted, chattered, and sang from morning till night along the shore, and beat the linen hard, as they do in our day. This is not the least part of the gaiety of Paris.

The University presented a huge mass to the eye. From one end to the other it was a compact and homogeneous whole. The myriad roofs, close-set, angular, adherent, almost all composed of the same geometrical elements, looked from above like a crystallization of one substance. The fantastic hollows of the streets divided this pastry of houses into tolerably equal slices. The forty-two colleges were distributed about quite evenly, there being some in every quarter. The delightfully varied pinnacles of these fine structures were the product of the same art as the simple roofs which they crowned, being really but a multiplication of the square or cube of the same geometrical figure. In this way they made the sum total more intricate without rendering it confused, and completed without overloading the general effect. Geometry is harmony. Certain handsome mansions here and there stood out superbly among the picturesque garrets on the left bank of the river— the Nevers house, the house of Rome, the Rheims house, which have all disappeared; the Hôtel de Cluny, still standing for the consolation of artists, and the tower of which was so stupidly lowered some years since. That Roman palace near Cluny, with its beautiful arches, was formerly the Baths of Julian. There were also a number of abbeys of a beauty more religious, a grandeur more severe, than the mansions, but no less splendid, no less spacious. Those first attracting the eye were the monastery of the Bernardines, with its three spires; Saint-Geneviève, whose square tower, still standing, makes us regret the rest so much; the Sorbonne, half college, half monastery, of which the fine nave still remains; the elegant quadrangular cloister of the Mathurin friars; its neighbor, the cloister of St. Benedict, within the walls of which a theatre has been knocked up in the interval between the seventh and eighth editions of this book; the Franciscan abbey, with its three enormous gables side by side; the house of the Austin friars, whose graceful spire was, after the Tour de Nesle, the second lofty landmark on this side of Paris, looking westward.

Trans. unknown (Boston: Estes and Lauriat, n.d.)

PART FOUR

Romantic Nature

THE CULT OF NATURE

I love thee, Nature, with a boundless
love.

—John Clare

Romantic Tourism

[FROM THE *Letters*]

CHARLES LAMB

To THOMAS MANNING

September 24, 1802

Since the date of my last letter, I have been a traveller. A strong desire seized me of visiting remote regions. My first impulse was to go and see Paris. It was
a trivial objection to my aspiring mind, that I did not
understand a word of the language, since I certainly
intend some time in my life to see Paris, and equally
certainly intend never to learn the language; therefore
that could be no objection. However, I am very glad
I did not go, because you had left Paris (I see) before
I could have set out. I believe, Stoddart promising to
go with me another year, prevented that plan. My next
scheme (for to my restless ambitious mind London
was become a bed of thorns) was to visit the far-

famed peak in Derbyshire, where the Devil sits, they
say, without breeches. *This* my purer mind rejected as
indelicate. And my final resolve was, a tour to the lakes.
I set out with Mary to Keswick, without giving Coleridge any notice, for my time, being precious, did not
admit of it. He received us with all the hospitality in
the world, and gave up his time to show us all the
wonders of the country. He dwells upon a small hill by
the side of Keswick, in a comfortable house, quite enveloped on all sides by a net of mountains: great
floundering bears and monsters they seem'd, all couch-
ant and asleep. We got in in the evening, travelling in
a post chaise from Penrith, in the midst of a gorgeous
sunshine, which transmuted all the mountains into colours, purple, &c. &c. We thought we had got into fairy
land. But that went off (and it never came again; while
we stayed we had no more fine sunsets); and we entered Coleridge's comfortable study just in the dusk,
when the mountains were all dark with clouds upon
their heads. Such an impression I never received from
objects of sight before, nor do I suppose I can ever
again. Glorious creatures, fine old fellows, Skiddaw,
&c. I never shall forget ye, how ye lay about that night,
like an intrenchment; gone to bed, as it seemed for
the night, but promising that ye were to be seen in the
morning. Coleridge had got a blazing fire in his study,
which is a large, antique, ill-shaped room, with an old-
fashioned organ, never play'd upon, big enough for a
church, shelves of scattered folios, an Eolian harp, and
an old sofa, half bed, &c. And all looking out upon the
fading view of Skiddaw, and his broad-breasted brethren: what a night! Here we staid three full weeks, in
which time I visited Wordsworth's cottage, where we
stayed a day or two with the Clarksons (good people,
and most hospitable, at whose house we tarried one day
and night), and saw Lloyd. The Wordsworths were
gone to Calais. They have since been in London, and

past much time with us: he is now gone into Yorkshire
to be married. So we have seen Keswick, Grasmere,
Ambleside, Ulswater, (where the Clarksons live), and
a place at the other end of Ulswater; I forget the name;
to which we travelled on a very sultry day, over the
middle of Helvellyn. We have clambered up to the top
of Skiddaw, and I have waded up the bed of Lodore.
In fine, I have satisfied myself that there is such a thing
as that which tourists call *romantic*, which I very much
suspected before: they make such a spluttering about it,
and toss their splendid epithets around them, till they
give as dim a light as at four o'clock next morning the
lamps do after an illumination. Mary was excessively
tired, when she got about half way up Skiddaw, but we
came to a cold rill, (than which nothing can be imagined more cold, running over cold stones), and with
the reinforcement of a draught of cold water, she sur-
mounted it most manfully. O, its fine black head, and
the bleak air atop of it, with a prospect of mountains
all about and about, making you giddy; then Scotland
afar off, and the border countries so famous in song
and ballad! It was a day that will stand out, like a
mountain, I am sure, in my life. But I am returned, (I
have now been come home near three weeks—I was a
month out), and you cannot conceive the degradation
I felt at first, from being accustomed to wander free as
air among mountains, and bathe in rivers without being
controul'd by any one, to come home and *work*. I felt
very *little*. I had been dreaming I was a very great
man. But that is going off, and I find I shall conform in
time to that state of life to which it has pleased God to
call me. Besides, after all, Fleet Street and the Strand
are better places to live in for good and all than amidst
Skiddaw.

"*Ye Presences of Nature*"

[FROM *The Prelude,* Book I]

WILLIAM WORDSWORTH

1805

Not seldom from the uproar I retired
Into a silent bay, or sportively
Glanced sideway, leaving the tumultuous throng,
To cut across the image of a star
That gleam'd upon the ice: and oftentimes
When we had given our bodies to the wind,
And all the shadowy banks, on either side,
Came sweeping through the darkness, spinning still
The rapid line of motion; then at once
Have I, reclining back upon my heels,
Stopp'd short, yet still the solitary Cliffs
Wheeled by me, even as if the earth had roll'd
With visible motion her diurnal round;
Behind me did they stretch in solemn train
Feebler and feebler, and I stood and watch'd
Till all was tranquil as a dreamless sleep.

Ye Presences of Nature, in the sky
And on the earth! Ye Visions of the hills!
And Souls of lonely places! can I think
A vulgar hope was yours when Ye employ'd
Such ministry, when Ye through many a year
Haunting me thus among my boyish sports,
On caves and trees, upon the woods and hills,
Impress'd upon all forms the characters

Of danger or desire, and thus did make
The surface of the universal earth
With triumph, and delight, and hope, and fear,
Work like a sea?
        Not uselessly employ'd,
I might pursue this theme through every change
Of exercise and play, to which the year
Did summon us in its delightful round.

  We were a noisy crew, the sun in heaven
Beheld not vales more beautiful than ours,
Nor saw a race in happiness and joy
More worthy of the ground where they were sown.
I would record with no reluctant voice
The woods of autumn and their hazel bowers
With milk-white clusters hung; the rod and line,
True symbol of the foolishness of hope,
Which with its strong enchantment led us on
By rocks and pools, shut out from every star
All the green summer, to forlorn cascades
Among the windings of the mountain brooks. . . .

  Nor, sedulous as I have been to trace
How Nature by extrinsic passion first
Peopled my mind with beauteous forms or grand,
And made me love them, may I here forget
How other pleasures have been mine, and joys
Of subtler origin; how I have felt,
Not seldom, even in that tempestuous time,
Those hallow'd and pure motions of the sense
Which seem, in their simplicity, to own
An intellectual charm, that calm delight
Which, if I err not, surely must belong
To those first-born affinities that fit
Our new existence to existing things,
And, in our dawn of being, constitute
The bond of union betwixt life and joy.

Yes, I remember, when the changeful earth,
And twice five seasons on my mind had stamp'd
The faces of the moving year, even then,
A Child I held unconscious intercourse
With the eternal Beauty, drinking in
A pure organic pleasure from the lines
Of curling mist, or from the level plain
Of waters colour'd by the steady clouds.

Unchanging Essences

[FROM *Nature*]

RALPH WALDO EMERSON

1836

Our age is retrospective. It builds the sepulchres of the fathers. It writes biographies, histories, and criticism. The foregoing generations beheld God and nature face to face; we, through their eyes. Why should not we also enjoy an original relation to the universe? Why should not we have a poetry and philosophy of insight and not of tradition, and a religion by revelation to us, and not the history of theirs? Embosomed for a season in nature, whose floods of life stream around and through us, and invite us, by the powers they supply, to action proportioned to nature, why should we grope among the dry bones of the past, or put the living generation into masquerade out of its faded wardrobe? The sun shines to-day also. There is more wool and flax in the fields. There are new lands, new men, new thoughts. Let us demand our own works and laws and worship.

Undoubtedly we have no questions to ask which are

unanswerable. We must trust the perfection of the creation so far as to believe that whatever curiosity the order of things has awakened in our minds, the order of things can satisfy. Every man's condition is a solution in hieroglyphic to those inquiries he would put. He acts it as life, before he apprehends it as truth. In like manner, nature is already, in its forms and tendencies, describing its own design. Let us interrogate the great apparition that shines so peacefully around us. Let us inquire, to what end is nature?

All science has one aim, namely, to find a theory of nature. We have theories of races and of functions, but scarcely yet a remote approach to an idea of creation. We are now so far from the road to truth, that religious teachers dispute and hate each other, and speculative men are esteemed unsound and frivolous. But to a sound judgment, the most abstract truth is the most practical. Whenever a true theory appears, it will be its own evidence. Its test is, that it will explain all phenomena. Now many are thought not only unexplained but inexplicable; as language, sleep, madness, dreams, beasts, sex.

Philosophically considered, the universe is composed of Nature and the Soul. Strictly speaking, therefore, all that is separate from us, all which Philosophy distinguishes as the NOT ME, that is, both nature and art, all other men and my own body, must be ranked under this name, NATURE. In enumerating the values of nature and casting up their sum, I shall use the word in both senses;—in its common and in its philosophical import. In inquiries so general as our present one, the inaccuracy is not material; no confusion of thought will occur. *Nature,* in the common sense, refers to essences unchanged by man; space, the air, the river, the leaf. *Art* is applied to the mixture of his will with the same things, as in a house, a canal, a statue, a picture. But his operations taken together are so insignificant, a little

chipping, baking, patching, and washing, that in an
impression so grand as that of the world on the human
mind, they do not vary the result.

NATURE

To go into solitude, a man needs to retire as much
from his chamber as from society. I am not solitary
whilst I read and write, though nobody is with me. But
if a man would be alone, let him look at the stars. The
rays that come from those heavenly worlds will separate between him and what he touches. One might
think the atmosphere was made transparent with this
design, to give man, in the heavenly bodies, the perpetual presence of the sublime. Seen in the streets of cities,
how great they are! If the stars should appear one night
in a thousand years, how would men believe and adore;
and preserve for many generations the remembrance of
the city of God which had been shown! But every night
come out these envoys of beauty, and light the universe
with their admonishing smile.

The stars awaken a certain reverence, because though
always present, they are inaccessible; but all natural
objects make a kindred impression, when the mind is
open to their influence. Nature never wears a mean
appearance. Neither does the wisest man extort her
secret, and lose his curiosity by finding out all her perfection. Nature never became a toy to a wise spirit. The
flowers, the animals, the mountains, reflected the wisdom of his best hour, as much as they had delighted
the simplicity of his childhood.

When we speak of nature in this manner, we have
a distinct but most poetical sense in the mind. We mean
the integrity of impression made by manifold natural
objects. It is this which distinguishes the stick of timber
of the wood-cutter, from the tree of the poet. The
charming landscape which I saw this morning is in-
dubitably made up of some twenty or thirty farms.

Miller owns this field, Locke that, and Manning the woodland beyond. But none of them owns the landscape. There is a property in the horizon which no man has but he whose eye can integrate all the parts, that is, the poet. This is the best part of these men's farms, yet to this their warranty-deeds give no title.

To speak truly, few adult persons can see nature. Most persons do not see the sun. At least they have a very superficial seeing. The sun illuminates only the eye of the man, but shines into the eye and the heart of the child. The lover of nature is he whose inward and outward senses are still truly adjusted to each other; who has retained the spirit of infancy even into the era of manhood. His intercourse with heaven and earth becomes part of his daily food. In the presence of nature a wild delight runs through the man, in spite of real sorrows. Nature says,—he is my creature, and maugre all his impertinent griefs, he shall be glad with me. Not the sun or the summer alone, but every hour and season yields its tribute of delight; for every hour and change corresponds to and authorizes a different state of the mind, from breathless noon to grimmest midnight. Nature is a setting that fits equally well a comic or a mourning piece. In good health, the air is a cordial or incredible virtue. Crossing a bare common, in snow puddles, at twilight, under a clouded sky, without having in my thoughts any occurrence of special good fortune, I have enjoyed a perfect exhilaration. I am glad to the brink of fear. In the woods, too, a man casts off his years, as the snake his slough, and at what period soever of life, is always a child. In the woods is perpetual youth. Within these plantations of God, a decorum and sanctity reign, a perennial festival is dressed, and the guest sees not how he should tire of them in a thousand years. In the woods, we return to reason and faith. There I feel that nothing can befall me in life,—no disgrace, no calamity (leaving me my eyes), which nature cannot repair. Standing on the bare ground,—my head bathed by the blithe air, and uplifted into infinite space,—all mean egotism vanishes. I become a transparent eye-ball; I am nothing; I see all; the currents of the Universal Being circulate through me; I am part or parcel of God. The name of the nearest friend sounds then foreign and accidental: to be brothers, to be acquaintances, master or servant, is then a trifle and a disturbance. I am the lover of uncontained and immortal beauty. In the wilderness, I find something more dear and connate than in streets or villages. In the tranquil landscape, and especially in the distant line of the horizon, man beholds somewhat as beautiful as his own nature.

An Island Paradise

[FROM *Musings of a Solitary Stroller*]

JEAN-JACQUES ROUSSEAU

1777

FIFTH PROMENADE

. . . I found my existence so charming, and led a life so agreeable to my humor, that I resolved here to end my days. My only source of disquiet was whether I should be allowed to carry my project out. . . . In the midst of the presentiments that disturbed me, I would fain have had people make a perpetual prison of my refuge, to confine me in it for all the rest of my life. I longed for them to cut off all chance and all hope of leaving it; to forbid my holding any communication with the mainland, so that knowing nothing of what was going on in the world, I might have forgotten the world's existence, and people might have forgotten mine too.

They suffered me to pass only two months in the island, but I could have passed two years, two centuries, and all eternity, without a moment's weariness; though I had not, with my companion, any other society than that of the steward, his wife, and their servants. They were in truth honest souls and nothing more, but that was just what I wanted. . . .

Carried thither in a violent hurry, alone and without a thing, I afterwards sent for my housekeeper, my books, and my scanty possessions—of which I had the delight of unpacking nothing—leaving my boxes and chests just as they had come, and dwelling in the house where I counted on ending my days exactly as if it were an inn whence I must set forth on the morrow. All things went so well, just as they were, that to think of ordering them better were to spoil them. One of my greatest joys was to leave my books fastened up in their boxes, and to be without even a case for writing. When any luckless letter forced me to take up a pen for an answer, I grumblingly borrowed the steward's inkstand, and hurried to give it back to him with all the haste I could, in the vain hope that I should never have need of the loan any more. Instead of meddling with those weary quires and reams and piles of old books, I filled my chamber with flowers and grasses; for I was then in my first fervor for botany. . . . Having given up employment that would be a task to me, I needed one that would be an amusement, nor cause me more pains than a sluggard might choose to take. I undertook to make the "Flora Petrinsularis"; and to describe every single plant on the island, in detail enough to occupy me for the rest of my days. . . . In consequence of this fine scheme, every morning after breakfast, which we all took in company, I used to go with a magnifying-glass in my hand, and my "Systema Naturae" under my arm, to visit some district of the island. I had divided it for that purpose into small squares, meaning to go through them one after another in each season of the year. . . . At the end of two or three hours I used to return laden with an ample harvest—a provision for amusing myself after dinner indoors, in case of rain. I spent the rest of the morning in going with the steward, his wife, and Thérèse, to see the laborers and the harvesting, and I generally set to work along with them: many a time when people from Berne came to see me, they found me perched on a high tree, with a bag fastened round my waist; I kept filling it with fruit, and then let it down to the ground with a rope. The exercise I had taken in the morning, and the good-humor that always comes from exercise, made the repose of dinner vastly pleasant to me. But if dinner was kept up too long, and fine weather invited me forth, I could not wait; but was speedily off to throw myself all alone into a boat, which, when the water was smooth enough, I used to pull out to the middle of the lake. There, stretched at full length in the boat's bottom, with my eyes turned up to the sky, I let myself float slowly hither and thither as the water listed, sometimes for hours together; plunged in a thousand confused delicious musings, which, though they had no fixed nor constant object, were not the less on that account a hundred times dearer to me than all that I had found sweetest in what they call the pleasures of life. Often warned by the going down of the sun that it was time to return, I found myself so far from the island that I was forced to row with all my might to get in before it was pitch dark. At other times, instead of losing myself in the midst of the waters, I had a fancy to coast along the green shores of the island, where the clear waters and cool shadows tempted me to bathe. But one of my most frequent expeditions was from the larger island to the smaller: there I disembarked and spent my afternoon—sometimes in limited rambles among wild elders, persicaries, willows, and shrubs of every species; sometimes settling myself on the top of a sandy knoll, covered with turf, wild thyme, flowers, even sainfoin and trefoil that had most likely been sown there in old days, making excellent quarters for rabbits. They might multiply in peace without either fearing anything or harming anything. I spoke of this to the steward. He at once had male and female rabbits brought from Neuchâtel, and we went in high state—his wife, one of his sisters, Thérèse, and I—to settle them in the little islet. . . . The foundation of our colony was a feast-day. The pilot of the Argonauts was not prouder than I, as I bore my company and the rabbits in triumph from our island to the smaller one. . . .

When the lake was too rough for me to sail, I spent my afternoon in going up and down the island, gathering plants to right and left; seating myself now in smiling lonely nooks to dream at my ease, now on little terraces and knolls, to follow with my eyes the superb and ravishing prospect of the lake and its shores, crowned on one side by the neighboring hills, and on the other melting into rich and fertile plains up to the feet of the pale-blue mountains on their far-off edge.

As evening drew on, I used to come down from the high ground, and sit on the beach at the water's brink in some hidden sheltering-place. There the murmur of the waves and their agitation charmed all my senses, and drove every other movement away from my soul: they plunged it into delicious dreamings, in which I was often surprised by night. The flux and reflux of the water, its ceaseless stir, swelling and falling at intervals, striking on ear and sight, made up for the internal movements which my musings extinguished; they were enough to give me delight in mere existence, without taking any trouble of thinking. From time to time arose some passing thought of the instability of the things of this world, of which the face of the waters offered an image: but such light impressions were swiftly effaced in the uniformity of the ceaseless motion, which rocked me as in a cradle; it held me with such fascination that even when called at the hour and by the signal appointed, I could not tear myself away without summoning all my force.

After supper, when the evening was fine, we used to go all together for a saunter on the terrace, to breathe the freshness of the air from the lake. We sat down in the arbor—laughing, chatting, or singing some old song —and then we went home to bed, well pleased with the day, and only craving another that should be exactly like it on the morrow. . . .

All is a continual flux upon the earth. Nothing in it keeps a form constant and determinate; our affections— fastening on external things—necessarily change and pass just as they do. Ever in front of us or behind us, they recall the past that is gone, or anticipate a future that in many a case is destined never to be. There is nothing solid to which the heart can fix itself. Here we have little more than a pleasure that comes and passes away; as for the happiness that endures, I cannot tell if it be so much as known among men. There is hardly in the midst of our liveliest delights a single instant when the heart could tell us with real truth, *"I would this instant might last forever."* And how can we give the name of happiness to a fleeting state that all the time leaves the heart unquiet and void,—that makes us regret something gone, or still long for something to come?

But if there is a state in which the soul finds a situation solid enough to comport with perfect repose, and with the expansion of its whole faculty, without need of calling back the past or pressing on towards the future; where time is nothing for it, and the present has no ending; with no mark for its own duration, and without a trace of succession; without a single other sense of privation or delight, of pleasure or pain, of desire or apprehension, than this single sense of existence—so long as such a state endures, he who finds himself in it may talk of bliss, not with a poor, relative, and imperfect happiness such as people find in the pleasures of life, but with a happiness full, perfect, and sufficing, that leaves in the soul no conscious unfilled void. Such a state was many a day mine in my solitary musings in the isle of St. Peter, either lying in my boat as it floated on the water, or seated on the banks of the broad lake, or in other places than the little isle—on the brink of some broad stream, or a rivulet murmuring over a gravel bed.

What is it that one enjoys in a situation like this? Nothing outside of one's self, nothing except one's self and one's own existence. . . . But most men, tossed as they are by unceasing passion, have little knowledge of such a state: they taste it imperfectly for a few moments, and then retain no more than an obscure confused idea of it, that is too weak to let them feel its charm.

Trans. H. E. H.

Nature in the New World

[FROM *Atala*]

FRANÇOIS RENÉ,
VICOMTE DE CHATEAUBRIAND

1801

France formerly possessed, in North America, a vast empire which extended from Labrador to the Floridas, and from the shores of the Atlantic to the remotest lakes of Upper Canada.

Four great rivers, having their sources in the same mountains, divide these immense regions; the river St. Lawrence, which loses itself in the East, in the gulf of its own name; the river of the West, which empties itself into unknown seas; the river Bourbon, which runs from South to North, and falls into Hudson's bay; the Meschaceba, which runs from North to South, and empties into the Gulf of Mexico.

This last river, through a course of more than a thousand leagues, waters a delightful country, which the inhabitants of the United States call New Eden, and to which the French have left the soft name of Louisiana. A thousand other rivers, tributary to the Meschaceba, the Missouri, the Illinois, the Akanza, the Ohio, the Wabash, the Tennessee, etc., enrich it with their slime, and fertilize it with their waters. When all these rivers are swelled by the rains and the melting of the snows; when the tempests have swept over the whole face of the country, Time collects, from every source,

the trees torn from their roots. He fastens them together with vines; he cements them with rich soil; he
plants upon them young shrubs, and launches his work
upon the waters. Transported by the swelling flood,
these rafts descend from all parts into the Meschaceba.
The old river takes possession of them, and pushes them
forward to his mouth, in order there to form with them
a new branch. Sometimes he raises his mighty voice
in passing between the mountains; expanding his
waters; overflowing the loftiest trees, those colonnades
of the forest, and deluging the pyramids of the Indian
tombs. This is the Nile of the deserts.

But in scenes of nature, elegance is always united
with magnificence; and while the middle current wafts
towards the sea the carcasses of pines and oaks, you
may see, all along each shore, floating islands of pistia
and nenuphar, ascending the river, by the force of
contrary currents; the yellow blossoms of which rise
into the appearance of little pavilions. Green serpents,
blue herons, flamingoes, young crocodiles, embark as
passengers on board these vessels of flowers; and the
little colony, displaying to the winds its golden sails,
gently glides towards the shore, and sleeps securely
in some retired creek.

From the mouth of the Meschaceba to its junction
with the Ohio, one continued picture covers its surface.
On the western shore, savannas open to view as far as
the sight extends. Their waving verdure, as the prospect
stretches, seems to reach the azure vault of heaven,
where it wholly disappears. In these boundless meadows
are seen, straying, droves of three or four thousand
wild buffaloes. Sometimes a bison, borne down with
years, cuts through the waves, and lands upon some
island of the Meschaceba, to sleep quietly among the
high grass. By his forehead, ornamented with two
crescents. and his grisly beard, you would take him for

the bellowing river god; who casts a look over the
waters and seems satisfied with the wild productions
which its shores so abundantly yield.

Such is the scene on the western shore; but it suddenly changes on the opposite side; and affords an admirable contrast. Bending over the banks of the river,
forming into little clusters upon the tops of the rocks,
and upon the summits of the mountains, scattered
through the valleys, trees of every shape, of every colour, and of every perfume, mingle and grow up together, rearing their tops to the clouds. Wild vines, such
as begonias, and coloquintidas, entwine together at
the roots of the trees, climb up the trunks, creep to
the extremity of the branches, and shoot from the maple
to the tulip, from the tulip to the elm; exhibiting the
appearance of a thousand grottos, a thousand alcoves,
a thousand piazzas.

It often happens that these lianes, in wandering
from tree to tree, cross branches of rivers, actually
forming arches and bridges, festooned with flowers. In
the midst of these massy columns, the superb magnolia
elevates its immoveable cone. Covered with its white
roses, it reigns supreme over all the forest, and has no
rival but the palm tree, which gently waves its verdant
branches near the other's lofty top.

A multitude of animals, placed by the hand of their
Creator, in these delightful retreats, diffuse life and
enchantment through the whole. From the skirts of the
groves are seen bears, intoxicated with grapes, reeling
upon the branches of the elms; flocks of caribeaus,
bathing in a lake; black squirrels playing among the
thick foliage. Mock birds, and Virginia pigeons of the
size of a sparrow, descend upon the grass plats, painted
with strawberries. Green paroquets, with yellow heads,
red cardinals, and purple woodpeckers, climb, after
many times encircling, to the tops of the cypresses.
Humming birds sparkle upon the jessamine of the

Floridas; and the bird-catching serpents hiss, as they swing suspended from the leafy domes, resembling the twining lianes.

If all is silence and repose in the savannas, on the other side of the river, here, on the contrary, all is movement and murmur. Strokes of the beak against the trunk of the oaks, the rustling of beasts, which hurry through the woods, browsing, and grinding between their teeth, the seeds and stones of various fruits; the roaring of the waters, the feeble groanings, hoarse bellowings, and soft murmurings, fill these deserts with a wild and pleasant harmony. But when a breeze begins to animate these solitudes, to put in motion all these floating bodies, to confound all these masses of white, azure, green, and red; to blend all colours, unite all murmurs, then there proceed from the recesses of these forests such noises, and the spectator is presented with such a view, as it would be in vain for me to attempt to describe to those who have never traversed over these primitive fields of nature.

Trans. Caleb Bingham (Boston: 1802).

The Castalian Fountain

[FROM *Walden*]

HENRY DAVID THOREAU

1854

The scenery of Walden is on a humble scale, and, though very beautiful, does not approach to grandeur, nor can it much concern one who has not long frequented it or lived by its shore; yet this pond is so remarkable for its depth and purity as to merit a partic-

ular description. It is a clear and deep green well, half
a mile long and a mile and three quarters in circumference, and contains about sixty-one and a half acres;
a perennial spring in the midst of pine and oak woods,
without any visible inlet or outlet except by the clouds
and evaporation. The surrounding hills rise abruptly
from the water to the height of forty to eighty feet,
though on the southeast and east they attain to about
one hundred and one hundred and fifty feet respec-
tively, within a quarter and a third of a mile. They
are exclusively woodland. All our Concord waters have
two colors at least; one when viewed at a distance,
and another, more proper, close at hand. The first de-
pends more on the light, and follows the sky. In clear
weather, in summer, they appear blue at a little distance, especially if agitated, and at a great distance all
appear alike. In stormy weather they are sometimes of
a dark slate-color. The sea, however, is said to be blue
one day and green another without any perceptible
change in the atmosphere. I have seen our river, when,
the landscape being covered with snow, both water and
ice were almost as green as grass. Some consider blue
"to be the color of pure water, whether liquid or solid."
But, looking directly down into our waters from a boat,
they are seen to be of very different colors. Walden is
blue at one time and green at another, even from the
same point of view. Lying between the earth and the
heavens, it partakes of the color of both. Viewed from
a hilltop it reflects the color of the sky; but near at
hand it is of a yellowish tint next the shore where you
can see the sand, then a light green, which gradually
deepens to a uniform dark green in the body of the
pond. In some lights, viewed even from a hilltop, it is
of a vivid green next the shore. Some have referred this
to the reflection of the verdure; but it is equally green
there against the railroad sandbank, and in the spring,
before the leaves are expanded, and it may be simply

the result of the prevailing blue mixed with the yellow
of the sand. Such is the color of its iris. This is that portion, also, where in the spring, the ice being warmed by
the heat of the sun reflected from the bottom, and also
transmitted through the earth, melts first and forms a
narrow canal about the still frozen middle. Like the
rest of our waters, when much agitated, in clear
weather, so that the surface of the waves may reflect
the sky at the right angle, or because there is more light
mixed with it, it appears at a little distance of a darker
blue than the sky itself; and at such a time, being on its
surface, and looking with divided vision, so as to see
the reflection, I have discerned a matchless and indescribable light blue, such as watered or changeable
silks and sword blades suggest, more cerulean than the
sky itself, alternating with the original dark green on
the opposite sides of the waves, which last appeared but
muddy in comparison. It is a vitreous greenish blue, as
I remember it, like those patches of the winter sky seen
through cloud vistas in the west before sundown. Yet
a single glass of its water held up to the light is as colorless as an equal quantity of air. It is well known that a
large plate of glass will have a green tint, owing, as the
makers say, to its "body," but a small piece of the same
will be colorless. How large a body of Walden water
would be required to reflect a green tint I have never
proved. The water of our river is black or a very dark
brown to one looking directly down on it, and, like that
of most ponds, imparts to the body of one bathing in
it a yellowish tinge; but this water is of such crystalline
purity that the body of the bather appears of an alabas-
ter whiteness, still more unnatural, which, as the limbs
are magnified and distorted withal, produces a monstrous effect, making fit studies for a Michael Angelo.

The water is so transparent that the bottom can easily
be discerned at the depth of twenty-five feet or thirty
feet. Paddling over it, you may see, many feet beneath

the surface, the schools of perch and shiners, perhaps only an inch long, yet the former easily distinguished by their transverse bars, and you think that they must be ascetic fish that find a subsistence there. Once, in the winter, many years ago, when I had been cutting holes through the ice in order to catch pickerel, as I stepped ashore I tossed my axe back on to the ice, but, as if some evil genius had directed it, it slid four or five rods directly into one of the holes, where the water was twenty-five feet deep. Out of curiosity, I lay down on the ice and looked through the hole, until I saw the axe a little on one side standing on its head, with its helve erect and gently swaying to and fro with the pulse of the pond; and there it might have stood erect and swaying till in the course of time the handle rotted off, if I had not disturbed it. Making another hole directly over it with an ice chisel which I had, and cutting down the longest birch which I could find in the neighborhood with my knife, I made a slip-noose, which I attached to its end, and, letting it down carefully, passed it over the knob of the handle, and drew it by a line along the birch, and so pulled the axe out again.

The shore is composed of a belt of smooth rounded white stones like paving-stones, excepting one or two short sand beaches, and is so steep that in many places a single leap will carry you into water over your head; and were it not for its remarkable transparency, that would be the last to be seen of its bottom till it rose on the opposite side. Some think it is bottomless. It is nowhere muddy, and a casual observer would say that there were no weeds at all in it; and of noticeable plants, except in the little meadows recently overflowed, which do not properly belong to it, a closer scrutiny does not detect a flag nor a bulrush, nor even a lily, yellow or white, but only a few small heart-leaves and potamogetons, and perhaps a water-target or two; all which however a bather might not perceive; and these plants are clean and bright like the element they grow in. The stones extend a rod or two into the water, and then the bottom is pure sand, except in the deepest parts, where there is usually a little sediment, probably from the decay of the leaves which have been wafted on to it so many successive falls and a bright green weed is brought up on anchors even in midwinter.

We have one other pond just like this, White Pond, in Nine Acre Corner, about two and a half miles westerly; but, though I am acquainted with most of the ponds within a dozen miles of this centre, I do not know a third of this pure and well-like character. Successive nations perchance have drank at, admired, and fathomed it, and passed away, and still its water is green and pellucid as ever. Not an intermitting spring! Perhaps on that spring morning when Adam and Eve were driven out of Eden Walden Pond was already in existence, and even then breaking up in a gentle spring rain accompanied with mist and a southerly wind, and covered with myriads of ducks and geese, which had not heard of the fall, when still such pure lakes sufficed them. Even then it had commenced to rise and fall, and had clarified its waters and colored them of the hue they now wear, and obtained a patent of Heaven to be the only Walden Pond in the world and distiller of celestial dews. Who knows in how many unremembered nations' literatures this has been the Castalian Fountain? or what nymphs presided over it in the Golden Age? It is a gem of the first water which Concord wears in her coronet.

Ode to the West Wind

PERCY BYSSHE SHELLEY

1820

I

O wild West Wind, thou breath of Autumn's being,
Thou, from whose unseen presence the leaves dead
Are driven, like ghosts from an enchanter fleeing.

Yellow, and black, and pale, and hectic red,
Pestilence-stricken multitudes: O thou,
Who chariotest to their dark wintry bed

The wingèd seeds, where they lie cold and low,
Each like a corpse within its grave, until
Thine azure sister of the spring shall blow

Her clarion o'er the dreaming earth, and fill
(Driving sweet buds like flocks to feed in air)
With living hues and odours plain and hill:

Wild Spirit, which art moving everywhere;
Destroyer and preserver; hear, Oh hear!

II

Thou on whose stream, mid the steep sky's commotion,
Loose clouds like earth's decaying leaves are shed,
Shook from the tangled boughs of Heaven and Ocean,

Angels of rain and lightning; there are spread
On the blue surface of thine airy surge,
Like the bright hair uplifted from the head

Of some fierce Maenad, even from the dim verge
Of the horizon to the zenith's height
The locks of the approaching storm. Thou dirge

Of the dying year, to which this closing night
Will be the dome of a vast sepulchre,
Vaulted with all thy congregated might

Of vapours, from whose solid atmosphere
Black rain, and fire, and hail will burst; Oh hear!

III

Thou who didst waken from his summer dreams
The blue Mediterranean, where he lay,
Lulled by the coil of his crystalline streams,

Beside a pumice isle in Baiae's bay,
And saw in sleep old palaces and towers
Quivering within the wave's intenser day,

All overgrown with azure moss and flowers
So sweet, the sense faints picturing them! Thou
For whose path the Atlantic's level powers

Cleave themselves into chasms, while far below
The sea-blooms and the oozy woods which wear
The sapless foliage of the ocean, know

Thy voice, and suddenly grow gray with fear,
And tremble and despoil themselves: Oh hear!

IV

If I were a dead leaf thou mightest bear;
If I were a swift cloud to fly with thee;
A wave to pant beneath thy power, and share

The impulse of thy strength, only less free
Than thou, O uncontrollable! If even
I were as in my boyhood, and could be

The comrade of thy wanderings over heaven,
As then when to outstrip thy skiey speed
Scarce seemed a vision; I would ne'er have striven

As thus with thee in prayer in my sore need.
Oh lift me as a wave, a leaf, a cloud!
I fall upon the thorns of life! I bleed!

A heavy weight of hours has chained and bowed
One too like thee: tameless, and swift, and proud.

v

Make me thy lyre, even as the forest is:
What if my leaves are falling like its own!
The tumult of thy mighty harmonies

Will take from both a deep, autumnal tone,
Sweet though in sadness. Be thou, spirit fierce,
My spirit! Be thou me, impetuous one!

Drive my dead thoughts over the universe
Like withered leaves to quicken a new birth!
And, by the incantation of this verse,

Scatter, as from an unextinguished hearth
Ashes and sparks, my words among mankind!
Be through my lips to unawakened earth

The trumpet of a prophecy! O, wind,
If Winter comes, can Spring be far behind?

Glorious Forms

[FROM *The Sorrows of Young Werther*]

Johann Wolfgang von
GOETHE

1774

August 18, 1771

Must it be ever thus—that the source of happiness
must also be the fountain of our misery? The rich and
ardent feeling which filled my heart with a love of
Nature, overwhelmed me with a torrent of delight, and
brought all paradise before me, has now become an
insupportable torment—a demon which perpetually
pursues me. When I used to gaze from these rocks
upon the mountains across the river and upon the
green valley before me, and saw everything around
budding and bursting; the hills clothed from foot to
peak with tall, thick trees; the valleys in all their variety, shaded with the loveliest woods; and the river
gently gliding along among the whispering reeds, mir-
roring the clouds which the soft evening breeze wafted
across the sky—when I heard the groves about me
melodious with the music of birds, and saw the million swarms of insects dancing in the last golden beams
of the sun, whose setting rays awoke the humming
beetles from their grassy beds, while the subdued tumult around me drew my attention to the ground, and
I there observed the hard rock giving nourishment to
the dry moss, while the heather flourished upon the
arid sands below me—all this conveyed to me the holy
fire which animates all Nature, and fil'ed and glowed

within my heart. I felt myself exalted by this overflowing fullness to the perception of the Godhead, and the glorious forms of an infinite universe stirred within my soul! Stupendous mountains encompassed me, abysses yawned at my feet, and cataracts fell headlong down before me; rivers rolled through the plains below, and rocks and mountains resounded from afar. In the depths of the earth I saw the mysterious powers at work; on its surface, and beneath the heavens there teemed ten thousand living creatures. Everything is alive with an infinite variety of forms; mankind safeguards itself in little houses and settles and rules in its own way over the wide universe. Poor fool! in whose petty estimation of all things are little. From the inaccessible mountains, across the wilderness which no mortal foot has trod, far as the confines of the unknown ocean, breathes the spirit of the eternal Creator; and every speck of dust which He has made finds favor in His sight— Ah, how often at that time has the flight of a crane, soaring above my head, inspired me with the desire to be transported to the shores of the immeasurable ocean, there to quaff the pleasures of life from the foaming goblet of the Infinite, and to realize, if but for a moment with the confined powers of my soul, the bliss of that Creator Who accomplishes all things in Himself, and through Himself!

Trans. Victor Lange (New York: Rinehart & Co., 1949).

The Perfect Image of a Mighty Mind

[FROM *The Prelude*, Book XI]

WILLIAM WORDSWORTH

1805

Even like this Maid before I was call'd forth
From the retirement of my native hills
I lov'd whate'er I saw; nor lightly lov'd,
But fervently, did never dream of aught
More grand, more fair, more exquisitely fram'd
Than those few nooks to which my happy feet
Were limited. I had not at that time
Liv'd long enough, nor in the least survived
The first diviner influence of this world,
As it appears to unaccustom'd eyes;
I worshipp'd then among the depth of things
As my soul bade me; could I then take part
In aught but admiration, or be pleased
With any thing but humbleness and love;
I felt, and nothing else; I did not judge,
I never thought of judging, with the gift
Of all this glory fill'd and satisfi'd.
And afterwards, when through the gorgeous Alps
Roaming, I carried with me the same heart:
In truth, this degradation, howsoe'er
Induced, effect in whatsoe'er degree
Of custom, that prepares such wantonness
As makes the greatest things give way to least.
Or any other cause which hath been named;
Or lastly, aggravated by the times,
Which with their passionate sounds might often make

The milder minstrelsies of rural scenes
Inaudible, was transient; I had felt
Too forcibly, too early in my life,
Visitings of imaginative power
For this to last: I shook the habit off
Entirely and for ever, and again
In Nature's presence stood, as I stand now,
A sensitive, and a creative soul.

There are in our existence spots of time,
Which with distinct pre-eminence retain
A vivifying Virtue, whence, depress'd
By false opinion and contentious thought,
Or aught of heavier or more deadly weight,
In trivial occupations, and the round
Of ordinary intercourse, our minds
Are nourished and invisibly repair'd,
A virtue by which pleasure is enhanced
That penetrates, enables us to mount
When high, more high, and lifts us up when fallen.
This efficacious spirit chiefly lurks
Among those passages of life in which
We have had deepest feeling that the mind
Is lord and master, and that outward sense
Is but the obedient servant of her will.
Such moments worthy of all gratitude,
Are scatter'd everywhere, taking their date
From our first childhood: in our childhood even
Perhaps are most conspicuous. . . .

ROMANTIC PRIMITIVISM, OR THE NOBLE SAVAGE

A race of real children.
—William Wordsworth

"A Child of Nature"

[FROM *Typee*]

HERMAN MELVILLE

1846

Toward the sea my progress was barred by an express prohibition of the savages; and after having made two or three ineffectual attempts to reach it, as much to gratify my curiosity as anything else, I gave up the idea. It was in vain to think of reaching it by stealth, since the natives escorted me in numbers wherever I went, and not for one single moment that I can recall to mind was I ever permitted to be alone.

The green and precipitous elevations that stood ranged around the head of the vale where Marheyo's habitation was situated effectually precluded all hope of escape in that quarter, even if I could have stolen away from the thousand eyes of the savages.

But these reflections now seldom obtruded upon me; I gave myself up to the passing hour, and if ever disagreeable thoughts arose in my mind, I drove them away. When I looked around the verdant recess in which I was buried, and gazed up to the summits of the lofty eminence that hemmed me in, I was well disposed to think that I was in the "Happy Valley," and that beyond those heights there was naught but a world of care and anxiety.

As I extended my wanderings in the valley and grew more familiar with the habits of its inmates, I was fain to confess that, despite the disadvantages of his condition, the Polynesian savage, surrounded by all the luxurious provisions of nature, enjoyed an infinitely happier, though certainly a less intellectual existence, than the self-complacent European.

The naked wretch who shivers beneath the bleak skies, and starves among the inhospitable wilds of Tierra del Fuego, might indeed be made happier by civilization, for it would alleviate his physical wants. But the voluptuous Indian, with every desire supplied, whom Providence has bountifully provided with all the sources of pure and natural enjoyment, and from whom are removed so many of the ills and pains of life—what has he to desire at the hands of Civilization? She may "cultivate his mind," may "elevate his thoughts"—these I believe are the established phrases—but will he be the happier? Let the once smiling and populous Hawaiian islands with their now diseased, starving, and dying natives, answer the question. The missionaries may seek to disguise the matter as they will, but the facts are incontrovertible; and the devoutest Christian who visits that group with an unbiased mind, must go away mournfully asking—"Are these, alas! the fruits of twenty-five years of enlightening?"

In a primitive state of society, the enjoyments of life, though few and simple, are spread over a great extent, and are unalloyed; but Civilization, for every advantage she imparts, holds a hundred evils in reserve

—the heart burnings, the jealousies, the social rivalries, the family dissensions, and the thousand self-inflicted discomforts of refined life, which make up in units the swelling aggregate of human misery, are unknown among these unsophisticated people.

Among the permanent inmates of the house were likewise several lovely damsels, who instead of thrumming pianos and reading novels, like more enlightened young ladies, substituted for these employments the manufacture of a fine species of tappa; but for the greater portion of the time were skipping from house to house, gadding and gossiping with their acquaintances.

From the rest of these, however, I must except the beauteous nymph Fayaway, who was my peculiar favorite. Her free, pliant figure was the very perfection of female grace and beauty. Her complexion was a rich and mantling olive, and when watching the glow upon her cheeks I could almost swear that beneath the transparent medium there lurked the blushes of a faint vermilion. The face of this girl was a rounded oval, and each feature as perfectly formed as the heart or imagination of man could desire. Her full lips, when parted with a smile, disclosed teeth of dazzling whiteness; and when her rosy mouth opened with a burst of merriment, they looked like the milk-white seeds of the "arta," a fruit of the valley, which, when cleft in twain, shows them reposing in rows on either side, imbedded in the rich and juicy pulp. Her hair of the deepest brown, parted irregularly in the middle, flowed in natural ringlets over her shoulders, and whenever she chanced to stoop, fell over and hid from view her lovely bosom. Gazing into the depths of her strange blue eyes, when she was in contemplative mood, they seemed most placid yet unfathomable; but when illuminated by some lively emotion, they beamed upon the beholder like stars. The hands of Fayaway were as soft and deli-

cate as those of any countess; for an entire exemption
from rude labor marks the girlhood and even prime of a
Typee woman's life. Her feet, though wholly exposed,
were as diminutive and fairly shaped as those which
peep from beneath the skirts of a Lima lady's dress.
The skin of this young creature, from continual ablu-
tions and the use of mollifying ointments, was incon-
ceivably smooth and soft.

I may succeed, perhaps, in particularizing some of the
individual features of Fayaway's beauty, but that general
loveliness of appearance which they all contributed to
produce I will not attempt to describe. The easy un-
studied graces of a child of nature like this, breathing
from infancy an atmosphere of perpetual summer, and
nurtured by the simple fruits of the earth; enjoying a
perfect freedom from care and anxiety, and removed
effectually from all injurious tendencies, strike the eye
in a manner which cannot be portrayed. This picture
is no fancy sketch; it is drawn from the most vivid recollections of the person delineated.

Children as Models

[FROM *The Sorrows of Young Werther*]

JOHANN WOLFGANG VON
GOETHE

1774

June 29, 1771

The day before yesterday the physician came from
the town to pay a visit to the judge. He found me on
the floor playing with Charlotte's brothers and sisters.
Some of them were scrambling over me, and others

romped with me; and as I caught and tickled them, they made a great uproar. The doctor is the sort of person who adjusts his stuffy cuffs, and continually settles his frill while he is talking; he thought my conduct beneath the dignity of a sensible man. I could see it in his face; but I did not let myself be disturbed, and allowed him to continue his wise talk, while I rebuilt the children's card houses as fast as they threw them down. He went about the town afterwards, complaining that the judge's children were spoiled enough, but that now Werther was completely ruining them.

Yes, Wilhelm, nothing on this earth is closer to my heart than children. When I watch their doings; when I see in the little creatures the seeds of all those virtues and qualities, which they will one day find so indispensable; when I see in their obstinacy all the future firmness and constancy of a noble character, in their capriciousness that gaiety of temper which will carry them over the dangers and troubles of life so simple and unspoiled, I always remember the golden words of the Great Teacher of mankind, "Unless ye become even as one of these." And yet, my friend, these children, who are our equals, whom we ought to consider models—we treat them as though they were our inferiors. They are supposed to have no will of their own! And have we none ourselves? Whence our superiority? Is it because we are older and more experienced? Great God! from the height of Thy Heaven Thou beholdest great children and little children, and no others; and Thy Son has long since declared which afford Thee greater pleasure. But they will not believe in Him, and hear Him not—that, too, is an old story; and they train their children after their own image, and—

Adieu, Wilhelm, I must not continue this useless talk.

Trans. Victor Lange (New York: Rinehart & Co., 1949).

Youth

FRIEDRICH HÖLDERLIN

1799

In my days of boyhood
A god saved me often
From the shouts and the rod of mankind.
Then, safe and virtuous, I played
With flowers of the forest,
And the breezes of Heaven
Played with me.

And as you delight
The hearts of flowers
When towards you
They stretch their slender arms,
So you delighted my heart,
Father Helios! And like Endymion
I was your darling,
Holy Luna.

O all ye faithful
Most kindly gods!
Would that you knew
How my soul loved you then.

Though then not yet I called
You by your names, and you
Addressed me never, as men do,
As though they knew each other,

Yet I knew you better
Than ever I knew men;

I understood the Aether's stillness,
But never have I comprehended human words.

I was reared by the melody
Of rustling woods,
And learned to love
Amongst the flowers;
In the arms of the gods I grew.

Trans. Michael Hamburger (New York: Pantheon Press, 1952).

The Voices of Children

WILLIAM BLAKE

[FROM *Songs of Innocence*]

1788-94

THE LITTLE BLACK BOY

My mother bore me in the southern wild,
And I am black, but O! my soul is white;
White as an angel is the English child,
But I am black, as if bereav'd of light.

My mother taught me underneath a tree,
And sitting down before the heat of day,
She took me on her lap and kissed me,
And pointing to the east, began to say:

"Look on the rising sun: there God does live,
And gives his light, and gives his heat away;
And flowers and trees and beasts and man receive
Comfort in morning, joy in the noonday.

"And we are put on earth a little space,
That we may learn to bear the beams of love;

And these black bodies and this sunburnt face
Is but a cloud, and like a shady grove.

"For when our souls have learn'd that heat to bear,
The cloud will vanish; we shall hear his voice,
Saying: 'Come out from the grove, my love & care,
And round my golden tent like lambs rejoice.' "

Thus did my mother say, and kissed me;
And thus I say to little English boy:
When I from black and he from white cloud free,
And round the tent of God like lambs we joy,

I'll shade him from the heat, till he can bear
To lean in joy upon our father's knee;
And then I'll stand and stroke his silver hair,
And be like him, and he will then love me.

Infant Joy

"I have no name:
I am but two days old."
What shall I call thee?
"I happy am,
Joy is my name."
Sweet joy befall thee!

Pretty joy!
Sweet joy but two days old,
Sweet joy I call thee:
Thou dost smile,
I sing the while,
Sweet joy befall thee!

Laughing Song

When the green woods laugh with the voice of joy,
And the dimpling stream runs laughing by;

When the air does laugh with our merry wit,
And the green hill laughs with the noise of it;

When the meadows laugh with lively green,
And the grasshopper laughs in the merry scene,
When Mary and Susan and Emily
With their sweet round mouths sing "Ha, Ha, He!"

When the painted birds laugh in the shade,
Where our table with cherries and nuts is spread,
Come live & be merry, and join with me,
To sing the sweet chorus of "Ha, Ha, He!"

HOLY THURSDAY

'Twas on a Holy Thursday, their innocent faces clean,
The children walking two & two, in red & blue & green,
Grey-headed beadles walk'd before, with wands as
    white as snow,
Till into the high dome of Paul's they like Thames'
    waters flow.

O what a multitude they seem'd, these flowers of Lon-
    don town!
Seated in companies they sit with radiance all their own.
The hum of multitudes was there, but multitudes of
    lambs,
Thousands of little boys & girls raising their innocent
    hands.

Now like a mighty wind they raise to heaven the voice
    of song,
Or like harmonious thunderings the seats of Heaven
    among.
Beneath them sit the aged men, wise guardians of the
    poor;
Then cherish pity, lest you drive an angel from your
    door.

[FROM *Songs of Experience*]

1788-94

HOLY THURSDAY

Is this a holy thing to see
In a rich and fruitful land,
Babes reduc'd to misery,
Fed with cold and usurous hand?

Is that trembling cry a song?
Can it be a song of joy?
And so many children poor?
It is a land of poverty!

And their sun does never shine,
And their fields are bleak & bare,
And their fields are fill'd with thorns:
It is eternal winter there.

For where-e'er the sun does shine,
And where-e'er the rain does fall,
Babe can never hunger there,
Nor poverty the mind appall.

THE CHIMNEY SWEEPER

A little black thing among the snow,
Crying ' 'weep! 'weep!' in notes of woe!
"Where are thy father & mother? say?"
"They are both gone up to church to pray.

"Because I was happy about the heath,
And smil'd among the winter's snow,
They clothed me in the clothes of death,
And taught me to sing the notes of woe.

"And because I am happy & dance & sing,
They think they have done me no injury,

And are gone to praise God & his Priest & King,
Who make up a heaven of our misery."

LONDON

I wander thro' each charter'd street,
Near where the charter'd Thames does flow,
And mark in every face I meet
Marks of weakness, marks of woe.

In every cry of every Man,
In every Infant's cry of fear,
In every voice, in every ban,
The mind-forg'd manacles I hear.

How the Chimney-sweepers' cry
Every black'ning Church appalls;
And the hapless Soldier's sigh
Runs in blood down Palace walls.

But most thro' midnight streets I hear
How the youthful Harlot's curse
Blasts the new born Infant's tear,
And blights with plagues the Marriage hearse.

INFANT SORROW

My mother groan'd! my father wept.
Into the dangerous world I leapt:
Helpless, naked, piping loud:
Like a fiend hid in a cloud.

Struggling in my father's hands,
Striving against my swadling bands,
Bound and weary I thought best
To sulk upon my mother's breast.

An Indian Chief

[FROM *The Last of the Mohicans*]

JAMES FENIMORE COOPER

1825

After a short and impressive pause, Chingachgook lighted a pipe whose bowl was curiously carved in one of the soft stones of the country, and whose stem was a tube of wood, and commenced smoking. When he had inhaled enough of the fragrance of the soothing weed, he passed the instrument into the hands of the scout. In this manner the pipe had made its rounds three several times, amid the most profound silence, before either of the party opened his lips. Then the Sagamore, as the oldest and highest in rank, in a few calm and dignified words proposed the subject for deliberation. He was answered by the scout, and Chingachgook rejoined when the other objected to his opinions. But the youthful Uncas continued a silent and respectful listener, until Hawkeye, in complaisance, demanded his opinion. Heyward gathered from the manners of the different speakers that the father and son espoused one side of a disputed question, while the white man maintained the other. The contest gradually grew warmer, until it was quite evident the feelings of the speakers began to be somewhat enlisted in the debate.

Notwithstanding the increasing warmth of the amicable contest, the most decorous Christian assembly, not even excepting those in which its reverend ministers are collected, might have learned a wholesome lesson of moderation from the forbearance and courtesy of the disputants. The words of Uncas were received with the same deep attention as those which fell from the maturer wisdom of his father; and so far from manifesting any impatience, neither spoke in reply, until a few moments of silent meditation were, seemingly, bestowed in deliberating on what had already been said.

The language of the Mohicans was accompanied by gestures so direct and natural, that Heyward had but little difficulty in following the thread of their argument. On the other hand, the scout was obscure; because, from the lingering pride of color, he rather affected the cold and artificial manner which characterizes all classes of Anglo-Americans, when unexcited. By the frequency with which the Indians described the marks of a forest trail, it was evident they urged a pursuit by land, while the repeated sweep of Hawkeye's arm towards the Horican denoted that he was for a passage across its waters.

The latter was, to every appearance, fast losing ground, and the point was about to be decided against him, when he arose to his feet, and shaking off his apathy, he suddenly assumed the manner of an Indian, and adopted all the arts of native eloquence. Elevating an arm, he pointed out the track of the sun, repeating the gesture for every day that was necessary to accomplish their object. Then he delineated a long and painful path, amid rocks and water-courses. The age and weakness of the slumbering and unconscious Munro were indicated by signs too palpable to be mistaken. Duncan perceived that even his own powers were spoken lightly of, as the scout extended his palm and mentioned him by the appellation of the "Open Hand"— a name his liberality had purchased of all the friendly tribes. Then came a representation of the light and graceful movements of a canoe, set in forcible contrast to the tottering steps of one enfeebled and tired. He concluded by pointing to the scalp of the Oneida, and apparently urging the necessity of their departing speedily, and in a manner that should leave no trail.

The Mohicans listened gravely, and with countenances that reflected the sentiments of the speaker. Conviction gradually wrought its influence, and towards the close of Hawkeye's speech, his sentences were accompanied by the customary exclamation of commendation. In short, Uncas and his father became converts to his way of thinking, abandoning their own previously expressed opinions with a liberality and candor that, had they been the representatives of some great and civilized people, would have infallibly worked their political ruin, by destroying forever their reputation for consistency.

The instant the matter in discussion was decided, the debate, and everything connected with it, except the result, appeared to be forgotten. Hawkeye, without looking round to read his triumph in applauding eyes very composedly stretched his tall frame before the dying embers, and closed his own organs in sleep.

Left now in a measure to themselves, the Mohicans, whose time had been so much devoted to the interests of others, seized the moment to devote some attention to themselves. Casting off, at once, the grave and austere demeanor of an Indian chief, Chingachgook commenced speaking to his son in the soft and playful tones of affection. Uncas gladly met the familiar air of his father; and before the hard breathing of the scout announced that he slept, a complete change was effected in the manner of his two associates.

It is impossible to describe the music of their language, while thus engaged in laughter and endearments, in such a way as to render it intelligible to those whose ears have never listened to its melody. The compass of their voices, particularly that of the youth, was wonderful, extending from the deepest bass to tones that were even feminine in softness. The eyes of the father followed the plastic and ingenious movements of the son with open delight, and he never failed to smile in reply to the other's contagious, but low laughter. While under the influence of these gentle and natural feelings, no trace of ferocity was to be seen in the softened features of the Sagamore. His figured panoply of death looked more like a disguise assumed in mockery, than a fierce annunciation of a desire to carry destruction in his footsteps.

Another Indian Chief

[FROM *Man as He Is Not; or, Hermsprong*]

ROBERT BAGE

1796

It appears to me, said Hermsprong, that the story I am telling you is very tedious, and totally uninteresting. The ladies, with more politeness than veracity perhaps, assured him to the contrary. I cannot, says he, make it entertaining; I must make it short.

My father was well received. The head man of the village, whose name was Lontac, and who had acquired the appellation of the Great Beaver, received him into his tent. There was a commerce of civility, but none of language. To remedy this, my father availed himself of the son's assistance, and during the winter months learned enough of their language to be able to communicate all the ideas he believed would be necessary for their mutual accommodation.

Early in spring, my father sent for stores; and having distributed presents of rum and tobacco, there was a meeting of head men from all the Nawdoessie villages, whom the Great Beaver addressed thus: Six moons ago, a man from the American people came hither, brought by my son to strengthen peace betwixt us. He has learned our language. He loves our customs. He will reside with us a vast number of moons; perhaps till the Great Spirit calls him away. He has a wife and people. We must build him a wigwam; large, that it may be unto us a storehouse of all the good things we want from the European people. He will be our friend. When we go to war, he will aid us with his counsel. When we return from hunting, he will buy our skins. So we shall have powder and guns, cloth to warm us in winter, and rum to cheer us.

The Great Beaver's speech was well received. The wigwam was built, large and commodious. The stores were deposited. My mother and myself, for I had made my appearance in this best of worlds, arrived safe, with our European servants, our books, our music, our instruments of drawing, and every thing that could be supposed to alleviate the solitude my mother had pictured to herself.

This afflicting solitude, however, did not arrive. The people were civil and attentive; Lontac's family obliging; and there was novelty in the scene. My father even found it difficult to procure leisure for the studies and amusements he most liked. When he could, he read, wrote, drew the rude scenes around him, and kept up a correspondence of philosophy as well as business with Mr. Germersheim.

My mother was a very good woman; not without her prejudices indeed, but a good woman, and a zealous catholic. She loved my father; she saw him in a place of safety and happy. She was happy herself, except when she thought of France, her father, and the convent. The last disturbed her most. She feared she had committed a crime; she had no confessor, and could not absolve herself. She confessed indeed to my father, who consoled her always, and would have given her absolution, had she been pleased to accept it. At length it came into her mind, that greater sins than hers might be expiated, by a conversion to Christianity of a few Nawdoessie females. How did she know but she might be the agent appointed by God, for producing this salutary change in a whole people?

Lodiquashow, the wife of Lontac, the best of squaws, the most obedient of wives, had never presumed to sit down in the presence of the Great Beaver till she had brought him six children. With her my mother determined to begin the great work, and applied herself to learn the language with an assiduity which surprised my father. Perhaps she began her pious labour before she had attained sufficient powers of explanation; for although Lodiquashow heard my mother with the most patient attention, nor once offended by interruption, contradiction, or remark; all the assent my mother was ever able to attain, was, The Great Spirit and Lontac only know.

Unable to produce any effect upon the stupid Lodiquashow, or on the two daughters, who still remained ungiven away in marriage, she determined to try her powers on Lontac himself. Sixty moons, however, passed away before she durst venture; partly owing to a fear she had not yet acquired the full force of the Nawdoessie tongue, and partly to a sort of awe of this venerable chief, who was himself an orator, and who was much beloved, respected, and obeyed.

At length my mother asked an audience and obtained it. It appeared indeed to Lontac to be an inversion of order, that the Great Beaver should lend his ear to a woman for instruction; but there is in these people a politeness derived from education, as well as ours, which qualifies them for patient hearers to a degree I have never observed in more polished nations.

What most of all astonished my mother, was, that though Lontac, after a few lectures, seemed himself to put her on speaking and to be amused, if not instructed, she could seldom obtain an answer; and when she did, it was only to thank her for the pains she took on his account. It is true, he did not always understand; when he understood, he did not always approve; but it is only for a native American to arrive at so high a degree of politeness, as to testify disapprobation, only by a respectful silence.

Wondering that any human creature should be deaf to persuasion, and blind to the sublime truth she had now so oft explained, she began at times to be angry, and ladies are seldom angry, without a little gentle abuse. Intreated, almost commanded, to answer, Lontac spoke with all possible gravity, and the greatest respect, as follows:

One day's journey west of this place, there is, as you have heard, a large lake called the White Bear; because white bears were numerous on its banks, and disputed the sovereignty of the adjacent lands with man. About a thousand moons ago, when the war had lasted many generations of bears and men, the two powers agreed upon a truce, and met on a certain bank of the lake, in order to have a talk. When the orators on both sides—

On both sides! exclaimed my mother.

Lontac proceeded—were preparing to speak, a figure arose from the midst of the lake, of vast dimensions; viewed on one side, it seemed to be a bear; on the other, it seemed to be a man. The white bear part of this awful figure waved its paw into the air to command silence, then said with a terrific voice—

Was ever any thing so preposterous! cries my mother. Sure it is impossible you should believe it!

Why impossible? answered Lontac; it is tradition handed down to us from our fathers. We believe because they said it.

Bears speak! again exclaimed my mother.

A serpent, answered Lontac, spake to the first woman; an ass spake to a prophet; you have said so, and therefore I believe it.

But, said my mother, they were inspired.

So was the half white bear. The Great Spirit inspires everything.

But this is so excessively absurd, said my mother.

I have not called your wonders absurd, Lontac replied; I thought it more decent to believe.

What have I told you preposterous? asked my mother.

Many things far removed from the ordinary course of nature, Lontac replied; I do not presume to call them preposterous; it is better to believe than contradict.

Such obstinacy of politeness provoked my mother, almost as much as contradiction could have done; she told my father what a stupid creature she had undertaken to instruct; and desired that he would endeavour to bring him to the light of truth. My father answered, My dear, they have had missionaries, whose holy lips have hitherto failed. Perhaps our mysteries are too refined for their gross understanding; perhaps the time appointed by Providence for their conversion is not yet come.

I despise them, said my mother, prodigiously.

Do, my dear, my father replied, as much as you can with civility for people who are always doing you services, and showing their regard. I despised them myself, till I found them my equals in knowledge of many things of which I believed them ignorant; and my superiors in the virtues of friendship, hospitality, and integrity.

I shall never be easy among them, said my mother.

You will indeed, my dear, answered my father, when you don't think of converting them.

"George Washington Cannibalistically Developed"

[FROM *Moby Dick*]

HERMAN MELVILLE

1851

Returning to the Spouter-Inn from the chapel I found Queequeg there quite alone; he having left the Chapel before the benediction some time. He was sitting on a bench before the fire, with his feet on the stove hearth, and in one hand was holding close up to his face that little negro idol of his, peering hard into its face, and with a jack-knife gently whittling away at its nose, meanwhile humming to himself in his heathenish way.

But being now interrupted, he put up the image, and pretty soon, going to the table, took up a large book there, and placing it on his lap began counting the pages with deliberate regularity; at every fiftieth page —as I fancied—stopping a moment, looking vacantly around him, and giving utterance to a long-drawn gurgling whistle of astonishment. He would then begin again at the next fifty; seeming to commence at number one each time, as though he could not count more than fifty, and it was only by such a large number of fifties being bound together, that his astonishment at the multitude of pages was excited.

With much interest I sat watching him. Savage though he was, and hideously marred about the face— at least to my taste—his countenance yet had a something in it which was by no means disagreeable. You

cannot hide the soul. Through all his unearthly tattoo-
ings, I thought I saw the traces of a simple honest
heart; and in his large, deep eyes, fiery black and bold,
there seemed tokens of a spirit that would dare a thousand devils. And besides all this, there was a certain
lofty bearing about the Pagan, which even his uncouth-
ness could not altogether maim. He looked like a man
who had never cringed and never had had a creditor.
Whether it was, too, that his head being shaved, his
forehead was drawn out in freer and brighter relief,
and looked more expansive than it other wise would,
this I will not venture to decide; but certain it was his
head was phrenologically an excellent one. It may seem
ridiculous, but it reminded me of General Washington's head, as seen in the popular busts of him. It had
the same long regularly graded retreating slope from
above the brows, which were likewise very projecting,
like two long promontories thickly wooded on top.
Queequeg was George Washington cannibalistically developed.

Whilst I was thus closely scanning him, half-pre-
tending meanwhile to be looking out at the storm from
the casement, he never heeded my presence, never
troubled himself with so much as a single glance; but
appeared wholly occupied with counting the pages of
the marvellous book. Considering how sociably we had
been sleeping together the night previous, and especially the affectionate arm I had found thrown over me
upon waking in the morning, I thought this indifference
of his very strange. But savages are strange beings; at
times you do not know exactly how to take them. At
first they are overawing; their calm self-collectedness
of simplicity seems a Socratic wisdom. I had noticed
also that Queequeg never consorted at all, or but very
little, with the other seamen in the inn. He made no
advances whatever; appeared to have no desire to en-
large the circle of his acquaintances. All this struck me

as mighty singular; yet, upon second thoughts, there
was something almost sublime in it. Here was a man
some twenty thousand miles from home, by the way of
Cape Horn, that is—which was the only way he could
get there—thrown among people as strange to him as
though he were in the planet Jupiter; and yet he
seemed entirely at his ease; preserving the utmost
serenity; content with his own companionship; always
equal to himself. Surely this was a touch of fine philosophy; though no doubt he had never heard there was
such a thing as that. But, perhaps, to be true philosophers, we mortals should not be conscious of so living
or so striving. So soon as I hear that such or such a
man gives himself out for a philosopher, I conclude
that, like the dyspeptic old woman, he must have
"broken his digester."

As I sat there in that now lonely room; the fire burning low, in that mild stage when, after its first intensity has warmed the air, it then only glows to be looked
at; the evening shades and phantoms gathering round
the casements, and peering in upon us silent, solitary
twain; the storm booming without in solemn swells; I
began to be sensible of strange feelings. I felt a melting in me. No more my splintered heart and maddened
hand were turned against the wolfish world. This soothing savage had redeemed it. There he sat, his very indifference speaking a nature in which there lurked no
civilized hypocrisies and bland deceits. Wild he was;
a very sight of sights to see; yet I began to feel myself
mysteriously drawn towards him. And those same things
that would have repelled most others, they were the
very magnets that thus drew me. I'll try a pagan friend,
thought I, since Christian kindness has proved but hollow courtesy. I drew my bench near him, and made
some friendly signs and hints, doing my best to talk
with him meanwhile. At first he little noticed these

advances; but presently, upon my referring to his last night's hospitalities, he made out to ask me whether we were again to be bedfellows. I told him yes; whereat I thought he looked pleased, perhaps a little complimented.

THE ROMANTIC VOYAGE

O my brave soul!
O farther farther sail!
O daring joy, but safe! are they not
all the seas of God?
O farther, farther, farther sail!

—Walt Whitman

Anywhere Out of the World

[FROM *The Spleen of Paris*]

CHARLES BAUDELAIRE

1869

Life is a hospital where every invalid wants to exchange his bed for someone else's. One person wishes to suffer next to a stove; another believes he will be cured if he lies beneath a window.

It occurs to me that I would always be happy where I am not, and this problem of changing one's residence I argue endlessly with my own soul.

"Tell me, soul, you poor cold little soul, how would you like to live in Lisbon? It is supposed to be warm there, and you could cheer yourself up like any lizard. It is a city on the water; they say it is built of marble, and the people hate vegetation so much that all the trees are pulled up. Certainly here is a country to suit your taste: a landscape composed of light and minerals, with water there to reflect them both!"

My soul does not answer.

"Well, since you like quiet so much along with the presence of motion, how about Holland, that blissful land? You might be amused in that country whose paintings have so often pleased you in museums. What about Rotterdam, for instance, you who like forests of masts and ships moored to the very foundations of houses?"

My soul remained speechless.

"Would Batavia please you better? There, moreover, we might discover where the mind of Europe has married the beauty of the tropics."

Not a word. Is my soul dead?

"Well, have you reached that state of torpor where you are happy with your sickness? If that is so, then flee to those regions analogous to Death itself. I labor my point, poor little soul! Why don't we pack up our trunks for Tornio. Or go even farther, to the very end of the Baltic Sea; still farther from existence, if that is possible; we might set ourselves up at the North Pole. After all, there the sun only crisps the earth obliquely, and the slowly alternating light and darkness reduce variety and augment monotony, that half of nonexistence. There we might take long baths made up of shadows, while meantime, to amuse us, the aurora borealis would now and then display scarlet sheaves, just like reflections from fireworks in Hell!"

Finally my soul burst out, and wisely said to me, "I don't care where! Only let it be any place out of this world!"

Trans. H. E. H.

"The Advantages of Looking at Mankind"

[FROM *Letters and Journals*]

GEORGE GORDON,
LORD BYRON

[TO HIS MOTHER, FROM ATHENS]

January 14, 1811

My Dear Madam,—I seize an occasion to write as usual, shortly, but frequently, as the arrival of letters, where there exists no regular communication, is, of course, very precarious. . . . I have lately made several small tours of some hundred or two miles about the Morea, Attica, &c., as I have finished my grand giro by the Troad, Constantinople, &c., and am returned down again to Athens. I believe I have mentioned to you more than once, that I swam (in imitation of Leander, though without his lady) across the Hellespont, from Sestos to Abydos. Of this, and all other particulars, Fletcher, whom I have sent home with papers, &c., will apprize you. I cannot find that he is any loss; being tolerably master of the Italian and modern Greek languages, which last I am also studying with a master, I can order and discourse more than enough for a reasonable man. Besides, the perpetual lamentations after beef and beer, the stupid, bigoted contempt for every thing foreign, and insurmountable incapacity of acquiring even a few words of any language, rendered him, like all other English servants, an incumbrance. I do assure you, the plague of speaking for him, the comforts he required (more than myself by far), the pilaws (a Turkish dish of rice and meat) which he could not eat, the wines which he could not drink, the beds where he could not sleep, and the long list of calamities, such as stumbling horses, want of *tea*! ! ! &c., which assailed him, would have made a lasting source of laughter to a spectator, and inconvenience to a master. After all, the man is honest enough, and, in Christendom, capable enough; but in Turkey, Lord forgive me! my Albanian soldiers, my Tartars and Jannizary, worked for him and us too, as my friend Hobhouse can testify.

It is probable I may steer homewards in spring; but to enable me to do that, I must have remittances. My own funds would have lasted me very well; but I was obliged to assist a friend, who, I know, will pay me; but, in the mean time, I am out of pocket. At present, I do not care to venture a winter's voyage, even if I were otherwise tired of travelling; but I am so convinced of the advantages of looking at mankind instead of reading about them, and the bitter effects of staying at home with all the narrow prejudices of an islander, that I think there should be a law amongst us, to set our young men abroad, for a term, among the few allies our wars have left us.

Here I see and have conversed with French, Italians, Germans, Danes, Greeks, Turks, Americans, &c., &c., &c.; and without losing sight of my own, I can judge of the countries and manners of others. Where I see the superiority of England (which, by the by, we are a good deal mistaken about in many things), I am pleased, and where I find her inferior, I am at least enlightened. Now, I might have staid, smoked in your towns, or fogged in your country, a century, without being sure of this, and without acquiring any thing more useful or amusing at home. I keep no journal, nor have I any intention of scribbling my travels. I have done with authorship, and if, in my last production, I have convinced the critics or the world I was something more than they took me for, I am satisfied: nor will I hazard *that reputation* by a future effort. It is true I have some others in manuscript, but I leave them for those who come after me; and, if deemed worth publishing, they may serve to prolong my memory when I myself shall cease to remember. I have a famous Bavarian artist taking some views of Athens, &c., &c., for me. This will be better than scribbling, a disease I hope myself cured of. I hope, on my return, to lead a quiet, recluse life, but God knows and does best for us all; at least, so they say, and I have nothing to object, as, on the whole, I have no reason to complain of my lot. I am convinced, however, that men do more harm to themselves than ever the devil could do to them. I trust this will find you well, and as happy as can be; you will, at least, be pleased to hear I am so, and yours ever.

George Gordon, Lord Byron

The Friendly Ocean

[FROM *Childe Harold*]

GEORGE GORDON,
LORD BYRON

1816

In my youth's summer I did sing of One,
The wandering outlaw of his own dark mind;
Again I seize the theme, then but begun,

And bear it with me, as the rushing wind
Bears the cloud onwards: in that Tale I find
The furrows of long thought, and dried-up tears,
Which, ebbing, leave a sterile track behind,
O'er which all heavily the journeying years
Plod the last sands of life,—where not a flower appears.

. . . .

Something too much of this:—but now 'tis past,
And the spell closes with its silent seal.
Long absent Harold re-appears at last;
He of the breast which fain no more would feel,
Wrung with the wounds which kill not, but ne'er
    heal;
Yet Time, who changes all, had alter'd him
In soul and aspect as in age: years steal
Fire from the mind as vigour from the limb;
And life's enchanted cup but sparkles near the brim.

His had been quaff'd too quickly, and he found
The dregs were wormwood; but he fill'd again,
And from a purer fount, on holier ground,
And deem'd its spring perpetual; but in vain!
Still round him clung invisibly a chain
Which gall'd for ever, fettering though unseen,
And heavy though it clank'd not; worn with pain,
Which pined although it spoke not, and grew keen,
Entering with every step he took through many a scene.

Secure in guarded coldness, he had mix'd
Again in fancied safety with his kind,
And deem'd his spirit now so firmly fix'd
And sheath'd with an invulnerable mind,
That, if no joy, no sorrow lurk'd behind;
And he, as one, might 'midst the many stand
Unheeded, searching through the crowd to find
Fit speculation; such as in strange land
He found in wonder-works of God and Nature's hand.

But who can view the ripen'd rose, nor seek
To wear it? who can curiously behold
The smoothness and the sheen of beauty's cheek,
Nor feel the heart can never all grow old?
Who can contemplate Fame through clouds unfold
The star which rises o'er her steep, nor climb?
Harold, once more within the vortex, roll'd
On with the giddy circle, chasing Time,
Yet with a nobler aim than in his youth's fond prime.

But soon he knew himself the most unfit
Of men to herd with Man; with whom he held
Little in common; untaught to submit
His thoughts to others, though his soul was quell'd
In youth by his own thoughts, still uncompell'd,
He would not yield dominion of his mind
To spirits against whom his own rebell'd;
Proud though in desolation; which could find
A life within itself, to breathe without mankind.

Where rose the mountains, there to him were friends;
Where roll'd the ocean, thereon was his home;
Where a blue sky, and glowing clime, extends,
He had the passion and the power to roam;
The desert, forest, cavern, breaker's foam,
Were unto him companionship; they spake
A mutual language, clearer than the tome
Of his land's tongue, which he would oft forsake
For Nature's pages glass'd by sunbeams on the lake.

Like the Chaldean, he could watch the stars,
Till he had peopled them with beings bright
As their own beams; and earth, and earthborn jars,
And human frailties, were forgotten quite:
Could he have kept his spirit to that flight
He had been happy; but this clay will sink
Its spark immortal, envying it the light

To which it mounts, as if to break the link
That keeps us from yon heaven which woos us to its
    brink.

But in Man's dwellings he became a thing
Restless and worn, and stern and wearisome,
Droop'd as a wild-born falcon with clipt wing,
To whom the boundless air alone were home:
Then came his fit again, which to o'er-come,
As eagerly the barr'd-up bird will beat
His breast and beak against his wiry dome
Till the blood tinge his plumage, so the heat
Of his impeded soul would through his bosom eat.

Self-exiled Harold wanders forth again,
With nought of hope left, but with less of gloom;
The very knowledge that he lived in vain,
That all was over on this side the tomb,
Had made Despair a smilingness assume,
Which, though 'twere wild,—as on the plunder'd
    wreck
When mariners would madly meet their doom
With draughts intemperate on the sinking deck,—
Did yet inspire a cheer, which he forbore to check.

Canto III, Stanzas 3, 8-16.

"My Roving Passion"

[FROM *The Sketch Book*]

WASHINGTON IRVING

1819-20

I was always fond of visiting new scenes, and observing strange characters and manners. Even when a

mere child I began my travels, and made many tours of discovery into foreign parts and unknown regions of my native city, to the frequent alarm of my parents, and the emolument of the town-crier. As I grew into boyhood, I extended the range of my observations. My holiday afternoons were spent in rambles about the surrounding country. I made myself familiar with all its places famous in history and fable. I knew every spot where a murder or robbery had been committed, or a ghost seen. I visited the neighboring villages, and added greatly to my stock of knowledge, by noting their habits and customs, and conversing with their sages and great men. I even journeyed one long summer's day to the summit of the most distant hill, whence stretched my eye over many a mile of *terra incognita*, and was astonished to find how vast a globe I inhabited.

The rambling propensity strengthened with my years. Books of voyages and travels became my passion, and in devouring their contents, I neglected the regular exercises of the school. How wistfully would I wander about the pier-heads in fine weather and watch the parting ships, bound to distant climes—with what longing eyes would I gaze after their lessening sails, and waft myself in imagination to the ends of the earth.

Further reading and thinking, though they brought this vague inclination into more reasonable bounds, only served to make me more decided. I visited various parts of my own country; and had I been merely a lover of fine scenery, I should have felt little desire to seek elsewhere its gratification: for on my country have the charms of nature been most prodigally lavished. Her mighty lakes, like oceans of liquid silver; her mountains, with their bright aerial tints; her valleys, teeming with wild fertility; her tremendous cataracts, thundering in their solitudes; her boundless plains, waving with spontaneous verdure; her broad deep rivers, rolling in solemn silence to the ocean; her trackless forests, where vegetation puts forth all its magnificence; her skies kindling with the magic of summer clouds and glorious sunshine;—no, never need an American long beyond his own country for the sublime and beautiful of natural scenery.

But Europe held forth the charms of storied and poetical association. There were to be seen the master-pieces of art, the refinements of highly cultivated society, the quaint peculiarities of ancient and local custom. My native country was full of youthful promise: Europe was rich in the accumulated treasures of age. Her very ruins told the history of times gone by, and every mouldering stone was a chronicle. I longed to wander over the scenes of renowned achievement— to tread, as it were, in the footsteps of antiquity—to loiter about the ruined castle—to meditate on the falling tower—to escape, in short, from the common-place realities of the present, and lose myself among the shadowy grandeurs of the past.

I had, beside all this, an earnest desire to see the great men of the earth. We have, it is true, our great men in America: not a city but has an ample share of them. I have mingled among them in my time, and been almost withered by the shade into which they cast me; for there is nothing so baleful to a small man as the shade of a great one, particularly the great man of a city. But I was anxious to see the great men of Europe; for I had read in the works of various philosophers, that all animals degenerated in America, and man among the number. A great man of Europe, thought I, must therefore be as superior to a great man of America, as a peak of the Alps to a highland of the Hudson; and in this idea I was confirmed, by observing the comparative importance and swelling magnitude of many English travellers among us, who, I was as-

sured, were very little people in their own country. I
will visit this land of wonders, thought I, and see the
gigantic race from which I am degenerated.

It had been either my good or evil lot to have my
roving passion gratified. I have wandered through different countries, and witnessed many of the shifting
scenes of life. I cannot say that I have studied them
with the eye of a philosopher; but rather with the
sauntering gaze with which humble lovers of the picturesque stroll from the window of one print-shop to
another; caught sometimes by the delineations of
beauty, sometimes by the distortions of caricature, and
sometimes by the loveliness of landscape. As it is the
fashion for modern tourists to travel pencil in hand,
and bring home their portfolios filled with sketches, I
am disposed to get up a few for the entertainment of
my friends. When, however, I look over the hints and
memorandums I have taken down for the purpose, my
heart almost fails me at finding how my idle humor
has led me aside from the great objects studied by every
regular traveller who would make a book. I fear I shall
give equal disappointment with an unlucky landscape
painter, who had travelled on the continent, but, following the bent of his vagrant inclination, had sketched
in nooks, and corners, and by places. His sketch book
was accordingly crowned with cottages, and landscapes,
and obscure ruins; but he had neglected to paint St.
Peter's, or the Coliseum; the cascade of Terni, or the
bay of Naples; and had not a single glacier or volcano
in his whole collection.

On Wings of Song

[FROM *The Lyrical Intermezzo*]

HEINRICH HEINE

1822-23

9

On wings of song, my dearest,
Far from here shall we go,
Where the Ganges' plains are broadest—
The most beautiful place I know.

There grow crimson-petaled flowers
Beneath the quiet moonlight;
The lotus buds count the hours
Till they with their sister unite.

Small violets dally and titter
And longingly look toward the stars;
Roses secretly chatter
In each other's fragrant ears.

Now listening, now leaping,
Romp innocent gazelles;
And far away is the sweeping
Sound of the sacred falls.

There finally we'd sail
To live 'neath spreading palms,
And love and rest inhale,
And dream our blessed dreams.

43

Age-old fairy tales
Beckon with pale hands,
In musical portrayals
To tell of magic lands:

Where glorious flowers languish
When twilight makes them gilt,
And mutually lavish
The looks of a bride-elect;

Where trees make conversation
And carol merrily,
And streams, in high elation,
Move in dance melody;

Where all love's sweet devices
Appear as if first time,
Mere longing there suffices
To drive one from one's mind!

Ah, could I ever get there
To put my heart at rest,
And abdicate each fret there
And be both free and blessed!

Ah! Land of such surprises,
So real in many a dream;
When morning sunlight rises,
It melts like frothy foam.

Trans. H. E. H.

Meditation and Water

[FROM *Moby Dick*]

HERMAN MELVILLE

1851

Call me Ishmael. Some years ago—never mind how long precisely—having little or no money in my purse, and nothing particular to interest me on shore, I thought I would sail about a little and see the watery part of the world. It is a way I have of driving off the spleen, and regulating the circulation. Whenever I find myself growing grim about the mouth; whenever it is a damp, drizzly November in my soul; whenever I find myself involuntarily pausing before coffin warehouses, and bringing up the rear of every funeral I meet; and especially whenever my hypos get such an upper hand of me, that it requires a strong moral principle to prevent me from deliberately stepping into the street, and methodically knocking people's hats off—then, I account it high time to get to sea as soon as I can. This is my substitute for pistol and ball. With a philosophical flourish Cato throws himself upon his sword; I quietly take to the ship. There is nothing surprising in this. If they but knew it, almost all men in their degree, some time or other, cherish very nearly the same feelings towards the ocean with me.

There now is your insular city of the Manhattoes, belted round by wharves as Indian isles by coral reefs —commerce surrounds it with her surf. Right and left, the streets take you waterward. Its extreme down-town is the battery, where that noble mole is washed by waves, and cooled by breezes, which a few hours previous were out of sight of land. Look at the crowds of water-gazers there.

Circumambulate the city of a dreamy Sabbath afternoon. Go from Corlears Hook to Coenties Slip, and from thence, by Whitehall, northward. What do you see?—Posted like silent sentinels all around the town, stand thousands upon thousands of mortal men fixed in ocean reveries. Some leaning against the spiles; some seated upon the pier-heads; some looking over the bulwarks of ships from China; some high aloft in the rigging, as if striving to get a still better seaward peep. But these are all landsmen; of week days pent up in lath and plaster—tied to counters, nailed to benches, clinched to desks. How then is this? Are the green fields gone? What do they here?

But look! here come more crowds, pacing straight for the water, and seemingly bound for a dive. Strange! Nothing will content them but the extremest limit of the land; loitering under the shady lee of yonder warehouses will not suffice. No. They must get just as nigh the water as they possibly can without falling in. And there they stand—miles of them—leagues. Inlanders all, they come from lanes and alleys, streets and avenues—north, east, south, and west. Yet here they all unite. Tell me, does the magnetic virtue of the needles of the compasses of all those ships attract them thither?

Once more. Say, you are in the country; in some high land of lakes. Take almost any path you please, and ten to one it carries you down in a dale, and leaves you there by a pool in the stream. There is magic in it. Let the most absent-minded of men be plunged in his deepest reveries—stand that man on his legs, set his feet a-going, and he will infallibly lead you to water, if water there be in all that region. Should you ever be athirst in the great American desert, try this experiment, if your caravan happens to be supplied with a metaphysical professor. Yes, as every one knows, meditation' and water are wedded for ever.

An Ancient Ship

["Ms. Found in a Bottle"]

EDGAR ALLAN POE

1833

Qui n'a plus qu'un moment à vivre
N'a plus rien à dissimuler.
—Quinault, *Atys*

Of my country and of my family I have little to say. Ill usage and length of years have driven me from the one, and estranged me from the other. Hereditary wealth afforded me an education of no common order, and a contemplative turn of mind enabled me to methodize the stores which early study very diligently garnered up.—Beyond all things, the study of the German moralists gave me great delight; not from any ill-advised admiration of their eloquent madness, but from the ease with which my habits of rigid thought enabled me to detect their falsities. I have often been reproached with the aridity of my genius; a deficiency of imagination has been imputed to me as a crime; and the Pyrrhonism of my opinions has at all times rendered me notorious. Indeed, a strong relish for physical philosophy has, I fear, tinctured my mind with a very common error of this age—I mean the habit of referring occurrences, even the least susceptible of such reference, to the principles of that science. Upon the whole, no person could be less liable than myself to be led away from the severe precincts of truth by the *ignes fatui* of superstition. I have thought proper to premise thus much, lest the incredible tale I have to tell should be considered rather the raving of a crude imagination, than the positive experience of a mind to which the reveries of fancy have been a dead letter and a nullity.

After many years spent in foreign travel, I sailed in the year 18—, from the port of Batavia, in the rich and populous island of Java, on a voyage to the Archipelago of the Sunda islands. I went as passenger—having no other inducement than a kind of nervous restlessness which haunted me as a fiend.

Our vessel was a beautiful ship of about four hundred tons, copper-fastened, and built at Bombay of Malabar teak. She was freighted with cotton-wool and oil, from the Lachadive islands. We had also on board coir, jaggeree, ghee, cocoa-nuts, and a few cases of opium. The stowage was clumsily done, and the vessel consequently crank.

We got under way with a mere breath of wind, and for many days stood along the eastern coast of Java, without any other incident to beguile the monotony of our course than the occasional meeting with some of the small grabs of the Archipelago to which we were bound.

One evening, leaning over the taffrail, I observed a very singular, isolated cloud, to the N. W. It was remarkable, as well for its color, as from its being the first we had seen since our departure from Batavia. I watched it attentively until sunset, when it spread all at once to the eastward and westward, girting in the horizon with a narrow strip of vapor, and looking like a long line of low beach. My notice was soon afterwards attracted by the dusky-red appearance of the moon, and the peculiar character of the sea. The latter was undergoing a rapid change, and the water seemed more than usually transparent. Although I could distinctly see the bottom, yet, heaving the lead, I found the ship in fifteen fathoms. The air now became intolerably hot, and was loaded with spiral exhalations similar to those arising from heated iron. As night came on, every breath of wind died away, and a more entire calm it is impossible to conceive. The flame of a candle burned upon the poop without the least perceptible motion, and a long hair, held between the finger and thumb, hung without the possibility of detecting a vibration. However, as the captain said he could perceive no indication of danger, and as we were drfting in bodily to shore, he ordered the sails to be furled, and the anchor let go. No watch was set, and the crew, consisting principally of Malays, stretched themselves deliberately upon deck. I went below—not without a full presentiment of evil. Indeed, every appearance warranted me in apprehending a Simoon. I told the captain my fears; but he paid no attention to what I said, and left me without deigning to give a reply. My uneasiness, however, prevented me from sleeping, and about midnight I went upon deck.— As I placed my foot upon the upper step of the companion-ladder, I was startled by a loud, humming noise, like that occasioned by the rapid revolution of a mill-wheel, and before I could ascertain its meaning, I found the ship quivering to its centre. In the next instant, a wilderness of foam hurled us upon our beam-ends, and, rushing over us fore and aft, swept the entire decks from stem to stern.

The extreme fury of the blast proved, in a great measure, the salvation of the ship. Although completely water-logged, yet, as her masts had gone by the board, she rose, after a minute, heavily from the sea, and, staggering awhile beneath the immense pressure of the tempest, finally righted.

By what miracle I escaped destruction, it is impossible to say. Stunned by the shock of the water, I found myself, upon recovery, jammed in between the stern-post and rudder. With great difficulty I gained my feet, and looking dizzily around, was, at first, struck with the idea of our being among breakers; so terrific, beyond the wildest imagination, was the whirlpool of mountainous and foaming ocean within which we were engulfed. After a while, I heard the voice of an old Swede, who had shipped with us at the moment of our leaving port. I hallooed to him with all my strength, and presently he came reeling aft. We soon discovered that we were the sole survivors of the accident. All on deck, with the exception of ourselves, had been swept overboard;—the captain and mates must have perished as they slept, for the cabins were deluged with water. Without assistance, we could expect to do little for the security of the ship, and our exertions were at first paralyzed by the momentary expectation of going down. Our cable had, of course, parted like pack-thread, at the first breath of the hurricane, or we should have been instantaneously overwhelmed. We scudded with frightful velocity before the sea, and the water made clear breaches over us. The frame-work of our stern was shattered excessively, and, in almost every respect, we had received considerable injury; but to our extreme joy we found the pumps unchoked, and that we had made no great shifting of our ballast. The main fury of the blast had already blown over, and we apprehended little danger from the violence of the wind; but we looked forward to its total cessation with dismay; well believing, that, in our shattered condition, we should inevitably perish in the tremendous swell which would ensue. But this very just apprehension seemed by no means likely to be soon verified. For five entire days and nights—during which our only subsistence was a small quantity of jaggeree, procured with great difficulty from the forecastle—the hulk flew at a rate defying computation, before rapidly succeeding flaws of wind, which, without equalling the first violence of the Simoon, were still more terrific than any tempest I had before encountered. Our course for the first four days was, with trifling variations, S. E. and by S.; and we must have run down the coast of New Holland.—On the fifth day the cold became extreme, although the wind had hauled round a point more to the northward.—The sun arose with a sickly yellow lustre, and clambered a very few degrees above the horizon— emitting no decisive light.—There were no clouds apparent, yet the wind was upon the increase, and blew with a fitful and unsteady fury. About noon, as nearly as we could guess, our attention was again arrested by the appearance of the sun. It gave out no light, properly so called, but a dull and sullen glow without reflection, as if all its rays were polarized. Just before sinking within the turgid sea, its central fires suddenly went out, as if hurriedly extinguished by some unaccountable power. It was a dim, silver-like rim, alone, as it rushed down the unfathomable ocean.

We waited in vain for the arrival of the sixth day— that day to me has not arrived—to the Swede, never did arrive. Thenceforward we were enshrouded in pitchy darkness, so that we could not have seen an object at twenty paces from the ship. Eternal night continued to envelop us, all unrelieved by the phosphoric sea-brilliancy to which we had been accustomed in the tropics. We observed too, that, although the tempest continued to rage with unabated violence, there was no longer to be discovered the usual appearance of surf, or foam, which had hitherto attended us. All around were horror, and thick gloom, and a black sweltering desert of ebony.—Superstitious terror crept by degrees into the spirit of the old Swede, and my own soul was wrapped up in silent wonder. We neglected all care of the ship, as worse than useless, and securing ourselves, as well as possible, to the stump of the mizen-mast, looked out bitterly into the world of ocean. We had no means of calculating time, nor could we form any guess of our situation. We were, however, well aware of having made farther to the southward than any previous navi-

gators, and felt great amazement at not meeting with
the usual impediments of ice. In the meantime every
moment threatened to be our last—every mountainous
billow hurried to overwhelm us. The swell surpassed
anything I had imagined possible, and that we were
not instantly buried is a miracle. My companion spoke
of the lightness of our cargo, and reminded me of the
excellent qualities of our ship; but I could not help feeling the utter hopelessness of hope itself, and prepared
myself gloomily for that death which I thought nothing
could defer beyond an hour, as, with every knot of way
the ship made, the swelling of the black stupendous seas
became more dismally appalling. At times we gasped
for breath at an elevation beyond the albatross—at
times became dizzy with the velocity of our descent
into some watery hell, where the air grew stagnant, and
no sound disturbed the slumbers of the kraken.

We were at the bottom of one of these abysses, when
a quick scream from my companion broke fearfully upon
the night. "See! see!" cried he, shrieking in my ears, "Almighty God! see! see!" As he spoke, I became aware of
a dull, sullen glare of red light which streamed down
the sides of the vast chasm where we lay, and threw a
fitful brilliancy upon our deck. Casting my eyes upwards, I beheld a spectacle which froze the current of
my blood. At a terrific height directly above us, and
upon the very verge of the precipitous descent, hovered
a gigantic ship of, perhaps, four thousand tons. Although upreared upon the summit of a wave more
than a hundred times her own altitude, her apparent
size still exceeded that of any ship of the line or East
Indiaman in existence. Her huge hull was of a deep
dingy black, unrelieved by any of the customary carv-
ings of a ship. A single row of brass cannon protruded
from her open ports, and dashed from their polished
surfaces the fires of innumerable battle-lanterns, which
swung to and fro about her rigging. But what mainly

inspired us with horror and astonishment, was that she bore up under a press of sail in the very teeth of that supernatural sea, and of that ungovernable hurricane. When we first discovered her, her bows were alone to be seen, as she rose slowly from the dim and horrible gulf beyond her. For a moment of intense terror she paused upon the giddy pinnacle, as if in contemplation of her own sublimity, then trembled and tottered, and —came down.

At this instant, I know not what sudden self-possession came over my spirit. Staggering as far aft as I could, I awaited fearlessly the ruin that was to overwhelm. Our own vessel was at length ceasing from her struggles, and sinking with her head to the sea. The shock of the descending mass struck her, consequently, in that portion of her frame which was already under water, and the inevitable result was to hurl me, with irresistible violence, upon the rigging of the stranger.

As I fell, the ship hove in stays, and went about; and to the confusion ensuing I attributed my escape from the notice of the crew. With little difficulty I made my way unperceived to the main hatchway, which was partially open, and soon found an opportunity of secreting myself in the hold. Why I did so I can hardly tell. An indefinite sense of awe, which at first sight of the navigators of the ship had taken hold of my mind, was perhaps the principle of my concealment. I was unwilling to trust myself with a race of people who had offered, to the cursory glance I had taken, so many points of vague novelty, doubt, and apprehension. I therefore thought proper to contrive a hiding-place in the hold. This I did by removing a small portion of the shifting-boards, in such a manner as to afford me a convenient retreat between the huge timbers of the ship.

I had scarcely completed my work, when a footstep in the hold forced me to make use of it. A man passed by my place of concealment with a feeble and unsteady

gait. I could not see his face, but had an opportunity
of observing his general appearance. There was about
it an evidence of great age and infirmity. His knees tottered beneath a load of years, and his entire frame
quivered under the burthen. He muttered to himself, in
a low broken tone, some words of a language which I
could not understand, and groped in a corner among a
pile of singular-looking instruments, and decayed charts
of navigation. His manner was a wild mixture of the
peevishness of second childhood, and the solemn dignity of a God. He at length went on deck, and I saw
him no more.

A feeling, for which I have no name, has taken possession of my soul—a sensation which will admit of
no analysis, to which the lessons of by-gone times are
inadequate, and for which I fear futurity itself will
offer me no key. To a mind constituted like my own, the
latter consideration is an evil. I shall never—I know
that I shall never—be satisfied with regard to the nature
of my conceptions. Yet it is not wonderful that these
conceptions are indefinite, since they have their origin
in sources so utterly novel. A new sense—a new entity
is added to my soul.

It is long since I first trod the deck of this terrible
ship, and the rays of my destiny are, I think, gathering
to a focus. Incomprehensible men! Wrapped up in meditations of a kind which I cannot divine, they pass me
by unnoticed. Concealment is utter folly on my part, for
the people *will not* see. It was just now that I passed
directly before the eyes of the mate—it was no long
while ago that I ventured into the captain's own private
cabin, and took thence the materials with which I write,
and have written. I shall from time to time continue this
journal. It is true that I may not find an opportunity of
transmitting it to the world, but I will not fail to make

the endeavour. At the last moment I will enclose the
MS. in a bottle, and cast it within the sea.

An incident has occurred which has given me new
room for meditation. Are such things the operation of
ungoverned Chance? I had ventured upon deck and
thrown myself down, without attracting any notice,
among a pile of ratlin-stuff and old sails, in the bottom
of the yawl. While musing upon the singularity of my
fate, I unwittingly daubed with a tar-brush the edges
of a neatly-folded studding-sail which lay near me on a
barrel. The studding-sail is now bent upon the ship, and
the thoughtless touches of the brush are spread out into
the word DISCOVERY. . . .

I have made many observations lately upon the structure of the vessel. Although well armed, she is not, I
think, a ship of war. Her rigging, build, and general
equipment, all negative a supposition of this kind. What
she *is not*, I can easily perceive—what she *is* I fear it
is impossible to say. I know not how it is, but in scruti-
nizing her strange model and singular cast of spars, her
huge size and overgrown suits of canvass, her severely
simple bow and antiquated stern, there will occasionally
flash across my mind a sensation of familiar things, and
there is always mixed up with such indistinct shadows
of recollection, an unaccountable memory of old foreign
chronicles and ages long ago. . . .

I have been looking at the timbers of the ship. She
is built of a material to which I am a stranger. There is
a peculiar character about the wood which strikes me
as rendering it unfit for the purpose to which it has
been applied. I mean its extreme *porousness,* considered
independently of the worm-eaten condition which is a
consequence of navigation in these seas, and apart from
the rottenness attendant upon age. It will appear perhaps an observation somewhat over-curious, but this
wood would have every characteristic of Spanish oak, if

Spanish oak were distended by any unnatural means.

In reading the above sentence a curious apothegm of an old weather-beaten Dutch navigator comes full upon my recollection. "It is as sure," he was wont to say, when any doubt was entertained of his veracity, "as sure as there is a sea where the ship itself will grow in bulk like the living body of the seaman." . . .

About an hour ago, I made bold to thrust myself among a group of the crew. They paid me no manner of attention, and, although I stood in the very midst of them all, seemed utterly unconscious of my presence. Like the one I had at first seen in the hold, they all bore about them the marks of a hoary old age. Their knees trembled with infirmity; their shoulders were bent double with decrepitude; their shrivelled skins rattled in the wind; their voices were low, tremulous and broken; their eyes glistened with the rheum of years; and their gray hairs streamed terribly in the tempest. Around them, on every part of the deck, lay scattered mathematical instruments of the most quaint and obsolete construction. . . .

I mentioned some time ago the bending of a studding-sail. From that period the ship, being thrown dead off the wind, has continued her terrific course due south, with every rag of canvass packed upon her, from her trucks to her lower studding-sail booms, and rolling every moment her top-gallant yard-arms into the most appalling hell of water which it can enter into the mind of man to imagine. I have just left the deck, where I find it impossible to maintain a footing, although the crew seem to experience little inconvenience. It appears to me a miracle of miracles that our enormous bulk is not swallowed up at once and forever. We are surely doomed to hover continually upon the brink of Eternity, without taking a final plunge into the abyss. From billows a thousand times more stupendous than any I have ever seen, we glide away with the facility of the arrowy

sea-gull; and the colossal waters rear their heads above
us like demons of the deep, but like demons confined to
simple threats and forbidden to destroy. I am lead to
attribute these frequent escapes to the only natural
cause which can account for such effect.—I must suppose the ship to be within the influence of some strong
current, or impetuous under-tow. . . .

I have seen the captain face to face, and in his own
cabin—but, as I expected, he paid me no attention. Although in his appearance there is, to a casual observer,
nothing which might bespeak him more or less than
man—still a feeling of irrepressible reverence and awe
mingled with the sensation of wonder with which I regarded him. In stature he is nearly my own height; that
is, about five feet eight inches. He is of a well-knit and
compact frame of body, neither robust nor remarkably
otherwise. But it is the singularity of the expression
which reigns upon the face—it is the intense, the wonderful, the thrilling evidence of old age, so utter, so
extreme, which excites within my spirit a sense—a sentiment ineffable. His forehead, although little wrinkled,
seems to bear upon it the stamp of a myriad of years.—
His gray hairs are records of the past, and his grayer
eyes are Sybils of the future. The cabin floor was thickly
strewn with strange, iron-clasped folios, and mouldering instruments of science, and obsolete long-forgotten
charts. His head was bowed down upon his hands, and
he pored, with a fiery unquiet eye, over a paper which I
took to be a commission, and which, at all events, bore
the signature of a monarch. He muttered to himself, as
did the first seaman whom I saw in the hold, some low
peevish syllables of a foreign tongue, and although the
speaker was close at my elbow, his voice seemed to
reach my ears from the distance of a mile. . . .

The ship and all in it are imbued with the spirit of
Eld. The crew glide to and fro like the ghosts of buried
centuries; their eyes have an eager and uneasy mean-

ing; and when their fingers fall athwart my path in the
wild glare of the battle-lanterns, I feel as I have never
felt before, although I have been all my life a dealer in
antiquities, and have imbibed the shadows of fallen
columns at Balbec, and Tadmor, and Persepolis, until
my very soul has become a ruin. . . .

When I look around me I feel ashamed of my former
apprehensions. If I trembled at the blast which has
hitherto attended us, shall I not stand aghast at a war-
ring of wind and ocean, to convey any idea of which the
words tornado and Simoon are trivial and ineffective?
All in the immediate vicinity of the ship is the blackness
of eternal night, and a chaos of foamless water; but,
about a league on either side of us, may be seen, indis-
tinctly and at intervals, stupendous ramparts of ice,
towering away into the desolate sky, and looking like
the walls of the universe. . . .

As I imagined, the ship proves to be in a current; if
that appellation can properly be given to a tide which,
howling and shrieking by the white ice, thunders on to
the southward with a velocity like the headlong dashing of a cataract. . . .

To conceive the horror of my sensations is, I presume,
uttery impossible; yet a curiosity to penetrate the mysteries of these awful regions, predominates even over
my despair, and will reconcile me to the most hideous
aspect of death. It is evident that we are hurrying onwards to some exciting knowledge—some never-to-be-
imparted secret, whose attainment is destruction. Perhaps this current leads us to the southern pole itself. It
must be confessed that a supposition apparently so wild
has every probability in its favor. . . .

The crew pace the deck with unquiet and tremulous
step; but there is upon their countenances an expression
more of the eagerness of hope than of the apathy of
despair.

In the meantime the wind is still in our poop, and, as

we carry a crowd of canvass, the ship is at times lifted
bodily from out the sea—Oh, horror upon horror! the
ice opens suddenly to the right, and to the left, and we
are whirling dizzily, in immense concentric circles,
round and round the borders of a gigantic amphitheatre,
the summit of whose walls is lost in the darkness and
the distance. But little time will be left me to ponder
upon my destiny—the circles rapidly grow small—we
are plunging madly within the grasp of the whirlpool
—and amid a roaring, and bellowing, and thundering of
ocean and of tempest, the ship is quivering, oh God!
and—going down.

NOTE. The "MS Found in a Bottle," was originally published in
1831 [1833], and it was not until many years afterwards that I
became acquainted with the maps of Mercator, in which the ocean
is represented as rushing, by four mouths, into the (northern) Polar
Gulf, to be absorbed into the bowels of the earth; the Pole itself
being represented by a black rock, towering to a prodigious height.
[E. A. P.]

PART FIVE

The Romantic Revolutions

THE REVOLUTION IN MANNERS AND MORALS

The world is weary of the past,
Oh, might it die or rest at last!

—Percy Bysshe Shelley

Man Requires a New Selfhood

[FROM *Jerusalem*]

WILLIAM BLAKE

1804-1820

He never can be a Friend to the Human Race who is the Preacher of Natural Morality or Natural Religion; he is a flatterer who means to betray, to perpetuate Tyrant Pride & the Laws of that Babylon which he foresees shall shortly be destroyed, with the Spiritual and not the Natural Sword. He is in the State named Rahab, which State must be put off before he can be the Friend of Man.

You, O Deists, profess yourselves the Enemies of Christianity, and you are so; you are also the Enemies of the Human Race & of Universal Nature. Man is born a Spectre or Satan & is altogether an Evil, & requires a new Selfhood continually, & must continually be changed into his direct Contrary. But your Greek Phi-

losophy (which is a remnant of Druidism) teaches that
Man is Righteous in his Vegetated Spectre: an Opinion
of fatal & accursed consequence to Man, as the Ancients
saw plainly by Revelation, to the intire abrogation of
Experimental Theory; and many believed what they
saw and Prophecied of Jesus.

Man must & will have Some Religion: if he has not
the Religion of Jesus, he will have the Religion of
Satan & will erect the Synagogue of Satan, calling the
Prince of this World, God, and destroying all who do
not worship Satan under the Name of God. Will any
one say, "Where are those who worship Satan under
the Name of God?" Where are they? Listen! Every
Religion that Preaches Vengeance for Sin is the Religion of the Enemy & Avenger and not of the Forgiver
of Sin, and their God is Satan, Named by the Divine
Name. Your Religion, O Deists! Deism, is the worship
of the God of this World by the means of what you
call Natural Religion and Natural Philosophy, and of
Natural Morality or Self-Righteousness, the Selfish Virtues of the Natural Heart. This was the Religion of
the Pharisees who murder'd Jesus. Deism is the same &
ends in the same.

Voltaire, Rousseau, Gibbon, Hume, charge the Spiritually Religious with Hypocrisy; but how a Monk, or
a Methodist either, can be a Hypocrite, I cannot conceive. We are Men of like passions with others & pretend not to be holier than others; therefore, when a
Religious Man falls into Sin, he ought not to be call'd
a Hypocrite; this title is more properly to be given to a
Player who falls into Sin, whose profession is Virtue &
Morality & the making Men Self-Righteous. Foote in
calling Whitefield, Hypocrite, was himself one; for
Whitefield pretended not to be holier than others, but
confessed his Sins before all the World. Voltaire! Rousseau! You cannot escape my charge that you are Pharisees & Hypocrites, for you are constantly talking of the

Virtues of the Human Heart and particularly of your own, that you may accuse others, & especially the Religious, whose errors you, by this display of pretended Virtue, chiefly design to expose. Rousseau thought Men Good by Nature: he found them Evil & found no friend. Friendship cannot exist without Forgiveness of Sins continually. The Book written by Rousseau call'd his Confessions, is an apology & cloke for his sin & not a confession.

But you also charge the poor Monks & Religious with being the causes of War, while you acquit & flatter the Alexanders & Caesars, the Lewis's & Fredericks, who done are its causes & its actors. But the Religion of Jesus, Forgiveness of Sin, can never be the cause of a War nor of a single Martyrdom.

Those who Martyr others or who cause War are Deists, but never can be Forgivers of Sin. The Glory of Christianity is To Conquer by Forgiveness. All the Destruction, therefore, in Christian Europe has arisen from Deism, which is Natural Religion.

"Oh, You Rationalists!"

[FROM *The Sorrows of Young Werther*]

JOHANN WOLFGANG VON GOETHE

1774

August 12, 1771
. . . On this occasion Albert was deeply immersed in his subject; I finally ceased to listen to him, and became lost in reverie. With a sudden motion I pointed the mouth of the pistol to my forehead, over the right

eye. "What are you doing?" cried Albert, turning the pistol away. "It is not loaded," said I. "Even so," he asked with impatience, "what is the meaning of this? I cannot imagine how a man can be so mad as to shoot himself; the very idea of it shocks me."

"Oh, you people!" I said, "why should you always have to label an action and call it mad or wise, good or bad? What does it all mean? Have you fathomed the motives of our actions? Can you explain the causes and make them inevitable? If you could, you would be less hasty with your 'labels.' "

"But you will admit," said Albert, "that some actions are vicious, let them spring from whatever motives they may." I granted it, and shrugged my shoulders.

"Still," I continued, "there are some exceptions here too. Theft is a crime; but the man who commits it from extreme poverty to save his family from starvation, does he deserve pity or punishment? Who shall throw the first stone at a husband who in just resentment sacrifices his faithless wife and her perfidious seducer; or at the young girl who in an hour of rapture forgets herself in the overwhelming joys of love? Even our laws, cold and pedantic as they are, relent in such cases, and withhold their punishment."

"That is quite another thing," said Albert, "because a man under the influence of violent passion loses all reasoning power and is regarded as drunk or insane."

"Oh, you rationalists," I replied, smiling. "Passion! Drunkenness! Madness! You moral creatures, so calm and so righteous! You abhor the drunken man, and detest the eccentric; you pass by, like the Levite, and thank God, like the Pharisee, that you are not like one of them. I have been drunk more than once, my passions have always bordered on madness; I am not ashamed to confess it; I have learned in my own way that all extraordinary men who have done great and improbable things have ever been decried by the world as drunk or insane. And in ordinary life, too, is it not intolerable that no one can undertake anything noble or generous without having everybody shout, 'That fellow is drunk, he is mad'? Shame on you, ye sages!"

"Here you go again," said Albert; "you always exaggerate, and in this matter you are undoubtedly wrong; we were speaking of suicide, which you compare with great actions, when actually it is impossible to regard it as anything but weakness. It is much easier to die than to bear a life of misery with fortitude."

I was on the point of breaking off the conversation, for nothing puts me off so completely as when someone utters a wretched commonplace when I am talking from the depths of my heart. However, I controlled myself, for I had often heard the same observation with sufficient vexation; I answered him, therefore, with some heat, "You call this a weakness—don't be led astray by appearances. When a nation which has long groaned under the intolerable yoke of a tyrant rises at last and throws off its chains, do you call that weakness? The man who, to save his house from the flames, finds his physical strength redoubled, so that he can lift burdens with ease which normally he could scarcely move; he who under the rage of an insult attacks and overwhelms half a dozen of his enemies—are these to be called weak? My friend, if a display of energy be strength, how can the highest exertion of it be a weakness?"

Albert looked at me and said, "Do forgive me, but I do not see that the examples you have produced bear any relation to the question." "That may be," I answered; "I have often been told that my method of argument borders a little on the absurd. But let us see if we cannot place the matter in another light by inquiring what may be a man's state of mind who resolves to free himself from the burden of life—a burden which often seems so pleasant to bear. Surely, we are justified in discussing a subject such as this only in so far as we can put ourselves in another man's situation."

"Human nature," I continued, "has its limits. It can endure a certain degree of joy, sorrow, and pain, but collapses as soon as this is exceeded. The question, therefore, is not whether a man is strong or weak, but whether he is able to endure the measure of his suffering, moral or physical; and in my opinion it is just as absurd to call a man a coward who kills himself as to call a man a coward who dies of a malignant fever."

Trans. Victor Lange (New York: Rinehart & Co., 1949).

"Simplicity, Simplicity, Simplicity!"

[FROM *Walden*]

HENRY DAVID THOREAU

1854

Every morning was a cheerful invitation to make my life of equal simplicity, and I may say innocence, with Nature herself. I have been as sincere a worshipper of Aurora as the Greeks. I got up early and bathed in the pond; that was a religious exercise, and one of the best things which I did. They say that characters were engraven on the bathing tub of King Tching-thang to this effect: "Renew thyself completely each day; do it again, and again, and forever again." I can understand that. Morning brings back the heroic ages. I was as much affected by the faint hum of a mosquito making its invisible and unimaginable tour through my apartment at earliest dawn, when I was sitting with door and windows open, as I could be by any trumpet that ever sang of fame. It was Homer's requiem; itself

an Iliad and Odyssey in the air, singing its own wrath
and wanderings. There was something cosmical about
it; a standing advertisement, till forbidden, of the everlasting vigor and fertility of the world. The morning,
which is the most memorable season of the day, is the
awakening hour. Then there is least somnolence in us;
and for an hour, at least, some part of us awakes which
slumbers all the rest of the day and night. Little is to
be expected of that day, if it can be called a day, to
which we are not awakened by our Genius, but by the
mechanical nudgings of some servitor, are not awakened by our own newly acquired force and aspirations
from within, accompanied by the undulations of celestial music, instead of factory bells, and a fragrance
filling the air—to a higher life than we fell asleep
from; and thus the darkness bear its fruit, and prove
itself to be good, no less than the light. That man who
does not believe that each day contains an earlier, more
sacred, and auroral hour than he has yet profaned, has
despaired of life, and is pursuing a descending and
darkening way. After a partial cessation of his sensuous life, the soul of man, or its organs rather, are reinvigorated each day, and his Genius tries again what
noble life it can make. All memorable events, I should
say, transpire in morning time and in a morning atmosphere. The Vedas say, "All intelligences awake with the
morning." Poetry and art, and the fairest and most
memorable of the actions of men, date from such an
hour. All poets and heroes, like Memnon, are the children of Aurora, and emit their music at sunrise. To him
whose elastic and vigorous thought keeps pace with the
sun, the day is a perpetual morning. It matters not
what the clocks say or the attitudes and labors of men.
Morning is when I am awake and there is a dawn in
me. Moral reform is the effort to throw off sleep. Why
is it that men give so poor an account of their day if they
have not been slumbering? They are not such poor cal-

culators. If they had not been overcome with drowsiness, they would have performed something. The millions are awake enough for physical labor; but only one in a million is awake enough for effective intellectual exertion, only one in a hundred millions to a poetic or divine life. To be awake is to be alive. I have never yet met a man who was quite awake. How could I have looked him in the face?

We must learn to reawaken and keep ourselves awake, not by mechanical aids, but by an infinite expectation of the dawn, which does not forsake us in our soundest sleep. I know of no more encouraging fact than the unquestionable ability of man to elevate his life by a conscious endeavor. It is something to be able to paint a particular picture, or to carve a statue, and so to make a few objects beautiful; but it is far more glorious to carve and paint the very atmosphere and medium through which we look, which morally we can do. To affect the quality of the day, that is the highest of arts. Every man is tasked to make his life, even in its details, worthy of the contemplation of his most elevated and critical hour. If we refused, or rather used up, such paltry information as we get, the oracles would distinctly inform us how this might be done.

I went to the woods because I wished to live deliberately, to front only the essential facts of life, and see if I could not learn what it had to teach, and not, when I came to die, discover that I had not lived. I did not wish to live what was not life, living is so dear; nor did I wish to practice resignation, unless it was quite necessary. I wanted to live deep and suck out all the marrow of life, to live so sturdily and Spartan-like as to put to rout all that was not life, to cut a broad swath and shave close, to drive life into a corner, and reduce it to its lowest terms, and, if it proved to be mean, why then to get the whole and genuine meanness of it, and publish its meanness to the world; or if it were sublime, to know it by experience, and be able to give a true account of it in my next excursion. For most men, it appears to me, are in a strange uncertainty about it, whether it is of the devil or of God, and have *somewhat hastily* concluded that it is the chief end of man here to "glorify God and enjoy him forever."

Still we live meanly, like ants; though the fable tells us that we were long ago changed into men; like pygmies we fight with cranes; it is error upon error, and clout upon clout, and our best virtue has for its occasion a superfluous and evitable wretchedness. Our life is fritted away by detail. An honest man has hardly need to count more than his ten fingers, or in extreme cases he may add his ten toes, and lump the rest. Simplicity, simplicity, simplicity! I say, let your affairs be as two or three, and not a hundred or a thousand; instead of a million count half a dozen, and keep your accounts on your thumb-nail. In the midst of this chopping sea of civilized life, such are the clouds and storms and quicksands and thousand-and-one items to be allowed for, that a man has to live, if he would not founder and go to the bottom and not make his port at all, by dead reckoning, and he must be a great calculator indeed who succeeds. Simplify, simplify. Instead of three meals a day, if it be necessary eat but one; instead of a hundred dishes, five; and reduce other things in proportion. Our life is like a German Confederacy, made up of petty states, with its boundary forever fluctuating, so that even a German cannot tell you how it is bounded at any moment. The nation itself, with all its so-called internal improvements, which, by the way, are all external and superficial, is just such an unwieldy and overgrown establishment, cluttered with furniture and tripped by its own traps, ruined by luxury and heedless expense, by want of calculation and a worthy aim, as the million households in the land;

and the only cure for it, as for them, is in a rigid economy, a stern and more than Spartan simplicity of life
and elevation of purpose.

Let us spend one day as deliberately as Nature, and
not be thrown off the track by every nutshell and mosquito's wing that falls on the rails. Let us rise early and
fast, or break fast, gently and without perturbation;
let company come and let company go, let the bells
ring and the children cry,—determined to make a day
of it. Why should we knock under and go with the
stream? Let us not be upset and overwhelmed in that
terrible rapid and whirlpool called a dinner, situated in
the meridian shallows. Weather this danger and you
are safe, for the rest of the way is down hill. With un-
relaxed nerves, with morning vigor, sail by it, looking
another way, tied to the mast like Ulysses. If the engine
whistles, let it whistle till it is hoarse for its pains. If
the bell rings, why should we run? We will consider
what kind of music they are like. Let us settle ourselves,
and work and wedge our feet downward through the
mud and slush of opinion, and prejudice, and tradition,
and delusion, and appearance, that alluvion which covers the globe, through Paris and London, through New
York and Boston and Concord, through Church and
State, through poetry and philosophy and religion, till
we come to a hard bottom and rocks in place, which
we can call *reality*, and say, This is, and no mistake;
and then begin, having a *point d'appui*, below freshet
and frost and fire, a place where you might found a
wall or a state, or set a lamp-post safely, or perhaps a
gauge, not a Nilometer, but a Realometer, that future
ages might know how deep a freshet of shams and appearances had gathered from time to time. If you stand
right fronting and face to face to a fact, you will see
the sun glimmer on both its surfaces, as if it were a
cimeter, and feel its sweet edge dividing you through

the heart and marrow, and so you will happily conclude your mortal career. Be it life or death, we crave only reality. If we are really dying, let us hear the rattle in our throats and feel cold in the extremities; if we are alive, let us go about our business.

Vegetarian Reformation

[NOTE FROM *Queen Mab: A Philosophical Poem*]

PERCY BYSSHE SHELLEY

1813

There is no disease, bodily or mental, which adoption of vegetable diet and pure water has not infallibly mitigated, wherever the experiment has been fairly tried. Debility is gradually converted into strength, disease into healthfulness, madness in all its hideous variety, from the ravings of the fettered maniac to the unaccountable irrationalities of ill-temper, that make a hell cf domestic life, into a calm and considerate evenness of temper, that alone might offer a certain pledge of the future moral reformation of society. On a natural system of diet, old age would be our last and our only malady; the term of our existence would be protracted; we should enjoy life, and no longer preclude others from the enjoyment of it; all sensational delights would be infinitely more exquisite and perfect; the very sense of being would then be a continued pleasure, such as we now feel it in some few and favoured moments of our youth. By all that is sacred in our hopes for the human race, I conjure those who love happiness and truth to give a fair trial to the vegetable system! Reasoning is surely superfluous on a subject whose merits an experience of six months would set for ever at rest. But it is only among the enlightened and benevolent that so great a sacrifice of appetite and prejudice can be expected, even though its ultimate excellence should not admit of dispute. It is found easier, by the short-sighted victims of disease, to palliate their torments by medicine, than to prevent them by regimen. The vulgar of all ranks are invariably sensual and indocile; yet I cannot but feel myself persuaded that, when the bene-fits of vegetable diet are mathematically proved; when it is as clear, that those who live naturally are exempt from premature death, as that one is not nine, the most sot-tish of mankind will feel a preference towards a long and tranquil, contrasted with a short and painful, life. On the average, out of sixty persons, four die in three years. Hopes are entertained that, in April, 1814, a statement will be given, that sixty persons, all having lived more than three years on vegetables and pure water, are then in *perfect health*. More than two years have now elapsed; *not one of them has died;* no such example will be found in any sixty persons taken at random. Seventeen persons of all ages (the families of Dr. Lambe and Mr. Newton) have lived for seven years on this diet without a death, and almost without the slightest illness. Surely when we consider that some of these were infants, and one a martyr to asthma, now nearly subdued, we may challenge any seventeen per-sons taken at random in this city to exhibit a parallel case. Those, who may have been excited to question the rectitude of established habits of diet by these loose remarks, should consult Mr. Newton's luminous and eloquent essay.

When these proofs come fairly before the world, and are clearly seen by all who understand arithmetic, it is scarcely possible that abstinence from aliment de-monstrably pernicious should not become universal. In proportion to the number of proselytes, so will be the weight of evidence; and, when a thousand persons can be produced, living on vegetables and distilled water, who have to dread no disease but old age, the world will be compelled to regard animal flesh and fermented liquors as slow but certain poisons.

Commonplace Existences

[FROM *The Eternal Philistine*]

CLEMENS BRENTANO

1810

Our daily life consists chiefly of ever-recurrent, self-preserving activities. This circle of commonplace deeds is merely a means to one chief end, principally to guarantee our earthly existence, which is itself a blend of various ways of existing.

Philistines live solely commonplace existences. To them the means of survival seem the only end. They do everything in terms of their earthly lives, in terms of how these appear for them; yet these are the sole terms they can conceive of. Philistines mix poetry into their lives as a necessity, only if they are accustomed to having it as a regular interruption. According to the rules, such an interruption occurs once every seven days. It might well be called a seven-day fever. Work stops every Sunday; that day they all live a little easier, and this Sunday ecstasy terminates in a deeper sleep than they usually enjoy. Then Monday they can work better than ever. Their social life has to be conventional, just like everyone else's, and stylish; even their pleasures they manufacture the way they do everything— laboriously and formally.

The Philistine achieves the highest grade of his poetical existence when he takes a trip, goes to a wedding or to a baptism, or attends church. Here his boldest desires are pacified; indeed, they are often surpassed.

The revolutionary Philistines are the worst. They belong to a covetous race which is the scum of the aforementioned group.

Coarse selfishness results from such spiritually impoverished limitation. The liveliest sensation always must be the present one; the highest sensation has to be the one that is the most pity-evoking. But the Philistine knows nothing better.

The word *Philistine* has its roots in the universities. There the youth—those enthusiastic, marriage-intoxicated lion-lacerators—have discovered the honey of wisdom in the very jaws of a beleaguered beast; there the youth—those eternally-rejuvenated Samsons—surrender themselves to the force of a wind from heaven, happy in their confidence in divine stars and in the well-planned navigation of their fragile barks; and flying daringly over the mirror-like surface of God's own ocean on wings of enthusiasm, repeatedly sink Philistine barges to the bottom. These, provided with excellent passports and deckloads of pot-house politicians, are in the process of making the trip between the butter market and the cheese market. We can also call all those Philistines who have never been students. We use the word student in its broadest sense: one who thirsts after knowledge, one who doesn't cement up his life's dwelling like a snail, as do the real Philistines; a man who is in the process of investigating the eternal verities, whether those of God or man, who joyfully allows all the beams of light to play over his spirit, who is reverent before ideas—even when the Philistines oppose him. All are Philistines who are not students in this broadest sense of the word.

They call *nature* only that which falls into their circle of vision, or rather into their little corner of vision; since they understand only quadrangular things, and say that everything else is either unnatural or sheer fanaticism. They don't understand anything about dinner but lay great stress on studying bread.

Philistines have a taste only for dull, trifling, ungraceful and goatish music. They think Beethoven is completely crazy. Bad paintings, allegories piled together any which way where the story is carefully sketched out with a slate pencil, a couple of gelatinous angels striking poses, an altar taken from a genealogical register or a tiny little temple in bucolic Greek taste—these are their architectural ideals. The infinite, the omnipotent filled with art, the single and rapturous greatness of buildings inspired by Christianity, they call Gothic and barbarian abortions, born out of bad taste.

When they speak of a lovely locale, they prefer to say, "I have my copy of Horace in my pocket, but I never take it out to read it." They tell each other happily about their youthful pranks, which then are just like those of Justice Shallow in Shakespeare's *Henry the Fourth*. And they never get intoxicated about anything without drinking, and then they must always get very drunk. If they get frightened, they immediately make water. They never can understand any original piece of poetry, but they scorn it and parody it and then write watery imitations. They have imitated *Werther* with the most sentimental novels, *Götz* with plays about knights, *Ardinghello* and *Wilhelm Meister* with novels about artists, *Lucinda* with lewd transcendentalism. . . .

Trans. H. E. H.

Two Civilizations Face to Face

[FROM *History of Romanticism*]

THEOPHILE GAUTIER

1874

HERNANI

[1830]

"Ah! Goodness! From the very first word we have an orgy! He breaks the rhymes and throws them out the window," said a classicist, admirer of Voltaire, with wisdom's indulgent smile for madness.

Nevertheless he was tolerant, and didn't object to prudent innovations, providing that these showed a respect for the language; but such negligence at the very beginning of a piece had to be censure for a poet, whatever his principles might be, liberal or royalist.

"But this was not negligence, this was beautiful," answered a Romantic who belonged to Devéria's studio, a young man tanned like Cordoba leather, whose thick red hair was dressed like some portrait by Giorgione.

"Don't you understand that this word *hidden*, run-on as if hanging in the middle of a line, admirably describes this amorous staircase and the mystery that encloses its spirals within the ramparts of the manor-house! Such marvelous architectonic science! What feeling for the art of the sixteenth century! What a profound knowledge of an entire civilization! . . ."

Despite the terror that Hugo's crew inspired with their little sorties, their easily recognizable eccentric acts and their ferocious manners, in the theater there buzzed a rumbling suggestion of excited crowds that was no more understandable than that of the ocean. The emotions owned by a room always display themselves and are revealed through unmistakeable signs. One only had to look at the public to convince one's self that this was no mere ordinary performance: two systems, two parties, two armies, indeed two civilizations —I do not go too far—were face to face, hated each other cordially, as one hates in a literary fashion, and only cried out for open warfare, ready as they were to jump on each other. The general attitude was hostile, the muscles were already flexing, the slightest contact would have begun the fight; and it wasn't hard to see that the young man with flowing hair found the well-shaved gentlemen a disastrous cretin, nor would he hide his personal opinion much longer. . . .

The Legend of the Red Waistcoat

The red waistcoat! They still talk about it after more than forty years, and they will be talking about it in years to come, so deeply has this flash of color permeated the public eye. If you utter the name of Théophile Gautier in front of a Philistine, even if he has only read two verses and a single line of ours, he knows us at least by that red waistcoat we wore at the first performance of *Hernani*, and he will say with great satisfaction at being so well informed, "Oh, yes! That young man with the red waitscoat and the long hair!" This is the idea of ourself we have bequeathed to the world. Our poems, our books, our articles, our travels shall be forgotten; but they will always recall that red waistcoat. . . .

The First Performance of "Hernani"

February 25, 1830! This date remains inscribed on the foundation of our past as if in flaming letters: the

date of the first performance of *Hernani!* That evening
which determined our whole life! There we received
the impetus that still drives us after so many years, the
same that shall move us up to the very end of our career. Much time has passed since, but our astonishment
is always the same. The enthusiasm of our youth has
never abated, and every time the magical horn-call re-
sounds, we prick up our ears like some old war-horse
ready to begin his former combats.

The young poet, with his proud audacity and his
great genius, preferring moreover fame to success, had
stubbornly refused the help of those paid cohorts who
share the triumphs and ward off the defeats. Claques,
like academicians, have their tastes. They would have
applauded Victor Hugo only reluctantly: at that time
their men were Casimir Delavigne and Scribe; and the
author ran the risk of being abandoned at the height
of the battle if the business went badly. People talked
of cabals, of shadowy-plotted intrigues, almost of am-
bushes intended to murder the play and to do away with
the new School with one stroke. Literary hatreds are
indeed more ferocious than political hatreds, for they
vibrate the most ticklish chords of self-esteem, and the
triumph of one's adversary proclaims one to be an imbecile. . . .

We couldn't, however, no matter how brave he might
be, let *Hernani* struggle all alone against an unrecep-
tive and noisy pit, against loges calmer in appearance
but no less dangerous in their hostile politeness, whose
sneers would hum so importunately beneath the hissing
that would be franker, at least, in its attack. The young
Romantics, filled with zeal and made fanatic by the
preface to *Cromwell*, were resolved to support "the
mountain hawk," as Alarcon says in *Tisserand of Se-
govia*; and they offered themselves to the master, who
accepted them. No doubt so much impetuosity and pas-

sion were to be feared, but timidity was not that period's defect. They organized themselves into small
squadrons in which each man had for a pass a square
of red paper stamped with the word *Hierro* [Iron].

In the small newspapers and polemical magazines of
that date, they were happy to describe these young
men (all of good families, educated, well brought up,
mad about art and poetry, some of them writers, some
of them painters, here a few musicians, there sculptors
and architects, others critics and engaged in some sort
of literary activity) as a crowd of sordid tramps. It
wasn't Attila's Huns who camped in front of the *Thé-
âtre Français,* slovenly, ferocious, bristling, stupid; but
rather here were the knights of the future, champions
of ideas, defenders of independent art; and they were
handsome, independent, and young. True, they had
hair—and you can't be born with a wig—and they had
a great deal of it which tumbled down in soft and
brilliant curls, for they were very well groomed. Some
wore thin mustaches and others had full beards. . . .

These intellectual thieves (the remark was made by
Philothée O'Neddy) didn't look like well-dressed lawyers, we must confess; but their dress, were individual
eccentricies of taste governed with a genuine feeling
for color, borrowed a great deal from painting. Satin,
velvet, sashes, brandenburgs, fur cuffs—all these are
well worth black coats with codfish tails, excessively
short silk waistcoats climbing up the stomach, the
starched muslin scarf in which the throat is buried,
and the points of white linen collars making eyelets for
gold spectacles. Even the soft felt hat and the boating
jacket on the youngest rakes who were not yet wealthy
enough to make their dreams come true about a Rubens
or Velasquez costume, were certainly more elegant than
the stovepipe hats and the old suits with wrinkled
creases worn by the aged customers of the *Comédie*

Française, who horrifiedly amassed themselves against the invasion of these young Shakespearian barbarians. . . .

We piled ourselves as best as we could way up aloft, in obscure corners in the semi-circle, on the rear-most benches in the galleries, in all those suspicious and dangerous places where there might be some ambush in the shadows, where some ardent member of a claque might be sheltered, some ordinary middle-class type. . . .

It was a long time to wait, six or seven hours in semi-darkness, or at least in the penumbra of a room not yet lighted; it was a long time, even at the start of that night when *Hernani* was to rise like the radiant sun. . . .

We began to feel hungry. The shrewdest had brought chocolate and cookies, others—*proh! pudor*—cold cuts, which the ill-disposed classicists said were full of garlic. . . . Supper being finished, a few of Hugo's ballads were sung. . . .

The orchestra and the balcony were paved with academic and classical skulls. The hint of a storm growled and rumbled in the room, for it was time for the curtain to be raised; so great was the animosity felt on both sides that they might well, all of them, have walked on their hands and knees to see the play. Finally the three strokes resounded. The curtain slowly parted and we saw, in a seventeenth-century bedroom, Donna Josefa Duarte illuminated by a small lamp, she dressed in black. . . .

> Is he already there? Upon those hidden
> Stairs—

Already the fight was on. This word thrown unmannerly into the next line, this daring, indeed impertinent, enjambment, seemed like some professional assassin, a

Saltabadil, a Scoronconcolo giving a flick to Classicism's
nose in order to provoke him to a duel.

Trans. H. E. H.

The Romantic Reformer

[FROM *Nightmare Abbey*]

THOMAS LOVE PEACOCK

1818

Scythrop was left alone in Nightmare Abbey. He was
a burnt child, and dreaded the fire of female eyes. He
wandered about the ample pile, or along the garden
terrace, with "his cogitative faculties immersed in cogi-
bundity of cogitation." The terrace terminated at the
southwestern tower, which, as we have said, was ruin-
ous and full of owls. Here would Scythrop take his
evening seat on a fallen fragment of mossy stone, with
his back resting against the ruined wall—a thick canopy of ivy, with an owl in it, over his head—and the
Sorrows of Werther in his hand. He had some taste for
romance reading before he went to the university,
where, we must confess, in justice to his college, he
was cured of the love of reading in all its shapes; and
the cure would have been radical, if disappointment
in love, and total solitude, had not conspired to bring
on a relapse. He began to devour romances and German tragedies, and, by the recommendation of Mr.
Flosky, to pore over ponderous tomes of transcendental
philosophy, which reconciled him to the labour of
studying them by their mystical jargon and necro-
mantic imagery. In the congenial solitude of *Nightmare*

Abbey, the distempered ideas of metaphysical romance and romantic metaphysics had ample time and space to germinate into a fertile crop of chimeras, which rapidly shot up into vigorous and abundant vegetation.

He now became troubled with the *passion for reforming the world.* He built many castles in the air, and peopled them with secret tribunals, and bands of *illuminati,* who were always the imaginary instruments of his projected regeneration of the human species. As he intended to institute a perfect republic, he invested himself with absolute sovereignty over these mystical dispensers of liberty. He slept with Horrid Mysteries under his pillow, and dreamed of venerable eleutherarchs and ghastly confederates holding midnight conventions in subterranean caves. He passed whole mornings in his study, immersed in gloomy reverie, stalking about the room in his nightcap, which he pulled over his eyes like a cowl, and folding his striped calico dressing gown about him like the mantle of a conspirator.

"Action," thus he soliloquised, "is the result of opinion, and to new-model opinion would be to new-model society. Knowledge is power; it is in the hands of a few, who employ it to mislead the many, for their own selfish purposes of aggrandisement and appropriation. What if it were in the hands of a few who should employ it to lead the many? What if it were universal, and the multitude were enlightened? No. The many must be always in leading-strings; but let them have wise and honest conductors. A few to think, and many to act; that is the only basis of perfect society. So thought the ancient philosophers: they had their esoterical and exoterical doctrines. So thinks the sublime Kant, who delivers his oracles in a language which none but the initiated can comprehend. Such were the views of those secret associations of *illuminati,* which were the terror of superstition and tyranny, and which, carefully selecting wisdom and genius from the great wilderness of society, as the bee selects honey from the flowers of the thorn and the nettle, bound all human excellence in a chain, which, if it had not been prematurely broken, would have commanded opinion, and regenerated the world."

Scythrop proceeded to meditate on the practicability of reviving a confederation of regenerators. To get a clear view of his own ideas, and to feel the pulse of the wisdom and genius of the age, he wrote and published a treatise, in which his meanings were carefully wrapt up in the monk's hood of transcendental technology, but filled with hints of matter deep and dangerous, which he thought would set the whole nation in a ferment; and he awaited the result in awful expectation, as a miner who has fired a train awaits the explosion of a rock. However, he listened and heard nothing; for the explosion, if any ensued, was not sufficiently loud to shake a single leaf of the ivy on the towers of *Nightmare Abbey*; and some months afterwards he received a letter from his bookseller, informing him that only seven copies had been sold, and concluding with a polite request for the balance.

Scythrop did not despair. "Seven copies," he thought, "have been sold. Seven is a mystical number, and the omen is good. Let me find the seven purchasers of my seven copies, and they shall be the seven golden candlesticks with which I will illuminate the world."

Scythrop had a certain portion of mechanical genius, which his romantic projects tended to develop. He constructed models of cells and recesses, sliding panels and secret passages, that would have baffled the skill of the Parisian police. He took the opportunity of his father's absence to smuggle a dumb carpenter into the *Abbey*, and between them they gave reality to one of these models in Scythrop's tower. Scythrop foresaw that a great leader of human regeneration would be involved in fearful dilemmas, and determined, for the benefit of mankind in general, to adopt all possible precautions for the preservation of himself.

The servants, even the women, had been tutored into silence. Profound silence reigned throughout and around the *Abbey*, except when the occasional shutting of a door would peal in long reverberations through the galleries, or the heavy tread of the pensive butler would wake the hollow echoes of the hall. Scythrop stalked about like the grand inquisitor, and the servants flitted past him like familiars. In his evening meditations on the terrace, under the ivy of the ruined tower, the only sounds that came to his ear were the rustling of the wind in the ivy, the plaintive voices of the feathered choristers, the owls, the occasional striking of the *Abbey* clock, and the monotonous dash of the sea on its low and level shore. In the mean time, he drank Madeira, and laid deep schemes for a thorough repair of the crazy fabric of human nature.

The Immanent Realm

["The Meadow"]

NOVALIS
(Friedrich von Hardenberg)

1798

The meadow clothed itself in green,
About the hedgerows blooms were seen;
Day in, day out new plants grew there,
The heavens were happy, and mild the air:
Yet what this was, or what befell,
I do not know, I cannot tell.

Darker, darker grew the wood
Where dwelled the feathered songsters' brood,
And soon their song, in that sweet air,
Impelled me here, impelled me there.
Yet what this was, or what befell,
I do not know, I cannot tell.

There gushed and poured from all around
Pure life and color, scent and sound;
Each seemed so happy to unite
In synthesis of pure delight.
Yet what this was, or what befell,
I do not know, I cannot tell.

I thought: Is some soul come alive
Some vivifying force, to strive
With countless flowers, countless treasure,
For self-revelatory pleasure?
Yet what this was, or what befell,
I do not know, I cannot tell.

Perhaps some realm is immanent
Where spongy dust becomes the plant,
The beast transmigrates from the tree
And where beast was, now man shall be.
Yet what this was, or what befell,
I do not know, I cannot tell.

While thus I stood in rapt repose,
A mighty force within me rose.
Then toward me came a friendly maid
And all my thoughts her own she made.
Yet what this was, or what befell,
I do not know, I cannot tell.

Sunshine suddenly filled the wood.
Springtime! Now I understood;

In brief, I saw that soon on earth
Mankind with gods would share their birth.
Now what this was, and what befell,
I know so well, I now can tell.

Trans. H. E. H.

Mental Fight

[FROM *Milton*]

WILLIAM BLAKE

1804-1808

And did those feet in ancient time
    Walk upon England's mountains green?
And was the holy Lamb of God
    On England's pleasant pastures seen?

And did the Countenance Divine
    Shine forth upon our clouded hills?
And was Jerusalem builded here
    Among these dark Satanic Mills?

Bring me my Bow of burning gold!
    Bring me my Arrows of desire!
Bring me my Spear: O clouds, unfold!
    Bring me my Chariot of fire!

I will not cease from Mental Fight,
    Nor shall my Sword sleep in my hand
Till we have built Jerusalem
    In England's green and pleasant Land.

REVOLUTIONARY YEARS:
1789, 1830, 1848

Wail, for the world's wrong.

—Percy Bysshe Shelley

A Spirit Not to Be Withstood

[FROM *The Prelude*, Book IX]

WILLIAM WORDSWORTH

1805

But though not deaf and obstinate to find
Error without apology on the side
Of those who were against us, more delight
We took, and let this freely be confess'd,
In painting to ourselves the miseries
Of royal Courts, and that voluptuous life
Unfeeling, where the Man who is of soul
The meanest thrives the most, where dignity,
True personal dignity, abideth not,
A light and cruel world, cut off from all
The natural inlets of just sentiment,
From lowly sympathy, and chastening truth,
Where good and evil never have that name,
That which they ought to have, but wrong prevails,
And vice at home. We added dearest themes,
Man and his noble nature, as it is

489

The gift of God and lies in his own power,
His blind desires and steady faculties
Capable of clear truth, the one to break
Bondage, the other to build Liberty
On firm foundations, making social life,
Through knowledge spreading and imperishable,
As just in regulation, and as pure
As individual in the wise and good.
We summon'd up the honorable deeds
Of ancient Story, thought of each bright spot
That could be found in all recorded time
Of truth preserv'd and error pass'd away,
Of single Spirits that catch the flame from Heaven,
And how the multitude of men will feed
And fan each other, thought of Sects, how keen
They are to put the appropriate nature on,
Triumphant over every obstacle
Of custom, language, Country, love and hate,
And what they do and suffer for their creed,
How far they travel, and how long endure,
How quickly mighty Nations have been form'd
From least beginnings, how, together lock'd
By new opinions, scatter'd tribes have made
One body spreading wide as clouds in heaven. . . .

  Yet not the less,
Hatred of absolute rule, where will of One
Is law for all, and of that barren pride
In them who, by immunities unjust,
Betwixt the Sovereign and the People stand,
His helper and not theirs, laid stronger hold
Daily upon me, mix'd with pity too
And love; for where hope is there love will be
For the abject multitude. And when we chanc'd
One day to meet a hunger-bitten Girl,
Who crept along, fitting her languid gait
Unto a Heifer's motion, by a cord

Tied to her arm, and picking thus from the lane
Its sustenance, while the girl with her two hands
Was busy knitting, in a heartless mood
Of solitude, and at the sight my Friend
In agitation said, ' 'Tis against *that*
Which we are fighting.' I with him believed
Devoutly that a spirit was abroad
Which could not be withstood, that poverty
At least like this, would in a little time
Be found no more, that we should see the earth
Unthwarted in her wish to recompense
The industrious, and the lowly Child of Toil,
All institutes for ever blotted out
That legalised exclusion, empty pomp
Abolish'd, sensual state and cruel power
Whether by edict of the one or few,
And finally, as sum and crown of all,
Should see the People having a strong hand
In making their own Laws, whence better days
To all mankind. . . .

An Experiment in
Human Perfectability

[FROM *The Friend*]

SAMUEL TAYLOR COLERIDGE

1809-10

Truth I pursued, as fancy sketch'd the way,
And wiser men than I went worse astray.

I was never myself, at any period of my life, a convert to the Jacobinical system. From my earliest manhood, it was an axiom in politics with me, that in every

country where property prevailed, property must be the grand basis of the government; and that that government was the best, in which the power or political influence of the individual was in proportion to his property, provided that the free circulation of property was not impeded by any positive laws or customs, nor the tendency of wealth to accumulate in abiding masses unduly encouraged. I perceived, that if the people at large were neither ignorant nor immoral, there could be no motive for a sudden and violent change of government; and if they were, there could be no hope but of a change for the worse. The temple of despotism, like that of the Mexican God, would be rebuilt with human skulls, and more firmly, though in a different style of architecture. Thanks to the excellent education which I had received, my reason was too clear not to draw this circle of power round me, and my spirit too honest to attempt to break through it. My feelings, however, and imagination did not remain unkindled in this general conflagration; and I confess I should be more inclined to be ashamed than proud of myself, if they had. I was a sharer in the general vortex, though my little world described the path of its revolution in an orbit of its own. What I dared not expect from constitutions of government and whole nations, I hoped from religion and a small company of chosen individuals. I formed a plan, as harmless as it was extravagant, of trying the experiment of human perfectibility on the banks of the Susquehanna; where our little society, in its second generation, was to have combined the innocence of the patriarchal age with the knowledge and genuine refinements of European culture; and where I dreamed that in the sober evening of my life, I should behold the cottages of independence in the undivided dale of industry,—

> And oft, soothed sadly by some dirgeful wind,
> Muse on the sore ills I had left behind!

Strange fancies, and as vain as strange! yet to the intense interest and impassioned zeal, which called forth and strained every faculty of my intellect for the organization and defence of this scheme, I owe much of whatever I at present possess, my clearest insight into the nature of individual man, and my most comprehensive views of his social relations, of the true uses of trade and commerce, and how far the wealth and relative power of nations promote or impede their welfare and inherent strength. Nor were they less serviceable in securing myself, and perhaps some others, from the pitfalls of sedition: and when we at length alighted on the firm ground of common sense from the gradually exhausted balloon of youthful enthusiasm, though the air-built castles, which we had been pursuing, had vanished with all their pageantry of shifting forms and glowing colours, we were yet free from the stains and impurities which might have remained upon us, had we been travelling with the crowd of less imaginative malcontents, through the dark lanes and foul by-roads of ordinary fanaticism.

An Experiment in Naval Mutiny

[The Petition of the Spithead Mutineers]

1797

To the Right Honourable the Lords Commissioners of the Admiralty.

We, the Seamen of his Majesty's navy, take the liberty of addressing your Lordships in an humble petition, shewing the many hardships and oppressions we have laboured under for many years, and which we hope your Lordships will redress as soon as possible.

We flatter ourselves that your Lordships, together with the nation in general, will acknowledge our worth and good services, both in the American war and the present; for which service your Lordships' petitioners do unanimously agree in opinion, that their worth to the nation, and laborious industry in defence of their country, deserve some better encouragement than that we meet at present, or from any we have experienced. We your petitioners, do not boast of our good services for any other purpose, than that of putting you and the nation in mind of the respect due to us; nor do we ever intend to deviate from our former character; so far from any thing of that kind, or that an Englishman or men should turn their coats; we likewise agree in opinion, that we should suffer double the hardships we have hitherto experienced, before we would suffer the crown of England to be in the least imposed upon by that of any other power in the world; we therefore beg leave to inform your Lordships of the grievances which we at present labour under.

We your humble petitioners relying, that your Lordships will take into early consideration the grievances of which we complain; and do not in the least doubt but your Lordships will comply with our desires, which are every way reasonable.

The first grievance which we have to complain of is, that our wages are too low, and ought to be raised, that we might be better able to support our wives and families in a manner comfortable, and whom we are in duty bound to support as far as our wages will allow, which, we trust, will be looked into by your Lordships and the honourable House of Commons in parliament assembled.

We your petitioners beg that your Lordships will take

into consideration the grievances of which we complain, and now lay before you.

First, that our provisions be raised to the weight of sixteen ounces to the pound, and of a better quality; and that our measures may be the same as those used in the commercial trade of this country.

Secondly, that your petitioners request your honours will please to observe, there should be no flour served while we are in harbour, or any port whatever under the command of the British flag; and also that there be granted a sufficient quantity of vegetables of such kind as may be the most plentiful in the ports to which we go, which we grievously complain and lie under the want of.

Thirdly, that your Lordships will be pleased seriously to look into the state of the sick on board his Majesty's ships, that they be better attended to, and that they may have the use of such necessaries as are allowed for them in time of their sickness; and that these necessaries be not on any account embezzled.

Fourthly, that your Lordships will be so kind as to look into this affair, which is no ways unreasonable; and that we may be looked upon as a number of men standing in defence of our country; and that we may in some wise have granted an opportunity to taste the sweets of liberty on shore when in any harbour; and when we have completed the duty of our ships, after our return from sea; and that no man may incroach upon his liberty, there shall be a boundary limited, and those trespassing any further, without a written order from the commanding officer, shall be punished according to the rules of the navy; which is a natural request, and congenial to the heart of man, and certainly to us, that you make the boast of being the guardians of the land.

Fifthly, that if any man is wounded in action, his pay

be continued until he is cured and discharged; and if any ship has any real grievances to complain of, we hope your Lordships will readily redress them, as far as in your power, to prevent any disturbances.

It is also unanimously agreed by the fleet, that from this day no grievance shall be received, in order to convince the nation at large, that we know when to cease to ask, as well as when to begin; and that we ask nothing but what is moderate, and may be granted, without detriment to the nation, or injury to the service.

Given on board the Queen Charlotte, by the Delegates of the Fleet, this 18th day of April, 1797.[1]

The Yoke upon Us

[FROM *Childe Harold's Pilgrimage*]

GEORGE GORDON,
LORD BYRON

1818

I speak not of men's creeds—they rest between
Man and his Maker—but of things allow'd,
Averr'd and known,—and daily, hourly, seen—
The yoke that is upon us doubly bow'd,
And the intent of tyranny avow'd,
The edict of Earth's rulers, who are grown
The apes of him who humbled once the proud,
And shook them from their slumbers on the throne,
Too glorious, were this all his mighty arm had done.

[1] The Petition was rejected, and the leaders hanged. [H.E.H.'s note.]

Can tyrants but by tyrants conquer'd be,
And Freedom find no champion and no child
Such as Columbia saw arise when she
Sprung forth a Pallas, arm'd and undefiled?
Or must such minds be nourish'd in the wild,
Deep in the unpruned forest, 'midst the roar
Of cataracts, where nursing Nature smiled
On infant Washington? Has Earth no more
Such seeds within her breast, or Europe no such shore?

But France got drunk with blood to vomit crime,
And fatal have her Saturnalia been
To Freedom's cause, in every age and clime;
Because the deadly days which we have seen,
And vile Ambition, that built up between
Man and his hopes an adamantine wall,
And the base pageant last upon the scene,
Are grown the pretext for the eternal thrall
Which nips life's tree, and dooms man's worst—his
   second fall.

Yet, Freedom! yet thy banner, torn, but flying,
Streams like the thunder-storm *against* the wind;
Thy trumpet voice, though broken now and dying,
The loudest still the tempest leaves behind;
Thy tree hath lost its blossoms, and the rind,
Chopp'd by the axe, looks rough and little worth,
But the sap lasts,—and still the seed we find
Sown deep, even in the bosom of the North;
So shall a better spring less bitter fruit bring forth.

England in 1819

PERCY BYSSHE SHELLEY

An old, mad, blind, despised, and dying king,—
Princes, the dregs of their dull race, who flow
Through public scorn,—mud from a muddy spring,—
Rulers who neither see, nor feel, nor know,
But leech-like to their fainting country cling,
Till they drop, blind in blood, without a blow,—
A people starved and stabbed in the untilled field,—
An army, which liberticide and prey
Makes as a two-edged sword to all who wield
Golden and sanguine laws which tempt and slay;
Religion Christless, Godless—a book sealed;
A Senate,—Time's worst statute unrepealed,—
Are graves, from which a glorious Phantom may
Burst, to illumine our tempestuous day.

The Distant Volcano

[FROM *The Masque of Anarchy*]

PERCY BYSSHE SHELLEY

1819

WRITTEN ON THE OCCASION OF THE MASSACRE
AT MANCHESTER

I

As I lay asleep in Italy
There came a voice from over the Sea,
And with great power it forth led me
To walk in the visions of Poesy.

II

I met Murder on the way—
He had a mask like Castlereagh—
Very smooth he looked, yet grim;
Seven blood-hounds followed him:

III

All were fat; and well they might
Be in admirable plight,
For one by one, and two by two,
He tossed them human hearts to chew
Which from his wide cloak he drew.

IV

Next came Fraud, and he had on,
Like Eldon, an ermined gown;
His big tears, for he wept well,
Turned to mill-stones as they fell.

V

And the little children, who
Round his feet played to and fro,
Thinking every tear a gem,
Had their brains knocked out by them.

VI

Clothed with the Bible, as with light,
And the shadows of the night,
Like Sidmouth, next, Hypocrisy
On a crocodile rode by.

VII

And many more Destructions played
In this ghastly masquerade,
All disguised, even to the eyes,
Like Bishops, lawyers, peers, and spies.

VIII

Last came Anarchy: he rode
On a white horse, splashed with blood;
He was pale even to the lips,
Like Death in the Apocalypse.

IX

And he wore a kingly crown;
And in his grasp a sceptre shone;
On his brow this mark I saw—
"I AM GOD, AND KING, AND LAW!"

X

With a pace stately and fast,
Over English land he passed,
Trampling to a mire of blood
The adoring multitude.

XI

And a mighty troop around,
With their trampling shook the ground,
Waving each a bloody sword,
For the service of their Lord.

XII

And with glorious triumph, they
Rode through England proud and gay,
Drunk as with intoxication
Of the wine of desolation.

XIII

O'er fields and towns, from sea to sea,
Passed the Pageant swift and free,
Tearing up, and trampling down;
Till they came to London town.

XIV

And each dweller, panic-striken,
Felt his heart with terror sicken
Hearing the tempestuous cry
Of the triumph of Anarchy.

XV

For with pomp to meet him came,
Clothed in arms like blood and flame,
The hired murderers, who did sing
"Thou art God, and Law, and King.

XVI

"We have waited, weak and lone
For thy coming, Mighty One!
Our purses are empty, our swords are cold,
Give us glory, and blood, and gold."

XVII

Lawyers and priests, a motley crowd,
To the earth their pale brows bowed;
Like a bad prayer not over loud,
Whispering—"Thou art Law and God."

XVIII

Then all cried with one accord,
"Thou art King, and God, and Lord;
Anarchy, to thee we bow,
Be thy name made holy now!"

XIX

And Anarchy, the Skeleton,
Bowed and grinned to every one,
As well as if his education
Had cost ten millions to the nation.

. . . .

LXXXII

"The old laws of England—they
Whose reverend heads with age are gray,
Children of a wiser day;
And whose solemn voice must be
Thine own echo—Liberty!

LXXXIII

"On those who first should violate
Such sacred heralds in their state
Rest the blood that must ensue,
And it will not rest on you.

LXXXIV

"And if then the tyrants dare
Let them ride among you there,
Slash, and stab, and maim, and hew,—
What they like, that let them do.

LXXXV

"With folded arms and steady eyes,
And little fear, and less surprise,
Look upon them as they slay
Till their rage has died away.

LXXXVI

"Then they will return with shame
To the place from which they came,
And the blood thus shed will speak
In hot blushes on their cheek.

LXXXVII

"Every woman in the land
Will point at them as they stand—
They will hardly dare to greet
Their acquaintance in the street.

LXXXVIII

"And the bold, true warriors
Who have hugged Danger in wars
Will turn to those who would be free,
Ashamed of such base company.

LXXXIX

"And that slaughter to the Nation
Shall steam up like inspiration,
Eloquent, oracular;
A volcano heard afar.

XC

"And these words shall then become
Like Oppression's thundered doom
Ringing through each heart and brain,
Heard again—again—again—

XCI

"Rise like Lions after slumber
In unvanquishable number—
Shake your chains to earth like dew
Which in sleep had fallen on you—
Ye are many—they are few."

"*Man Has Exploited Man*"

HENRI DE SAINT-SIMON

[FROM *Concerning the Organization of European Society*, by Henri de Saint-Simon and Augustin Thierry]

1814

There will doubtless come an age when all the people of Europe will feel that they must deal with issues of general interest before they come down to national concerns; at that time cares will diminish, troubles will abate, wars will cease. Toward this we aim without respite; toward this the path of the human spirit takes us! But which is worthier of man's prudence, that he run there or be pulled there?

The poetic imagination has placed the Golden Age within the cradle of the human race, amid the ignorance and rudeness of these early times; perhaps it would be better to relegate this period to the Iron Age. The Golden Age of the human race is not behind us at all, it is ahead, it lies in the perfection of the social order; our forefathers have never seen it, our children shall reach there some day. It is up to us to trace the path for them.

[FROM *The Doctrine of Saint-Simon*, composed by a group of his disciples]

1829

A new science, a science as *positive* as any that deserves the title, has been created by SAINT-SIMON: this science is that of the *human race*; its method is the same employed by astronomy and physics; the facts within it are grouped within a series of homogeneous classes, linked to each other within an order of *generalization* and *particularization*, in such a way as to bring out the special *proclivity* of each, that is to say, to demonstrate the law of *increase* and *decrease* to which all must submit.

A primary application of this science proves the tendency of the human race toward *universal association*, or, in other words, the constant diminution of *antagonism*, explained in succession by these words: *families, castes, cities, nations, HUMANITY*; whence results that societies, originally organized for *war*, tend to blend into a *peaceful* UNIVERSAL ASSOCIATION.

A general picture of the development of the human race, including Jewish monotheism, Greek and Roman polytheism, and Christianity up to the present, demonstrates with proof this law of PROGRESS.

Up to now, man has exploited man. Masters and slaves; patrician, plebeian; lords, serfs; owners, farmers; idlers and workers—behold the progressive history of humanity up to our day. Behold our future with UNIVERSAL ASSOCIATION: *to each according to his capacity, to each capacity according to its productivity*, behold the new LAW which replaces that of *conquest* and of BIRTH: man no longer exploits man; but man, linked to man, exploits the natural world delivered to his power.

Ah! What do our lawyers, political journalists, economists come to tell us today? Does not their science prove to us that wealth and misery shall always be *hereditary;* that wealth is a necessary *attribute* of idleness? Does it not also prove that the sons of the poor are as free as those of the rich? Free! When one needs bread! That they are all *equal before the law?* Equal before the law? When one has the right to live without working, and the other—if he doesn't work, has only the right to die.

They repeat to us without end that property is the foundation of the social order; we too proclaim this eternal truth. But who shall be the property owner? Shall it be the *lazy, ignorant,* IMMORAL son of a deceased man, or shall it be rather the man capable of fulfilling his social function with dignity? They claim that all privileges of birth have been destroyed. Ah! What is the transmission of a fortune from father to son, with no other reason than the link of blood, if it is not the most *immoral* of all privileges—that of *living in society without working,* and there to be rewarded above and beyond one's labor?

A sad science, which would have maintained slavery, which would have stopped JESUS from preaching human *brotherhood,* fearful that His words might have resounded in the ears of a slave; a sad science that in an age even more distant would have proclaimed the validity of cannibalism!

Yes, all our political theorists have their eyes on the past, even those who claim themselves to be worthy of the future; and when we have announced to them the arrival of the reign of WORK, and that the reign of idleness is over, they have treated us as dreamers; they tell us that sons have always inherited from their fathers, like a pagan saying that a free man has always owned slaves. But humanity has proclaimed through JESUS, NO MORE SLAVERY! Through SAINT-SIMON it now cries: *to each according to his capacity, to each capac-*

ity according to its productivity, NO MORE INHERIT-
ANCE!

All the members of the body social are men, but all
too are *artists, scholars,* or *businessmen;* in other words,
all *feel, think,* or *act.* This triple aspect of human life
provides the occasion for a triple division in general
and specialized education. This is the conception which
serves as a foundation for education in the future, for
which we have sketched the principal developments in
summary fashion.

Trans. H. E. H.

This Harmonious Revolution

[FROM THE *Memoirs*]

HECTOR BERLIOZ

1830

It was in the year 1830. I was just finishing my cantata when the Revolution broke out.

A number of families had taken shelter in the Palais
de l'Institut, and it looked strangely transformed—
with long-barreled muskets protruding from the barred
doors, and its façade riddled with bullets, the air filled
with the shrieks of women, and, in the lulls between
the discharges of musketry, the shrill twitter of the
swallows. I hurriedly dashed off the last pages of my
cantata to the tune of the dry thud of the bullets as
they struck close to my windows or on the walls of
my room; and on the 24th I was free to loaf about
Paris with the *"sacred rabble,"* and my pistol in my
pocket, till the next day.

I shall never forget the aspect of Paris during those memorable days—the wild bravado of the street Arabs, the enthusiasm of the men, the frenzy of the women, the mournful resignation of the Swiss and Royal Guards, the curious pride which the workmen exhibited in not pillaging Paris though they were masters of the situation, the astounding stories told by young fellows of their exploits, in which the real bravery of the deed was lost in the sense of the ridiculous aroused by the manner in which it was told; as, for instance, when they described the storming of the cavalry barracks of the Rue de Babylone—in which considerable loss had been incurred—with a gaiety worthy of Alexander's veterans, as "the capture of Babylon"—an abbreviation forced on them by the length of the real name. With what pompous prolongation of the "o" the name of "Babylon" was pronounced! . . . Oh Parisians, what buffoons you are! Great, if you will, but still buffoons! . . .

No words can give any idea of the music, the songs and the hoarse voices which rang through the streets!

And yet it was only a few days after this harmonious revolution that I received a most extraordinary musical impression, or shock. I was crossing the Palais Royal when I heard a tune which I seemed to recognize, issuing from among a crowd of people. As I drew nearer I perceived that ten or twelve young fellows were singing a war song of my own, the words of which, translated from one of Moore's *Irish Melodies*, happened exactly to suit the situation. Delighted at the discovery, and little used to that kind of success, I enter the circle of singers, and ask to be allowed to join. I am admitted, and a superfluous bass is interpolated into the chorus. I did not, of course, betray my identity; but I remember having a warm discussion with the leader as to the time in which he was taking my song. Luckily I recover his good graces by singing my part in Béranger's "*Vieux*

Drapeau," which he had set to music, and which we next performed, quite correctly. During the *entr'actes* of this improvised concert three National Guards, whose duty it was to keep the crowd away from the singers, went round, shako in hand, to make a collection for those who had been wounded during the Three Days. The Parisians, struck by the quaintness of the idea, contributed liberally, and there was a perfect hailstorm of five-franc pieces, which our music alone could hardly have charmed from the pockets of their owners. As the audience went on increasing it became more and more difficult to keep the necessary space clear for the performers, and an *armed force* soon became impotent to control the curious crowd. We find great difficulty in escaping; the crowd streams after us; and at last, when we reach the Galérie Colbert, leading to the *Rue Vivienne*, we are hunted out like bears at a fair, surrounded on all sides, and more songs demanded of us. The wife of a draper, over whose shop there is a semicircular glazed gallery, suggests that we should go up, and pour down our torrents of harmony on our ardent admirers from thence, without fear of being crushed to death. We agree, and begin with the "Marseillaise." The noisy crowd at our feet is hushed at once. The air is as still as it is in the Piazza of St. Peter's when the Pope pronounces the blessing, *urbi et orbi,* from the pontifical balcony. At the end of the second verse, still the same silence. At the end of the third again, not a sound. This was not at all what I wanted. When I beheld that vast concourse I suddenly remembered that I had just arranged Rouget de Lisle's song for full orchestra and double chorus, and had put in the margin: *For all who have voices, hearts, and blood in their veins.* "Ah!" I said to myself, "that is what we want." So I was greatly disappointed at this persistent silence, and at the end of the fourth verse, unable to contain myself, I shouted, "Why on earth don't you

sing?" Then the people roared out, "*Aux armes, cito-
yens!*" with the precision and power of a trained chorus.
You must remember that the gallery which opened into
the Rue Vivienne was crowded, so was the one opening
into the Rue Neuve des Petits Champs, so was the area
in the middle; and also that these four or five thousand
voices came reverberating back in the enclosed space,
from the closed shops below, the glass frames above,
and the pavement beneath their feet. You must not
forget either that the singers, men, women, and children, were hot from the combat of the previous day,
and you can imagine the effect produced by their thundering refrain. . . . I can only say that I actually fell
prostrate in the midst of our little band, who stood
completely dumbfounded by the explosion like birds
after a peal of thunder.

Trans. Rachel and Eleanor Holmes (London: Macmillan, 1884).

"Poor People, Brave People, All Fighters"

[FROM *Journal of a Poet*]

ALFRED DE VIGNY

1864

Tuesday, 27 July, 1830

Today begin the popular uprisings.—The cause is
the laws of the 25th.—The King has gone to Compiègne, leaving the Ministers to fire on the people.—I
hear this as I write.—I am happy that I left the Army;
thirteen years of badly paid service have left me quits
with the Bourbons.—Ever since the accession of Charles

X, I have predicted that he would try to achieve absolute rule.—He hates the Charter and doesn't understand it. Old women in the Court and favorites in the government.—Now he has put in M. de Polignac as minister and wants to keep him there despite everything.—He believes himself insulted that the 221 have been re-elected to the Chamber; he thinks he can act the role of Bonaparte: Bonaparte standing in front of his cannons at Saint-Roch. Charles X is at Compiègne. He said: "My brother gave away everything and fell; I shall resist and not fall." He is wrong, Louis XVI fell to the left and Charles X to the right. There is all the difference.

Wednesday, the 28th

I can no longer cross Paris. The workers have been let out, breaking the street lamps, breaking into the shops, killing, shot at and pursued by the Guard.— They say that the 50th Regiment of the Line has refused to fire on the people.

I approved of the Ministry of the Duc de Richelieu; that of M. de Martignac.—The only way to reconcile the *Restoration* and the *Revolution*, these two perpetual enemies, would be to govern with these two centers and wipe out the extremists from beneath.—Today, an extremist wins everything. Disorders. Illegality.— The ministers are *outlaws,* outside of the law, and have placed the King there too.—Why isn't he in Paris? Why is the Dauphin away?

From Wednesday to Thursday, the 29th

They have been fighting since this morning. The workers are a brave group from the *Vendée*; the soldiers are courageous Imperial Guards: all French. On the one hand zeal and intelligence, on the other hand, honor.—What is my duty? To protect my mother and my wife. What am I? Retired captain. I left the service five years ago. The Court gave me nothing during my service. My writings displeased it: the Court found them seditious. I described Louis XIII in such a way that I was often told: *You are a liberal.* From the Bourbons I received one promotion out of *seniority,* to the 5th Guard Regiment; the only one, for I entered as a lieutenant. Nevertheless, if the King came back to the Tuileries and the Dauphin put himself at the head of his troops, I would go forth to be killed with them.—The tocsin.—I saw the fire from the attic windows.—The fire will bring chaos.—Poor people, brave people, all fighters!

I have gotten my old uniform ready. If the King calls out all the officers, I shall go.—And his cause is a bad one; he is in his childhood, as is all his family: a childhood which does not understand the present time.— Why have I felt that I owe this death?—It's silly. He would know neither my name nor my death. But when I was still a child, my father made me kiss the cross of Saint-Louis, at the time of the Empire; superstition, political superstition, rootless, puerile, an old prejudice of feudal fidelity, of attachment to one's family, a kind of vassalage, the parenthood of seigneur to serf. But how could I not go tomorrow morning if he calls all of us? I served the king for thirteen years. That word: king—what does it mean? And to leave my old mother and my young wife who depend on me! But I shall leave them, it's quite wrong, but it is necessary.

The night is almost over.—Again cannon fire.

Thursday, the 29th

They are not coming to Paris, and people are dying for them. Oh race of Stuarts! Oh! I shall protect my family.

Attack on the barracks at Rue Verte and Pépinière. Unbelievable bravery on the part of the locksmith workers. I stuck my head out of the window to see if any wounded from either side were taking refuge at my doorstep. They've just fired on me, thinking that I wanted to shoot from my window. The three bullets have smashed the cornice of my window.—In twenty minutes, both barracks taken.

Friday, the 30th

Not a single prince has appeared. The poor brave fellows in the Guard have been abandoned without orders, without bread for two days, hunted out everywhere and fighting all the time. . . .

Saturday, the 31st

Thus in three days, the old throne is undermined! I have finished forever with inconvenient political superstitions. They can only bother my ideas now out of instinct.—If the Duc d'Enghien had been there, or only the Duc de Berry, I should have been dead. Perhaps that might have been too bad. Who knows what I shall do!

11th of August

They don't talk of those officers of the Guard who committed noble acts of bravery.—A lieutenant of the 6th Guards Regiment, receiving the order to fire, refused to do so because the street was full of women and children. The colonel reiterated the order to fire and threatened him with arrest: he took a pistol and shot his own brains out.

Le Motheux, captain in the 1st regiment, sent in his resignation the day of M. de Polignac's foolish laws. That evening, the fighting began; he went to find his colonel and begged him to act as if the resignation had not arrived.—His company was hunted down in the Madeleine, among these church columns they are building: they shouted at him to surrender; he refused and was shot.

These two instances can serve as a perfect symbol to explain the spiritual condition of the Royal Guard. They did their duty nobly, but reluctantly.

The day when there will be neither enthusiasm, love, adoration, nor devotion among mankind, let us scoop out the earth right to its center; then we shall place five hundred thousand barrels of powder there, and may she explode into pieces like a bomb in the middle of the firmament.

Oh, to flee! To flee from mankind and to retire among a few of the elect out of the millions and millions!

Trans. H. E. H.

"*Then Courage, European Revolter*"

[FROM *Leaves of Grass*]

WALT WHITMAN

TO A FOIL'D EUROPEAN REVOLUTIONAIRE

1856

Courage yet, my brother or my sister!
Keep on—Liberty is to be subserv'd whatever occurs;
That is nothing that is quell'd by one or two failures, or
   any number of failures,
Or by the indifference or ingratitude of the people, or
   by any unfaithfulness,
Or the show of the tushes of power, soldiers, cannon,
   penal statutes.

What we believe in waits latent forever through all the
   continents,

Invites no one, promises nothing, sits in calmness and
  light, is positive and composed, knows no discourage-
  ment,
Waiting patiently, waiting its time.

(Not songs of loyalty alone are these,
But songs of insurrection also,
For I am the sworn poet of every dauntless rebel the
  world over,
And he going with me leaves peace and routine behind
  him,
And stakes his life to be lost at any moment.)

The battle rages with many a loud alarm and frequent
  advance and retreat,
The infidel triumphs, or supposes he triumphs,
The prison, scaffold, garrote, handcuffs, iron necklace
  and lead-balls do their work,
The named and unnamed heroes pass to other spheres,
The great speakers and writers are exiled, they lie sick
  in distant lands,
The cause is asleep, the strongest throats are choked
  with their own blood,
The young men droop their eyelashes toward the
  ground when they meet;
But for all this Liberty has not gone out of the place,
  nor the infidel enter'd into full possession.

When Liberty goes out of a place it is not the first to
  go, nor the second or third to go,
It waits for all the rest to go, it is the last.

When there are no more memories of heroes and martyrs,
And when all life and all the souls of men and women
  are discharged from any part of the earth,

Then only shall liberty or the idea of liberty be dis-
    charged from that part of the earth,
And the infidel come into full possession.

Then courage, European revolter, revoltress!
For till all ceases neither must you cease.

I do not know what you are for, (I do not know what I
    am for myself, nor what any thing is for,)
But I will search carefully for it even in being foil'd,
In defeat, poverty, misconception, imprisonment—for
    they too are great.

Did we think victory great?
So it is—but now it seems to me, when it cannot be
    help'd, that defeat is great,
And that death and dismay are great.

EUROPE: THE 72ND AND 73RD YEARS OF THESE STATES

1850-1860

Suddenly out of its stale and drowsy lair, the lair of
    slaves,
Like lightning it le'pt forth half startled at itself,
Its feet upon the ashes and the rags, its hand tight to
    the throats of kings.

O hope and faith!
O aching close of exiled patriots' lives!
O many a sicken'd heart!
Turn back unto this day and make yourselves afresh.

And you, paid to defile the People—you liars, mark!
Not for numberless agonies, murders, lusts,
For court thieving in its manifold mean forms, worming
    from his simplicity the poor man's wages,
For many a promise sworn by royal lips and broken
    and laugh'd at in the breaking,

Then in their power not for all these did the blows
    strike revenge, or the heads of the nobles fall;
The People scorn'd the ferocity of kings.

But the sweetness of mercy brew'd bitter destruction,
    and the frighten'd monarchs come back,
Each comes in state with his train, hangman, priest,
    tax-gatherer,
Soldier, lawyer, lord, jailer, and sycophant.

Yet behind all lowering stealing, lo, a shape,
Vague as the night, draped interminably, head, front
    and form, in scarlet folds,
Whose face and eyes none may see,
Out of its robes only this, the red robes lifted by the
    arm,
One finger crook'd pointed high over the top, like the
    head of a snake appears.

Meanwhile corpses lie in new-made graves, bloody
    corpses of young men,
The rope of the gibbet hangs heavily, the bullets of
    princes are flying, the creatures of power laugh aloud,
And all these things bear fruits, and they are good.

Those corpses of young men,
Those martyrs that hang from the gibbets, those hearts
    pierc'd by the gray lead,
Cold and motionless as they seem live elsewhere with
    unslaughter'd vitality.

They live in other young men, O kings!
They live in brothers again ready to defy you,
They were purified by death, they were taught and
    exalted.

Not a grave of the murder'd for freedom but grows
    seed for freedom, in its turn to bear seed,

Which the winds carry afar and re-sow, and the rains
and the snows nourish.

Not a disembodied spirit can the weapons of tyrants let
loose,
But it stalks invisibly over the earth, whispering, coun-
seling, cautioning.

Liberty, let others despair of you— I never despair of
you.
Is the house shut? is the master away?
Nevertheless, be ready, be not weary of watching,
He will soon return, his messengers come anon.

Paris in 1848

[FROM *The Sentimental Education*]

GUSTAVE FLAUBERT

1869

He was abruptly roused from sleep by the noise of
a discharge of musketry; and, in spite of Rosanette's
entreaties, Frédéric was fully determined to go and
see what was happening. He hurried down to the
Champs Élysées, from which shots were being fired.
At the corner of the Rue Saint-Honoré some men in
blouses ran past him, exclaiming, "No! not that way!
to the Palais-Royal!"

Frédéric followed them. The grating of the Convent
of the Assumption had been torn away. A little further
on he noticed three paving-stones in the middle of the
street, the beginning of a barricade, no doubt; then
fragments of bottles and bundles of iron-wire, to ob-
struct the cavalry; and, at the same moment, there

rushed suddenly out of a lane a tall young man of pale complexion, with his black hair flowing over his shoulders, and with a sort of pea-coloured swaddling-cloth thrown round him. In his hand he held a long military musket, and he dashed along on the tips of his slippers with the air of a somnambulist and with the nimbleness of a tiger. At intervals a detonation could be heard.

On the evening of the day before, the spectacle of the wagon containing five corpses picked up from amongst those that were lying on the Boulevard des Capucines had charged the disposition of the people; and, while at the Tuileries the aides-de-camp succeeded each other, and M. Molé, having set about the composition of a new Cabinet, did not come back, and M. Thiers was making efforts to constitute another, and while the King was cavilling and hesitating, and finally assigned the post of commander-in-chief to Bugeaud in order to prevent him from making use of it, the insurrection was organising itself in a formidable manner, as if it were directed by a single arm.

Men endowed with a kind of frantic eloquence were engaged in haranguing the populace at the street corners, others were in the churches ringing the tocsin loudly as ever they could. Lead was cast for bullets, cartridges were rolled about. The trees on the boulevards, the urinals, the benches, the gratings, the gas-burners, everything was torn off and thrown down. Paris, that morning, was covered with barricades. The resistance which was offered was of short duration, so that at eight o'clock the people, by voluntary surrender or by force, had got possession of five barracks, nearly all the municipal buildings, the most favourable strategic points. Of its own accord, without any effort, the Monarchy was melting away in rapid dissolution, and now an attack was made on the guard-house of the Château d'Eau, in order to liberate fifty prisoners, who were not there.

Frédéric was forced to stop at the entrance to the square. It was filled with groups of armed men. The Rue Saint-Thomas and the Rue Fromanteau were occupied by companies of the Line. The Rue de Valois was choked up by an enormous barricade. The smoke which fluttered about at the top of it partly opened. Men kept running overhead, making violent gestures; they vanished from sight; then the firing was again renewed. It was answered from the guard-house without anyone being seen inside. Its windows, protected by oaken window-shutters, were pierced with loop-holes; and the monument with its two storeys, its two wings, its fountain on the first floor and its little door in the centre, was beginning to be speckled with white spots under the shock of the bullets. The three steps in front of it remained unoccupied.

At Frédéric's side a man in a Greek cap, with a cartridge-box over his knitted vest, was holding a dispute with a woman with a Madras neckerchief round her shoulders. She said to him, "Come back now! Come back!"

"Leave me alone!" replied the husband. "You can easily mind the porter's lodge by yourself. I ask, citizen, is this fair? I have on every occasion done my duty— in eighteen thirty, in thirty-two, in thirty-four, and in thirty-nine! Today they're fighting again. I must fight! Go away!"

And the porter's wife ended by yielding to his remonstrances and to those of a National Guard near them— a man of forty, whose simple face was adorned with a circle of white beard. He loaded his gun and fired while talking to Frédéric, as cool in the midst of the outbreak as a horticulturist in his garden. A young lad with a packing-cloth thrown over him was trying to coax this man to give him a few caps, so that he might make use of a gun he had, a fine fowling-piece which a "gentleman" had made him a present of.

"Catch on behind my back," said the good man, "and keep yourself from being seen, or you'll get yourself killed!"

The drums beat for the charge. Sharp cries, hurrahs of triumph burst forth. A continual ebbing to and fro made the multitude sway backwards and forwards. Frédéric, caught between two thick masses of people, did not move an inch, all the time fascinated and exceedingly amused by the scene around him. The wounded who sank to the ground, the dead lying at his feet, did not seem like persons really wounded or really dead. The impression left on his mind was that he was looking on at a show.

In the midst of the surging throng, above the sea of heads, could be seen an old man in a black coat, mounted on a white horse with a velvet saddle. He held in one hand a green bough, in the other a paper, and he kept shaking them persistently; but at length, giving up all hope of obtaining a hearing, he withdrew from the scene.

The soldiers of the Line had gone, and only the municipal troops remained to defend the guard-house. A wave of dauntless spirits dashed up the steps; they were flung down; others came on to replace them, and the gate resounded under blows from iron bars. The municipal guards did not give way. But a wagon stuffed full of hay, and burning like a gigantic torch, was dragged against the walls. Faggots were speedily brought, then straw, and a barrel of spirits of wine. The fire mounted up to the stones along the wall; the building began to send forth smoke on all sides like the crater of a volcano; and at its summit, between the balustrades of the terrace, huge flames escaped with a harsh noise. The first storey of the Palais-Royal was occupied by National Guards. Shots were fired through every window in the square; the bullets whizzed, the water of the fountain, which had burst, was mingled with the blood, forming little pools on the ground. People slipped in the mud over clothes, shakos, and weapons. Frédéric felt something soft under his foot. It was the hand of a sergeant in a grey great-coat, lying on his face in the stream that ran along the street. Fresh bands of people were continually coming up, pushing on the combatants at the guard-house. The firing became quicker. The wine-shops were open; people went into them from time to time to smoke a pipe and drink a glass of beer, and then came back again to fight. A lost dog began to howl. This made the people laugh.

Frédéric was shaken by the impact of a man falling on his shoulder with a bullet through his back and the death-rattle in his throat. At this shot, perhaps directed against himself, he felt himself stirred up to rage; and he was plunging forward when a National Guard stopped him.

" 'Tis useless! the King has just gone! Ah! if you don't believe me, go and see for yourself!"

This assurance calmed Frédéric. The Place du Carrousel had a tranquil aspect. The Hôtel de Nantes stood there as fixed as ever; and the houses in the rear, the dome of the Louvre in front, the long gallery of wood at the right, and the waste plot of ground that ran unevenly as far as the sheds of the stall-keepers were, so to speak, steeped in the grey hues of the atmosphere, where indistinct murmurs seemed to mingle with the fog; while, at the opposite side of the square, a stiff light, falling through the parting of the clouds on the façade of the Tuileries, cut out all its windows into white patches. Near the Arc de Triomphe a dead horse lay on the ground. Behind the gratings groups consisting of five or six persons were chatting. The doors leading into the château were open, and the servants at the thresholds allowed the people to enter.

The meeting exhibited great respect for the president. He was one of those who, on the 25th of February, had desired an immediate organisation of labour. On the following day, at the Prado, he had declared himself in favour of attacking the Hôtel de Ville; and, as every person at that period took some model for imitation, one copied Saint-Just, another Danton, another Marat; as for him, he tried to be like Blanqui, who imitated Robespierre. His black gloves, and his hair brushed back, gave him a rigid aspect exceedingly becoming.

He opened the proceedings with the declaration of the Rights of Man and of the Citizen—a customary act of faith. Then, a vigorous voice struck up Béranger's "*Souvenirs du Peuple.*"

Other voices were raised: "No! no! not that!"

" '*La Casquette!*' " the patriots at the bottom of the apartment began to howl.

And they sang in chorus the favourite lines of the period:

> "Doff your hat before my cap—
> Kneel before the working man!"

At a word from the president the audience became silent.

One of the secretaries proceeded to inspect the letters.

Some young men announced that they burned a number of the *Assemblée Nationale* every evening in front of the Panthéon, and they urged on all patriots to follow their example.

"Bravo! adopted!" responded the audience.

The Citizen Jean Jacques Langreneux, a printer in the Rue Dauphin, would like to have a monument raised to the memory of the martyrs of Thermidor.

Michel Evariste Népomucène, ex-professor, gives expression to the wish that the European democracy should adopt unity of language. A dead language might be used for that purpose—as, for example, improved Latin.

"No—no Latin!" exclaimed the architect.

"Why?" said the college-usher.

And these two gentlemen engaged in a discussion, in which the others also took part, each putting in a word of his own for effect; and the conversation on this topic soon became so tedious that many went away. But a little old man, who wore at the end of his prodigiously high forehead a pair of green spectacles, asked permission to speak in order to make an important communication.

It was a memorandum on the assessment of taxes. The figures flowed on in a continuous stream, as if they were never going to end. The impatience of the audience found vent at first in murmurs, in whispered talk. He allowed nothing to put him out. Then they began hissing; they catcalled him. Sénécal called the persons who were interrupting to order. The orator went on like a machine. It was necessary in order to stop him to catch him by the shoulder. The old fellow looked as if he were waking out of a dream, and, placidly lifting his spectacles: "Pardon me, citizens! pardon me! I am going—a thousand excuses!"

Frédéric was disconcerted with the failure of the old man's attempts to read this written statement. He had his own address in his pocket, but an extemporaneous speech would have been preferable.

Finally the president announced that they were about to pass on to the important matter, the electoral question. They would not discuss the big Republican lists. However, the "Club of Intellect" had every right, like every other, to form one, "with all respect for the pachas of the Hôtel de Ville," and the citizens who solicited the popular mandate might set forth their claims.

"Go on, now!" said Dussadier.

A man in a cassock, with woolly hair and a petulant expression on his face, had already raised his hand. He said, with a stutter, that his name was Ducretot, priest and agriculturist, and author of a work entitled *Manures*. He was told to send it to a horticultural club.

Then a patriot in a blouse climbed up into the rostrum. He was a plebian, with broad shoulders, a big face, very mild-looking, and long black hair. He cast on the assembly an almost voluptuous glance, flung back his head, and, finally, spreading out his arms: "You have repelled Ducretot, O my brothers! and you have done right; but it was not through irreligion, for we are all religious."

Many of those present listened open-mouthed, with the air of catechumens and in ecstatic attitudes.

"It is not either because he is a priest, for we, too, are priests! The workman is a priest, just as the founder of Socialism was—the Master of us all, Jesus Christ!"

The time had arrived to inaugurate the Kingdom of God. The Gospel led directly to '89. After the abolition of slavery, the abolition of the proletariat. They had had the age of hate—the age of love was going to begin.

"Christianity is the keystone and the foundation of the new edifice."

"You are making game of us?" exclaimed the traveller in wines. "Who has given me such a priest's cap?"

This interruption gave great offence. Nearly all the audience got on benches, and, shaking their fists, shouted, "Atheists! aristocrat! low rascal!" whilst the president's bell kept ringing continuously, and the cries of "Order! order!" redoubled. But, aimless, and, moreover, fortified by "three cups of coffee" which he had swallowed before coming to the meeting, he struggled in the midst of the others. "What? I an aristocrat? Come, now!"

When, at length, he was permitted to give an explanation, he declared that he would never be at peace with the priests; and, since something had just been said about economical measures, it would be a splendid one to put an end to the churches, the sacred pyxes, and finally all creeds.

Somebody raised the objection that he was going very far.

"Yes! I am going very far! But, when a vessel is caught suddenly in a storm—"

Without waiting for the conclusion of this simile, another made a reply to his observation: "Granted! But this is to demolish at a single stroke, like a mason devoid of judgment—"

"You are insulting the masons!" yelled a citizen covered with plaster. And persisting in the belief that provocation had been offered to him, he vomited forth insults, and wanted to fight, clinging tightly to the bench whereon he sat. It took no less than three men to put him out.

Trans. D. F. Hannigan (London: H. S. Nichols, 1898).

The Right of Revolution

[FROM "On the Duty of Civil Disobedience"]

HENRY DAVID THOREAU

1849

I heartily accept the motto, "That government is best which governs least"; and I should like to see it acted up to more rapidly and systematically. Carried out, it finally amounts to this, which also I believe, "That government is best which governs not at all"; and when men are prepared for it, that will be the kind of government which they will have. Government is at best but an expedient; but most governments are usually, and all governments are sometimes, inexpedient. The objections which have been brought against a standing army, and they are many and weighty, and deserve to prevail, may also at last be brought against a standing government. The standing army is only an arm of the standing government. The government itself, which is only the mode which the people have chosen to execute their will, is equally liable to be abused and perverted before the people can act through it. Witness the present Mexican war, the work of comparatively a few individuals using the standing government as their tool; for, in the outset, the people would not have consented to this measure.

This American government—what is it but a tradition, though a recent one, endeavoring to transmit itself unimpaired to posterity, but each instant losing some of its integrity? It has not the vitality and force of a single living man; for a single man can bend it to his will. It is a sort of wooden gun to the people themselves. But it is not the less necessary for this; for the people must have some complicated machinery or other, and hear its din, to satisfy that idea of government which they have. Governments show thus how successfully men can be imposed on, even impose on themselves, for their own advantage. It is excellent, we must all allow. Yet this government never of itself furthered any enterprise, but by the alacrity with which it got out of its way. *It* does not keep the country free. *It* does not settle the West. *It* does not educate. The character inherent in the American people has done all that has been accomplished; and it would have done somewhat more, if the government had not sometimes got in its way. For government is an expedient by which men would fain succeed in letting one another alone; and, as has been said, when it is most expedient, the governed are most let alone by it. Trade and commerce, if they were not made of India-rubber, would never manage to bounce over the obstacles which legislators are continually putting in their way; and, if one were to judge these men wholly by the effects of their actions and not partly by their intentions, they would deserve to be classed and punished with those mischievous persons who put obstructions on the railroads.

But, to speak practically and as a citizen, unlike those who call themselves no-government men, I ask for, not at once no government, but *at once* a better government. Let every man make known what kind of government would command his respect, and that will be one step toward obtaining it.

After all, the practical reason why, when the power is once in the hands of the people, a majority are permitted, and for a long period continue, to rule is not because they are most likely to be in the right, nor because this seems fairest to the minority, but because they are physically the strongest. But a government in which the majority rule in all cases cannot be based on justice, even as far as men understand it. Can there not be a government in which majorities do not virtually decide right and wrong, but conscience?—in which majorities decide only those questions to which the rule of expediency is applicable? Must the citizen ever for a moment, or in the least degree, resign his conscience to the legislator? Why has every man a conscience, then? I think that we should be men first, and subjects afterward.

How does it become a man to behave toward this American government today? I answer, that he cannot without disgrace be associated with it. I cannot for an instant recognize that political organization as *my* government which is the *slave's* government also.

All men recognize the right of revolution; that is, the right to refuse allegiance to, and to resist, the government, when its tryranny or its inefficiency are great and unendurable. But almost all say that such is not the case now. But such was the case, they think, in the Revolution of '75. If one were to tell me that this was a bad government because it taxed certain foreign commodities brought to its ports, it is most probable that I should not make an ado about it, for I can do without them. All machines have their friction; and possibly this does enough good to counterbalance the evil. At any rate, it is a great evil to make a stir about it. But when the friction comes to have its machine, and oppression and robbery are organized, I say, let us not have such a machine any longer. In other words, when a sixth of the population of a nation which has undertaken to be the refuge of liberty are slaves, and a whole country is unjustly overrun and conquered by a foreign army, and subjected to military law, I think that it is not too soon for honest men to rebel and revolutionize. What makes this duty the more urgent is the fact that the country so overrun is not our own, but ours is the invading army.

The authority of government, even such as I am willing to submit to—for I will cheerfully obey those who know and can do better than I, and in many things even those who neither know nor can do so well—is still an impure one: to be strictly just, it must have the sanction and consent of the governed. It can have no pure right over my person and property but what I concede to it. The progress from an absolute to a limited monarchy, from a limited monarchy to a democracy, is a progress toward a true respect for the individual. Even the Chinese philosopher was wise enough to regard the individual as the basis of the empire. Is a democracy, such as we know it, the last improvement possible in government? Is it not possible to take a step further towards recognizing and organizing the rights of man? There will never be a really free and enlightened State until the State comes to recognize the individual as a higher and independent power, from which all its own power and authority are derived, and treats him accordingly. I please myself with imagining a State at last which can afford to be just to all men, and to treat the individual with respect as a neighbor; which even would not think it inconsistent with its own repose if a few were to live aloof from it, not meddling with it, nor embraced by it, who fulfilled all the duties of neighbors and fellow-men. A State which bore this kind of fruit, and suffered it to drop off as fast as it ripened, would prepare the way for a still more perfect and glorious State, which also I have imagined, but not yet anywhere seen.

PART SIX

The Romantic Artist

IMAGINATION:
THE POETIC PRINCIPLE

The Divine Arts of Imagination, Imagination, the real & eternal world of which this Vegetable Universe is but a faint shadow.

—William Blake

Poets Are Unacknowledged Legislators

[FROM *A Defence of Poetry*]

PERCY BYSSHE SHELLEY

182.

The exertions of Locke, Hume, Gibbon, Voltaire, Rousseau, and their disciples, in favour of oppressed and deluded humanity, are entitled to the gratitude of mankind. Yet it is easy to calculate the degree of moral and intellectual improvement which the world would have exhibited, had they never lived. A little more nonsense would have been talked for a century or two; and perhaps a few more men, women, and children, burnt as heretics. We might not at this moment have been congratulating each other on the abolition of the

Inquisition in Spain. But it exceeds all imagination to conceive what would have been the moral condition of the world if neither Dante, Petrarch, Boccaccio, Chaucer, Shakespeare, Calderon, Lord Bacon, nor Milton, had ever existed; if Raphael and Michael Angelo had never been born; if the Hebrew poetry had never been translated; if a revival of the study of Greek literature had never taken place; if no monuments of ancient sculpture had been handed down to us; and if the poetry of the religion of the ancient world had been extinguished together with its belief. The human mind could never, except by the intervention of these excitements, have been awakened to the invention of the grosser sciences, and that application of analytical reasoning to the aberrations of society, which it is now attempted to exalt over the direct expression of the inventive and creative faculty itself.

We have more moral, political and historical wisdom, than we know how to reduce into practice; we have more scientific and economical knowledge than can be accommodated to the just distribution of the produce which it multiplies. The poetry in these systems of thought, is concealed by the accumulation of facts and calculating processes. There is no want of knowledge respecting what is wisest and best in morals, government, and political economy, or at least, what is wiser and better than what men now practise and endure. But we let *"I dare not* wait upon *I would,* like the poor cat in the adage." We want the creative faculty to imagine that which we know; we want the generous impulse to act that which we imagine; we want the poetry of life: our calculations have outrun conception; we have eaten more than we can digest. The cultivation of those sciences which have enlarged the limits of the empire of man over the external world, has, for want of the poetical faculty, proportionally circumscribed those of the internal world; and man, having enslaved the

elements, remains himself a slave. To what but a cultivation of the mechanical arts in a degree dispropor-
tioned to the presence of the creative faculty, which
is the basis of all knowledge, is to be attributed the
abuse of all invention for abridging and combining
labour, to the exasperation of the inequality of mankind? From what other cause has it arisen that the discoveries which should have. lightened, have added a
weight to the curse imposed on Adam? Poetry, and the
principle of Self, of which money is the visible incarnation, are the God and Mammon of the world.

The functions of the poetical faculty are two-fold; by
one it creates new materials of knowledge and power
and pleasure; by the other it engenders in the mind a
desire to reproduce and arrange them according to a
certain rhythm and order which may be called the
beautiful and the good. The cultivation of poetry is
never more to be desired than at periods when, from
an excess of the selfish and calculating principle, the
accumulation of the materials of external life exceed
the quantity of the power of assimilating them to the
internal laws of human nature. The body has then become too unwieldy for that which animates it.

Poetry is indeed something divine. It is at once the
centre and circumference of knowledge; it is that which
comprehends all science, and that to which all science
must be referred. It is at the same time the root and
blossom of all other systems of thought; it is that from
which all spring, and that which adorns all; and that
which, if blighted, denies the fruit and the seed, and
withholds from the barren world the nourishment and
the succession of the scions of the tree of life. It is the
perfect and consumate surface and bloom of all things;
it is as the odour and the colour of the rose to the tex-
ture of the elements which compose it, as the form and
splendour of unfaded beauty to the secrets of anatomy
and corruption. What were virtue, love, patriotism,

friendship—what were the scenery of this beautiful universe which we inhabit; what were our consolations on this side of the grave—and what were our aspirations beyond it, if poetry did not ascend to bring light and fire from those eternal regions where the owl-winged faculty of calculation dare not ever soar? Poetry is not like reasoning, a power to be exerted according to the determination of the will. A man cannot say, "I will compose poetry." The greatest poet even cannot say it; for the mind in creation is as a fading coal, which some invisible influence, like an inconstant wind, awakens to transitory brightness; this power arises from within, like the colour of a flower which fades and changes as it is developed, and the conscious portions of our natures are unprophetic either of its approach or its departure. Could this influence be durable in its original purity and force, it is impossible to predict the greatness of the results; but when composition begins, inspiration is already on the decline, and the most glorious poetry that has ever been communicated to the world is probably a feeble shadow of the original conceptions of the poet. I appeal to the greatest poets of the present day, whether it is not an error to assert that the finest passages of poetry are produced by labour and study. The toil and the delay recommended by critics, can be justly interpreted to mean no more than a careful observation of the inspired moments, and an artificial connexion of the spaces between their suggestions by the intertexture of conventional expressions; a necessity only imposed by the limitedness of the poetical faculty itself; for Milton conceived the *Paradise Lost* as a whole before he executed it in portions. We have his own authority also for the muse having "dictated" to him the "unpremeditated song." And let this be an answer to those who would allege the fifty-six various readings of the first line of the *Orlando Furioso*. Compositions so produced are to poetry what mosaic is

to painting. This instinct and intuition of the poetical
faculty is still more observable in the plastic and pic-
torial arts; a great statue or picture grows under the
power of the artist as a child in the mother's womb;
and the very mind which directs the hands in forma-
tion is incapable of accounting to itself for the origin,
the gradations, or the media of the process.

Poetry is the record of the best and happiest moments of the happiest and best minds. We are aware of
evanescent visitations of thought and feeling sometimes
associated with place or person, sometimes regarding our
own mind alone, and always arising unforeseen and departing unbidden, but elevating and delightful beyond
all expression: so that even in the desire and regret they
leave, there cannot but be pleasure, participating as it
does in the nature of its object. It is as it were the
interpenetration of a diviner nature through our own;
but its footsteps are like those of a wind over the sea,
which the coming calm erases, and whose traces remain
only, as on the wrinkled sand which paves it. These
and corresponding conditions of being are experienced
principally by those of the most delicate sensibility and
the most enlarged imagination; and the state of mind
produced by them is at war with every base desire. The
enthusiasm of virtue, love, patriotism, and friendship,
is essentially linked with such emotions; and whilst they
ast, self appears as what it is, an atom to a universe.
Poets are not only subject to these experiences as spirits
of the most refined organization, but they can colour
all that they combine with the evanescent hues of this
ethereal world; a word, a trait in the representation of
a scene or a passion, will touch the enchanted chord,
and reanimate, in those who have ever experienced
these emotions, the sleeping, the cold, the buried image of the past. Poetry thus makes immortal all that is
best and most beautiful in the world; it arrests the
vanishing apparitions which haunt the interlunations of

life, and veiling them, or in language or in form, sends them forth among mankind, bearing sweet news of kindred joy to those with whom their sisters abide— abide, because there is no portal of expression from the caverns of the spirit which they inhabit into the universe of things. Poetry redeems from decay the visitations of the divinity in man.

Poetry turns all things to loveliness; it exalts the beauty of that which is most beautiful, and it adds beauty to that which is most deformed; it marries exultation and horror, grief and pleasure, eternity and change; it subdues to union under its light yoke, all irreconcilable things. It transmutes all that it touches, and every form moving within the radiance of its presence is changed by wondrous sympathy to an incarnation of the spirit which it breathes: its secret alchemy turns to potable gold the poisonous waters which flow from death through life; it strips the veil of familiarity from the world, and lays bare the naked and sleeping beauty, which is the spirit of its forms.

All things exist as they are perceived; at least in relation to the percipient. "The mind is its own place, and of itself can make a heaven of hell, a hell of heaven." But poetry defeats the curse which binds us to be subjected to the accident of surrounding impressions. And whether it spreads its own figured curtain, or withdraws life's dark veil from before the scene of things, it equally creates for us a being within our being. It makes us the inhabitants of a world to which the familiar world is a chaos. It reproduces the common universe of which we are portions and percipients, and it purges from our inward sight the film of familiarity which obscures from us the wonder of our being. It compels us to feel that which we perceive, and to imagine that which we know. It creates anew the universe, after it has been annihilated in our minds by the recurrence of impressions blunted by reiteration. It justifies the bold and true words of Tasso: *Non merita nome di creatore, se non Iddio ed il Poeta.*

A poet, as he is the author to others of the highest wisdom, pleasure, virtue and glory, so he ought personally to be the happiest, the best, the wisest, and the most illustrious of men. As to his glory, let time be challenged to declare whether the fame of any other institutor of human life be comparable to that of a poet. That he is the wisest, the happiest, and the best, inasmuch as he is a poet, is equally incontrovertible: the greatest poets have been men of the most spotless virtue, of the most consummate prudence, and, if we would look into the interior of their lives, the most fortunate of men: and the exceptions, as they regard those who possessed the poetic faculty in a high yet inferior degree, will be found on consideration to confine rather than destroy the rule. Let us for a moment stoop to the arbitration of popular breath, and usurping and uniting in our own persons the incompatible characters of accuser, witness, judge, and executioner, let us decide without trial, testimony, or form, that certain motives of those who are "there sitting where we dare not soar," are reprehensible. Let us assume that Homer was a drunkard, that Virgil was a flatterer, that Horace was a coward, that Tasso was a madman, that Lord Bacon was a peculator, that Raphael was a libertine, that Spenser was a poet laureate. It is inconsistent with this division of our subject to cite living poets, but posterity has done ample justice to the great names now referred to. Their errors have been weighed and found to have been dust in the balance; if their sins "were as scarlet, they are now white as snow": they have been washed in the blood of the mediator and redeemer, Time. Observe in what a ludicrous chaos the imputations of real or fictitious crime have been confused in the contemporary calumnies against poetry and poets; consider how little is, as it appears—or appears, as it is; look to your own motives, and judge not, lest ye be judged.

Poetry, as has been said, differs in this respect from logic, that it is not subject to the control of the active powers of the mind, and that its birth and recurrence have no necessary connexion with the consciousness or will. It is presumptuous to determine that these are the necessary conditions of all mental causation, when mental effects are experienced unsusceptible of being referred to them. The frequent recurrence of the poetical power, it is obvious to suppose, may produce in the mind a habit of order and harmony correlative with its own nature and with its effects upon other minds. But in the intervals of inspiration, and they may be frequent without being durable, a poet becomes a man, and is abandoned to the sudden reflux of the influences under which others habitually live. But as he is more delicately organized than other men, and sensible to pain and pleasure, both his own and that of others, in a degree unknown to them, he will avoid the one and pursue the other with an ardour proportioned to this difference. And he renders himself obnoxious to calumny, when he neglects to observe the circumstances under which these objects of universal pursuit and flight have disguised themselves in one another's garments.

But there is nothing necessarily evil in this error, and thus cruelty, envy, revenge, avarice, and the passions purely evil, have never formed any portion of the popular imputations on the lives of poets.

I have thought it most favourable to the cause of truth to set down these remarks according to the order in which they were suggested to my mind, by a consideration of the subject itself, instead of observing the formality of a polemical reply; but if the view which they contain be just, they will be found to involve a refutation of the arguers against poetry, so far at least as regards the first division of the subject. I can readily conjecture what should have moved the gall of some learned and intelligent writers who quarrel with certain versifiers; I confess myself, like them, unwilling to be stunned by the Theseids of the hoarse Codri of the day. Bavius and Maevius undoubtedly are, as they ever were, insufferable persons. But it belongs to a philosophical critic to distinguish rather than confound.

The first part of these remarks has related to poetry in its elements and principles; and it has been shown, as well as the narrow limits assigned them would permit, that what is called poetry, in a restricted sense, has a common source with all other forms of order and of beauty, according to which the materials of human life are susceptible of being arranged, and which is poetry in a universal sense.

The second part will have for its object an application of these principles to the present state of the cultivation of poetry, and a defence of the attempt to idealize the modern forms of manners and opinions, and compel them into a subordination to the imaginative and creative faculty. For the literature of England, an energetic development of which has ever preceded or accompanied a great and free development of the national will, has arisen as it were from a new birth. In spite of the low-thoughted envy which would undervalue contemporary merit, our own will be a memorable age in intellectual achievements, and we live among such philosophers and poets as surpass beyond comparison any who have appeared since the last national struggle for civil and religious liberty. The most unfailing herald, companion, and follower of the awakening of a great people to work a beneficial change in opinion or institution, is poetry. At such periods there is an accumulation of the power of communicating and receiving intense and impassioned conceptions respecting man and nature. The persons in whom this power resides may often, as far as regards many portions of their nature, have little apparent correspondence with that spirit of good of which they are the ministers. But even whilst they deny and abjure, they are yet compelled to serve, the power which is seated on the throne of their own soul. It is impossible to read the compositions of the most celebrated writers of the present day without being startled with the electric life which burns within their words. They measure the circumference and sound the depths of human nature with a comprehensive and all-penetrating spirit, and they are themselves perhaps the most sincerely astonished at its manifestations; for it is less their spirit than the spirit of the age. Poets are the hierophants of an unapprehended inspiration; the mirrors of the gigantic shadows which futurity casts upon the present; the words which express what they understand not; the trumpets which sing to battle, and feel not what they inspire; the influence which is moved not, but moves. Poets are the unacknowledged legislators of the world.

The Primacy of the Imagination

[FROM *The Statesman's Manual*
AND *Biographia Literaria*]

SAMUEL TAYLOR COLERIDGE

1816-17

1. The histories and political economy of the present and preceding century partake in the general contagion of its mechanistic philosophy, and are the produce of an unenlivened generalizing understanding. In the Scriptures they are the living educts of the imagination; of that reconciling and mediatory power, which

incorporating the reason in images of the sense, and organizing (as it were) the flux of the senses by the permanence and self-circling energies of the reason, gives birth to a system of symbols, harmonious in themselves, and consubstantial with the truths of which they are the conductors. These are the *wheels* which Ezekiel beheld, when the hand of the Lord was upon him, and he saw the visions of God as he sate among the captives by the river of Chebar. *Whithersoever the Spirit was to go, the* wheels *went, and thither was their spirit to go:—for the spirit of the living creature was in the* wheels *also.*

II. Repeated meditations led me first to suspect, (and a more intimate analysis of the human faculties, their appropriate marks, functions, and effects matured my conjecture into full conviction) that fancy and imagination were two distinct and widely different faculties, instead of being, according to the general belief, either two names with one meaning, or, at furthest, the lower and higher degree of one and the same power. It is not, I own, easy to conceive a more opposite translation of the Greek *Phantasia* than the Latin Imaginatio; but it is equally true that in all societies there exists an instinct of growth, a certain collective, unconscious good sense working progressively to desynonymize those words originally of the same meaning, which the conflux of dialects had supplied to the more homogeneous languages, as the Greek and German: and which the same cause, joined with accidents of translation from original works of different countries, occasion in mixt languages like our own. The first and most important point to be proved is, that two conceptions perfectly distinct are confused under one and the same word, and (this done) to appropriate that word exclusively to one meaning, and the synonyme (should there be one) to the other. But if (as will be often the case in the arts and sciences) no synonyme exists, we must either invent or borrow a word. In the present instance the appropriation has already begun, and been legitimated in the derivative adjective: Milton had a highly *imaginative*, Cowley, a very *fanciful* mind. If therefore I should succeed in establishing the actual existences of two faculties generally different, the nomenclature would be at once determined. To the faculty by which I had characterized Milton, we should confine the term *imagination*; while the other would be contradistinguished as *fancy*. Now were it once fully ascertained, that this division is no less grounded in nature, than that of delirium from mania, or Otway's

> Lutes, lobsters, seas of milk, and ships of amber,

from Shakespeare's

> What! have his daughters brought him to this pass?

or from the preceding apostrophe to the elements; the theory of the fine arts, and of poetry in particular, could not, I thought, but derive some addition and important light. It would in its immediate effects furnish a torch of guidance to the philosophical critic; and ultimately to the poet himself. In energetic minds, truth soon changes by domestication into power; and from directing in the discrimination and appraisal of the product, becomes influencive in the production. To admire on principle, is the only way to imitate without loss of originality.

III. The IMAGINATION then, I consider either as primary, or secondary. The primary IMAGINATION I hold to be the living Power and prime Agent of all human Perception, and as a repetition in the finite mind of the eternal act of creation in the infinite I AM. The secondary Imagination I consider as an echo of the former, coexisting with the conscious will, yet still as identical with the primary in the *kind* of its agency, and differing only in *degree*, and in the *mode* of its operation. It dissolves, diffuses, dissipates, in order to recreate; or where this process is rendered impossible, yet still at all events it struggles to idealize and to unify. It is essentially *vital*, even as all objects (*as* objects) are essentially fixed and dead.

FANCY, on the contrary, has no other counters to play with, but fixities and definites. The Fancy is indeed no other than a mode of Memory emancipated from the order of time and space; while it is blended with, and modified by the empirical phenomenon of the will, which we express by the word CHOICE. But equally with the ordinary memory the Fancy must receive all its materials ready made from the law of association.

Imaginative Footnotes

SAMUEL TAYLOR COLERIDGE

[FROM THE *Gutch Memorandum Book*]

1795-98

a dusky light—a purple *flash*
crystalline splendor—light blue—
Green lightnings—
in that eternal and delirious misery
wrath fires—
inward desolations
an horror of great darkness
great things—on the ocean
counterfeit infinity—

[FROM *Anima Poetae*]

1895

If a man could pass through Paradise in a dream, and have a flower presented to him as a pledge that

his soul had really been there, and if he found that
flower in his hand when he awoke— Aye! and what
then?

Kubla Khan:
or, A Vision in a Dream

A Fragment

SAMUEL TAYLOR COLERIDGE

1798

In the summer of the year 1797, the Author, then in ill-
health, had retired to a lonely farm-house between Porlock
and Linton, on the Exmoor confines of Somerset and Devon-
shire. In consequence of a slight indisposition, an anodyne
had been prescribed, from the effect of which he fell asleep
in his chair at the moment he was reading the following
sentence, or words of the same substance, in Purchas's Pilgrimage: "Here the Khan Kubla commanded a palace to be
built, and a stately garden thereunto: and thus ten miles of
fertile ground were inclosed with a wall." The Author continued for about three hours in a profound sleep, at least of
the external senses, during which time he has the most vivid
confidence, that he could not have composed less than from
two to three hundred lines; if that indeed can be called composition in which all the images rose up before him as things,
with a parallel production of the correspondent expressions,
without any sensation or consciousness of effort. On awaking
he appeared to himself to have a distinct recollection of the
whole, and taking his pen, ink, and paper, instantly and
eagerly wrote down the lines that are here preserved. At this
moment he was unfortunately called out by a person on business from Porlock, and detained by him above an hour, and
on his return to his room, found, to his no small surprise and

mortification, that though he still retained some vague and dim recollection of the general purport of the vision, yet, with the exception of some eight or ten scattered lines and images, all the rest had passed away like the images on the surface of a stream into which a stone had been cast, but, alas! without the after restoration of the latter:

> Then all the charm
> Is broken—all that phantom-world so fair,
> Vanishes, and a thousand circlets spread,
> And each mis-shape[s] the other. Stay awhile,
> Poor youth! who scarcely dar'st lift up thine eyes—
> The stream will soon renew its smoothness, soon
> The visions will return! And lo! he stays,
> And soon the fragments dim of lovely forms
> Come trembling back, unite, and now once more
> The pool becomes a mirror.
>   [From "The Picture"]

Yet from the still surviving recollections in his mind, the Author has frequently purposed to finish for himself what had been originally, as it were, given to him Αὔριον ἄδιον ἄσω: but the to-morrow is yet to come.

> In Xanadu did Kubla Khan
> A stately pleasure-dome decree:
> Where Alph, the sacred river, ran
> Through caverns measureless to man
>   Down to a sunless sea.
> So twice five miles of fertile ground
> With walls and towers were girdled round:
> And there were gardens bright with sinuous rills,
> Where blossom'd many an incense-bearing tree,
> And here were forests ancient as the hills,
> Enfolding sunny spots of greenery.
>
> But oh! that deep romantic chasm which slanted
> Down the green hill athwart a cedarn cover!
> A savage place! as holy and enchanted
> As e'er beneath a waning moon was haunted

By woman wailing for her demon-lover!
And from this chasm, with ceaseless turmoil seething,
As if this earth in fast thick pants were breathing,
A mighty fountain momently was forced:
Amid whose swift half-intermitted burst
Huge fragments vaulted like rebounding hail,
Or chaffy grain beneath the thresher's flail:
And 'mid these dancing rocks at once and ever
It flung up momently the sacred river.
Five miles meandering with a mazy motion
Through wood and dale the sacred river ran,
Then reach'd the caverns measureless to man,
And sank in tumult to a lifeless ocean:
And 'mid this tumult Kubla heard from far
Ancestral voices prophesying war!
  The shadow of the dome of pleasure
  Floated midway on the waves;
  Where was heard the mingled measure
  From the fountain and the caves.
It was a miracle of rare device,
A sunny pleasure-dome with caves of ice!

  A damsel with a dulcimer
  In a vision once I saw:
  It was an Abyssinian maid,
  And on her dulcimer she play'd,
  Singing of Mount Abora.
Could I revive within me
Her symphony and song,
To such a deep delight 'twould win me
That with music loud and long,
I would build that dome in air,
That sunny dome! those caves of ice!
And all who heard should see them there,
And all should cry, Beware! Beware!
His flashing eyes, his floating hair!

Weave a circle round him thrice,
And close your eyes with holy dread,
For he on honey-dew hath fed,
And drunk the milk of Paradise.

The Imagination Amplified

EDGAR ALLAN POE

[FROM "The Philosophy of Composition"]

1846

There is a radical error, I think, in the usual mode of constructing a story. Either history affords a thesis —or one is suggested by an incident of the day—or, at best, the author sets himself to work in the combination of striking events to form merely the basis of his narrative—designing, generally, to fill in with description, dialogue, or autorial comment, whatever crevices of fact, or action, may, from page to page, render themselves apparent.

I prefer commencing with the consideration of an *effect*. Keeping originality *always* in view—for he is false to himself who ventures to dispense with so obvious and so easily attainable a source of interest—I say to myself, in the first place, "Of the innumerable effects, or impressions, of which the heart, the intellect, or (more generally) the soul is susceptible, what one shall I, on the present occasion, select?" Having chosen a novel, first, and secondly a vivid effect, I consider whether it can be best wrought by incident or tone— whether by ordinary incidents and peculiar tone, or the converse, or by peculiarity both of incident and tone—

afterward looking about me (or rather within) for such combinations of event, or tone, as shall best aid me in the construction of the effect.

I have often thought how interesting a magazine paper might be written by any author who would—that is to say who could—detail, step by step, the processes by which any one of his compositions attained its ultimate point of completion. Why such a paper has never been given to the world, I am much at a loss to say—but, perhaps, the autorial vanity has had more to do with the omission than any one other cause. Most writers—poets in especial—prefer having it understood that they compose by a species of fine frenzy—an ecstatic intuition—and would positively shudder at letting the public take a peep behind the scenes, at the elaborate and vascillating crudities of thought—at the true purposes seized only at the last moment—at the innumerable glimpses of idea that arrived not at the maturity of full view—at the fully matured fancies discarded in despair as unmanageable—at the cautious selections and rejections—at the painful erasures and interpolations—in a word, at the wheels and pinions—the tackle for scene-shifting—the step-ladders and demon-traps—the cock's feathers, the red paint and the black patches, which, in ninety-nine cases out of the hundred, constitute the properties of the literary *histrio.*

I am aware, on the other hand, that the case is by no means common, in which an author is at all in condition to retrace the steps by which his conclusions have been attained. In general, suggestions, having arisen pell-mell, are pursued and forgotten in a similar manner.

For my own part, I have neither sympathy with the repugnance alluded to, nor at any time the least difficulty in recalling to mind the progressive steps of any of my compositions; and, since the interest of an analysis, or reconstruction, such as I have considered a *desideratum*, is quite independent of any real or fancied interest in the thing analyzed, it will not be regarded as a breach of decorum on my part to show the *modus operandi* by which some one of my own works was put together. I select "The Raven," as most generally known. It is my design to render it manifest that no one point in its composition is referrible either to accident or intuition—that the work proceeded, step by step, to its completion with the precision and rigid consequence of a mathematical problem.

[FROM *Marginalia*]

FANCY AND IMAGINATION

[n.d.]

A new poem from Moore calls to mind that critical opinion respecting him which had its origin, we believe, in the dogmatism of Coleridge—we mean the opinion that he is essentially the poet of *fancy*—the term being employed in contradistinction to *imagination*. "The fancy," says the author of the "Ancient Mariner," in his *Biographia Literaria*, "the fancy combines, the imagination creates." And this was intended, and has been received, as a distinction. If so at all, it is one without a difference; without even a difference of *degree*. The fancy as nearly creates as the imagination; and neither creates in any respect. All novel conceptions are merely unusual combinations. The mind of man can *imagine* nothing which has not really existed; and this point is susceptible of the most positive demonstration—see the Baron de Bielfeld, in his *"Premiers Traits de L'Erudition Universelle,"* 1767. It will be said, perhaps, that we can imagine a *griffin*, and that a griffin does not exist. Not the griffin certainly, but its component parts. It is a mere compendium of known limbs and features—of known qualities. Thus with all which seems to be *new*—which appears to be a *creation* of intellect. It is resoluble into the old. The wildest and most vigorous effort of mind cannot stand the test of this analysis.

We might make a distinction, *of degree*, between the fancy and the imagination, in saying that the latter is the former *loftily employed*. But experience proves this distinction to be unsatisfactory. What we *feel* and *know* to be fancy, will be found still only *fanciful*, whatever be the theme which engages it. It retains its idiosyncrasy under all circumstances. No *subject* exalts it into the ideal. . . .

Many a schoolboy . . . admires the imagination displayed in Jack the Giant-Killer . . . is finally rejoiced at discovering his own imagination to surpass that of the author, since the monsters destroyed by Jack are only about forty feet in height, and he himself has no trouble in imagining some of one hundred and forty. The fairy of Shelley is not a mere compound of incongruous natural objects, inartificially put together, and unaccompanied by any *moral* sentiment; but a being, in the illustration of whose nature some physical elements are used collaterally as adjuncts, while the main conception springs immediately, *or thus apparently springs*, from the brain of the poet, enveloped in the moral sentiments of grace, of colour, of motion —of the beautiful, of the *mystical*, of the august—in short, of the ideal.

The truth is that the just distinction between the fancy and the imagination (and which is still but a distinction *of degree*) is involved in the consideration of the *mystic*. We give this as an idea of our own, altogether. We have no authority for our opinion—but do not the less firmly hold it. The term *mystic* is here employed in the sense of Augustus William Schlegel, and of most other German critics. It is applied by them to that class of composition in which there lies beneath the transparent upper current of meaning an under or *suggestive* one. What we vaguely term the *moral* of any sentiment is its mystic or secondary expression. It has the vast force of an accompaniment in music. This vivifies the air; that spiritualizes the *fanciful* conception, and lifts it into the *ideal*.

This theory will bear, we think, the most rigorous tests which can be made applicable to it, and will be acknowledged as tenable by all who are themselves imaginative. If we carefully examine those poems, or portions of poems, or those prose romances, which mankind have been accustomed to designate as *imaginative* (for an instinctive feeling leads us to employ properly the term whose full import we have still never been able to define), it will be seen that all so designated are remarkable for the *suggestive* character which we have discussed. They are strongly *mystic*, in the proper sense of the word. We will here only call to the reader's mind, the "Prometheus Vinctus" of Æschylus; the *Inferno* of Dante; the "Destruction of Numantia" by Cervantes; the "Comus" of Milton; the "Ancient Mariner," the "Christabel," and the "Kubla Khan" of Coleridge; the "Nightingale" of Keats; and, most especially, the "Sensitive Plant" of Shelley, and the *Undine* of De La Motte Fouqué. These two latter poems (for we call them both such) are the finest possible examples of the purely *ideal*. There is little of fancy here, and everything of imagination. With each note of the lyre is heard a ghostly, and not always a distinct, but an august and soul-exalting *echo*. In every glimpse of beauty presented, we catch, through long and wild vistas, dim bewildering visions of a far more ethereal beauty *beyond*. But not so in poems which the world has always persisted in terming *fanciful*. Here the upper current is often exceedingly brilliant and beautiful; but then men *feel* that this upper current *is all*. No Naiad voice addresses them *from below*. The notes of the air

of the song do not tremble with the according tones of
the accompaniment.

The Opium Dream

[FROM *Confessions of an English Opium-Eater*]

THOMAS DE QUINCEY

1821

Under the connecting feeling of tropical heat and
vertical sun-lights, I brought together all creatures,
birds, beasts, reptiles, all trees and plants, usages and
appearances, that are found in all tropical regions, and
assembled them together in China or Indostan. From
kindred feelings, I soon brought Egypt and all her gods
under the same law. I was stared at, hooted at, grinned
at, chattered at, by monkeys, by paroquets, by cocka-
toos. I ran into pagodas: and was fixed, for centuries,
at the summit, or in secret rooms; I was the idol; I was
the priest; I was worshipped; I was sacrificed. I fled
from the wrath of Brama through all the forests of Asia:
Vishnu hated me: Seeva laid wait for me. I came suddenly upon Isis and Osiris: I had done a deed, they
said, which the ibis and the crocodile trembled at. I
was buried, for a thousand years, in stone coffins, with
mummies and sphynxes, in narrow chambers at the
heart of eternal pyramids. I was kissed, with cancerous
kisses, by crocodiles; and laid, confounded with all unutterable slimy things, amongst reeds and Nilotic mud.

I thus give the reader some slight abstraction of my
oriental dreams, which always filled me with such
amazement at the monstrous scenery, that horror
seemed absorbed, for a while, in sheer astonishment.

Sooner or later, came a reflux of feeling that swallowed up the astonishment, and left me, not so much in terror, as in hatred and abomination of what I saw. Over every form, and threat, and punishment, and dim sightless incarceration, brooded a sense of eternity and infinity that drove me into an oppression as of madness. Into these dreams only, it was, with one or two slight exceptions, that any circumstances of physical horror entered. All before had been moral and spiritual terrors. But here the main agents were ugly birds, or snakes, or crocodiles; especially the last. The cursed crocodile became to me the object of more horror than almost all the rest. I was compelled to live with him; and (as was always the case almost in my dreams) for centuries. I escaped sometimes, and found myself in Chinese houses, with cane tables, &c. All the feet of the tables, sophas, &c. soon became instinct with life: the abominable head of the crocodile, and his leering eyes, looked out at me, multiplied into a thousand repetitions: and I stood loathing and fascinated. And so very often did this hideous reptile haunt my dreams, that many times the very same dream was broken up in the very same way: I heard gentle voices speaking to me (I hear every thing when I am sleeping); and instantly I awoke: it was broad noon; and my children were standing, hand in hand, at my bed-side; come to show me their coloured shoes, or new frocks or to let me see them dressed for going out. I protest that so awful was the transition from the damned crocodile, and the other unutterable monsters and abortions of my dreams, to the sight of innocent *human* natures and of infancy, that, in the mighty and sudden revulsion of mind, I wept, and could not forbear it, as I kissed their faces.

As a final specimen, I cite one of a different character, from 1820.

The dream commenced with a music which now I often heard in dreams—a music of preparation and of awakening suspense; a music like the opening of the Coronation Anthem, and which, like *that*, gave the feeling of a vast march—of infinite cavalcades filing off— and the tread of innumerable armies. The morning was come of a mighty day—a day of crisis and of final hope for human nature, then suffering some mysterious eclipse, and labouring in some dread extremity. Somewhere, I knew not where—somehow, I knew not how —by some beings, I knew not whom—a battle, a strife, an agony, was conducting,—was evolving like a great drama, or piece of music; with which my sympathy was the more insupportable from my confusion as to its place, its cause, its nature, and its possible issue. I, as is usual in dreams (where, of necessity, we make ourselves central to every movement), had the power, and yet had not the power, to decide it. I had the power, if I could raise myself, to will it; and yet again, had not the power, for the weight of twenty Atlantics was upon me, or the oppression of inexpiable guilt. "Deeper than ever plummet sounded," I lay inactive. Then, like a chorus, the passion deepened. Some greater interest was at stake; some mightier cause than ever yet the sword had pleaded, or trumpet had proclaimed. Then came sudden alarms: hurryings to and fro: trepidations of innumerable fugitives, I knew not whether from the good cause or the bad: darkness and lights: tempests and human faces; and at last, with the sense that all was lost, female forms, and the features that were worth all the world to me, and but a moment allowed,—and clasped hands, and heart-breaking partings, and then— everlasting farewells! and with a sigh, such as the caves of hell sighed when the incestuous mother uttered the abhorred name of death, the sound was reverberated— everlasting farewells! and again, and yet again reverberated—everlasting farewells!

And I awoke in struggles, and cried aloud—"I wil sleep no more!"

The Elevation of a Moment

JOHN KEATS

[FROM THE *Letters*]

TO BENJAMIN BAILEY

November 22, 1817

I am certain of nothing but of the holiness of the Heart's affections and the truth of Imagination— What the imagination seizes as Beauty must be truth—whether it existed before or not—for I have the same Idea of all our Passions as of Love they are all in their sublime, creative of essential Beauty. . . . The Imagination may be compared to Adam's dream—he awoke and found it truth. I am the more zealous in this affair, because I have never yet been able to perceive how any thing can be known for truth by consequitive reasoning—and yet it must be. Can it be that even the greatest Philosopher ever arrived at his goal without putting aside numerous objections. However it may be, O for a Life of Sensations rather than of Thoughts! It is 'a Vision in the form of Youth' a Shadow of reality to come—and this consideration has further convinced me for it has come as auxiliary to another favorite Speculation of mine, that we shall enjoy ourselves here after by having what we called happiness on Earth repeated in a finer tone and so repeated. And yet such a fate can only befall those who delight in Sensation rather than hunger as you do after Truth.

Adam's dream will do here and seems to be a conviction that Imagination and its empyreal reflection is the
same as human Life and its Spiritual repetition. But as
I was saying—the simple imaginative Mind may have
its rewards in the repeti[ti]on of its own silent Working
coming continually on the Spirit with a fine Sudden-
ness—to compare great things with small—have you
never by being Surprised with an old Melody—in a
delicious place—by a delicious voice, fe[l]t over again
your very Speculations and Surmises at the time it first
operated on your Soul—do you not remember forming
to yourself the singer's face more beautiful than it was
possible and yet with the elevation of the Moment you
did not think so—even then you were mounted on the
Wings of Imagination so high—that the Prototype must
be here after—that delicious face you will see. What
a time! I am continually running away from the subject—sure this cannot be exactly the case with a complex Mind—one that is imaginative and at the same
time careful of its fruits—who would exist partly on
Sensation partly on thought—to whom it is necessary
that years should bring the philosophic Mind—such an
one I consider your's and therefore it is necessary to
your eternal Happiness that you not only drink this old
Wine of Heaven, which I shall call the redigestion of
our most ethereal Musings on Earth; but also increase
in knowledge and know all things.

[FROM *Endymion*]

1817

    A thing of beauty is a joy for ever:
Its loveliness increases; it will never
Pass into nothingness; but still will keep
A bower quiet for us, and a sleep
Full of sweet dreams, and health, and quiet breathing.
Therefore, on every morrow, are we wreathing

all good poetry is the spontaneous overflow of powerful feelings: and though this be true, Poems to which any value can be attached were never produced on any variety of subjects but by a man who, being possessed of more than usual organic sensibility, had also thought long and deeply. For our continued influxes of feeling are modified and directed by our thoughts, which are indeed the representatives of all our past feelings; and, as by contemplating the relation of these general representatives to each other, we discover what is really important to men, so, by the repetition and continuance of this act, our feelings will be connected with important subjects, till at length, if we be originally possessed of much sensibility, such habits of mind will be produced, that, by obeying blindly and mechanically the impulses of those habits, we shall describe objects, and utter sentiments, of such a nature, and in such connexion with each other, that the understanding of the Reader must necessarily be in some degree enlightened, and his affections strengthened and purified.

Having dwelt thus long on the subjects and aim of these Poems, I shall request the Reader's permission to apprise him of a few circumstances relating to their *style,* in order, among other reasons, that he may not censure me for not having performed what I never attempted. The Reader will find that personifications of abstract ideas rarely occur in these volumes; and are utterly rejected, as an ordinary device to elevate the style, and raise it above prose. My purpose was to imitate, and, as far as possible, to adopt the very language of men; and assuredly such personifications do not make any natural or regular part of that language. They are, indeed, a figure of speech occasionally prompted by passion, and I have made use of them as such; but have endeavoured utterly to reject them as a mechanical device of style, or as a family language which Writ-

A flowery band to bind us to the earth,
Spite of despondence, of the inhuman dearth
Of noble natures, of the gloomy days,
Of all the unhealthy and o'er-darkened ways
Made for our searching: yes, in spite of all,
Some shape of beauty moves away the pall
From our dark spirits. Such the sun, the moon,
Trees old, and young, sprouting a shady boon
For simple sheep; and such are daffodils
With the green world they live in; and clear rills
That for themselves a cooling covert make
'Gainst the hot season; the mid forest brake,
Rich with a sprinkling of fair musk-rose blooms:
And such too is the grandeur of the dooms
We have imagined for the mighty dead;
All lovely tales that we have heard or read:
An endless fountain of immortal drink,
Pouring unto us from the heaven's brink.
   Nor do we merely feel these essences
For one short hour; no, even as the trees
That whisper round a temple become soon
Dear as the temple's self, so does the moon,
The passion poesy, glories infinite,
Haunt us till they become a cheering light
Unto our souls, and bound to us so fast,
That, whether there be slime, or gloom o'ercast,
They always must be with us, or we die.

Ideas Associated with Excitement

[FROM Preface to the Second Edition
of the *Lyrical Ballads*]

WILLIAM WORDSWORTH

1800

The principal object, then, proposed in these Poems was to choose incidents and situations from common life, and to relate or describe them, throughout, as far as was possible in a selection of language really used by men, and, at the same time, to throw over them a certain colouring of imagination, whereby ordinary things should be presented to the mind in an unusual aspect; and, further, and above all, to make these incidents and situations interesting by tracing in them, truly though not ostentatiously, the primary laws of our nature: chiefly, as far as regards the manner in which we associate ideas in a state of excitement. Humble and rustic life was generally chosen, because, in that condition, the essential passions of the heart find a better soil in which they can attain their maturity, are less under restraint, and speak a plainer and more emphatic language; because in that condition of life our elementary feelings co-exist in a state of greater simplicity, and, consequently, may be more accurately contemplated, and more forcibly communicated; because the manners of rural life germinate from those elementary feelings, and, from the necessary character of rural occupations, are more easily comprehended, and are more durable; and, lastly, because in that condition the passions of men are incorporated with the beautiful and permanent forms of nature. The lan-

guage, too, of these men has been adopted indeed from what appear to be its real def all lasting and rational causes of dislike or di cause such men hourly communicate with objects from which the best part of languag nally derived; and because, from their rank and the sameness and narrow circle of their in being less under the influence of social vanity, vey their feelings and notions in simple and rated expressions. Accordingly, such a languag out of repeated experience and regular feeli more permanent, and a far more philosoph guage, than that which is frequently substitut by Poets, who think that they are conferring upon themselves and their art, in proportion separate themselves from the sympathies of m indulge in arbitrary and capricious habits of exp in order to furnish food for fickle tastes, and fi petites, of their own creation.

I cannot, however, be insensible to the prese cry against the triviality and meanness, both of t and language, which some of my contemporarie occasionally introduced into their metrical compo and I acknowledge that this defect, where it ex more dishonourable to the Writer's own characte false refinement or arbitrary innovation, though I contend at the same time, that it is far less pern in the sum of its consequences. From such vers Poems in these volumes will be found distinguish least by one mark of difference, that each of ther a worthy *purpose*. Not that I always began to with a distinct purpose formally conceived; but h of meditation have, I trust, so prompted and regu my feelings, that my descriptions of such object strongly excite those feelings, will be found to along with them a *purpose*. If this opinion be err ous, I can have little right to the name of a Poet.

ers in metre seem to lay claim to by prescription. I have wished to keep the Reader in the company of flesh and blood, persuaded that by so doing I shall interest him. Others who pursue a different track will interest him likewise; I do not interfere with their claim, but wish to prefer a claim of my own. There will also be found in these volumes little of what is usually called poetic diction; as much pains has been taken to avoid it as is ordinarily taken to produce it; this has been done for the reason already alleged, to bring my language near to the language of men; and further, because the pleasure which I have proposed to myself to impart, is of a kind very different from that which is supposed by many persons to be the proper object of poetry. Without being culpably particular, I do not know how to give my Reader a more exact notion of the style in which it was my wish and intention to write, than by informing him that I have at all times endeavoured to look steadily at my subject; consequently, there is I hope in these Poems little falsehood of description, and my ideas are expressed in language fitted to their respective importance. Something must have been gained by this practice, as it is friendly to one property of all good poetry, namely, good sense: but it has necessarily cut me off from a large portion of phrases and figures of speech which from father to son have long been regarded as the common inheritance of Poets. I have also thought it expedient to restrict myself still further, having abstained from the use of many expressions, in themselves proper and beautiful, but which have been foolishly repeated by bad Poets, till such feelings of disgust are connected with them as it is scarcely possible by any art of association to overpower.

It was previously asserted, that a large portion of the language of every good poem can in no respect differ from that of good Prose. We will go further. It may be safely affirmed, that there neither is, nor can be, any *essential* difference between the language of prose and metrical composition. We are fond of tracing the resemblance between Poetry and Painting, and, accordingly, we call them Sisters: but where shall we find bonds of connexion sufficiently strict to typify the affinity betwixt metrical and prose composition? They both speak by and to the same organs; the bodies in which both of them are clothed may be said to be of the same substance, their affections are kindred, and almost identical, not necessarily differing even in degree; Poetry sheds no tears "such as Angels weep," but natural and human tears; she can boast of no celestial ichor that distinguishes her vital juices from those of prose; the same human blood circulates through the veins of them both.

If it be affirmed that rhyme and metrical arrangement of themselves constitute a distinction which overturns what has just been said on the strict affinity of metrical language with that of prose, and paves the way for other artificial distinctions which the mind voluntarily admits, I answer that the language of such Poetry as is here recommended is, as far as is possible, a selection of the language really spoken by men; that this selection, wherever it is made with true taste and feeling, will of itself form a distinction far greater than would at first be imagined, and will entirely separate the composition from the vulgarity and meanness of ordinary life; and, if metre be superadded thereto, I believe that a dissimilitude will be produced altogether sufficient for the gratification of a rational mind. What other distinction would we have? Whence is it to come? And where is it to exist? Not, surely, where the Poet speaks through the mouths of his characters: it cannot be necessary here, either for elevation of style, or any of its supposed ornaments: for, if the Poet's subject be judiciously chosen, it will naturally, and upon fit occasion, lead him to passions the language of which, if selected truly and judiciously, must necessarily be dignified and variegated, and alive with metaphors and figures. I forbear to speak of an incongruity which would shock the intelligent Reader, should the Poet interweave any foreign splendour of his own with that which the passion naturally suggests: it is sufficient to say that such addition is unnecessary. And, surely, it is more probable that those passages, which with propriety abound with metaphors and figures, will have their due effect, if, upon other occasions where the passions are of a milder character, the style also be subdued and temperate.

I have said that poetry is the spontaneous overflow of powerful feelings: it takes its origin from emotion recollected in tranquility: the emotion is contemplated till, by a species of reaction, the tranquility gradually disappears, and an emotion, kindred to that which was before the subject of contemplation, is gradually produced, and does itself actually exist in the mind. In this mood successful composition generally begins, and in a mood similar to this it is carried on; but the emotion, of whatever kind, and in whatever degree, from various causes, is qualified by various pleasures, so that in describing any passions whatsoever, which are voluntarily described, the mind will, upon the whole, be in a state of enjoyment. If Nature be thus cautious to preserve in a state of enjoyment a being so employed, the Poet ought to profit by the lesson held forth to him, and ought especially to take care, that, whatever passions he communicates to his Reader, those passions, if his Reader's mind be sound and vigorous, should always be accompanied with an overbalance of pleasure. Now the music of harmonious metrical language, the sense of difficulty overcome, and the blind association of pleasure which has been previously received from works of rhyme or metre of the same or similar construction, an indistinct perception perpetually renewed of language closely resembling that of real life, and yet, in the circumstance of metre, differing from it so widely—all these imperceptibly make up a complex feeling of delight, which is of the most important use in tempering the painful feeling always found intermingled with powerful descriptions of the deeper passions. This effect is always produced in pathetic and impassioned poetry; while, in lighter compositions, the ease and gracefulness with which the Poet manages his numbers are themselves confessedly a principal source of the gratification of the Reader. All that it is *necessary* to say, however, upon this subject, may be effected by affirming, what few persons will deny, that, of two descriptions, either of passions, manners, or characters, each of them equally well executed, the one in prose and the other in verse, the verse will be read a hundred times where the prose is read once.

The Visionary Gleam

["Ode: Intimations of Immortality from Recollections of Early Childhood"]

WILLIAM WORDSWORTH

1802-1806

> *The Child is father of the Man;*
> *And I could wish my days to be*
> *Bound each to each by natural piety.*

There was a time when meadow, grove, and stream,
The earth, and every common sight,

        To me did seem
     Apparelled in celestial light,
The glory and the freshness of a dream.
It is not now as it hath been of yore;—
     Turn wheresoe'er I may,
       By night or day,
The things which I have seen I now can see no more.

     The Rainbow comes and goes
     And lovely is the Rose;
     The Moon doth with delight
Look round her when the heavens are bare,
     Waters on a starry night
     Are beautiful and fair;
     The sunshine is a glorious birth;
     But yet I know, where'er I go,
That there hath past away a glory from the earth.

Now, while the birds thus sing a joyous song,
     And while the young lambs bound
      As to the tabor's sound,
To me alone there came a thought of grief:
A timely utterance gave that thought relief,
     And I again am strong:
The cataracts blow their trumpets from the steep;
No more shall grief of mine the season wrong;
I hear the Echoes through the mountains throng,
The Winds come to me from the fields of sleep,
     And all the earth is gay;
      Land and sea
     Give themselves up to jollity,
      And with the heart of May
     Doth every Beast keep holiday;—
      Thou Child of Joy,
Shout round me, let me hear thy shouts, thou happy
     Shepherd-boy!

Ye blessèd Creatures, I have heard the call
    Ye to each other make; I see
The heavens laugh with you in your jubilee;
    My heart is at your festival,
    My head hath its coronal,
The fulness of your bliss, I feel—I feel it all.
    Oh evil day! if I were sullen
    While Earth herself is adorning,
        This sweet May-morning,
        And the Children are culling
            On every side,
        In a thousand valleys far and wide,
        Fresh flowers; while the sun shines warm,
And the Babe leaps up on his Mother's arm:—
    I hear, I hear, with joy I hear!
    —But there's a Tree, of many, one,
A single Field which I have looked upon,
Both of them speak of something that is gone:
        The Pansy at my feet
        Doth the same tale repeat:
Whither is fled the visionary gleam?
Where is it now, the glory and the dream?

Our birth is but a sleep and a forgetting:
The Soul that rises with us, our life's Star,
        Hath had elsewhere its setting,
        And cometh from afar:
        Not in entire forgetfulness,
        And not in utter nakedness,
But trailing clouds of glory do we come
        From God, who is our home:
Heaven lies about us in our infancy!
Shades of the prison-house begin to close
        Upon the growing Boy,
But He beholds the light, and whence it flows,
        He sees it in his joy;

The Youth, who daily farther from the east
  Must travel, still is Nature's Priest,
   And by the vision splendid
    Is on his way attended;
At length the Man perceives it die away,
And fade into the light of common day.

Earth fills her lap with pleasures of her own;
Yearnings she hath in her own natural kind,
And, even with something of a Mother's mind,
   And no unworthy aim,
   The homely Nurse doth all she can
To make her Foster-child, her Inmate, Man,
   Forget the glories he hath known,
And that imperial palace whence he came.

Behold the Child among his new-born blisses,
A six years' Darling of a pigmy size!
See, where 'mid work of his own hand he lies,
Fretted by sallies of his mother's kisses,
With light upon him from his father's eyes!
See, at his feet, some little plan or chart,
Some fragment from his dream of human life,
Shaped by himself with newly-learned art;
   A wedding or a festival,
   A mourning or a funeral;
    And this hath now his heart,
   And unto this he frames his song:
    Then will he fit his tongue
To dialogues of business, love, or strife;
    But it will not be long
    Ere this be thrown aside,
    And with new joy and pride
The little Actor cons another part;
Filling from time to time his "humorous stage"
With all the Persons, down to palsied Age,

That Life brings with her in her equipage;
>As if his whole vocation
>Were endless imitation.

Thou, whose exterior semblance doth belie
>Thy Soul's immensity;
Thou best Philosopher, who yet dost keep
Thy heritage, thou Eye among the blind,
That, deaf and silent, read'st the eternal deep,
Haunted for ever by the eternal mind,—
>Mighty Prophet! Seer blest!
>On whom those truths do rest,
Which we are toiling all our lives to find,
In darkness lost, the darkness of the grave;
Thou, over whom thy Immortality
Broods like the Day, a Master o'er a Slave,
A presence which is not to be put by;
>To whom the grave
Is but a lonely bed without the sense or sight
>Of day or the warm light
A place of thought where we in waiting lie;
Thou little Child, yet glorious in the might
Of heaven-born freedom on thy being's height,
Why with such earnest pains dost thou provoke
The years to bring the inevitable yoke,
Thus blindly with thy blessedness at strife?
Full soon thy Soul shall have her earthly freight,
And custom lie upon thee with a weight,
Heavy as frost, and deep almost as life!

>O joy! that in our embers
>Is something that doth live,
>That nature yet remembers
>What was so fugitive!
The thought of our past years in me doth breed
Perpetual benediction: not indeed
For that which is most worthy to be blest;

Delight and liberty, the simple creed
Of Childhood, whether busy or at rest,
With new-fledged hope still fluttering in his breast—
          Not for these I raise
          The song of thanks and praise;
     But for those obstinate questionings
          Of sense and outward things,
          Fallings from us, vanishings;
          Blank misgivings of a Creature
Moving about in worlds not realized,
High instincts before which our mortal Nature
Did tremble like a guilty Thing surprised:
          But for those first affections,
          Those shadowy recollections,
     Which, be they what they may,
Are yet the fountain-light of all our day,
Are yet a master-light of all our seeing;
          Uphold us, cherish, and have power to make
Our noisy years seem moments in the being
Of the eternal Silence: truths that wake,
          To perish never:
Which neither listlessness, nor mad endeavour,
          Nor Man nor Boy,
Nor all that is at enmity with joy,
Can utterly abolish or destroy!
          Hence in a season of calm weather
          Though inland far we be,
Our Souls have sight of that immortal sea
          Which brought us hither,
          Can in a moment travel thither,
And see the Children sport upon the shore,
And hear the mighty waters rolling evermore.

Then sing, ye Birds, sing, sing a joyous song!
          And let the young Lambs bound
          As to the tabor's sound!
We in thought will join your throng,

Ye that pipe and ye that play,
Ye that through our hearts to-day
Feel the gladness of the May!
What though the radiance which was once so bright
Be now for ever taken from my sight,
Though nothing can bring back the hour
Of splendour in the grass, of glory in the flower;
We will grieve not, rather find
Strength in what remains behind;
In the primal sympathy
Which having been must ever be;
In the soothing thoughts that spring
Out of human suffering;
In the faith that looks through death,
In years that bring the philosophic mind.

And O, ye Fountains, Meadows, Hills, and Groves,
Forebode not any severing of our loves!
Yet in my heart of hearts I feel your might;
I only have relinquished one delight
To live beneath your more habitual sway.
I love the Brooks which down their channels fret,
Even more than when I tripped lightly as they;
The innocent brightness of a new-born Day
Is lovely yet;
The Clouds that gather round the setting sun
Do take a sober colouring from an eye
That hath kept watch o'er man's mortality;
Another race hath been, and other palms are won.
Thanks to the human heart by which we live,
Thanks to its tenderness, its joys, and fears,
To me the meanest flower that blows can give
Thoughts that do often lie too deep for tears.

THE ARTIST IN PERSON

Gods of Love who tame the chaos.
—Samuel Taylor Coleridge

The Hero as Poet

[FROM *On Heroes, Hero-Worship, and the Heroic in History*]

THOMAS CARLYLE

1840

Poet and Prophet differ greatly in our loose modern notions of them. In some old languages, again, the titles are synonymous; *Vates* means both Prophet and Poet: and indeed at all times, Prophet and Poet, well understood, have much kindred of meaning. Fundamentally indeed they are still the same; in this most important respect especially, that they have penetrated both of them into the sacred mystery of the Universe; what Goethe calls "the open secret." "Which is the great secret?" asks one.—"The *open* secret,"—open to all, seen by almost none. That divine mystery, which lies everywhere in all Beings, "the Divine Idea of the World," that which lies at "the bottom of Appearance," as Fichte styles it; of which all Appearance, from the starry sky to the grass of the field, but especially the Appearance of Man and his work, is but the *vesture*,

573

the embodiment that renders it visible. This divine mystery *is* in all times and in all places; veritably *is*. In most times and places it is greatly overlooked; and the Universe, definable always in one or the other dialect, as the realized Thought of God, is considered a trivial, inert, commonplace matter,—as if, says the Satirist, it were a dead thing, which some upholsterer had put together! It could do no good, at present, to *speak* much about this; but it is a pity for every one of us if we do not know it, live ever in the knowledge of it. Really a most mournful pity;—a failure to live at all, if we live otherwise!

But now, I say, whoever may forget this divine mystery, the *Vates,* whether Prophet or Poet, has penetrated into it; is a man sent hither to make it more impressively known to us. That always is his message; he is to reveal that to us,—that sacred mystery which he more than others lives ever present with. While others forget, he knows it;—I might say, he has been driven to know it; without consent asked of *him,* he finds himself living in it, bound to live in it. Once more, here is no Hearsay, but a direct Insight and Belief; this man too could not help being a sincere man! Whosoever may live in the shows of things, it is for him a necessity of nature to live in the very fact of things. A man once more, in earnest with the Universe, though all others were but toying with it. He is a *Vates,* first of all, in virtue of being sincere. So far Poet and Prophet, participators in the "open secret," are one.

With respect to their distinction again the *Vates* Prophet, we might say, has seized that sacred mystery rather on the moral side, as Good and Evil, Duty and Prohibition; the *Vates* Poet on what the Germans call the aesthetic side, as Beautiful, and the like. The one we may call a revealer of what we are to do, the other of what we are to love. But indeed these two provinces run into one another, and cannot be disjoined. The Prophet too has his eye on what we are to love: how else shall he know what it is we are to do? The highest Voice ever heard on this earth said withal, "Consider the lilies of the field; they toil not, neither do they spin: yet Solomon in all his glory was not arrayed like one of these." A glance, that, into the deepest deep of Beauty.

He Is a Seer

[FROM Preface to the 1855 Edition of *Leaves of Grass*]

WALT WHITMAN

Of all nations the United States with veins full of poetical stuff most need poets and will doubtless have the greatest and use them the greatest. Their Presidents shall not be their common referee so much as their poets shall. Of all mankind the great poet is the equable man. Not in him but off from him things are grotesque or eccentric or fail of their sanity. Nothing out of its place is good and nothing in its place is bad. He bestows on every object or quality its fit proportions neither more nor less. He is the arbiter of the diverse and he is the key. He is the equalizer of his age and land . . . he supplies what wants supplying and checks what wants checking. If peace is the routine out of him speaks the spirit of peace, large, rich, thrifty, building vast and populous cities, encouraging agriculture and the arts and commerce—lighting the study of man, the soul, immortality—federal, state or municipal government, marriage, health, freetrade, intertravel by

land and sea . . . nothing too close, nothing too far off
. . . the stars not too far off. In war he is the most
deadly force of the war. Who recruits him recruits horse
and foot . . . he fetches parks of artillery the best
that engineer ever knew. If the time becomes slothful
and heavy he knows how to arouse it . . . he can make
every word he speaks draw blood. Whatever stagnates
in the flat of custom or obedience or legislation he
never stagnates. Obedience does not master him, he
masters it. High up out of reach he stands turning a
concentrated light . . . he turns the pivot with his
finger . . . he baffles the swiftest runners as he stands
and easily overtakes and envelops them. The time
straying toward infidelity and confections and persiflage
he withholds by his steady faith . . . he spreads out
his dishes . . . he offers the sweet firmfibred meat that
grows men and women. His brain is the ultimate brain.
He is no arguer . . . he is judgment. He judges not as
the judge judges but as the sun falling around a helpless thing. As he sees the farthest he has the most faith.
His thoughts are the hymns of the praise of things. In
the talk on the soul and eternity and God off of his equal
plane he is silent. He sees eternity less like a play with
a prologue and denouement . . . he sees eternity in
men and women . . . he does not see men and women
as dreams or dots. Faith is the antiseptic of the soul
. . . it pervades the common people and preserves
them . . . they never give up believing and expecting
and trusting. There is that indescribable freshness and
unconsciousness about an illiterate person that humbles
and mocks the power of the noblest expressive genius.
The poet sees for a certainty how one not a great artist
may be just as sacred as the greatest artist. . . . The
power to destroy or remould is freely used by him but
never the power of attack. What is past is past. If he
does not expose superior models and prove himself by
every step he takes he is not what is wanted. The

presence of the greatest poet conquers . . . not parley-
ing or struggling or any prepared attempts. Now he has
passed that way see after him! there is not left any
vestige of despair or misanthropy or cunning or exclu-
siveness or the ignominy of a nativity or color or delusion of hell or the necessity of hell . . . and no man
thenceforward shall be degraded for ignorance or
weakness or sin.

The greatest poet hardly knows pettiness or triviality.
If he breathes into any thing that was before thought
small it dilates with the grandeur and life of the universe. He is a seer . . . he is individual . . . he is
complete in himself . . . the others are as good as he,
only he sees it and they do not. He is not one of the
chorus . . . he does not stop for any regulations . . .
he is the president of regulation.

The poet shall not spend his time in unneeded work.
He shall know that the ground is always ready plowed
and manured . . . others may not know it but he shall.
He shall go directly to the creation. His trust shall
master the trust of everything he touches . . . and
shall master all attachment.

The known universe has one complete lover and that
is the greatest poet. He consumes an eternal passion
and is indifferent which chance happens and which
possible contingency of fortune or misfortune and per-
suades daily and hourly his delicious pay. What balks
or breaks others is fuel for his burning progress to
contact and amorous joy. Other proportions of the
reception of pleasure dwindle to nothing to his proportions. All expected from heaven or from the highest he
is rapport with in the sight of the daybreak or a scene
of the winter-woods or the presence of children playing
or with his arm round the neck of a man or woman. His
love above all love has leisure and expanse . . . he
leaves room ahead of himself. He is no irresolute or

suspicious lover . . . he is sure . . . he scorns intervals. His experience and the showers and thrills are not for nothing. Nothing can jar him . . . suffering and darkness cannot—death and fear cannot. To him complaint and jealousy and envy are corpses buried and rotten in the earth . . . he saw them buried. The sea is not surer of the shore or the shore of the sea than he is of the fruition of his love and of all perfection and beauty.

The greatest poet has less a marked style and is more the channel of thoughts and things without increase or diminution, and is the free channel of himself. He swears to his art, I will not be meddlesome, I will not have in my writing any elegance or effect or originality to hang in the way between me and the rest like curtains. I will have nothing hang in the way, not the richest curtains. What I tell I tell for precisely what it is. Let who may exalt or startle or fascinate or sooth I will have purposes as health or heat or snow has and be as regardless of observation. What I experience or portray shall go from my composition without a shred of my composition. You shall stand by my side and look in the mirror with me.

The old red blood and stainless gentility of great poets will be proved by their unconstraint. A heroic person walks at his ease through and out of that custom or precedent or authority that suits him not. Of the traits of the brotherhood of writers savants musicians inventors and artists nothing is finer than silent defiance advancing from new free forms. In the need of poems philosophy politics mechanism science behaviour, the craft of art, an appropriate native grand-opera, shipcraft, or any craft, he is greatest forever and forever who contributes the greatest original practical example. The cleanest expression is that which finds no sphere worthy of itself and makes one.

The messages of great poets to each man and woman are, Come to us on equal terms, Only then can you understand us, We are no better than you, What we enclose you enclose, What we enjoy you may enjoy. Did you suppose there could be only one Supreme? We affirm there can be unnumbered Supremes, and that one does not countervail another any more than one eyesight countervails another . . . and that men can be good or grand only of the consciousness of their supremacy within them.

The direct trial of him who would be the greatest poet is today. If he does not flood himself with the immediate age as with vast oceanic tides . . . and if he does not attract his own land body and soul to himself and hang on its neck with incomparable love and plunge his semitic muscle into its merits and demerits . . . and if he be not himself the age transfigured . . . and if to him is not opened the eternity which gives similitude to all periods and locations and processes and animate and inanimate forms, and which is the bond of time, and rises up from its inconceivable vagueness and infiniteness in the swimming shape of today, and is held by the ductile anchors of life, and makes the present spot the passage from what was to what shall be, and commits itself to the representation of this wave of an hour and this one of the sixty beautiful children of the wave—let him merge in the general run and wait his development. . . . Still the final test of poems or any character or work remains. The prescient poet projects himself centuries ahead and judges performer or performance after the changes of time. Does it live through them? Does it still hold on untired? Will the same style and the direction of genius to similar points be satisfactory now? Has no new discovery in science or arrival at superior planes of thought and judgment and behaviour fixed him or his so that either can be looked down upon? Have the marches of tens and hundreds and thousands of years made willing detours to the right hand and the left hand for his sake? Is he beloved long and long after he is buried? Does the young man think often of him? and the young woman think often of him? and do the middle-aged and the old think of him?

A great poem is for ages and ages in common and for all degrees and complexions and all departments and sects and for a woman as much as a man and a man as much as a woman. A great poem is no finish to a man or woman but rather a beginning. Has any one fancied he could sit at last under some due authority and rest satisfied with explanations and realize and be content and full? To no such terminus does the greatest poet bring . . . he brings neither cessation or sheltered fatness and ease. The touch of him tells in action. Whom he takes he takes with firm sure grasp into live regions previously unattained . . . thenceforward is no rest . . . they see the space and ineffable sheen that turn the old spots and lights into dead vacuums.

The poems distilled from other poems will probably pass away. The coward will surely pass away. The expectation of the vital and great can only be satisfied by the demeanor of the vital and great. The swarms of the polished deprecating and reflectors and the polite float off and leave no remembrance. America prepares with composure and goodwill for the visitors that have sent word. It is not intellect that is to be their warrant and welcome. The talented, the artist, the ingenious, the editor, the statesman, the erudite . . . they are not unappreciated . . . they fall in their place and do their work. The soul of the nation also does its work. No disguise can pass on it . . . no disguise can conceal from it. It rejects none, it permits all. Only toward as good as itself and toward the like of itself will it advance half-way. An individual is as superb as a nation when he has the qualities which make a superb nation. The soul of the largest and wealthiest and proudest nation may well go half-way to meet that of its poets. The signs are effectual. There is no fear of mistake. If the one is true the other is true. The proof of a poet is that his country absorbs him as affectionately as he has absorbed it.

The Unpoetical Poet

[FROM THE *Letters*]

JOHN KEATS

Tuesday 27 Oct. 1818

My Dear Woodhouse,

Your Letter gave me a great satisfaction; more on account of its friendliness, than any relish of that matter in it which is accounted so acceptable in the "genus irritable." The best answer I can give you is in a clerk-like manner to make some observations on two principle points, which seem to point like indices into the midst of the whole pro and con, about genius, and views and atchievements and ambition and cœtera. 1st. As to the poetical Character itself (I mean that sort of which, if I am any thing, I am a Member; that sort distinguished from the wordsworthian or egotistical sublime; which is a thing per se and stands alone) it is not itself—it has no self—it is every thing and nothing—It has no character—it enjoys light and shade; it lives in gusto, be it foul or fair, high or low, rich or poor, mean or elevated—It has as much delight in conceiving an Iago as an Imogen. What shocks the virtuous philosopher, delights the camelion Poet. It does no harm from its relish of the dark side of things any more than from its taste for the bright one; because they both end in speculation. A Poet is the most unpoetical of any thing in existence; because he has no Identity—he is continually in for—and filling some other Body—The Sun, the Moon, the Sea and Men and Women who are creatures of impulse are poetical and have about them an unchangeable attribute—the poet has none; no identity—he is certainly the most unpoetical of all God's Creatures. If then he has no self, and if I am a Poet, where is the Wonder that I should say I would write no more? Might I not at that very instant have been cogitating on the Characters of Saturn and Ops? It is a wretched thing to confess; but is a very fact that not one word I ever utter can be taken for granted as an opinion growing out of my identical nature—how can it, when I have no nature? When I am in a room with People if I ever am free from speculating on creations of my own brain, then not myself goes home to myself: but the identity of every one in the room begins to press upon me that I am in a very little time an[ni]hilated—not only among Men; it would be the same in a Nursery of children: I know not whether I make myself wholly understood: I hope enough so to let you see that no dependence is to be placed on what I said that day.

In the second place I will speak of my views, and of the life I purpose to myself. I am ambitious of doing the world some good: if I should be spared that may be the work of maturer years—in the interval I will assay to reach to as high a summit in Poetry as the nerve bestowed upon me will suffer. The faint conceptions I have of Poems to come brings the blood frequently into my forehead. All I hope is that I may not lose all interest in human affairs—that the solitary

indifference I feel for applause even from the finest
Spirits, will not blunt any acuteness of vision I may
have. I do not think it will—I feel assured I should
write from the mere yearning and fondness I have for
the Beautiful even if my night's labours should be burnt
every morning, and no eye ever shine upon them. But
even now I am perhaps not speaking from myself: but
from some character in whose soul I now live. I am
sure however that this next sentence is from myself. I
feel your anxiety, good opinion and friendliness in the
highest degree, and am

Your's most sincerely
John Keats

"An Immortal Evening"

[FROM *Autobiography and Memoirs*]

BENJAMIN ROBERT HAYDON

1817.—On December 28th the immortal dinner came
off in my painting-room, with Jerusalem towering up
behind us as a background. Wordsworth was in fine
cue, and we had a glorious set-to—on Homer, Shakespeare, Milton and Virgil. Lamb got exceedingly merry
and exquisitely witty; and his fun in the midst of
Wordsworth's solemn intonations of oratory was like the
sarcasm and wit of the fool in the intervals of Lear's
passion. He made a speech and voted me absent, and
made them drink my health. "Now," said Lamb, "you
old lake poet, you rascally poet, why do you call Voltaire dull?" We all defended Wordsworth, and affirmed

there was a state of mind when Voltaire would be dull. "Well," said Lamb, "here's to Voltaire—the Messiah of the French nation, and a very proper one too."

He, then, in a train of humour beyond description, abused me for putting Newton's head into my picture; "a fellow," said he, "who believed nothing unless it was as clear as the three sides of a triangle." And then he and Keats agreed he had destroyed all the poetry of the rainbow by reducing it to the prismatic colours. . . .

By this time the other friends joined, amongst them poor Ritchie who was going to penetrate by Fezzan to Timbuctoo. I introduced him to all as "a gentleman going to Africa." Lamb seemed to take no notice; but all of a sudden he roared out: "Which is the gentleman we are going to lose?" We then drank the victim's health, in which Ritchie joined. . . .

It was indeed an immortal evening. Wordsworth's fine intonation as he quoted Milton and Virgil, Keats' eager inspired look, Lamb's quaint sparkle of lambent humour, so speeded the stream of conversation, that in my life I never passed a more delightful time. . . . It was a night worthy of the Elizabethan age, and my solemn Jerusalem flashing up by the flame of the fire, with Christ hanging over us like a vision, all made up a picture which will long glow upon

> that inward eye
> Which is the bliss of solitude.

Keats made Ritchie promise he would carry his *Endymion* to the great desert of Sahara and fling it in the midst.

The Dying Keats

[FROM *Autobiography and Memoirs*]

BENJAMIN ROBERT HAYDON

March 29th, 1821.—Keats too is gone! He died at Rome, the 23rd February, aged twenty-five. A genius more purely poetical never existed!

In fireside conversation he was weak and inconsistent, but he was in his glory in the fields. The humming of a bee, the sight of a flower, the glitter of the sun, seemed to make his nature tremble. . . . He began life full of hopes, fiery impetuous and ungovernable, expecting the world to fall at once beneath his powers. Poor fellow! his genius had no sooner begun to bud than hatred and malice spat their poison on its leaves, and sensitive and young it shrivelled beneath their effusions. Unable to bear the sneers of ignorance or the attacks of envy, not having strength of mind enough to buckle himself together like a porcupine and present nothing but his prickles to his enemies, he began to despond and flew to dissipation as a relief, which after a temporary elevation of spirits plunged him into deeper despondency than ever. For six weeks he was scarcely sober, and— to show what a man does to gratify his appetites when once they get the better of him—once covered his tongue and throat as far as he could reach with cayenne pepper in order to appreciate the "delicious coldness of claret in all its glory"—his own expression. . . . The last time I ever saw him was at Hampstead lying in a white bed with a book, hectic and on his back, irritable at his weakness and wounded at the way he had been used. He seemed to be going out of life with a contempt for this world and no hopes for the other.

"*These Initiated Men*"

[FROM "Concerning the Situation of Artists and Their Condition in Society," *Paris Musical Gazette,* May 3, 1835]

FRANZ LISZT

To determine today with scope and precision what the situation of artists in our social order;—to define their individual, political, and religious relationships; —to relate their woes and miseries, their exhaustion and their disappointments;—to rip off the bandages from all their ever-bleeding wounds and to protest with energy against the oppressive iniquity or the stupid insolence that brands them, tortures them and, even worse, deigns to use them as playthings; to look into their past, prophesy their future, to set forth all their titles of glory; to teach the public, a forgetful and materialistic society (those men and women to whom we give pleasure and who *buy our wares*) from whence we come, where we are going, what our mission is, what finally we really are! . . . what these elected men are who seem to be chosen by God Himself to bear witness to the grandest feelings of humanity, and leave these behind them as a noble legacy . . .

These predestined men, struck down and chained, who have stolen the sacred fire of Heaven, who have given life to inanimate matter, form to thought, and by their cognizance of the ideal have lifted us up through their unconquerable sympathies toward enthusiasm and divine visions . . . These initiated men, these apostles, these priests belonging to an ineffable, mysterious, eternal religion which is conceived and grows without ceasing in every heart . . . Oh! To do all that, to say and to shout all these things, which are themselves self-evident, in such a way that even those most deaf would be constrained to listen, certainly that would be a beautiful and noble task to undertake. I must confess that often I have been strongly attracted by the importance, and, if I may say it, the flagrancy of the problem; but I have been too directly involved in the special studies of composing and performing, and have been able (for lack of time and talent) only to sketch very tentatively these questions of a different order. . . .

With the certitude of our acquired convictions we cry out without respite that a great task, a great religious and social MISSION has been imposed upon the artist.

Now, lest we are reproached for using these words loosely, in a vague or indeterminate manner—in order to express in a meaningful fashion the general feeling that the uninterrupted parallelism of the progress of art and the moral and intellectual progress of artists can only serve to augment and enhance each day of our lives; finally to help as much as we can the realization of that future we foresee and so desire, we call on the MUSICIANS, all those possessing a large, profound feeling for art, to establish among themselves a common, brotherly, and religious band, to *set up a universal society,* having for its aims:

1. The provoking, encouraging, and activating of

the forward movement, the extension and indefinite development of music.

2. The betterment and ennobling of the condition of artists, by remedying the abuses and the injustices that befall them, and deciding upon the necessary measures for the upholding of their dignity.

Trans. H. E. H.

The Poet's Solitude

[FROM *Stello*]

ALFRED DE VIGNY

1832

"SEPARATE POETICAL LIFE FROM POLITICAL LIFE."
And, to succeed in doing so:

1. Render unto Caesar that which belongs to Caesar, that is to say the right to be in every hour of every day reviled on the streets, cheated in the palace; fought secretly, undermined at large, beaten quickly, and chased with violence.

Because, to attack him or to flatter him with the triple power of the arts would be to degrade his work and to impress upon him how fragile and transitory are the day's ordinary events. It is easier to leave this task to a critic in the morning paper, who is dead by evening, or the evening critic who is dead the next morning.— Render unto all the Caesars the market square, and let them play their roles and go away, as long as they don't disturb your night's work or your day's rest.—Pity them with all your heart if they are compelled to place on their foreheads this crown of Caesar's, which no longer has leaves and crushes the skull. Pity them still more if they wanted it; the awakening they shall have afterward will be all the crueller after a long, beautiful dream. Pity them if they are perverted by Power; for there is nothing that might falsify this ancient and perhaps necessary Falseness, whence spring so many evils.—Watch this light die out, and stay awake: happy if your vigils may help humanity to consolidate and to unite about a purer brightness!

II. ALONE AND FREE, TO ACCOMPLISH ONE'S MISSION. Follow the conditions of your own being, detached from the influence of any Associations, even the most attractive.

Because Solitude is the source of all inspirations.

SOLITUDE IS HOLY. All Associations have the defects of convents. They tend to classify and direct the intelligence, and they create little by little a tyrannous authority which—taking liberty and individuality away from the intelligence, without which it is nothing—suffocates genius itself under an empire of corporate jealousy.

In Assemblies, Bodies, Companies, Schools, Academies, and everything that resembles them, intriguing mediocrities succeed step by step in dominating through their gross and material activity, and by that kind of cunning to which large and generous spirits can never lower themselves.

The Imagination cannot live save from spontaneous and special emotions, generated from each one's own penchants and character.

The Republic of letters is the only one that may ever be created from truly free citizens; for it is made up of isolated thinkers, each separated, and often mutually unknown to each other.

Poets and Artists alone, among all men, possess the happiness to accomplish their mission in solitude. Long may they rejoice in this happiness of not being overwhelmed in that society which mills about the slightest celebrity, appropriates him for themselves, encompasses him, unites with him, clasps him, and then tells him: US.

Yes, the Poet's imagination is as unstable as that of a person of fifteen who senses the first impressions of love. The Imagination of the Poet cannot be guided, because it is not taught. Take away his wings and you will make him die.

The mission of the Poet or the Artist is to produce, and everything that he produces is useful, if that is admirable.

A Poet shows his worth by his work, a man attached to Power can show his worth only by the functions that he fulfills. Happiness for the former, misery for the latter; for if any progress is made within these two heads, one rushes suddenly ahead by creating a work, the other is forced to follow the slow progression afforded by life's daily events and the gradual steps of his career.

ALONE AND FREE, TO ACCOMPLISH ONE'S MISSION.

III. Avoid the vagrant and sickly dream that misleads the spirit, and employ all the powers of the will to keep from sight the excessively facile enterprises of the active life.

Because the discouraged man falls often, out of laziness of mind, into the desire to act and to entangle himself with common interests, when he sees how they are inferior to him and how easy it would be to make his mark there. It is thus that he strays from his path; and if he strays too often, he loses it forever.

The Neutrality of the solitary thinker is an Armed Neutrality which awakens at a moment of need.

He places one finger on the scales and weights the balance. The more he presses, the more he impedes the will of a nation; he inspires public actions or protests against them, according to how it is revealed to him to act out of the percipience he has of the future. What matter to him if his head is exposed when he throws himself to the rear or the van?

He speaks the word he has to speak, and light is created.

He speaks this word from the far distant, and as soon as the word reverberates he goes back to his silent work and thinks no more about what he has done.

iv. Always have in the forefront of one's thought the pictures, chosen out of a thousand, of Gilbert, of Chatterton, and André Chénier.

Because with these three young shadows unceasingly before you, each one of them will keep you from those political pathways where you might entangle your feet. The first of these beloved phantoms shall show you his key, the second his vial of poison, and the last his guillotine. They will cry out the following:

"The Poet is accursed in his life and blessed in his name. The Poet, apostle of an always youthful truth, casts an eternal shadow over the man of Power, apostle of an aged fiction; because one owns inspiration, the other merely concentration or aptitude of the mind; because the Poet shall bequeath a work where shall be written a judgment of public actions and their actors; because at that same moment when these actors disappear forever, a long life begins for the author. Follow your calling. Your kingdom is not of this world, on which your eyes are open, but of that which shall be when your eyes are closed."

HOPE IS THE GREATEST OF OUR DELUSIONS.

Ah! what may one expect from a world to which one comes with the assurance of seeing one's father and mother die?

From a world where of two beings who love each other and give each other their lives, it is certain that one shall lose the other and see him die?

Then these melancholy phantoms shall cease talking to unite their voices in chorus, as in a sacred hymn; for Reason speaks, but Love sings.

And you shall hear the following:

CONCERNING SWALLOWS

See what the swallows do, birds of passage even as are we. They say to men: "Protect us, but don't touch us."

And men have for them, as they do for us, a superstitious respect.

Swallows seek shelter in a marble palace or the thatch of a cottage; but neither the man in the palace nor the man in the cottage dares lay a hand on their nest, because then they would lose forever the bird who brings happiness to their dwelling, as with us who dwell in lands where the people venerate us.

Only for a moment do the swallows touch the ground with their feet, and they swim in the skies all their life, just as easily as the dolphins do in the sea.

And if they look at the earth, it is from the height of a firmament that they look; and the trees and the mountains, and the cities and monuments, are no more elevated in their eyes than are the plains and the streams, even as in the celestial sight of the Poet everything on earth blends into a single globe lit by a beam of light from on high.

"Listen to them, and if you are inspired, write a book."

Do not hope that a great work be conceived, that a book be read, as books have been.

If your book is written in solitude, in study and composure, I desire for you that it be read in composure, study, and solitude: but be almost certain that it shall be read on the busy street, in the café, in a carriage, amid chatter, arguments, drinking, games, and bursts of laughter—or not at all.

And if it is original, God spare you from pale imitators, that harmful and innumerable crew of tainted, awkard apes.

And after all, you have given the light of day to a volume which, like all of men's works that have never expressed but a question and a sigh, shall be infallibly reduced to two words that never cease expressing our doubtful and sad destiny:

WHY? and ALAS!

Trans. H. E. H.

He Reads the Course

[FROM *Chatterton*]

ALFRED DE VIGNY

1835

CHATTERTON:

Character: A young man of eighteen, pale, face marked by energy, delicate build, worn-out by excessive thinking and late hours, both simple and elegant in manner, timid and tender when he is with Kitty Bell, amicable and kind with the Quaker, proud with all others and on the defensive with the world; his speech and accent passionate and serious.

Costume: Black coat, black waistcoat, gray trousers, soft leather boots; unpowdered brown hair slightly in disorder; his mien at once military and ecclesiastical. . . .

THE QUAKER: In your case, constant dreaming has killed action.

CHATTERTON: Ah! What does it matter, if one hour of such dreaming produces more works than twenty days of activity does with others! Who can judge between them and me? Is physical work all there is for man? Is not cerebral labor worthy of some pity? Ah! Good God! Is the sole science of the mind the science of numbers? Is Pythagoras the God of the universe? Must I say to burning inspiration: "Don't come near me, you are useless?"

THE QUAKER: She has inscribed your forehead with her fatal character. I don't blame you, my child, but I weep for you.

CHATTERTON (*sits down*): Good Quaker, does your fraternal and religious group have pity for those who are carried away by the passion of ideas? I think so. I have noted your indulgence toward me, your severity toward the rest of the world, and this calms me a little. (*Rachel enters and sits on Chatterton's lap.*) In all truth, I have almost been happy here for the past three months; no one knows my name, no one talks to me about myself, and I see lovely children on my knees.

THE QUAKER: My friend, I love you for your serious nature. You could be a worthy member of our religious group, where there is neither idolatrous papist agitation nor puerile protestant singing. I love you because I surmise that the world hates you. A contemplative soul is a burden for all the idle good-for-nothings who infest the globe. Imagination and contemplation are two ailments for which no one has pity! You don't even know the names of those secret enemies who prowl about you; but I know some persons who hate you all the more for not knowing you.

CHATTERTON (*heatedly*): But don't I also have the right to be loved by my brothers, I who work for them day and night, I who wearily seek amid patriotic ruins for a few blossoms of poetry from which I might extract lasting perfume; I who wish to add one more pearl to England's crown, and who dive deeply in sea and river to find it? (*Rachel leaves Chatterton; she goes to sit on a little table at the Quaker's feet and looks at the pictures.*) If only you knew how hard I work! . . . I've made my room into a cloistered cell; I've made my life and my thoughts into something holy and sanctified; I have curtailed my vision and shut from my eyes the light of our own age; I have simplified my heart; I have taught myself the pristine speech of ancient times; like Harold of England to William of Normandy, I have written verse half in Saxon, half in Old French. Finally, I have placed the tenth-century Muse, the religious Muse, in a reliquary as if she were a saint. They would have smashed her had they thought the poems were from my pen; now they love her because they believe the writing to belong to a monk who never even existed, whom I have named Rowley. . . .

CHATTERTON: It was I, Milord, who wrote to you.

MR. BECKFORD: Ah, so it was you, my dear boy! Come a little nearer that I may look at you. I knew your father, a fine man if ever there was one; an impoverished soldier who bravely followed his calling. Ah! So you are Thomas Chatterton? Well, you've had fun writing poetry, my young friend. That's fine for a short while, but it must not last. No one has ever really believed in that foolishness. Ha-ha! I was just like you in my salad days, and never did Littleton, Swift, or Wilkes write more gallant and playful verse for the ladies than did I.

CHATTERTON: I don't doubt that, Milord.

MR. BECKFORD: But I only gave my spare time to the Muses. I remember well what Ben Jonson once said: the most beautiful Muse in the world still can't cook for a man, and those girls we ought to have for mistresses, but never for wives.

(*Lauderdale, Kingston, and the other Lords laugh.*)

LAUDERDALE: Brave, Milord! That's well put!

CHATTERTON: Nothing could be truer, as I see today, Milord.

MR. BECKFORD: Your story is the same as that of a thousand other young men. You haven't been able to do anything save write these blasted poems, and what good are they, I ask you? I want to talk to you like a father, I do. . . . What good are they? A good Englishman should be of value to his country. Pause and think a minute. What notion do you have of the duty we all owe to everybody, each one of us?

CHATTERTON (aside): For her! For her! I will drink the bitter draught to the bottom. (Aloud) I think I understand, Milord. England is a ship. Our island even has that shape: the bow heads north, and it is as if she were anchored in the middle of the ocean, looking at the Continent. At her sides small ships built to resemble her endlessly tie up only to go forth again to represent her in all the corners of the earth. But our chief labor lies aboard the large vessel. The King, the Lords, and the Commons are on the poop deck, at the helm and behind the compass; the rest of us must haul on the lines, climb the masts, handle the sails, and shoot the cannon. We are all part of the crew and no one is superfluous when our glorious ship is being maneuvered.

MR. BECKFORD: Not bad, not bad! Let him make more poetry; still, even as I admit your idea, you must still see that I am right. What the devil does the poet do amid all this maneuvering?

(There is a short pause.)

CHATTERTON: From the stars, he reads the course pointed by the finger of God.

LORD TALBOT: What do you say to that, Milord? Doesn't that make you wrong? The pilot isn't useless.

MR. BECKFORD: Sheer imagination, my dear fellow! Or madness, which is the same thing. You are good for nothing, and this sort of nonsense has made you so.

I have information about you . . . to speak frankly
. . . and—

LORD TALBOT: Milord, he is a friend of mine, and you
would oblige me if you treated him kindly. . . .

Trans. H. E. H.

From Gladness to Madness

[FROM "Resolution and Independence"]

WILLIAM WORDSWORTH

1802

I thought of Chatterton, the marvellous Boy,
The sleepless Soul that perished in his pride;
Of Him who walked in glory and in joy
Following his plough, along the mountain-side:
By our own spirits are we deified:
We poets in our youth begin in gladness;
But thereof come in the end despondency and mad-
ness. . . .

"Extreme Sensibility"

[FROM *On the Character of Rousseau*]

WILLIAM HAZLITT

1816

Madame de Staël, in her Letters on the Writings and
Character of Rousseau, gives it as her opinion, "that

the imagination was the first faculty of his mind, and that this faculty even absorbed all the others." And she farther adds, "Rousseau had great strength of reason on abstract questions, or with respect to objects, which have no reality but in the mind." Both these opinions are radically wrong. Neither imagination nor reason can properly be said to have been the original predominant faculties of his mind. The strength both of imagination and reason, which he possessed, was borrowed from the excess of another faculty; and the weakness and poverty of reason and imagination, which are to be found in his works, may be traced to the same source, namely, that these faculties in him were artificial, secondary, and dependent, operating by a power not theirs, but lent to them. The only quality which he possessed in an eminent degree, which alone raised him above ordinary men, and which gave to his writings and opinions an influence greater, perhaps, than has been exerted by any individual in modern times, was extreme sensibility, or an acute and even morbid feeling of all that related to his own impressions, to the objects and events of his life. He had the most intense consciousness of his own existence. No object that had once made an impression on him was ever after effaced. Every feeling in his mind become a passion. His craving after excitement was an appetite and a disease. His interest in his own thoughts and feelings was always wound up to the highest pitch; and hence the enthusiasm which he excited in others. . . . Hence the tenaciousness of his logic, the acuteness of his observations, the refinement and the inconsistency of his reasoning. Hence his keen penetration, and his strange want of comprehension of mind: for the same intense feeling which enabled him to discern the first principles of things, and seize some one view of a subject in all its ramifications, prevented him from admitting the operation of other causes which interfered with his favourite purpose, and involved him in endless wilful contradictions. Hence his excessive egotism, which filled all objects with himself, and would have occupied the universe with his smallest interest. Hence his jealousy and suspicion of others; for no attention, no respect or sympathy, could come up to the extravagant claims of his self-love. Hence his dissatisfaction with himself and with all around him; for nothing could satisfy his ardent longings after good, his restless appetite of being. Hence in part also his quarrel with the artificial institutions and distinctions of society, which opposed so many barriers to the unrestrained indulgence of his will, and allured his imagination to scenes of pastoral simplicity or of savage life, where the passions were either not excited or left to follow their own impulse,—where the petty vexations and irritating disappointments of common life had no place,—and where the tormenting pursuits of arts and sciences were lost in pure animal enjoyment, or indolent repose. Thus he describes the first savage wandering for ever under the shade of magnificent forests, or by the side of mighty rivers, smit with the unquenchable love of nature!

Rousseau, in all his writings, never once lost sight of himself. He was the same individual from first to last. The spring that moved his passions never went down, the pulse that agitated his heart never ceased to beat. It was this strong feeling of interest, accumulating in his mind, which overpowers and absorbs the feelings of his readers. He owed all his power to sentiment. The writer who most nearly resembles him in our own times is the author of the *Lyrical Ballads*. We see no other difference between them, than that the one wrote in prose and the other in poetry; and that prose is perhaps better adapted to express those local and personal feelings, which are inveterate habits in the mind, than poetry, which embodies its imaginary creations. We conceive that Rousseau's exclamation, "*Ah, voilà de la pervenche*" ["Ah, there are periwinkles!"] comes more home to the mind than Mr. Wordsworth's discovery of the linnet's nest "with five blue eggs," or than his address to the cuckoo, beautiful as we think it is; and we will confidently match the Citizen of Geneva's adventures on the Lake of Bienne against the Cumberland Poet's floating dreams on the Lake of Grasmere. Both create an interest out of nothing, or rather out of their own feelings; both weave numberless recollections into one sentiment; both wind their own being round whatever object occurs to them.

Lamb on Blake

[FROM THE *Letters*]

CHARLES LAMB

To BERNARD BARTON

May 15, 1824

Blake is a real name, I assure you, and a most extraordinary man, if he be still living. He is the Robert [William] Blake, whose wild designs accompany a splendid folio edition of the "Night Thoughts," which you may have seen, in one of which he pictures the parting of soul and body by a solid mass of human form floating off, God knows how, from a lumpish mass (facsimile to itself) left behind on the dying bed. He paints in water colours marvellous strange pictures, visions of his brain, which he asserts that he has seen.

They have great merit. He has *seen* the old Welsh bards
on Snowden—he has seen the Beautifullest, the strongest, and the Ugliest Man, left alone from the Massacre
of the Britons by the Romans, and has painted them
from memory (I have seen his paintings), and asserts
them to be as good as the figures of Raphael and Angelo, but not better, as they had precisely the same
retro-visions and prophetic visions with themself [him-
self]. The painters in oil (which he will have it that
neither of them practised) he affirms to have been the
ruin of art, and affirms that all the while he was engaged in his Water paintings, Titian was disturbing
him, Titian the Ill Genius of Oil Painting. His Pictures
—one in particular, the Canterbury Pilgrims (far above
Stothard's)—have great merit, but hard, dry, yet with
grace. He has written a Catalogue of them with a most
spirited criticism on Chaucer, but mystical and full of
Vision. His poems have been sold hitherto only in Manuscript. I never read them; but a friend at my desire
procured the "Sweep Song." There is one to a tiger,
which I have heard recited, beginning:

> Tiger, Tiger, burning bright,
> Thro' the desarts of the night,

which is glorious, but, alas! I have not the book; for
the man is flown, whither I know not—to Hades or a
Mad House. But I must look on him as one of the most
extraordinary persons of the age. . . .

Baudelaire on Delacroix

[FROM "The Works and Life of Eugène Delacroix,"
reprinted in *Romantic Art*]

CHARLES BAUDELAIRE

1863

Eugène Delacroix was a curious mixture of skepticism, politeness, dandyism, a forceful will, craftiness, despotism, and finally of a type of personal kindliness and moderate tenderness which always accompanies genius. His father belonged to that race of powerful men whose last members we knew when we were children; half of them ardent disciples of Jean-Jacques Rousseau, the rest fervent disciples of Voltaire; and they all collaborated with equal zeal in the French Revolution. Their survivors, whether they were Jacobins or Cordeliers, all rallied with equally good faith (this is important to note) around Bonaparte's cause.

Eugène Delacroix always retained the traces of his revolutionary origin. It might be said of him, as of Stendhal, that he greatly feared being made a fool of. Skeptical and aristocratic, he was acquainted with passion and the supernatural only by dint of his forced intimacy with dreams. One who hated the masses, he really only considered them as iconoclasts; and the acts of violence done to some of his paintings in 1848 were scarcely able to convert him to the political sentimentality of our age. Concerning style, manners, and opinions, there was something of Victor Jacquemont about him. I realize that the comparison is rather offensive; therefore I want it to be made with extreme discretion. With Jacquemont, there is a nice touch of the rebellious bourgeois wit and a sullen sarcasm just as likely to puzzle the disciples of Brahma as those of Christ. Delacroix, restricted by the taste always inherent in genius, could never fall into these vulgarities. Thus my comparison relates only to the spirit of prudence and of sobriety which marked them both. Common to both, the hereditary marks which the 18th century had left upon his nature seemed above all to have been taken from that class which is as far distant from the utopians as it is from the fanatics: that class of polished skeptics, the victors and survivors, who, generally speaking, stemmed more from Voltaire than they did from Jean-Jacques. Thus at first glance, Eugène Delacroix simply looked like the *enlightened* man, to use the word in its honorable context, like a perfect *gentleman* with neither prejudice nor passion. Only when one cultivated his acquaintance more assiduously could one get beneath the varnish and guess at the hidden nooks and crannies of his soul. M. Mérimée might be a person to whom we could compare him more aptly, both as to outward appearance and manners. There was the same apparent, slightly affected, coldness; the same icy cloak which concealed a bashful sensitivity and a burning passion for the good and the beautiful; here too, beneath the same hypocritical pretense of egotism, was the same devotion to his personal friends and to his favorite ideas.

In Eugène Delacroix there was a good deal of the *savage;* this was the most precious part of his soul, the part completely dedicated to the painting of his dreams and to the cult of his artistry. He was also much the man of the world; that portion of him was destined to disguise the other part, and to get it excused. I think it was one of the great preoccupations of his life to conceal the rage he felt in his heart, and not to have the outward show of the man of genius. His domineering spirit, which it was quite legitimate and even necessary for him to possess, had almost entirely disappeared beneath a thousand acts of kindness. One couldn't help thinking of a volcanic crater artfully concealed with bouquets of flowers.

I have mentioned to you that what struck the watchful observer was the *natural* ingredient in Delacroix's soul, despite the mollifying veil of his civilized refinement. He was all energy, an energy stemming from his nerves and will-power, since physically he was frail and delicate. A tiger intent on his prey has less light in his eyes and less impatient muscles than one could observe with our great painter, when his whole soul hurled itself upon an idea or struggled to come into possession of a dream. Even his physiognomy, his Peruvian or Malay-like coloring; his great black eyes, which, however, through their concentrated blinking seemed smaller so that they appeared merely to sip the light; his thick and glossy hair, his stubborn forehead, his tight lips where unceasing tension of will gave the impression of cruelty: in short, his whole personality suggested some idea of exotic origins. More than once, when I looked at him, I thought of those ancient monarchs of Mexico, of Montezuma, whose hand, skilled in making sacrifices, could immolate three thousand human beings in a single day on the pyramidal altar of the Sun; or of one of those Hindu princes who, amid the splendor of his most brilliant feasts, betrays in the depths of his eyes a touch of insatiable craving and an inexplicable nostalgia, something like the memory and the regret of things not known.

Trans. H. E. H.

Beethoven on Goethe

[FROM THE *Letters*]

LUDWIG VAN BEETHOVEN

To Bettina von Arnim

Teplitz, August 15, 1812

Dearest, good Bettina!

Kings and princes can certainly create professors, privy councilors, and titles, and hang on ribbons of various orders, but they cannot create great men, master-minds which tower above the rabble; this is beyond them. Such men must therefore be held in respect. When two such as I and Goethe meet, these grand gentlemen are forced to note what greatness, in such as we are, means. Yesterday on the way home we met the whole Imperial family. We saw them from afar approaching, and Goethe slipped away from me and stood to one side. Say what I would, I could not induce him to advance another step, so I pushed my hat on my head, buttoned up my overcoat, and went, arms folded, into the thickest of the crowd. Princes and sycophants drew up a line; Duke Rudolph took off my hat, after the Empress had first greeted me. Persons of rank *know* me. To my great amusement I saw the procession defile past Goethe. Hat in hand, he stood at the side, deeply bowing. Then I mercilessly reprimanded him, cast his sins in his teeth, especially those of which he was guilty toward you, dearest Bettina, of whom we had just been speaking. Good heav-

ens! Had I been in your company, as he has, I should
have produced works of greater, far greater, importance. A musician is also a poet, and the magic of a
pair of eyes can suddenly cause him to feel transported
into a more beautiful world, where great spirits make
sport of him and set him mighty tasks. I cannot tell
what ideas came into my head when I made your acquaintance. In the little observatory during the splendid May rain—that was a fertile moment for me; the
most beautiful themes then glided from your eyes into
my heart, which one day will enchant the world when
Beethoven has ceased to conduct. If God grant me
yet a few years, then I must see you again, dear, dear
Bettina; so calls the voice within me which never errs.
Even minds can love each other. I shall always court
yours; your approval is dearer to me than anything in
the whole world. I gave my opinion to Goethe, that
approval affects such men as ourselves and that we
wish to be listened to with the intellect by those who
are our equals. Emotion is only for women (excuse this);
the flame of music must burst forth from the mind of
a man. Ah! my dearest child, we have now for a long
time been in perfect agreement about everything! The
only good thing is a beautiful, good soul, which is recognized in everything, and in presence of which there
need be no concealment. *One must be somebody if one
wishes to appear so.* The world is bound to recognize
one; it is not always unjust. To me, however, that is a
matter of no importance, for I have a higher aim. I
hope when I get back to Vienna to receive a letter
from you. Write soon, soon, and a very long one; in a
week from now I shall be there; the court goes tomorrow; there will be no more performance today. The
Empress rehearsed her part with him. His duke and
he both wished to play some of my music, but to both
I made refusal. They are mad about Chinese porcelain,
hence there is need for indulgence; for the intellect has

lost the whip-hand. I will not play to these silly folk, who never get over that mania, nor will I write at public cost any stupid stuff for princes. Adieu, adieu, dearest; your last letter lay on my heart for a whole night, and comforted me. *Everything* is allowed to musicians. Great heavens, how I love you!

Your sincerest friend and deaf brother,

Beethoven

Trans. J. S. Shedlock. The German Classics (New York: German Publications Society, 1913).

Rellstab on Beethoven

[FROM *From My Life*]

LUDWIG RELLSTAB

1861

[BEETHOVEN, CA. 1815]

When I entered, he was the first object to meet my glance. He sat idly on an unmade bed by the far wall of the room, on which he seemed to have just been reclining. In one hand he held Zelter's letter. The other hand he cordially held out to me; and this he did with such a benevolent, sorrowful look that I felt an oppressive partition-wall falling. I came up to him with the deepest reverence and with the whole warmth of my love. He stood up, shook hands in good hearty German fashion, and said, "You have brought me a fine letter from Zelter! He is a true protector of real art!"

Accustomed as he was to doing most of the talking, since he grasped the remarks of other people only with great difficulty, he continued: "I am not at all well!

I am really very ill! You will have a hard time talking to me, for I hear very badly!"

Beethoven invited me then to sit down. He himself took a chair in front of the bed and pushed it next to a table. There it was, two steps away from me, covered with treasures and the notes written in Beethoven's own hand—the very work with which he now was occupied. I sat in a chair right beside him. I took a quick look around the room. It is as large as the anteroom and has two windows. Beneath these stands a piano. Save for this, there is nothing else that might betray ease, comfort, any splendor or luxury. A writing-desk, a few chairs and tables, white walls with old and dusty carpeting—this is Beethoven's dwelling. But why should he be bothered with bronze statuary, mirrored paneling, divans, gold and silver? He, to whom all the splendor of this world's trumpery is but dust and ashes before a godlike flame; he, who shines out above everything with a radiance from within!

Thus I sat near the sick and melancholy sufferer. His almost completely gray hair stuck up bushy and disorderly from the crown of his head—not smooth, not curly, not stiff, but a mixture of all of these. Upon first glance his features did not seem particularly significant. His face was much smaller than I had imagined from all the powerful, compelling, wild, and genius-like portraits I had seen. I saw nothing to reveal the gruffness, the stormy unfettered quality that painters have lent his physiognomy in order to bring his face into consonance with his creations. But why must Beethoven's face resemble his scores?

His color was brownish: not that healthy, strong tan acquired by a hunter, but rather a sickly and yellowish cast. A small, sharp nose; a kindly mouth; small, pale gray, revealing eyes. I read melancholy, sorrow, and benevolence in his face. Yet—and I repeat this—no trace of harshness or that loftiness that often betokens an arrogance of spirit was perceptible. Here I cannot deceive the reader with fiction. I must tell the truth in order to present an affectionate mirror to a beloved countenance. Despite all that has been said, he was doing no penance for that secretly attractive power that binds us so irresistibly to the figures of great men. His sorrow—that mute and heavy anguish that revealed itself from within—was not the result of temporary ill-health. I always saw the same expression, even during those weeks when Beethoven enjoyed good health. Rather did it represent his whole, entire, fated existence, in which were blended the highest affirmative traits with the cruellest trials of self-denial. Did we not know the story of Raphael blinded at the height of his strength, Beethoven could not find his equal in health and sickness, either in the history of art or in the history of the world!

Therefore the sight of this quiet and deep sorrow, apparent on his melancholy brow and in his deep eyes, affected me with a nameless emotion. It required the strongest self-control for me to sit opposite him and restrain the tears that threatened to pour out. After we sat down, Beethoven handed me a tablet and a pencil, and said to me, "You have only to write down the main points of your conversation. Then I can follow you. I have been used to doing this for many years."

Trans. H. E. H.

Liszt on Chopin

[FROM *The Life of Chopin*]

FRANZ LISZT

1852

It was not without an effort, not without a slightly misanthropic repugnance, that Chopin could be persuaded to open his doors and his piano, even to those whose respectful and faithful friendship gave them some claim to urge with eagerness such a request. No doubt more than one of us can still recollect our first improvised evening with him, in spite of his refusal, when he lived in the Chaussée d'Antin. His apartment, which was invaded by surprise, was lit up only by some wax candles grouped around one of Pleyel's pianos, which he very much liked on account of their slightly veiled but silvery sonority and easy touch, permitting him to draw forth tones which one might almost have thought proceeded from one of those harmonicas, so ingeniously constructed by old German masters by the union of crystal and water, of which Germany has preserved a monopoly. The corners of the room were left in obscurity so that all idea of limit was lost, and there seemed to be no boundary save the darkness of space around. Some tall piece of furniture draped in white would reveal itself in this dim light—a form indistinct, lifting itself like a spectre to listen to the tones which had called it forth. The light concentrated round the piano, and falling on the floor, glided on like a spreading wave until it reached and mingled with the fitful flashes from the fire, from which orange-lined plumes rose and fell, like shifting gnomes attracted to the spot by mystic incantations in their own language. A single portrait of a pianist, who was an admiring and sympathising friend, seemed as if it were invited to be a constant auditor of the ebbing and flowing tide of sound which sighed, moaned, murmured, broke, and died upon the instrument near to which it always hung. By a curious coincidence, the polished surface of the mirror only reflected, in such manner as to double it to our vision, that beautiful oval with silky curls which so many pencils have drawn, and which has just been reproduced by the engraver for all who are charmed by works of such peculiar eloquence.

Grouped in the luminous zone immediately around the piano were several men of brilliant renown; Heine, that saddest of all humourists, listened with the eagerness of a fellow-countryman to the stories told him by Chopin of that mysterious country which also haunted his ethereal fancy, and the beautiful shores he too had explored. Chopin and Heine comprehended each other at a word, a tone, or a glance; the player responded to the questions which the poet murmured in his ear, and gave in tones the most astonishing revelations from those unknown realms respecting that "laughing nymph" about whom he enquired "Whether she still continued, with a coquetry so enticing, to wrap her silvery veil around the flowing locks of her green hair?" Familiar with all the love tales and gossip of those distant lands, he asked "Whether the old marine god with the long white beard still pursued this mischievous Naiad with his ridiculous love?" Full of information, too, as to all the exquisite fairy scenes to be beheld "down there—down there," he asked "Whether the roses always glowed there with so triumphant a flame? Whether trees at moonlight always sang so harmoniously?" When Chopin had replied, and they had conversed together for a long time about that aerial clime, they would relapse into gloomy silence, seized with that *mal du pays* which afflicted Heine when he likened himself to the Dutch captain of the phantom ship, eternally driven about with his crew upon the chilly waves, and "in vain sighing for the spices, the tulips, the hyacinths, the sea-foam pipes, the porcelain cups of Holland." . . .

In the autumn of 1837 Chopin was seized by an alarming illness, which left him almost without the power of supporting life. He was compelled by dangerous symptoms to travel southward to avoid the rigours of winter. Madame Sand, who was ever watchful over those whom she loved, and so full of compassion for their sufferings, saw that his state of health required great care, and she would not permit him to set out alone, but decided to go with him. They fixed upon the island of Majorca for a residence, because the sea air combined with the mild climate prevalent there is particularly salubrious for sufferers from lung disease. Though when he left Paris he was so weak that we had no hope he would ever return, and though he was long and dangerously ill after his arrival in Majorca, yet he derived so much benefit from the change that for several years his health was improved.

Was it the balmy climate alone which called him back to life, or was it not rather because his life was so blissful that he found strength to live? Did he not there regain strength simply because he so strongly desired to live? Who can tell the extent of the influence of the will upon the bodily frame? Who can say what subtle internal aroma the will had the power of setting free to preserve the sinking frame from decay, or what vital force it can breathe into the bodily organs? Who can tell where the dominion of mind over matter ceases, or how far our senses are dominated by our imagination, to what extent their powers may be augmented or their extinction accelerated by will power? It is of no moment *how* the imagination obtains its strange extension of power, whether it is by long and bitter exercise or whether it collects spontaneously its forgotten strength and concentrates its force in some new and decisive moment of destiny, as the rays of the sun can kindle a flame of celestial origin when they are concentrated in the focus of the burning-glass, brittle and fragile though that medium may be.

Upon this epoch in Chopin's life all the long-scattered rays of happiness were concentrated; is it then to be wondered at that they should have rekindled the flame of life, and that it should at this period have burned with the most intense lustre? The solitude, surrounded by the blue waves of the Mediterranean, and shaded by orange groves, seemed by its exceeding loveliness to be exactly adapted to the ardent vows of youthful lovers who still believed in their sweet and naïve illusions, and sighed for happiness in "some desert isle." Chopin there breathed that air for which natures unfit for the world, and who never feel happy in it, long with such painful homesickness; that air which we can find in every place where there is a sympathetic soul to breathe it with us, and which, without such a soul, can be found nowhere; the air which pervades our dream-land; the air which, in spite of all obstacles and of all bitter realities, is very easily found when two souls seek it together! It is the balmy air of that ideal land to which we so gladly lead the being we cherish, repeating with poor Mignon—*"Dahin! Dahin! . . . lasset uns ziehn!"*

While his illness continued Madame Sand never left his pillow. He loved her even unto death, with a clinging attachment which lost none of its intensity when it had lost all its joy, and which remained faithful to her even when all its memories had turned to pain; for it seemed as though this fragile being was absorbed and consumed by the strength of his love. . . . Some seek happiness in their attachments, and when they can find it no longer, the attraction gradually vanishes. In this they only resemble the rest of the world. But Chopin loved for the sake of loving; no amount of suffering could discourage him. "He could arrive at a new phase—that of woe; but he could never reach the phase of coldness. That would indeed have been a phase of physical agony; his love was his life; and whether it was sweet or bitter, he could not for one moment withdraw himself from its dominion." Madame Sand remained till Chopin's last moment, that woman of magic spells who had plucked him from the valley of the shadow of death, whose power over him had converted his physical agony into love's delicious languor.

Trans. John Broadhouse. (London: William Reeves, 1914.)

Goethe on Byron

[FROM J. P. Eckermann, *Conversations with Goethe*]

JOHANN WOLFGANG VON
GOETHE

1825-27

"Lord Byron," continued Goethe, "is to be regarded as a man, as an Englishman, and as a great talent. His good qualities belong chiefly to the man, his bad to the Englishman and the peer, his talent is incommensurable.

"All Englishmen are, as such, without reflection, properly so called; distractions and party spirit will not permit them to perfect themselves in quiet. But they are great as practical men.

"Thus, Lord Byron could never attain reflection on himself, and on this account his maxims in general are not successful, as is shown by his creed, 'much money, no authority,' for much money always paralyses authority.

"But where he will create, he always succeeds; with him inspiration supplies the place of reflection. He was obliged to go on poetizing; and then everything that came from the man, especially from his heart, was excellent. He produced his best things as women do pretty children, without thinking about it or knowing how it was done.

"He is a great talent, a born talent, and I never saw the true poetical power greater in any man. In the apprehension of external objects, and a clear penetration into past situations, he is quite as great as Shakespeare. But, as a pure individuality, Shakespeare is his superior. This was felt by Byron; and on this account he does not say much of Shakespeare, although he knows whole passages by heart. He would willingly have denied him altogether; for Shakespeare's cheerfulness is in his way, and he feels that he is no match for it. Pope he does not deny, for he had no cause to fear him: on the contrary, he mentions him, and shows him respect when he can; for he knows well enough that Pope is a mere foil to himself."

Goethe seemed inexhaustible on the subject of Byron. After a few digressions, he proceeded thus:

"His high rank as an English peer was very injurious to Byron; for every talent is oppressed by the outer world—how much more, then, when there is such high birth and so great a fortune? A middle rank is much more favourable to talent, so we find all great artists and poets in the middle classes. Byron's predilection for the unbounded could not have been nearly so dangerous with more humble birth and smaller means. As it was, he was able to put every fancy into practice, and this involved him in innumerable scrapes. Besides, how could one of such high rank be inspired with awe and respect by any rank whatever? He spoke out whatever he felt, and this brought him into ceaseless conflict with the world."

"I could not," said Goethe, "make use of any man as the representative of the modern poetical era except him, who undoubtedly is the greatest genius of our century. Again, Byron is neither antique nor romantic, but like the present day itself. This was the sort of man I required. Then he suited me on account of his unsatisfied nature and his warlike tendency, which led to his death at Missolonghi. A treatise upon Byron would be neither convenient nor advisable; but I shall not fail to pay him honour and to allude to him at proper times."

Trans. J. Oxenford.

Byron: The Feet of Clay

[FROM *Recollections of the Last Days of Shelley and Byron*]

E. J. TRELAWNEY

1858

[BYRON IN FLORENCE, 1822]

In external appearance Byron realized that ideal standard with which imagination adorns genius. He was in the prime of life, thirty-five; of middle height, five feet eight and a half inches; regular features, without a stain or furrow on his pallid skin, his shoulders broad, chest open, body and limbs finely proportioned. His small, highly-finished head and curly hair had an airy and graceful appearance from the massiveness and length of his throat; you saw his genius in his eyes and lips. In short, Nature could do little more than she had done for him, both in outward form and in the inward spirit she had given to animate it. But all these rare gifts to his jaundiced imagination only served to make his one personal defect (lameness) the more apparent, as a flaw is magnified in a diamond when polished; and he brooded over that blemish as sensitive minds will brood until they magnify a wart into a wen.

His lameness certainly helped to make him skeptical, cynical, and savage. There was no peculiarity in his dress, it was adapted to the climate; a tartan jacket braided,—he said it was the Gordon pattern, and that his mother was of that ilk. A blue velvet cap with a gold band, and very loose nankeen trousers, strapped down so as to cover his feet: his throat was not bare, as represented in drawings.

His conversation was anything but literary, except when Shelley was near him. The character he most commonly appeared in was of the free and easy sort, such as had been in vogue when he was in London, and George IV was regent; and his talk was seasoned with anecdotes of the great actors on and off the stage, boxers, gamblers, duellists, drunkards, etc., etc., appropriately garnished with the slang and scandal of that day. Such things had all been in fashion, and were at that time considered accomplishments by gentlemen; and of this tribe of Mohawks the Prince Regent was the chief, and allowed to be the most perfect specimen. Byron, not knowing that the tribe was extinct, still prided himself on having belonged to it; of nothing was he more indignant, than of being treated as a man of letters, instead of as a Lord and a man of fashion; this prevented foreigners and literary people from getting on with him, for they invariably so offended. His long absence had not effaced the mark John Bull brands his children with; the instant he loomed above the horizon, on foot or horseback, you saw at a glance he was a Britisher.

[MISSOLONGHI, 1824]

It was the 24th or 25th of April when I arrived; Byron had died on the 19th. I waded through the streets, between wind and water, to the house he had lived in; it was detached, and on the margin of the shallow slimy sea-waters. For three months this house had been besieged, day and night, like a bank that has a run upon it. Now that death had closed the door, it was as silent as a cemetery. No one was within the house but Fletcher, of which I was glad. As if he knew my wishes, he led me up a narrow stair into a small room, with nothing in it but a coffin standing on trestles. No word was spoken by either of us; he withdrew the black pall and the white shroud, and there lay the embalmed body of the Pilgrim—more beautiful in death than in life. The contraction of the muscles and skin had effaced every line that time or passion had ever traced upon it; few marble busts could have matched its stainless white, the harmony of its proportions, and perfect finish; yet he had been dissatisfied with that body, and longed to cast its slough. How often had I heard him curse it! He was jealous of the genius of Shakespeare—that might well be—but where had he seen the face or form worthy to excite his envy? I asked Fletcher to bring me a glass of water. On his leaving the room, to confirm or remove my doubts as to the cause of his lameness, I uncovered the Pilgrim's feet, and was answered—the great mystery was solved. Both his feet were clubbed, and his legs withered to the knee—the form and features of an Apollo, with the feet and legs of a sylvan satyr. This was a curse, chaining a proud and soaring spirit like his to the dull earth.

Shelley: The Enduring Heart

[FROM *Recollections of the Last Days of Shelley and Byron*]

E. J. TRELAWNEY

[1822]

1858

The soldiers collected fuel whilst I erected the furnace, and then the men of the Health Office set to work, shovelling away the sand which covered the body, while we gathered round, watching anxiously. The first indication of their having found the body, was the appearance of the end of a black silk handkerchief—I grubbed this out with a stick, for we were not allowed co touch any thing with our hands—then some shrouds of linen were met with, and a boot with the bone of the leg and the foot in it. On the removal of a layer of brushwood, all that now remained of my lost friend was exposed—a shapeless mass of bones and flesh. The limbs separated from the trunk on being touched.

"Is that a human body?" exclaimed Byron; "why it's more like the carcase of a sheep, or any other animal, than a man: this is a satire on our pride and folly. . . ."

Byron looked on, muttered, "The entrails of a worm

hold together longer than the potter's clay, of which man is made. Hold! let me see the jaw," he added, as they were removing the skull, "I can recognize any one by the teeth, with whom I have talked. I always watch the lips and mouth: they tell what the tongue and eyes try to conceal. . . ."

The funeral pyre was now ready; I applied the fire, and the materials being dry and resinous, the pine-wood burnt furiously, and drove us back. . . . We threw frankincense and salt into the furnace, and poured a flask of wine and oil over the body. The Greek oration was omitted, for we had lost our Hellenic bard. . . . At four o'clock the funeral pyre burnt low, and when we uncovered the furnace, nothing remained in it but dark-coloured ashes, with fragments of the larger bones. I gathered together the human ashes, and placed them in a small oak-box, bearing an inscription on a brass plate, screwed it down, and placed it in Byron's carriage. He returned with Hunt to Pisa, promising to be with us on the following day at Via Reggio. I returned with my party in the same way we came, and supped and slept at the inn. On the following morning we went on board the same boats, with the same things and party, and rowed the little river near Via Reggio to the sea, pulled along the coast towards Massa, then landed, and began our preparations as before.

The work went on silently in the deep and unresisting sand, not a word was spoken, for the Italians have a touch of sentiment, and their feelings are easily excited into sympathy. Even Byron was silent and thoughtful. We were startled and drawn together by a dull hollow sound that followed the blow of a mattock; the iron had struck a skull, and the body was soon uncovered. Lime had been strewn on it; this, or decomposition, had the effect of staining it a dark and ghastly indigo colour. Byron asked me to preserve the skull for him; but remembering that he had formerly used one as a drinking-cup, I was determined Shelley's should not be so profaned. . . . The heat from the sun and fire was so intense that the atmosphere was tremulous and wavy. The corpse fell open and the heart was laid bare. The frontal bone of the skull, where it had been struck with the mattock, fell off; and, as the back of the head rested on the red-hot bottom bars of the furnace, the brains literally seethed, bubbled, and boiled as in a cauldron, for a very long time. . . .

The only portions that were not consumed were some fragments of bones, the jaw, the skull, but what surprised us all, was that the heart remained entire. In snatching this relic from the fiery furnace, my hand was severely burnt; and had any one seen me do the act I should have been put into quarantine.